"PEOPLE OF VOA. THIS is Cyra Noavek. Thuvhe has declared war on Shotet. Hostiles incoming. Evacuate to the sojourn ship immediately. I repeat, evacuate to the sojourn ship immediately. Transmission complete."

With that, I bent at the waist, bracing myself on my knees, and struggled to breathe. I was in so much pain my legs felt like they would give out at any moment. Akos rushed forward, clutching first at my shoulders, and then at my hands. I braced myself against him, my head slotted next to his, my forehead against his shoulder.

"You did well," he said quietly. "You did well, I have you, I have you."

War was coming. And no matter what Akos said, no matter what anyone said from now on, *I* was the one who had urged it forward.

BOOKS BY
VERONICA ROTH

PRAISE FOR
THE FATES DIVIDE

"If you enjoyed *Carve the Mark* and this intricate world that Veronica Roth created, you'll definitely be a fan of *The Fates Divide*. This sequel takes a magnifying glass to all of the understated and unexplored aspects of the first novel, giving the reader a closer look while also setting parts of what we thought we knew about the world and the characters aflame."
—HYPABLE

"The expansive world Roth introduced in the series opener gets even bigger in this sequel, with a bevy of additional characters, deepened secrets, and complex interplanetary politics. Fans will be eager for a conclusion to Cyra and Akos's story . . . and they are likely to be satisfied."
—ALA *BOOKLIST*

"*The Fates Divide* features themes like hope and resilience, and is told from four perspectives, as the lives of its two heroes are ruled by their fates spoken by the oracles at their births. Of course, a little romance gets in the way as well."
—*ENTERTAINMENT WEEKLY*

ASSEMBLY SHIP

CURRENTSTREAM BARRIER · CURRENTSTREAM BARRIER · CURRENTSTREAM BARRIER · CURRENTSTREAM BARRIER · CURRENTSTREAM BARRIER

OGRA

KOLLANDE

TEFES

ESSANDER

TRELLA

OTHYR

SUN

ZOLD

PITHA

THUVHE

PIIO4

THE BRIM

THE
FATES
DIVIDE

VERONICA ROTH

HarperCollins *Children's Books*

First published in the US by Katherine Tegen Books in 2018
Katherine Tegen Books is an imprint of HarperCollins Publishers
First published in Great Britain by HarperCollins *Children's Books* in 2018
Published in this edition in 2019
HarperCollins *Children's Books* is a division of HarperCollins*Publishers* Ltd,
HarperCollins Publishers
1 London Bridge Street
London SE1 9GF

The HarperCollins website address is:
www.harpercollins.co.uk
1

ISBN 978–0–00–819221–1

Printed and bound by CPI Group (UK) Ltd, Croydon CR0 4YY

MIX
Paper from
responsible sources
FSC™ C007454

This book is produced from independently certified FSC™ paper
to ensure responsible forest management.

For more information visit: www.harpercollins.co.uk/green

To my dad, Frank, my brother, Frankie, and my sister, Candice:
we may not share blood, but I'm so lucky we're family.

PROLOGUE | EIJEH

"WHY SO AFRAID?" WE ask ourself.

"She is coming to kill us," we reply.

We were once alarmed by this feeling of being in two bodies at once. We have grown accustomed to it in the cycles since the shift occurred, since both our currentgifts dissolved into this new, strange one. We know how to pretend, now, that we are two people instead of one—though we prefer, when we are alone, to relax into the truth. We are one person in two bodies.

We are not on Urek, as we were the last time we knew our location. We are adrift in space, the bend of the blushing currentstream the only interruption in the blackness.

Only one of our two cells has a window. It is a narrow thing, with a thin mattress in it and a bottle of water. The other cell is a storage room that smells of disinfectant, harsh and acrid. The only light comes from the vents in the door, closed now but not fully sealed against the hallway glow.

We stretch two arms—one shorter and browner, the other long and pale—in unison. The former feels lighter, the latter clumsy and heavy. The drugs have faded from one body but not the other.

One heart pounds, hard, and the other maintains a steady rhythm.

"To kill us," we say to ourself. "Are we sure?"

"As sure as the fates. She wants us dead."

"The fates." There is dissonance here. Just as a person can love and hate something at once, we love and hate the fates, we believe and do not believe in them. "What was the word our mother used—" We have two mothers, two fathers, two sisters. And yet only one brother. "Accept your fate, or bear it, or—"

"'Suffer the fate,' she said," we reply. "'For all else is delusion.'"

Shithi. Verb. In Thuvhesit: "can/should/must"

CHAPTER 1 | CYRA

LAZMET NOAVEK, MY FATHER and former tyrant of Shotet, had been presumed dead for over ten seasons. We had held a funeral for him on the first sojourn after his passing, sent his old armor into space, because there was no body.

And yet my brother, Ryzek, imprisoned in the belly of this transport ship, had said, *Lazmet is still alive.*

My mother had called my father "Laz," sometimes. No one else would have dared but Ylira Noavek. "Laz," she would say, "let it go." And he obeyed her, as long as she didn't command him too often. He respected her, though he respected no one else, not even his own friends.

With her he had some softness, but with everyone else . . . well.

My brother—who had begun his life soft, and only later hardened into someone who would torture his own sister—had learned to cut out a person's eye from Lazmet. And how to store it, too, in a preservative, so it wouldn't rot. Before I truly understood what the jars in the Weapons Hall contained, I had gone there to look at them, on shelves high above my head, glinting in the low light. Green and brown and gray irises, afloat, like fish bobbing to the surface of a tank for food.

My father had never carved a piece of someone with his own hands. Nor had he ordered someone else to do it. He had used his currentgift to control their bodies, to force them to do it to themselves.

Death is not the only punishment you can give a person. You can also give them nightmares.

When Akos Kereseth came to find me, later, it was on the nav deck of the small transport ship that carried us away from my home planet, where my people, the Shotet, now stood on the verge of war with Akos's home nation of Thuvhe. I sat in the captain's chair, swiveling back and forth to soothe myself. I meant to tell him what Ryzek had told me, that my father—if he *was* my father, if Ryzek was even my brother—was alive. Ryzek seemed certain that he and I didn't actually share blood, that I was not truly a Noavek. That was why, he had said, I hadn't been able to open the gene lock that kept his rooms secure, why I hadn't been able to assassinate him the first time I tried.

But I didn't know how to begin. With the death of my father? With the body we had never found? With the niggling feeling that Ryzek and I were too dissimilar in features to have ever been related?

Akos didn't seem to want to talk, either. He spread a blanket he had found somewhere in the ship on the ground between the captain's chair and the wall, and we lay on top of it, side by side, staring out at nothingness. Currentshadows—my lively, painful ability—wrapped around my arms like black string, sending a deep ache all the way down to my fingertips.

I was not afraid of emptiness. It made me feel small. Barely worth a first glance, let alone a second. And there was comfort in that, because so often I worried that I was capable of causing too much damage. At least, if I was small and kept to myself, I wouldn't do any more harm. I wanted only what was within arm's reach.

Akos's index finger hooked around my pinkie. The shadows disappeared as his currentgift countered mine.

Yes, what was within arm's reach was definitely enough for me.

"Would you . . . say something in Thuvhesit?" he asked.

I turned my head toward him. He was still looking up at the window, a faint smile curling his lips. Freckles dotted his nose, and one of his eyelids, right near the lash line. I hesitated with my hand just lifted off the blanket, wanting to touch him but also wanting to stay in the wanting for a moment. Then I followed the line of his eyebrow across his face with a fingertip.

"I'm not a pet bird," I said. "I don't chirp on command."

"This is a request, not a command. A humble one," he said. "Just say my full name, maybe?"

I laughed. "Most of your name is Shotet, remember?"

"Right." He lunged at my hand with his mouth, snapping his teeth together. It startled a laugh from me. "What was hardest for you to say, when you were first learning?"

"Your city names, what a mouthful," I said as he let go of one of my hands to catch the other, holding me by pinkie and thumb with all his fingertips. He pressed a kiss to the center of my palm, where the skin was callused from holding currentblades. Strange, that something so simple, given to a hardened part of me, could suffuse me so completely, bringing life to every nerve.

I sighed, acquiescing.

"Fine, I'll say them. Hessa, Shissa, Osoc," I said. "There was a chancellor who called Hessa the very heart of Thuvhe. Her surname was Kereseth."

"The only Kereseth chancellor in Thuvhesit history," Akos said, bringing my palm to his cheek. I propped myself up on one elbow to lean over him, my hair slipping forward to frame both our faces, long on one side though I was now silverskinned on the other. "I do know that much."

"For a long time, there were only two fated families on Thuvhe," I said, "and yet, aside from that one exception, the leadership has only ever been with the Benesits, when the fates have named a chancellor at all. Is that not strange to you?"

"Maybe we aren't any good at leading."

"Maybe fate favors you," I said. "Maybe thrones are curses."

"Fate doesn't favor me," he said gently, so gently I almost didn't realize what he meant. His fate—*the third child of the family Kereseth will die in service to the family Noavek*—was to betray his home for my family, in serving us, and to die. How could anyone see that as anything but a hardship?

I shook my head. "I'm sorry, I wasn't thinking—"

"Cyra," he said. Then he paused, frowning at me. "Did you just apologize?"

"I do know the words," I replied, scowling back. "I'm not completely without manners."

He laughed. "I know the Essanderae word for 'garbage'; that doesn't mean I sound right saying it."

"Fine, I revoke my apology." I flicked his nose, hard, and when he cringed away, still laughing, I said, "What's the Essanderae word for 'garbage'?"

He said it. It sounded like a word reflected in a mirror, said once forward and once backward.

"I've found your weakness," he said. "I just have to taunt you with knowledge you don't have, and you're distracted immediately."

I considered that. "I guess you're allowed to know *one* of my weaknesses . . . considering you have so many to exploit."

He raised his eyebrows in question, and I attacked him with my fingers, jabbing his left side just under his elbow, his right side just above his hip, the tendon behind his right leg. I had learned these soft places when we were training—places he didn't protect well enough, or that made him cringe harder than usual when struck—but I teased him now with more gentleness than I had thought myself capable of, drawing from him laughs instead of cringes.

He pulled me on top of him, holding me by the hips. A few of his fingers slipped under the waistband of my pants, and it was a kind of agony I was unfamiliar with, a kind I didn't mind at all. I braced myself on the blanket, on either side of his head, and lowered myself slowly to kiss him.

We hadn't kissed more than a few times, and I had never kissed anyone but him, so each time was still a discovery. This time I found the edge of teeth, skimming, and the tip of a tongue; I found the slide of a knee between mine, and the weight of a hand at the back of my neck, urging me closer, further, faster. I didn't breathe, didn't want to take the time, and so I ended up gasping against the side of his neck before long, making him laugh.

"I'll take that as a good sign," he said.

"Don't get cocky, Kereseth."

I couldn't keep myself from smiling. Lazmet—and whatever questions I had about my parentage—didn't feel as close to me now. I was safe here, floating on a ship in the middle of nowhere, with Akos Kereseth.

And then: a scream, from somewhere deep in the ship. It sounded like Akos's sister, Cisi.

CHAPTER 2 | CISI

I KNOW WHAT IT is to watch your family die. I am Cisi Kereseth, after all.

I watched Dad die on our living room floor. I watched Eijeh and Akos get dragged away by Shotet soldiers. I watched Mom fade like fabric in the sun. There's not much I don't understand about loss. I just can't express it the way other people do. My currentgift keeps me all wrapped up tight.

So I'm a little bit jealous of how Isae Benesit, fated chancellor of Thuvhe and my friend, can let herself grieve. She wears herself out with emotion, and then we fall asleep, shoulder to shoulder, in the galley of the Shotet exile ship.

When I wake up, my back hurts from slumping against the wall for so long. I get up and lean to the left, to the right, while I take note of her.

Isae doesn't look right, which I guess makes sense, since her twin sister, Ori, died only yesterday, in an arena of Shotet all chanting for her blood.

She doesn't *feel* right, either, the texture around her all fuzzy like the way your teeth feel when you haven't brushed them. Her eyes skip back and forth over the room, dancing across my face and body, and not in a way that would make a person blush. I try to calm her with my currentgift, sending out a smooth feeling, like unrolling a skein of silk thread. It doesn't seem like it does much good.

My currentgift is an odd thing. I can't know how she feels, not really, but I can feel it, like it's a texture in the air. And I can't control how she feels, either, but I can make suggestions. Sometimes it takes a couple of tries, or a new way of thinking about it. So instead of silk, which had no effect, I try water, heavy, undulating.

It's a bust. She's too keyed up. Sometimes, when a person's feelings are too intense, it's hard for me to make an impact.

"Cisi, can I trust you?"

It's a funny word in Thuvhesit, *can*. It's *can* and *should* and *must* all squished together, and you can only suss out the true meaning from context. It leads to misunderstandings, sometimes, which is probably why our language is described by off-worlders as "slippery." That, and off-worlders are lazy.

So when Isae Benesit asks me in my mother tongue if she can trust me, I don't really know what she means. But regardless, there's only one answer.

"Of course."

"I mean it, Cisi," she says, in that low voice she uses when she's serious. I like that voice, the way it hums in my head. "There's something I have to do, and I want you to come with me, but I'm afraid you won't be—"

"Isae," I cut her off. "I'm here for you, whatever you need." I touch her shoulder with gentle fingers. "Okay?"

She nods.

She leads me out of the galley, and I try not to step on any kitchen knives. After she shut herself in here, she ripped all the drawers out, broke everything she could get her hands on. The floor is covered with shreds of fabric and pieces of glass and cracked plastic and unrolled bandages. I guess I don't blame her.

My currentgift keeps me from doing or saying things that I know will make people uncomfortable. Which means that, after my dad died, I couldn't cry unless I was alone. I couldn't say much of anything to my mom for months. So if I'd been able to destroy a kitchen, like Isae did, I probably would have.

I follow Isae out, quiet. We walk past Ori's body. It has a sheet tucked nicely around it, so it's just the slopes of her shoulders, the bump of her nose and chin. Just an impression of who she was. Isae stops there, draws a sharp breath. She feels even grittier now than she did before, like grains of sand against my skin. I know I can't soothe her, but I'm too worried about her not to try.

I send airy feathergrass tufts, and hard, polished wood. I send warm oil and rounded metal. Nothing works. I chafe against her, frustrated. Why can't I do *anything* to help her?

I think, for a tick, of asking for help. Akos and Cyra are right there on the nav deck. Mom's somewhere below. Even Akos and Cyra's renegade friend, Teka, is right there, stretched out on the bench seats with a sheet of white-blond hair sprawled across behind her. But I can't call out to any of them. For one thing,

I just can't—can't knowingly cause distress, thanks to my gift-curse—and for another, instinct tells me it's better if I can earn Isae's trust.

Isae leads us down below, where there are two storage rooms and a washroom. Mom's in the washroom, I can tell by the sound of the recycled water splattering. In one storage room—the one with the window, I made sure of that—is my other brother, Eijeh. It hurt me to see him again, so long after his kidnapping, and so small compared to the pale pillar of Ryzek Noavek next to him. You think when people get older, they're supposed to get stronger, fatter. Not Eijeh.

The other storage room—the one with all the cleaning supplies—holds Ryzek Noavek. Just knowing he's that close, the man who ordered my brothers taken and my dad killed, makes me tremble. Isae pauses between the two doors, and it hits me, then, that she's going in one of those rooms. And I don't want her to go in Eijeh's.

I know he's the one who killed Ori, technically. That is, he was holding the knife that did it. But I know my brother. He could never kill anyone, especially not his best friend from childhood. There has to be some other explanation for what happened. It has to be Ryzek's fault.

"Isae," I say. "What are you—"

She touches three fingers to her lips, telling me to hush.

She's right between the rooms. Deciding something, it seems like, judging by the faint buzz around her. She takes a key from her pocket—she must have lifted it off Teka, when she went out to make sure we were headed to Assembly Headquarters—and sticks it in the lock for Ryzek's cell. I reach for her hand.

"He's dangerous," I say.

"I can handle it," she replies. And then, softening around the eyes: "I won't let him hurt you, I promise."

I let her go. There's a part of me that's hungry to see him, to meet the monster at last.

She opens the door, and he's sitting against the back wall, sleeves rolled up, feet outstretched. He has long, skinny toes, and narrow ankles. I blink at them. Are sadistic dictators supposed to have vulnerable-looking feet?

If Isae's at all intimidated, she doesn't let on. She stands with her hands clasped in front of her and her head high.

"My, my," Ryzek says, running his tongue over his teeth. "Resemblance between twins never fails to shock me. You look just like Orieve Benesit. Except for those scars, of course. How old are they?"

"Two seasons," Isae says, stiff.

She's talking to him. She's *talking* to Ryzek Noavek, my sworn enemy, kidnapper of her sister, with a long line of kills tattooed on the outside of his arm.

"They will fade still, then," he says. "A shame. They made a lovely shape."

"Yes, I'm a work of art," she says. "The artist was a Shotet flesh-worm who had just finished digging around in a pile of garbage."

I stare at her. I've never heard her say something so hateful about the Shotet before. It's not like her.

"Fleshworm" is what people call the Shotet when they're reaching for the worst insult. Fleshworms are gray, wriggly things that feed on the living from the inside out. Parasites, all but eradicated by Othyrian medicine.

"Ah." His smile grows wider, forcing a dimple into his cheek. There's something about him that sparks in my memory. Maybe something he has in common with Cyra, though they don't look at all alike, at a glance. "So this grudge you have against my people isn't merely in your blood."

"No." She sinks into a crouch, resting her elbows on her knees. She makes it look graceful and controlled, but I'm worried about her. She's long and willowy in build, not near as strong as Ryzek, who is *big*, though thin. One wrong move and he could lunge at her, and what would I do to stop it? Scream?

"You know about scars, I suppose," she says, nodding to his arm. "Will you mark my sister's life?"

The inside of his forearm, the softer, paler part, doesn't have any scars—they start on the outside and work their way around, row by row. He has more than one row.

"Why, have you brought me a knife and some ink?"

Isae purses her lips. The sandpaper feeling she gave off a moment ago turns as jagged as a broken stone. By instinct, I press back against the door and find the handle behind my back.

"Do you always claim kills you didn't actually carry out?" Isae says. "Because last time I checked, you weren't the one on that platform with the knife."

Ryzek's eyes glint.

"I wonder if you've ever actually killed at all, or if all that work is done by others." Her head tilts. "Others who, unlike you, actually have the stomach for it."

It's a Shotet insult. The kind a Thuvhesit wouldn't even realize was insulting. Ryzek picks up on it, though, eyes boring into hers.

"Miss Kereseth," he says, without looking at me. "You look so much like the elder of your two brothers." He glances at me, then, appraising. "Are you not curious what's become of him?"

I want to answer coolly, like Ryzek is nothing to me. I want to meet his eyes with strength. I want a thousand fantasies of revenge to come suddenly to life like hushflowers at the Blooming.

I open my mouth, but nothing comes out.

Fine, I think, and I let out a peal of my currentgift, like a clap of my hands. I've come to understand that not everybody can control their currentgifts the way I can. I just wish I could master the part that keeps me from saying what I want to.

I see how he relaxes when my gift hits him. It has no effect on Isae—none that I can see, anyway—but maybe it will loosen his tongue. And whatever Isae is planning, she seems to need him to talk first.

"My father, the great Lazmet Noavek, taught me that people can be like blades, if you learn to wield them, but your best weapon should still be yourself," Ryzek says. "I have always taken that to heart. Some of the kills I have commanded have been carried out by others, Chancellor, but rest assured, those deaths are still mine."

He slumps forward over his knees, clasping his hands between them. He and Isae are just breaths apart.

"I will mark your sister's life on my arm," he says. "It will be a fine trophy to add to my collection."

Ori. I remember which tea she drank in the morning (harva bark, for energy and clarity) and how much she hated the chip in her front tooth. And I hear the chants of the Shotet in my ears: *Die, die, die.*

"That clarifies things," Isae says.

She holds her hand out for him to take. He gives her an odd look, and no wonder—what kind of person wants to shake hands with the man who just admitted to ordering her sister's death? And being *proud* of it?

"You really are an odd one," he says. "You must not have loved your sister very much, to offer your hand to me now."

I see the skin pull taut over the knuckles of her other hand, the one not held out to him. She opens her fist, and inches her fingers toward her boot.

Ryzek takes the hand she offered, then stiffens, eyes widening.

"On the contrary, I loved her more than anyone," Isae says. She squeezes him, hard, digging in her fingernails. And all the while, her left hand moves toward her boot.

I'm too stunned to realize what's happening until it's too late. With her left hand she tugs a knife out of her boot, from where it's strapped to her leg. With her right, she pulls him forward. Knife and man come together, and she presses, and the sound of his gurgling moan carries me to my living room, to my adolescence, to the blood that I scrubbed from the floorboards as I sobbed.

Ryzek slumps, and bleeds.

I slam my hand down on the door handle and stumble into the hallway. I am wailing, crying, pounding on the walls; no, I'm not, my currentgift won't let me.

All it allows me to do, in the end, is let out a single, weak scream.

CHAPTER 3 | CYRA

I RAN TOWARD CISI Kereseth's scream, Akos on my heels, not even bothering with the rungs of the ladder that took me below deck—I just jumped down. I went straight toward Ryzek's cell, knowing, of course, that he was likely the source of anything that caused screaming on this ship. I saw Cisi braced against the corridor wall, the storage room door across from her open. Behind her, Teka dropped down from the other end of the ship, beckoned here by the same noise. Isae Benesit stood inside Ryzek's cell, and below her, in a jumble of legs and arms, was my brother.

There was a certain amount of poetry in it, I supposed, that just as Akos had watched his father spill his life on the floor, so I now watched my brother do the same.

It took far longer for him to die than I anticipated. That was intentional, I assumed; Isae Benesit stood over his body the entire time, bloody knife in her fist, eyes blank but watchful. She had wanted to take her time with this moment, her moment of triumph over the one who killed her sister.

Well, *one* of the ones who killed her sister, because Eijeh, who had held the actual blade, was still in the next room.

Ryzek's eyes found mine, and almost as if he'd touched me, I was buoyed into a memory. Not one that he was taking from me, but one I had almost hidden from myself.

I was in the passage behind the Weapons Hall, with my eye pressed to the crack in the wall panel. I had gone there to spy on my father's meeting with a prominent Shotet businessman-turned-slumlord, because I often spied on my father's meetings when I was bored and curious about the happenings of this house. But this meeting had gone bad, which had never happened before when I peeked in. My father had stretched out a hand, two fingers held aloft, like a Zoldan ascetic about to give a blessing, and the businessman had drawn his own knife, his movements jerky, like he was fighting his own muscles.

He brought the knife to the inside corner of his eye.

"Cyra!" hissed a voice behind me, making me jerk to attention. A young, spotted Ryzek slid to his knees beside me. He cradled my face in his hands. I had not realized, before that moment, that I was crying. As the screaming started in the next room, he pressed his palms flat to my ears, and brought my face to his chest.

I struggled, at first, but he was too strong. All I could hear was the pounding of my own heart.

At last he pulled me away, wiped the tears from my cheeks, and said, "What does Mother always say? Those who go looking for pain . . ."

"Find it every time," I replied, completing the phrase.

Teka held me by the shoulders, and jostled me a little, saying my name. I looked at her, then, confused.

"What is it?" I said.

"Your currentshadows were . . ." She shook her head. "Never mind."

I knew what she meant. My currentgift had likely gone haywire, sending sprawling black lines all over me. The current-shadows had changed since Ryzek tried to use me to torture Akos in the cell block beneath the amphitheater. They drifted on top of my skin now, instead of burrowing beneath it like dark veins. But they were still painful, and I could tell this episode had been worse—my vision was blurry, and there were impressions of fingernails in my palms.

Akos was kneeling in my brother's blood, his fingers on the side of Ryzek's throat. I watched as his hand fell away, and he slumped, bracing himself on his thighs.

"It's done," Akos said, sounding thick, like his throat was coated in milk. "After everything Cyra did to help me—after *everything*—"

"I won't apologize," Isae said, finally looking away from Ryzek. She scanned all our faces—Akos, surrounded by blood; Teka, wide-eyed at my shoulder; me, arms streaked black; Cisi, holding her stomach near the wall. The air was pungent with the smell of sick.

"He murdered my sister," Isae said. "He was a tyrant and a torturer and a killer. I won't apologize."

"It's not about *him*. You think I didn't want him dead?" Akos lurched to his feet. Blood ran down the front of his pants, from knees to ankles. "Of course I did! He took more from me than he did from you!" He was so close to her I wondered if he would lash out, but he made a fitful motion with his hands, and that was all. "I wanted him to fix what he did first, I wanted him to set Eijeh right, I . . ."

It seemed to hit him all at once. Ryzek was—had been—my

brother, but the grief was his. He had persevered, carefully orchestrated every element of his brother's rescue, only to find himself
blocked, again and again, by people more powerful than he was.
And now, he had succeeded in getting his brother out of Shotet,
but he had not saved him, and all the planning, all the fighting, all
the *trying* . . . was for nothing.

Akos fell against the nearest wall to hold himself up, closed his
eyes, and swallowed a moan.

I found my way out of my trance.

"Go upstairs," I said to Isae. "Take Cisi with you."

She looked like she might object, for a moment, but it didn't
last. Instead, she dropped the murder weapon—a simple kitchen
knife—right where she stood, and went to Cisi's side.

"Teka," I said. "Would you get Akos upstairs, please?"

"Are you—" Teka started, and stopped. "Okay."

Isae and Cisi, Teka and Akos, they left me there, alone, with
my brother's body. He had died next to a mop and a bottle of
disinfectant. *How convenient*, I thought, and stifled a laugh. Or
tried to. But it wouldn't stay stifled. In moments my knees were
weak with laughter, and I fumbled through my hair for the side
of my head that was now silverskin, to remind myself how he had
sliced and diced me for the entertainment of a crowd, how he had
planted pieces of himself inside me, as if I was just a barren field
to sow with pain. My entire body carried the scars Ryzek Noavek
had given me.

And now, at last, I was free of him.

When I calmed, I set about cleaning up Isae Benesit's mess.

Ryzek's body didn't frighten me, and neither did blood. I

dragged him by his legs into the hallway, sweat tickling the back of my neck as I heaved and pulled. He was heavy, in death, as I was sure he had been in life, skeletal though he was. When Akos's oracle mother, Sifa, appeared to help me, I didn't say anything to her, just watched as she worked a sheet beneath him so we could wrap him in it. She produced a needle and thread from the storage room, and helped me stitch the makeshift burial sack closed.

Shotet funerals, when they took place on land, involved fire, like most cultures in our varied solar system. But it was a special honor to die in space, on the sojourn. We covered the bodies, all but the head, so the loved ones of whoever was lost could see and accept the person's death. When Sifa pulled the sheet back, away from Ryzek's face, I knew she had at least studied our customs.

"I see so many possibilities for how things will unfold," Sifa said finally, dragging her arm across her forehead to catch some of the sweat. "I didn't think this one was likely, or I might have warned you."

"No, you wouldn't have," I said, lifting a shoulder. "You only intervene when it suits your purposes. My comfort and ease don't matter to you."

"Cyra . . ."

"I don't care," I said. "I hated him. Just . . . don't pretend that you care about me."

"I am not pretending," she replied.

I had thought, surely, that I might see some of Akos in her. And in her mannerisms, yes, perhaps he was there. Mobile eyebrows and quick, decisive hands. But her face, her light brown skin, her modest stature, they were not his.

I didn't know how to evaluate her honesty, so I didn't bother.

"Help me carry him to the trash chute," I said.

I took the heavy side of his body, his head and shoulders, and she took his feet. It was lucky that the trash chute was only a few feet away, another unexpected convenience. We took it in stages, a few steps at a time. Ryzek's head lolled around, his eyes open but sightless, but there was nothing I could do about it. I set him down next to the chute, and pressed the button to open the first set of doors, at waist height. It was fortunate that he was so narrow, or his shoulders wouldn't have fit. Together Sifa and I folded him into the short channel, bending his legs so the inner doors would be able to close. Once they had, I pressed the button again, to open the outer doors and slide the tray in the chute forward to launch his body into space.

"I know the prayer, if you want me to say it," Sifa said.

I shook my head.

"They said that prayer at my mother's funeral," I said. "No."

"Then let us just acknowledge that he has suffered his fate," Sifa said. "To fall to the family Benesit. He no longer needs to fear it."

It was kind enough.

"I'm going to clean myself up," I said. The blood on my palms was beginning to dry, making them itch.

"Before you do," Sifa said, "I will warn you of this. Ryzek was not the only person the chancellor blamed for her sister's death. In fact, she likely began with him because she was saving the more important piece of retribution for later. And she won't stop there, either. I have seen enough of her to know her nature, and it is not forgiving."

I blinked at her for a moment before it made sense to me.

She was talking about Eijeh, still locked away in the other storage room. And not just Eijeh, but the rest of us—complicit, Isae believed, in Orieve's death.

"There is an escape pod," Sifa said. "We can put her in it, and someone from the Assembly will fetch her."

"Tell Akos to drug her," I said. "I don't feel up to a fight right now."

CHAPTER 4 | AKOS

AKOS WADED THROUGH THE cutlery that was all over the galley floor. The water was already heating, and the vial of sedative was ready to dump into the tea, he just had to get some dried herbs into the strainer. The ship bumped along, and he stepped on a fork, flattening the tines with his heel.

He cursed his stupid head, which couldn't stop telling him that there was still hope for Eijeh. *There are so many people across the galaxy, with so many gifts. Somebody will know how to put him right.* Truth was, Akos was tired of hanging on to hope. He'd been clawing at it since he first got to Shotet, and now he was ready to let go and just let fate take him where it wanted him to go. To death, and Noaveks, and Shotet.

All he'd promised his dad was that he would get Eijeh home. Maybe here—floating in space—was the best he could do. Maybe that would just have to be enough.

But—

"Shut up," he said to himself, and he dumped the herbs from the galley cabinet into a strainer. There weren't any iceflowers, but he'd learned enough about Shotet plants to make a simple calming blend. At this point, though, there was no artistry in it. He was just going through the motions, folding bits of garok root into powdered fenzu shell and squeezing a little nectar on top of it all, for taste. He didn't even know what to call the plants that made up the nectar—he'd taken to calling the little fragile flowers "mushflowers" while he was at the army training camp outside Voa, because of how easily they fell apart, but he'd never learned the right name for them. They tasted sweet, and that seemed to be their only use.

When the water was hot, he poured it through the strainer. The extract it left behind was a murky brown, perfect for hiding the yellow of the sedative. His mom had told him to drug Isae and he hadn't even asked why. He didn't care, as long as it got her out of his sight. He couldn't quite escape the image of her standing there watching Ryzek Noavek gush blood like it was some kind of show. Isae Benesit may have worn Ori's face, but she wasn't anything like her. He couldn't imagine Ori just standing there and watching someone die, no matter how much she hated them.

Once the extract was brewed and mixed with the drug, he brought it to Cisi, who was sitting alone on the bench just outside the galley.

"You waiting for me?" he said.

"Yeah," she said. "Mom told me to."

"Good," he said. "Will you take this to Isae? It's just to calm her down."

Cisi raised an eyebrow at him.

"Don't drink any of it yourself," he added.

She reached for it, but instead of taking the mug, she put her hand on his wrist. The look in her eyes changed—sharpened—like it always did when his currentgift dampened her own.

"What's left of Eijeh?" she asked.

Akos's whole body clenched up. He didn't want to think about what was left of Eijeh.

"Someone who served Ryzek Noavek," he said, with venom. "Who hated me, and Dad, and probably you and Mom, too."

"How is that possible?" She frowned. "He can't *hate* us just because someone put different memories into his head."

"You think I know?" Akos all but growled.

"Then, maybe—"

"He held me down while someone tortured me." Akos shoved the mug into her hands.

Some of the hot tea spilled on both their hands. Cisi jerked away, wiping her knuckles on her pants.

"Did I burn you?" he said, nodding to her hand.

"No," she said. The softness her currentgift brought to her expression was back. Akos didn't want tenderness of any kind, so he turned away.

"This won't hurt her, will it?" Cisi said, tapping a fingernail on the mug so he would hear the *ting ting ting*.

"No," he said. "It's to keep from having to hurt her."

"Then I'll give it to her," Cisi said.

Akos grunted a little. There was some more sedative in his pack, maybe he ought to take it. He'd never been so worn, like a half-finished weaving, light showing between all the threads. It would be easier just to sleep.

Instead of drugging himself to oblivion, though, he just took a dried hushflower petal from his pocket and stuck it between his cheek and his teeth. It wouldn't knock him out, but it would dull him some. Better than nothing.

Akos was coasting on hushflower an hour later when Cisi came back.

"It's done," she said. "She's out."

"All right," he said. "Then let's get her into the escape pod."

"I'm going with her," Cisi said. "If Mom's right, and we're headed into war——"

"Mom's right."

"Yeah," Cisi said. "Well, in that case, whoever's against Isae is against Thuvhe. So I'm going to stick with my chancellor."

Akos nodded.

"I take it you won't be," Cisi said.

"Fated traitor, remember?" he said.

"Akos." She crouched in front of him. At some point he had sat down on the bench, which was hard and cold and smelled like disinfectant. Cisi rested an arm on his knee. She had tied her hair back, messy, and a chunk of curls had come loose, falling around her face. She was pretty, his sister, her face a shade of cool brown that reminded him of Trellan pottery. A lot like Cyra's, and Eijeh's, and Jorek's. Familiar.

"You don't have to do anything you don't want to, just because Mom raised us fate-faithful and obedient to the oracles and all that," Cisi said. "You're a Thuvhesit. You should come with me. Leave everyone else to their war, and we'll go home and wait it out. No one needs us here."

He'd thought about it. He was as torn now as he'd ever been, and not just because of his fate. When he came out of the daze of the hushflower, he would remember how nice it felt to laugh with Cyra earlier that day, and how warm she was, pressed up against him. And he would remember that as much as he wanted to just be in his house again, walk up the creaky stairs and stoke the burnstones in the courtyard and send flour up into the air as he kneaded the bread, he had to live in the real world. In the real world, Eijeh was broken, Akos spoke Shotet, and his fate was still his fate.

"Suffer the fate," he said. "For all else is delusion."

Cisi sighed. "Thought you might say that. Sometimes delusion's nice, though."

"Stay safe, okay?" he said, taking her hand. "I hope you know I don't want to leave you again. It's pretty much the last thing I want."

"I know." She squeezed his thumb. "I still have faith, you know. That one day you'll come home, and Eijeh will be better, and Mom will stop with the oracle bullshit, and we can cobble together something again."

"Yeah." He tried to smile for her. He might have halfway accomplished it.

She helped him get Isae settled in the escape pod, and Teka told her how to send out a distress signal so the pod would be picked up by Assembly "goons," as Teka called them. Then Cisi kissed their mom good-bye, and wrapped her arms tight around Akos's middle until her warmth was pushed all the way through him.

"You're so damn tall," she said, softly, as she pulled away.

"Who told you that you could be so much taller than me?"

"I did it just to spite you," he replied with a grin.

Then she got in the pod, and closed the doors. And he didn't know when he would ever see her again.

Teka tripped up to the captain's chair on the nav deck and pried the cover of the control panel off with a wedge tool she kept on her belt. She did it while whistling.

"What are you doing?" Cyra asked. "Now's not really the time to take apart our ship."

"First, this is *my* ship, not 'ours,'" Teka said with a roll of her blue eye. "I designed most of the features that have kept us alive so far. Second, do you really still want to go to Assembly Headquarters?"

"No." Cyra sat in the first officer's chair, to Teka's right. "The last time I went there, I overheard the representative from Trella call my mother a piece of filth. She didn't think I could understand her, even though she was speaking Othyrian."

"Figures." Teka made a scoffing sound in the back of her throat as she pulled out a handful of wires from the control panel, then ran her fingers down them like she was petting an animal. She reached under the wires, to a part of the control panel Akos couldn't see, so far her entire arm disappeared. A projection of coordinates flashed up ahead, glowing right across the current-stream in their sights. The ship's nose—Akos was sure there was a technical name for it, but he didn't know it, so he called it a "nose"—drifted so they were moving toward the currentstream instead of away.

"You going to tell us where we're headed?" Akos said, stepping up to the nav deck. The control panel was lit up in all different colors, with levers and buttons and switches everywhere. If Teka had spread her arms wide, she still wouldn't have been able to reach all of them from where she sat.

"I guess I can, since we're all stuck in this together now," Teka said. She gathered her bright hair on top of her head, and tied it with a thick band she wore around her wrist. Swimming in a technician's coveralls, with her legs folded up beneath her on the captain's chair, she looked like a kid playing pretend. "We're going to the exile colony. Which is on Ogra."

Ogra. The "shadow planet," people called it. It was rare to meet an Ogran, let alone fly a ship in sight of Ogra. It was as far from Thuvhe as any planet could be without leaving the safe band of currentstream that encircled the solar system. No amount of surveillance could poke through its dense, dark atmosphere, and it was a wonder they could get any signal from the news feed. They never fed any stories into it, either, so almost no one had ever seen the planet's surface, even in images.

Cyra's eyes, of course, lit up at the information. "Ogra? But how do you communicate with them?"

"The easiest way to transmit messages without the government listening in is through people," Teka said. "That's why my mom was on board the sojourn ship—to represent the exiles' interests among the renegades. We were trying to work together. Anyway, the exile colony is a good place for us to regroup, figure out what's going on back in Voa."

"I have a guess," Akos said, crossing his arms. "Chaos."

"And then more chaos," Teka said with a sage nod. "With a short break in between. For chaos, of course."

He couldn't imagine what Voa looked like now that—the Shotet believed—Ryzek Noavek had been assassinated by his younger sister right in front of them. That was how it had looked, anyway, when Cyra appeared to cut her brother in the arena, waiting for the sleeping elixir she had arranged for him to drink that morning to kick in and knock him flat. The standing army might have taken over, under the leadership of Vakrez Noavek, Ryzek's older cousin, or those who lived on the outer edges of the city might have taken to the streets to fill the power vacuum. Either way, Akos imagined streets full of broken glass and blood spatter and ripped paper floating in the wind.

Cyra tipped her forehead into her hands. "And Lazmet," she said.

Teka's eyebrows popped up. "What?"

"Before Ryzek died . . ." Cyra gestured vaguely toward the other end of the ship, where Ryzek had met his end. "He told me my father is still alive."

Cyra didn't talk about Lazmet much, so all Akos knew was from history class, as a kid, and rumor, not that Thuvhesit rumors about the Shotet had proved to be all that accurate. The Noaveks hadn't been in power in Shotet before the oracles spoke the fates of the family Noavek for the first time, just two generations ago. When Lazmet's mother came of age, she had taken the throne by force, using her fate as justification for the coup. And later, when she had been sitting on the throne for at least ten seasons, she had killed off all her siblings so her own children would be guaranteed power. That was the kind of family Lazmet had come from, and he had been, by all accounts, every izit as brutal as his mother.

"Oh, honestly." Teka groaned. "Is it some kind of rule of the universe that at least one Noavek asshole has to be alive at any given time, or what?"

Cyra swiveled to face her. "What am I, then? Not alive?"

"Not an asshole," Teka replied. "Bicker with me much more and I'll change my mind."

Cyra looked faintly pleased. She wasn't used to people not considering her just another Noavek, Akos assumed.

"Whatever the rules of the universe pertaining to Noaveks," she said, "I don't know how Lazmet is still alive, just that Ryzek didn't appear to be lying when he told me. He wasn't trying to get anything in return, he was just . . . warning me, maybe."

Teka snorted. "Because, what, Ryzek loves doing favors?"

"Because he was scared of your dad," Akos said. When Cyra did talk about Ryzek, she always talked about how afraid he was. What could scare a man like Ryzek more than the man who had made him the way he was? "Right? He's more terrified than anyone. Or he was, anyway."

Cyra nodded.

"If Lazmet is alive . . ." Her eyes fluttered closed. "That needs to be corrected. As soon as possible."

That needs to be corrected. Like a math problem or a technical error. Akos didn't know how you could talk about your own dad that way. It rattled him more than it would have if Cyra had seemed scared. She couldn't even talk about him like he was a person. What had she seen him do, to make her talk about him that way?

"One problem at a time," Teka said, a little more gently than usual.

Akos cleared his throat. "Yeah, first let's survive getting through Ogra's atmosphere. *Then* we can assassinate the most powerful man in Shotet history."

Cyra opened her eyes, and laughed.

"Settle in for a long ride," Teka says. "We're bound for Ogra."

CHAPTER 5 | CISI

THE ESCAPE POD IS only just big enough for the two of us pressed together. As it is, my shoulder is still jammed up against the glass wall. I fumble on the little control panel for the switch that activates the distress signal. It's lit up pink, and it's one of only three switches in front of me, so it's not hard to find. I flip it up and hear a high-pitched whistling, which means the signal is transmitting, Teka said. Now all that's left to do is wait for Isae to wake up, and try not to panic.

Being on a little transport vessel like the one we just left is nerve-wracking enough for a Hessa girl who's only left the planet a couple times, but the escape pod is another thing. It's more window than floor, the clear glass curving up over my head and all the way down to my toes. I don't feel like I'm looking out at space so much as getting swallowed by it. I can't think about it or I'll panic.

I hope Isae wakes up soon.

She's limp on the bench seat next to me, and her body is framed by a blackness so complete, she really does look like the only thing in the entire universe. I've known her only a couple years, since Ori disappeared to take care of her after her face got cut with a Shotet knife. She grew up far away from Thuvhe, on a transporter ship that took goods from one end of the galaxy to the other, whatever they could haul.

It was a good thing Ori had been around to force us to talk to each other, in the beginning. I might never have talked to her otherwise. She was intimidating even *without* the title, tall and slim and beautiful, scars or no scars, and radiating *capability* like a machine.

I don't know how long it takes for her eyes to open. She drifts for a while, staring all bleary at what's in front of us, which is flat nothing in between the far-off wink of stars. Then she blinks at me.

"Cee?" she says. "Where are we?"

"We're in an escape pod, waiting for the Assembly to come get us," I say.

"An escape pod?" She frowns. "What did we need to escape from?"

"I think it's more that they wanted to escape from *us*," I say.

"Did you drug me?" She rubs her eyes with a fist, first the left one and then the right. "You gave me that tea."

"I didn't know there was anything in it." I'm a good liar, and I don't think twice. She wouldn't accept the truth—that I wanted to get her away from the rest of my family just as much as Akos did. Mom said Isae was going to try to kill Eijeh the same way she did Ryzek, and I wasn't willing to risk it. I don't want to lose Eijeh again, no matter how warped he is now. "Mom warned them you might try to hurt Eijeh, too."

Isae curses. "Oracles! It's a wonder we even let them have citizenship, with all the loyalty your mother shows her own chancellor."

I have nothing to say to that. She's frustrating, but she's my mother.

I continue, "They put you in the pod, and I told them I was going with you."

The scars that cross her face stay stiff while her brow furrows. She rubs them, sometimes, when she thinks no one is looking. She says it helps the scar tissue to stretch out, so one day she'll be able to move those parts of her face again. That's what the doctor said, anyway. I once asked her why she just let the scars form instead of getting reconstructive surgery on Othyr. It's not like she didn't have the resources. She told me she didn't want to get rid of them, that she liked them.

"Why?" she finally says after a long pause. "They're your family. Eijeh's your brother. Why would you come with me?"

Giving an honest answer isn't as easy as people say. There are so many answers to her question, all of them true. She's my chancellor, and I'm not going to oppose Thuvhe, like my brother is. I care about her, as a friend, as . . . whatever else we are to each other. I'm worried about the wild grief I saw in her right before she killed Ryzek Noavek, and she needs help to do what's right from now on rather than what satisfies her thirst for revenge. The list goes on, and the answer I choose is as much about what I want her to hear as it is about the truth.

"You asked me if you could trust me," I finally say. "Well, you can. I'm with you, no matter what. Okay?"

"I thought, after what you saw me do . . ." I think of the knife she used to kill Ryzek dropping to the floor, and push the memory away. "I thought you wouldn't want to be anywhere near me."

What she did to Ryzek didn't disgust me, it worried me. I don't care that he's dead, but I do care that she was able to kill him. I don't try to explain that to her, though.

"He killed Ori," I say.

"So did your brother," she whispers. "It was both of them, Cisi. There's something wrong with Eijeh. I saw it in Ryzek's head, right before—"

She chokes before she can finish her sentence.

"I know." I grab her hand and hold on tight. "I know."

She starts to cry. At first it's dignified, but then the beast of grief takes over, and she claws at my arms to get away from it, sobbing. But I know, I know as well as anybody that there's no escape. Grief is absolute.

"I got you," I say, rubbing circles on her back. "I got you."

She stops scratching after a while, stops sobbing. Just leans her face into my shoulder.

"What did you do?" she asks, voice muffled by my shirt. "After your dad died, after your brothers . . ."

"I . . . I just did things, for a long time. I ate, showered, worked, studied. But I wasn't really there, or at least, I didn't feel like I was. But . . . it was like when feeling comes back to a limb that's gone numb. It comes back in little prickles, little pieces at a time."

She lifts her head to look at me.

"I'm sorry I didn't tell you what I was about to do. I'm sorry I asked you to come see . . . *that*," she says. "I needed a witness, just in case it went wrong, and you were the only one I trusted."

I sigh, and push her hair behind her ears. "I know."

"Would you have stopped me, if you knew?"

I purse my lips. The real answer is that I don't know, but that's not the one I want to give her, not the one that will make her trust me. And she has to trust me, if I'm going to do any good in the war that's coming.

"No," I say. "I know you only do what you have to."

It was true. But it didn't mean I wasn't worried about how simple it had been to her, and the distant look in her eyes as she led me to that storage room, and the perfect hesitation she had shown Ryzek as she waited for just the right moment to stab him.

"They're not going to take our planet," she says to me, in a dark whisper. "I won't let them."

"Good," I say.

She takes my hand. We've held hands before, but that doesn't mean it doesn't still send a thrill through me when her skin slides over mine. She is still so capable. Smooth and strong. I want to kiss her, but this isn't the time, not when there's still Ryzek's blood drying under her fingernails.

So I just let the touch of her hand be enough, and we stare out together at nothingness.

CHAPTER 6 | AKOS

AKOS FUMBLED WITH THE chain around his neck. The ring of Jorek and Ara's family was a now-familiar weight right in the hollow of his throat. When he wore armor it made an imprint in his skin, like a brand. As if the mark on his arm wasn't enough to remind him of what he had done to Suzao Kuzar, Jorek's father and Ara's violent husband.

He wasn't sure why he thought of killing Suzao in the arena now, standing outside his brother's cell. It was time to decide if Eijeh ought to stay drugged—for how long? Until they got to Ogra? After that?—or if, now that Ryzek was dead, it was safe to risk Eijeh wandering around the ship clearheaded. Cyra and Teka had left the decision up to him and his mom.

His mom was right next to him, her head reaching just a few izits higher than his shoulder. Hair loose and messy around her shoulders, curled into knots. Sifa hadn't been much of anywhere since Ryzek died, holing up in the belly of the ship to whisper the future to herself, barefoot, pacing. Cyra and Teka had been alarmed, but he told them that's just how oracles were. Or at least, that was how his mother the oracle was. Sometimes sharp as a knife, sometimes half outside her own body, her own time.

"Eijeh's not how you remember him," he said to her. It was a useless warning. She knew it already, for one thing, and for another, she had probably seen him just the way he was now, and a hundred other ways besides.

Still, "I know" was all she said.

Akos tapped the door with his knuckles, then unlocked it with the key Teka had given him and walked in.

Eijeh sat cross-legged on the thin mattress they had thrown into the corner of the cell, an empty tray next to him with the dregs of soup left in a bowl on top of it. When he saw them he scrambled to his feet, hands held out like he might put them in fists and start pummeling. He was wan and red-eyed and shaky.

"What happened?" he said, eyes skirting Akos's. "W—I felt something. What happened?"

"Ryzek was killed," Akos replied. "You felt that?"

"Did *you* do it?" Eijeh asked with a sneer. "Wouldn't be surprised. You killed Suzao. You killed Kalmev."

"And Vas," Akos said. "You've got Vas somewhere in that memory stew, don't you?"

"He was a friend," Eijeh said.

"He was the man who *killed our father*," Akos spat.

Eijeh squinted, and said nothing.

"What about me?" Sifa said, voice flat. "Do you remember me, Eijeh?"

He looked at her like he had only just noticed she was there. "You're Sifa." He frowned. "You're Mom. I don't—there's gaps."

He stepped toward her and said, "Did I love you?"

Akos had never seen Sifa look hurt before, not even when they were younger and told her they hated her because she wouldn't let them go out with friends, or scolded them for bad scores on tests. He knew she got hurt, because she was a person as well as an oracle, and all people got hurt sometimes. But he wasn't quite ready for how the look pierced him, when it came, the furrowed brow and downturned mouth.

Did I love you? Akos knew, hearing those words, that he had definitely failed. He hadn't gotten Eijeh out of Shotet, as he had promised his father before he died. This wasn't really Eijeh, and what might have restored him was gone, now that Ryzek was dead.

Eijeh was gone. Akos's throat got tight.

"Only you can know," Sifa said. "Do you love me now?"

Eijeh twitched, made an aborted hand gesture. "I—maybe."

"Maybe." Sifa nodded. "Okay."

"You knew, didn't you. That I was the next oracle," he said. "You knew I would be kidnapped. You didn't warn me. You didn't get me ready."

"There are reasons for that," she said. "I doubt you would find any of them comforting."

"Comfort." Eijeh snorted. "I have no need for comfort."

He sounded like Ryzek then—that Shotet diction, put into Thuvhesit.

"But you do," Sifa said. "Everybody does."

Another snort, but no answer.

"Come here to drug me again, did you?" He nodded to Akos. "That's what you're good for, right? You're a poison-maker. And Cyra's whore."

Then Akos's hands were in fists in Eijeh's worn shirt, lifting him up, so his toes were just brushing the floor. He was heavy, but not too heavy for Akos, with the energy that burned inside him, energy that had nothing to do with the current.

Akos slammed him into the wall and growled, "Shut. Your. Mouth."

"Stop, both of you," Sifa said, her hand on Akos's shoulder. "Put him down. Now. If you can't stay calm, you'll have to leave."

Akos dropped Eijeh and stepped back. His ears were ringing. He hadn't meant to do that. Eijeh slid to the floor, and ran his hands over his buzzed head.

"I am not sure what Ryzek Noavek dumping his memories into your skull has to do with being so cruel to your brother," Sifa said to Eijeh. "Unless it's just the only way you know how to be, now. But I suggest you learn another way, and quickly, or I will devise a very creative punishment for you, as your mother and your superior, the sitting oracle. Understand?"

Eijeh looked her over for a few ticks, then his chin shifted, up and down, just a little.

"We are going to land in a few days," Sifa said. "We will keep you locked in here until our descent, at which point we will ensure you are safely strapped in with the rest of us. When we land, you will be my charge. You will do as I say. If you don't, I will have Akos drug you again. Our situation is too tenuous to risk you wreaking havoc." She turned to Akos. "How does that plan sound to you?"

"Fine," he said, teeth gritted.

"Good." She forced a smile that was completely without feeling. "Would you like anything to read while you're in here, Eijeh? Something to pass the time?"

"Okay," Eijeh said with a half shrug.

"I'll see what I can find."

She stepped toward him, making Akos tense up in case she needed his help. But Eijeh didn't stir as she picked up his empty tray, and he didn't look up at either of them when they left the room. Akos locked it behind him, and checked the handle twice to make sure the lock held. He was breathing fast. That was the Eijeh he remembered from Shotet, the one who walked around with Vas Kuzar like they were born friends instead of born enemies, and the one who held him down while Vas forced Cyra to torture him.

His eyes burned. He shut them.

"Had you seen him that way?" he said. "In visions, I mean."

"Yes," Sifa said, quiet.

"Did it help? To know it was coming?"

"It's not as straightforward as you think," she said. "I see so many paths, so many versions of people. . . . I'm always surprised to discover which future has come to pass. I am still not sure which Akos I am speaking to, for example. There are many that you could be."

She lapsed into quiet, and sighed.

"No," she said, finally. "It didn't help."

"I—" He gulped, and opened his eyes, not looking at his mother, but at the wall opposite him. "I'm sorry I couldn't stop it. I—I failed him."

"Akos—" She gripped his shoulder, and he let himself feel the warmth and the strength of her hand for a tick.

The cell that had held Ryzek was scrubbed clean, like nothing had ever happened. In some secret part of himself, he wished Eijeh had died, too. It would be easier than this, the constant reminder of how he'd messed it all up, and couldn't fix it.

"There's nothing you—"

"Don't," he said, more harshly than he meant to. "He's gone. And now there's nothing left to do but—bear it."

He turned, and left her standing there, caught between two sons who weren't quite the same as they used to be.

They took turns sitting on the nav deck to make sure the ship didn't steer straight into an asteroid or another spaceship or some other piece of debris. Sifa had the first shift, since Teka was exhausted from reprogramming the ship in the first place, and Cyra had spent the last several hours mopping up her own brother's blood. Akos cleared the floor of the galley and rolled out a blanket in the corner, near the medical supplies.

Cyra came to join him, her face scrubbed shiny and her hair in a braid over one shoulder. She lay shoulder to shoulder with him, and for a time neither of them said anything at all, just breathed in time together. It reminded him of being in her quarters on the sojourn ship, how he could always hear when she was up because the tossing and turning stopped and all he could hear were her breaths.

"I'm glad he's dead," Cyra said.

He turned to face her, propping himself up on one elbow. She had trimmed the hair neatly around the silverskin. He'd gotten used to it now, shining on one side of her head like a mirror. It suited her, really, even if he hated what had happened to her.

Her jaw was set. She started on the straps of the armor that covered her arm, working them back and forth until they were loose. When she shucked it, there was a new cut on her arm, right near her elbow, with a hash through it. He touched it, lightly, with a fingertip.

"You didn't kill him," he said to her.

"I know," she said. "But the chancellor isn't going to take note of him, and . . ." She sighed. "I guess I could have gotten some revenge from beyond death, if I had let him go unmarked. Dishonored him by pretending he never existed."

"But you couldn't do that," Akos supplied.

"I couldn't," Cyra agreed. "He's still my brother. His life is still . . . notable."

"And you're upset that you couldn't punish him."

"Sort of."

"Well, if my opinion counts for anything, I don't think you need to regret showing some mercy," he said. "I'm just sorry you went to all the trouble of sparing him for me, and then . . . it didn't even matter."

With a heavy sigh, he slumped to the ground again. Just another way that he'd failed.

She laid a hand on him, right over his sternum, right over his heart, with the scarred arm that said so much and so little about her at once.

"I'm not," she said. "Sorry, I mean."

"Well." He covered her hand with one of his own. "I'm not sorry you've got Ryzek's loss marked on your arm, even though I hated him."

The corners of her mouth twitched up. He was surprised to find that she had chipped off a little piece of his guilt, and he wondered if he'd done the same for her, in his way. They were both people who carried every scrap of everything around, but maybe they could help each other set things down, piece by piece.

It was good he felt this way, he thought. With Eijeh gone, all that he had left to do was meet his fate, and Cyra and his fate were inextricable. He would die for the family Noavek, and she was the last of them. She was a happy inevitability, brilliant and unavoidable.

Acting on impulse, Akos turned and kissed her. She stuck her fingers in one of his belt loops and pulled him tight against her, the way they had been earlier, when they were interrupted. But the door was closed, now, and Teka was fast asleep in some other part of the ship.

They were alone. Finally.

The chemical-floral smell of the ship was replaced with the smell of her, of the herbal shampoo she'd last used in the ship's shower, and sweat and sendes leaf. He ran potion-stained fingertips down the side of her throat and across the faint curve of her collarbone.

She pushed him over, so she was straddling him, and pinned his hips down for a tick, just to tug his shirt out from under his waistband. Her hands were so warm against him he could hardly breathe. They found the soft give of flesh around his middle, the taut muscle wrapped around his ribs. She undid buttons all the way up to his throat.

He'd thought of this when he helped her take her clothes off before that bath in the renegade safehouse, how it might be to take off their clothes when they weren't injured and fighting for their lives. He'd imagined something frantic, but she was taking her time, running her fingers over the bumps of his ribs, the tendons on the inside of his wrists as she freed the buttons on his cuffs, the bones that stuck out of his shoulders.

When he tried to touch her back, she pressed him away. That wasn't how she wanted it just then, it seemed like, and he was happy to give her what she wanted. She was the girl who couldn't touch people, after all. It sparked something inside him to know that he was the only one she'd done this with—not excitement, but something softer. Tender.

She was his only—and fate said she would be his last.

She pulled back to look at him, and he tugged at the hem of her shirt.

"May I?" he said.

She nodded.

He felt suddenly tentative as he started undoing her shirt buttons, from throat to waist. He sat up just enough to kiss the skin he revealed, izit by izit. Soft skin, for someone so strong, soft over hard muscle and bone and steely nerve.

He tipped them over, so he was leaning over her, leaving just enough space between them to feel her warmth without touching her. He stripped his shirt from his shoulders, and kissed her stomach again. He'd run out of shirt to unbutton.

He touched his nose to the inside of her hip and looked up at her.

"Yes?" he said.

"Yes," she said roughly.

His hands closed over her waistband, and he ran parted lips over the skin he exposed, izit by izit.

CHAPTER 7 | CISI

THE ASSEMBLY SHIP IS the size of a small planet, wide and round as a floater but so much bigger it's downright alarming. It fills the windows of the little patrol ship that picked up our escape pod, made of glass and smooth, pale metal.

"You've never seen it before?" Isae asks me.

"Only images," I say.

Its clear glass panels reflect the currentstream where it burns pink, and emptiness where it doesn't. Little red lights along the ship's borders blink on and off like inhales and exhales. Its movements around the sun are so slight it looks still.

"It's different in images," I say. "Much less impressive."

"I spent three seasons here as a child." Isae's knuckles skim the glass. "Learning how to be proper. I had that brim accent—they didn't like that."

I smile. "You still do, sometimes, when you forget to care. I like it."

"You like it because the brim accent is so much like your

Hessan one." She pokes her fingertip into my dimple, and I smack it away.

"Come on," she says. "Time to dock."

The ship's captain, a squat little man with sweat dotting his forehead, noses his little ship toward the massive Assembly one—to secure entrance B, I'd heard him say. The letter was painted above the doors, reflective. Two metal panels pull apart under the *B*, and an enclosed walkway reaches for our ship's hatch. Hatch and walkway lock together with a hiss. Another crew member seals the connection with the pull of a lever.

We all stand by the hatch doors as they open, making way for Isae to stand at the fore. It's a skeleton patrol crew that picked us up, meant to cruise around the middle band of the solar system in case someone's in trouble—or making it. There's just a captain, a first officer, and two others on board with us, and they don't talk much. Likely because their Othyrian isn't strong—they sound like Trellans to me when they do speak.

I skip ahead into the bright tunnel beyond the hatch doors to catch up to Isae. The glass walls are so clean. I feel like I'm floating in nothingness for a tick, but the floor holds firm.

I just make it to Isae's side when a group of official-looking people in pale gray uniforms greets us. At their sides are nonlethal channeling rods, designed to stun, not kill. The sight is reassuring. This is how things should be—controlled but not dangerous.

The one in front, with a row of medals on his chest, bows to Isae.

"Hello, Chancellor," he says in crisp Othyrian. "I am Captain Morel. The Assembly Leader has been informed of your arrival, and your quarters have been prepared, as well as those of your . . . guest."

Isae smooths her sweater down like that's going to get the folds out of it.

"Thank you, Captain Morel," she says, all traces of brim accent gone. "May I introduce Cisi Kereseth, a family friend from the nation-planet of Thuvhe."

"A pleasure," Captain Morel says to me.

I let my gift unfold right away. It's just instinct, at this point. Most people react well when I think of my currentgift as a blanket falling over their shoulders, and Captain Morel is no exception— he relaxes right in front of me, and his smile softens, like he actually means it. I think it works on Isae, too, for the first time in days. She looks a little softer around the eyes.

"Captain Morel," I say. "Thank you for the welcome."

"Allow me to escort you to your quarters," he says. "Thank you for delivering Chancellor Benesit safely here, sir," he adds to the captain who brought us here.

The man grunts a little, and nods at Isae and me as we turn to go.

Captain Morel's shoes snap when he walks, and when he turns corners, they slide a little as the balls of his feet twist into the floor. If he's here, it's because he was born into a rich family on whatever his home planet is, but doesn't have the disposition—or the stomach—for actual military service. He's just right for tasks like these, which require manners and diplomacy and polish.

When the captain delivers me to my room—right next to Isae's, for convenience—I sigh with relief. After the door shuts behind me, I let my jacket slide off my shoulders and fall to my feet.

The rooms have been set for us, clearly. That's the only explanation for the field of feathergrass, twitching in the wind, on the far wall. It's footage of Thuvhe. Right in front of it is a narrow bed with a thick brown blanket tucked around the mattress.

I put a hand on the touch panel near the door, flicking images and text forward until I find the one I want. *Wall footage*. I scroll until I find one of Hessa in the snow. The top of the hill sparkles red from the domed roof of the temple. I follow the bumps of house roofs all the way to the bottom of the hill, watching weather vanes spin as I do. All the buildings are hidden behind a white haze of snowflakes.

Sometimes I forget how beautiful my home is.

I see just the corner of the fields my dad farmed, and the image cuts off. Somewhere past them is the empty spot where we held Eijeh's and Akos's funerals. It wasn't my idea—Mom was the one who stacked the wood and burnstones, who said the prayer and lit it up. I just stood close by in my kutyah coat, the face shield on so I could cry without anyone seeing.

I hadn't thought of Eijeh and Akos as lost, truly lost, until then. If Mom was burning the pyres, I thought, that must mean she knew they were dead, in the way only an oracle could know things. But she hadn't known nearly as much as I thought.

I fall to the bed and stare up at the snow.

Maybe it wasn't smart to come here, to contend with a chancellor instead of following my own family. I don't know much about politics or government—I'm Hessa-born, so far out of my realm of knowledge it's almost funny. But I know Thuvhe. I know people.

And someone needs to look out for Isae before she loses herself in grief.

Isae's wall just looks like a window to space. Stars all glinting, little pricks of light, and the bend and swell of the currentstream. It reminds me of a fight we had, early on, before I knew her better.

You know nothing about my planet and its people, I said to her then. It was after she had gone public as chancellor. She and Ori had shown up at my apartment at school, and she had been rude to me for being so familiar with her sister. And for some reason, my currentgift had let me be rude back. *This is only your first season on its soil.*

The broken look she gave me then is a lot like the one she's giving me now, as I walk into her quarters—twice the size of the ones given to me, but that's not surprising. She sits on the end of her bed in an undershirt and underwear that's really just a pair of shorts clinging to her long, skinny legs. It's more casual than I've ever seen her before, and more vulnerable, somehow, like letting me see her right after waking ripped her open somehow.

All my life I have loved this planet, more fervently than my family or my friends or even myself, she had replied back then. *You have walked all your seasons on its skin, but I have buried myself deep in its guts, so don't you dare tell me that I don't know it.*

The thing about Isae is, her outer shell is so thick I don't always believe there's something under it. She's not like Cyra Noavek, who lets you see everything writhing just out of reach, or like Akos, whose emotions glitter in his eyes like precious metal caught in the bottom of a pan. Isae is just blank.

"My friend—the one I told you about—will be here soon," she says, her voice rough. "He wasn't far from here when I called."

She'd commandeered the nav deck for a while when the patrol ship first picked us up, saying she needed to make a call to an old friend, one she grew up with. Ast was his name. She said she could use someone's help, someone who wasn't tied to the Assembly or Thuvhe or Shotet. Ast was "brim spawn," as some people liked to call it, born out on some broken moon beyond the currentstream barrier.

"I'm glad," I say.

I try one of my favorite feelings on her now, to calm her— water, which is odd, since I don't know much about water, having grown up on an ice planet. But there was a hot spring in the basement of the temple in Hessa, to enhance the visions of the oracle, and Mom had taken me there once to learn to tread water. It was dark as a tomb down there, but the hot water had surrounded me, all soft, like silk, only heavier. I let that heavy silk fold around Isae now, watch that tension in her shoulders ebb away. I'm learning her, slowly, and it's easier, now that we're not on that little Shotet ship anymore.

"He was the mechanic's son, on the ship where I was raised," she says, rubbing her eyes with the back of a hand. Her trade vessel was always adrift, never staying anywhere for long. The perfect place for someone who needed to stay hidden. "He was there, too, during the attack. He lost his father. Some of his friends, too."

"What does he do now? Still a mechanic?"

"Yeah," she says. "He was just finishing up a job on a fueling station near here, though. Good timing."

Maybe it's the idea that she needs somebody else, even though I'm here, or maybe it's just plain jealousy, but I don't feel good about Ast. And I don't know what he'll make of me.

It's like thinking about him summons him, because the door buzzes right then. When Isae opens it, there's an Assembly-type standing right there, his eyes sliding down her bare legs. Behind him is a broad-shouldered man holding two big canvas bags. He puts the side of his hand against the Assembly man's shoulder, and what looks like a flying beetle whizzes out of his sleeve.

"Pazha!" Isae exclaims as the beetle lands on her outstretched hand. It's not a real bug—it's made of metal, and emits a constant clicking. It's a guide bot, meant to help the blind maneuver. Ast tilts his head toward it, following the sound, and drops his bags just inside the doorway. Isae, with the beetle perched on her knuckles, throws her arms around him.

Her currentgift is tied to memory—she can't take a person's memories, the way Ryzek could, but she can see their memories. Sometimes she sees them even when she doesn't want to. So I understand when she tucks her nose into his shoulder, taking a sniff of him. She told me once that because smells are so tied to memory, they're special to her; they turn the tide of memory she sees when she touches somebody into a little trickle. Controlled, for once.

It's not until Ast blinks that I notice his eyes. His irises are ringed with pale green light, and his pupils are circled with white. They're mechanical implants. They only move by shifting, incremental. I know they likely don't show him much—enough to help him, maybe, but they're just supplements, like the beetle Isae called Pazha.

"Nice new tech," Isae says to him.

"Yeah, they're the new fashion in Othyr," he drawls in a brim lilt. "Everybody who's anybody is cutting out their eyes with butter knives and replacing them with tech."

"Always with the sarcasm," Isae says. "Do they actually help?"

"Some. Depends on the light." Ast shrugs. "Seems like a nice setup in here." He flicks his fingers, sending Pazha away from Isae's fist and into the room. It flies the perimeter of the room, whistling at each corner. "Big. Smells clean. Surprised you're not wearing a crown, Chancellor."

"Didn't go with my outfit," Isae says. "Come on, meet my friend Cisi."

The beetle is whizzing toward me now, turning fast circles around my head, shoulders, stomach, legs. I try to hear the clicking like he does, how it reveals the shape and size of me to him, but my ears aren't trained for it.

He's dressed in so many layers I don't know what piece of clothing is what. Does the hood belong to his jacket, or the sweatshirt under it? How many T-shirts is he wearing, two or three? There's a screwdriver at his hip where a knife ought to be.

"Ast," he says to me, in almost a grunt. He holds out his hand, waiting for me to step forward and take it, and I do.

"Cisi," I say. His skin is warm, and he has a good grip, not too tight. By instinct I pick a currentgift feeling for him—waves of warmth, like ripples in the air.

Most of my textures work for people who aren't in some kind

of turmoil, at least a little, but the ones I like to use are the ones people don't detect. But judging by his little frown, he knows something isn't right.

"Whoa," he says to me. "What's that all about?"

"Oh, sorry," I say. "My currentgift is hard for me to control."

I always lie about that. Makes people less wary.

"Cisi is the daughter of the oracle of Thuvhe," Isae says.

"Sitting oracle," I correct automatically.

"There are different kinds?" Ast shrugs. "Didn't know that. We don't have oracles out there in the brim. Or fated nobility."

"Fated families aren't nobility on Thuvhe," I say. "Just unlucky."

"Unlucky." Ast raises his eyebrows. "I take it your fate doesn't meet with your approval?"

"No, it doesn't," I say softly.

He fusses at his lower lip. One of his fingernails is so bruised it looks painted.

"Sorry," he says after a beat. "Didn't mean to touch on a sore subject."

"It's fine."

It's not true, and I get the sense we both know that, but he doesn't press me.

Isae searches out her gown from the floor and pulls it over her shoulders, fastening it in front so the skirt is closed, though she doesn't bother with the dozen or so buttons that go up over her undershirt.

"You might have guessed that I didn't ask you here to bring me my old stuff," Isae says, folding her hands in front of her. She's switching into her formal speech, her chancellor posture. I can tell Ast notices something's different. He looks almost alarmed, his eyes twitching from side to side.

"I want to ask for your assistance. For a longer period," she says. "I don't know what you're doing, what you're leaving behind. But there aren't many people left I can trust—maybe just the people in this room, and—"

He puts up a hand to stop her.

"Quit it," he says. "Of course I'll stay. As long as you need."

"Really?"

He holds out his hand, and when she takes it, he shifts their grip, grasping her at the thumb, the way soldiers do. He brings their joined hands to his heart, like he's swearing an oath, but brim spawn don't swear oaths except by spitting, rumor has it.

"I'm sorry about your sister," he says. "I only met her once, I know, but I liked her."

It's beautiful, in its way. Straightforward and honest. I can tell why she likes him. I try another feeling, for him—an embrace of arms, locked around the chest. Firm but bracing.

"Now that's downright disconcerting, Cisi," he says. "No way to turn it off?"

"My brother's currentgift can, but I've never found anything else that does," I say. I've never met someone so aware of my gift before. I would ask him what his is, if that wasn't so impolite.

"Don't get so twitchy about it, Ast," Isae says. "Cisi's been helping me a lot."

"Well, good." He manages a small smile in my direction. "Isae's opinion about a person says a lot to me."

"It says a lot to me, too," I say. "I've heard a lot of stories about the ship you two grew up on."

"She probably told you it smelled like feet," he says.

"She did," I say. "But she also said it was charming in its way."

Isae reaches for my hand, sliding her fingers between mine.

"It's the three of us against the galaxy, now," she says. "Hope you're both ready."

"Don't be so dramatic," Ast says.

She purses her lips, tightens her hand on mine, and says, quietly:

"I'm not."

CHAPTER 8 | CISI

EVERY NOW AND THEN it hits me that most people don't make friends wherever they go. I do. Assembly Headquarters is like anywhere else—people just want to be heard, even if what they have to say is boring. And boy is it boring most of the time.

I get good information from it sometimes, though. The woman behind me in the cafeteria line that morning—piling synthetic eggs high on her plate and covering them with some kind of green sauce—tells me there's a greenhouse on the second level stocked with plants from all over the solar system, a different room for each planet. I inhale a bowl of cooked grains and head there as soon as I can. It's been such a long time since I saw a plant.

That's how I end up in the hallway just outside the room for Thuvhe. The corners of the windows are dusted with frost. I would need to put on protective gear to go in, so I stay just outside, crouched near the cluster of jealousies growing by the door. They're yellow and teardrop-shaped, but if you touch one at just the right time in its growth, it spits out a cloud of bright dust.

Judging by the swollen bellies of these, they're just about ready to burst.

"You know, try as we might, we can't seem to grow hushflowers here," a voice says from behind me.

The man is old—deep lines frame his eyes and mouth—and bald, the top of his head shiny. He wears pale gray slacks, like all the Assembly staff do, and a thin gray sweater. His skin, too, looks almost pale gray, like he got caught downwind of the wrong field on Zold. If I think hard enough about it, I can probably figure out where he's from by the color of his eyes, which are lavender—the only remarkable thing about him, as far as I can tell.

"Really?" I say, straightening. "What happens when you try? They die?"

"No, they just don't bloom," he says. "It's as if they know where they are, and they save all their beauty for Thuvhe."

I smile. "That's a romantic thought."

"Too romantic for an old man like me, I know." His eyes sparkle a little. "You must be a Thuvhesit, to look so fondly at these plants."

"I am," I say. "My name is Cisi Kereseth."

I offer him my hand. His own is dry as an old bone.

"I'm not permitted to tell you my name, as it would hint at my origins," he says. "But I am the Assembly Leader, Miss Kereseth, and it is lovely to meet you."

My hand goes limp in his. The Assembly Leader? I am not used to thinking of the person with that title as a real person, with a creaky voice and a wry smile. When they are selected from a pool of candidates by the representatives of all the planets, they are stripped of name and origin, so as not to show any bias. They serve the solar system in its entirety, it's said.

"I'm sorry I didn't recognize you," I say. Something about the man makes me think he will like a subtle manifestation of my currentgift: the touch of a warm breeze. He smiles at me, and I think it must have worked on him, since he doesn't look like a man given to smiling.

"I am not offended," he says. "So you are the daughter of an oracle, then."

I nod. "The sitting oracle of Thuvhe, yes."

"And the sister of an oracle, too, if Eijeh Kereseth still lives," he says. "Yes, I've memorized all the oracle names, though I confess I had to use a few memory techniques. It's quite a long mnemonic device. I would share it with you if it didn't have a few vulgarities thrown in to keep it interesting."

I laugh.

"You have come here with Isae Benesit?" he says. "Captain Morel told me she had brought two friends with her on this visit."

"Yes. I was close with her sister, Ori," I say. "Orieve, I mean."

He makes a soft, sad sound, lips closed. "I am deeply sorry for your loss, then."

"Thank you," I say. For now I can push the grief aside. It's not something this man would be comfortable seeing, so it wouldn't show even if I wanted it to, thanks to my gift.

"You must be very angry," he says. "The Shotet have taken your father, your brothers, and now your friend?"

It's a strange thing to say. It assumes too much.

"It's not 'the Shotet' who did it," I say. "It was Ryzek Noavek."

"True." He focuses on the frosty windows again. "But I can't help but think that a people who allow themselves to be ruled by a tyrant such as Ryzek Noavek deserves to shoulder some of the blame for his behavior."

I want to disagree with him. Supporters of the Noaveks, sure, I can blame them. But the renegades, the exiles, the poor and sick and desperate people living in the neighborhood around that building we used as a safe house? They're just as victimized by Ryzek as I am. After visiting the country, I'm not sure I can even think of "the Shotet" as one thing anymore. They're too varied to be lumped together. It would be like saying that the daughter of a Hessan farmer and a soft-handed Shissa doctor are the same.

I want to disagree, but I can't. My tongue is stuck, my throat swollen with my stupid currentgift. So I just look passively at the Assembly Leader and wait for him to talk again.

"I am meeting with Miss Benesit later today," he says at last. "I hope that you will attend. She is a bit thorny at times, and I sense your presence would soothe her."

"That's one of the things I like about her," I say. "That she's 'thorny.'"

"I am sure in friendship it is an entertaining quality." He smiles. "But in political discussions, it is often an impediment to progress."

I give in to the instinct to step back from him.

"That depends on how you define 'progress,' I suppose," I say, keeping my tone light.

"I hope that we will agree on a definition by the day's end," he says. "I will leave you to look at the plants, Miss Kereseth. Do stop by the Tepessar area—it's too hot to go in, but you've never seen anything like those specimens, I promise you."

I nod, and he takes his leave.

I remember where I've seen those eyes before: in pictures of the intellectual elite on Kollande. They take some kind of medicine designed to keep someone awake for longer than usual without suffering fatigue, and light-eyed people's irises often turn purple from prolonged use. That he's from Kollande doesn't tell me much about him—I've never been there, though I know the planet is wealthy and not particularly concerned about its oracles. But those eyes do. He's someone who values advancement over his own safety or vanity. He's focused and smart. And he probably thinks he knows better than the rest of us.

I understand, now, what Isae meant when she said it was me, Ast, and her against the galaxy. It's not just the Shotet we're up against, it's the Assembly, too.

Ast, Isae, and I sit on one side of a polished glass table, and the Assembly Leader sits on the other. It's so clean that his water glass, and the pitcher next to it, almost look like they're floating. I rammed my legs against the edge when I sat down, because I wasn't sure where the table ended. If it's supposed to disarm me, it worked.

"Let us first talk through what happened in Shotet," the Assembly Leader says as he pours himself a glass of water.

We're in the outer ring of the Assembly ship, which is arranged in concentric circles. All the outer walls are made of glass that turns opaque when the ship rotates to face the sun, so nobody's corneas get burned. The walls to my left are opaque now, and the room is heating up, so there's a ring of sweat around my collar. Ast keeps pinching the front of his shirt and pulling it away from his body to keep it from sticking.

"I am sure the footage the sights provided is more than suffi-cient," Isae says, clipped.

She's wearing chancellor clothes: a heavy Thuvhesit dress, long-sleeved, buttoned up to her throat. Tight boots that made her grimace while she laced them. Her hair is pinned to the back of her head, and shines like she lacquered it there. If she's hot—which she must be, that dress is made for Thuvhe, not . . . *this*—she doesn't show it. Maybe that's why she put such a dense layer of powder on her skin before we left.

"I understand your reticence to discuss it," the Assembly Leader says. "Perhaps Miss Kereseth can give us a summary instead? She was there, too, correct?"

Isae glances at me. I fold my hands in my lap and smile, remem-bering that the Assembly Leader's preferred texture was a warm breeze. That's how I need to be, too—all warm and casual, a layer of sweat you don't mind, a gust of air that almost tickles.

"Of course," I say. "Cyra Noavek challenged her brother Ryzek to a duel, and he accepted. But before either of them could hit each other, my brother Eijeh appeared—" I choke. I can't say the rest.

"Sorry," I say. "My currentgift isn't being cooperative."

"She can't always say what she wants to say," Isae clarifies. "Which is that Eijeh was holding a knife to my sister's throat. He killed her. The end."

"And Ryzek?"

"Also killed," Isae says, and for a tick I think she's going to tell him what she did on the ship, how she went into the storage room with a knife and teased a confession out of him and then stuck him with the blade like it was a stinger. But then she adds, "By his own sister, who then dragged the body aboard, I assume to keep it from being defiled by the mob that had erupted into chaos."

"And now, his body is . . . ?"

"Drifting through space, I assume," Isae says. "That is the preferred Shotet method of burial, no?"

"I don't familiarize myself with Shotet customs," the Assembly Leader says, leaning back in his chair. "Very well, that is all as I expected. As far as how the rest of the galaxy has responded . . . well, I have been fielding messages from the other leaders and representatives since your sister's death was broadcast. They have interpreted the killing as an act of war, and wish to know how we will proceed from here."

Isae laughs. It's the same bitter laugh she gave Ryzek before she cut him open.

"We?" she says. "Two seasons ago, I asked for support from the Assembly to declare war on Shotet in light of the killing of our falling oracle, and I was told that the 'civil dispute' between Shotet and Thuvhe, as you have termed it, is an intraplanetary matter. That I needed to handle it internally. And now you're wondering what *we* will be doing? There is no *we*, Assembly Leader."

The Assembly Leader looks to me, eyebrows raised. If he expects me to—what word did he use?—*soothe* her, he's going to be disappointed. I don't always get to control my currentgift, but I don't want to do something just because he says so. I'm not sure, yet, whether there's any advantage to Isae being *soothed*.

"Two seasons ago, Ryzek Noavek didn't kill a chancellor's sister," the Assembly Leader replies, all smooth and level. "Shotet was not in a state of total upheaval. The situation has changed."

The opaque panels on the left side of the chamber are starting to lighten up again, turning from wall to window.

"Do you know how long they've been attacking us?" Isae says. "Since before I was born. Over twenty seasons."

"I am aware of the history of conflict between Thuvhe and Shotet."

"So what was your thought process, then?" Isae says. "That we're just a bunch of thickheaded iceflower farmers, so who cares if we get attacked, as long as the product is safe?" She laughs, harshly. "The town of Hessa is decimated by guerilla warfare, and you call it a civil dispute. My face gets carved up and my parents get killed, and no one budges an inch except to send condolences. One of my oracles dies, and another is kidnapped, and it's my job to handle it. So why are you all hopping with excitement to help me now? What has everyone scared?"

His eye twitches a little.

"You must understand that to the rest of the galaxy, the Shotet were little more than an annoyance until the Noaveks came into power," he says. "When you came to us two seasons ago, describing vicious warriors, we thought of the sad wrecks who once came begging at another planet's doorstep, every season, to dig through our trash."

"They've been looting hospitals and attacking fueling outposts for longer than two seasons, on their sojourns," she replies. "This escaped the attention of every single planet's leadership until now?"

"Not precisely," the Assembly Leader says. "But we received information from a credible source that Lazmet Noavek is still alive, and will soon move to reclaim his place at Shotet's helm.

You have not been alive long enough to truly grasp this, but Ryzek was remarkably civil compared to his father. He inherited his mother's desire for diplomacy, if not her ease with it. It was under Lazmet that Shotet became fearsome. It was *still* under his guidance—from beyond the grave, apparently—that Ryzek pursued oracles and, indeed, your sister, at all."

"So you're all afraid of him. This one man." Ast frowns. "What can he do, shoot fire out of his ass?"

"Lazmet controls people—quite literally—using his current-gift," the Assembly Leader says. "His abilities, combined with the new strength of the Shotet fighting force, are not to be underestimated. We must treat the Shotet as an infestation, a blight on land that could otherwise be used for iceflower farming—for something useful and valuable."

His eyes glitter. I may not have grown up fancy, but I know how to speak Subtext. He wants the Shotet gone. At one point they were a husk of a people, clanking around the galaxy in their big, outdated ship, starved and sick and sagging. He wants that back. He wants more iceflowers, more valuable Thuvhesit land. More for him, and nothing for them, and he wants to use Isae to get it.

Mom used to tell me that all the galaxy once mocked the Shotet. "Dirty scavengers," they called them, and "fleshworms." They flew in circles around the solar system, chasing their own tails. Half the time they didn't even sound like they were saying words. I knew all this. I'd heard it, even said some of it myself.

But the Assembly Leader isn't just mocking the Shotet now.

"Then tell me," Isae says, "what disciplinary action the Assembly has planned for the Pithar, given that the Pithar leadership suggested it might be amenable to a trade agreement with Shotet not long ago?"

"Don't play the fool with me, Chancellor," the Assembly Leader says, but not like he's mad, more like he's tired. "You know that we can't act against Pitha. The galaxy cannot function without the materials Pitha provides."

I'd never given Pitha much thought before. I'd actually never thought about politics, period, until I fell back in with the Benesit sisters after my dad died. But the Assembly Leader is right—durable materials from Pitha make up almost all the good tech in the galaxy, including ships. And in Thuvhe, especially, with our frozen air, we rely on insulated Pithar glass for our windows. We can't afford to lose them any more than the rest of the Assembly of Nine Planets can.

"Pitha has retracted their willingness to engage with Shotet, and that will have to be enough. As for the rest of the nation-planets, they still believe the war effort should be headed up by Thuvhe, given that it *is* an intraplanetary matter. They are open to discussions about aid and support, however."

"So in other words," Ast says, "you'll throw money at her, but she still has to give you a wall of flesh between Shotet and the rest of you."

"My, you certainly do enjoy dramatic language, don't you, Mr. . . ." The Assembly Leader tilts his head. "Do you have a surname?"

"I don't need any kind of honorific," Ast says. "Call me Ast or don't call me anything."

"Ast," the Assembly Leader says, and he softens his voice like he's talking to a child. "Money is not the only form of aid the Assembly can offer. And if war is what confronts you, Miss Benesit, you are in no position to refuse our help."

"Maybe I don't want to fight a war," she says, sitting back in her chair. "Maybe I want to broker a peace."

"That is, of course, your prerogative," the Assembly Leader replies. "However, I will be forced to pursue an investigation I had hoped I would be able to avoid."

"An investigation into what?" Isae scowls.

"It would be quite simple for a person to consult the heat signatures in the Voa amphitheater at the time of Ryzek's alleged death. And if a person did, they might see that Ryzek was alive when he was taken aboard that transport ship," the Assembly Leader says. "Which means that if his body is adrift in space, as you say, someone else must have killed him. Not Cyra Noavek."

"Interesting theory," Isae says.

"I can't think of why you would lie to me, and tell me Cyra Noavek committed the crime in the arena, unless you needed to protect yourself, Miss Benesit," the Assembly Leader says. "And if you were to be investigated for murder—particularly premeditated murder against a self-declared sovereign—then you would not be permitted to rule Thuvhe until you were acquitted."

"So, just to clarify," Ast says, glowering, "you're threatening to tie Isae up in bureaucratic nonsense if she doesn't do as you say."

The Assembly Leader only smiles.

"If you would like me to proofread your declaration of war before you send it to the Shotet, I will happily take a look at it," he says. "I must now take my leave. Good day, Miss Benesit, Miss Kereseth . . . Ast."

His head bobs three times, once for each of us, and then he's gone. I glance at Isae.

"Would he really do that?" I say. "Charge you with murder?"

"I don't doubt it." Her mouth puckers. "Let's go."

CHAPTER 9 | CYRA

"CYRA." TEKA RAISED AN eyebrow at me outside the ship's little bathroom when I got up for my shift. I was dressed only in underwear and my sweater from the day before. I avoided her eyes as I searched the ship's storage room for a spare mechanic's uniform. We were all running out of clothes. Hopefully they would provide for us on Ogra.

Teka cleared her throat. She was leaning against the wall, arms folded, a plain black eye patch covering her missing eye.

"I don't have to worry about little Kereseth-Noavek spawn running around someday, do I?" She yawned. "Because I really don't want to."

"No," I said with a snort. "Like I'd take that risk."

"Never?" She frowned a little. "There's this thing called 'contraception,' you know."

I shook my head. "Nothing is certain."

The little mocking expression she always wore when she was looking at me faded, leaving her serious.

"My currentgift," I explained, holding up a hand to show her the shadows that curled around my knuckles, stinging me, "is an instrument of torture. You think I would risk inflicting that torture on something growing inside me? Even if it's a very limited risk?" I shook my head. "No."

She nodded. "That's very decent of you."

I added, "It's not like . . . *that* is the only thing you can do with someone, anyway."

She brought her hands up to her face, groaning.

"I did not want any information that specific!" she said, voice muffled.

"Then don't ask probing questions, genius."

I found a mechanic's jumpsuit buried under a stack of towels, and stood to hold it up to my body. The legs were too long, so I would have to roll them, but it would have to do. I dove back into the pile to look for underwear.

"How long until we get to Ogra?" I said. "Because we're going to run out of food pretty soon, you know."

"Food and toilet paper. The recycled water is starting to smell weird, too," Teka agreed. "I think we'll make it, without too much snacking. A few days."

"This ship's upgrades are pretty brilliant," I said. I found a pair of too-big underwear wedged into a corner of one of the shelves, and clutched the ball of clothes to my chest as pain burned across my back. "You did them all?"

"Jorek helped," she said. Her face fell a little. "Not sure where he is right now. He was supposed to send a message from Voa once he made sure his mother was safe."

I didn't know Jorek well, just that he was a more virtuous soul than his father had been and was, apparently, a renegade. So I didn't try to reassure her. My words would have been empty.

"We'll find out about a lot of things when we get to Ogra," I said. "Jorek's status, among them."

"Yeah." Teka shrugged. "Get to the nav deck, Noavek, your break is over."

The next few days passed in a haze. I spent most of the time sleeping, tucked in the galley near the sink, or sitting up in the first officer's chair while Akos took his shift. Our surroundings seemed designed to drive us all mad, they yielded so little of interest. The sky was dark and, without stars, planets, or drifting ships to break it up, completely flat. I often had to check the nav map to make sure we hadn't stalled.

I shared most of my waking time—when not in the captain's chair—with Teka, trying to distract myself from my currentgift. She taught me a game she usually played with multicolored stones, though we used handfuls of beans from the galley and drew dots on them, to tell them apart. We spent most of the time arguing over which beans were which, but I came to see that bickering was a sign of friendship with Teka, and mostly didn't mind it, as long as no one stormed out. Akos sometimes joined us before going to sleep, sitting too close to me and tucking his nose into my hair when he thought Teka wouldn't notice. She always did.

My nights I spent huddled together with Akos, when I could, and finding new places to kiss. Our first fumbles at intimacy had been full of awkward laughter and uncomfortable squirming—I was learning to touch another person, as well as to touch *him*, in particular, and it was difficult to learn everything at once. But we were both happy to practice. Despite his constant nightmares—he didn't wake screaming, but he often woke with a start, a sheen of sweat on his brow—and my lingering grief for the brother who had been twisted into a monster, we found snatches of happiness together, built largely on ignoring everything around us. It worked well.

It worked well, that was, until Ogra came into view.

"Why," Teka said, staring at the black hole of a planet we were headed toward, "would anyone ever settle here?"

Akos laughed. "You could say the same about Thuvhe."

"Don't call it that when we land," I said, cocking an eyebrow. "It's 'Urek' or nothing."

"Right."

Urek meant "empty," but said with reverence, not like an insult. Empty, to us, meant possibility; it meant freedom.

Ogra had come into sight as a small, dark gap in the stars ahead, and then the gap had turned into a hole, like a stray ember burned through fabric. And now it loomed darkly above the nav deck, devouring every fragment of light in its vicinity. I wondered how the first settlers had even known it was a planet. It looked more like a yawn.

"I take it it's not an easy landing," Akos said.

"No." Teka laughed. "No, it's not. The only way to get through it without getting ripped to shreds is to completely disable the ship's power and free-fall. Then I have to reactivate the ship's power before we all liquify on impact." She brought her hands together with a smack. "So we all need to strap in and say a prayer, or whatever makes you feel lucky."

Akos looked paler than usual. I laughed.

Sifa came up behind us, clutching a book to her stomach. There were few books aboard the ship—what use would they have had?—but those she had been able to rummage, she had brought to Eijeh one by one, along with his food. Akos didn't ask about him, and neither did I. I assumed his status was unchanged, and that the worst parts of my brother lived on in him. I needed no further updates.

"Luck," Sifa said, "is simply a construct to make people believe they are in control of some aspect of their destinies."

Teka appeared to consider this, but Akos just rolled his eyes.

"Or maybe it's just a word for what fate looks like to the rest of us," I said to her. I was the only one willing to argue with Sifa—Teka was too reverent, and Akos, too dismissive. "You've forgotten what it's like to stare at the future from this angle instead of your own."

Sifa smirked at me. She smirked at me often. "Perhaps you are correct."

"Everybody strap in," Teka said. "Oracle, I need you in the first officer's chair. You know the most about flying."

"Hey," I said.

"Currentgifts go haywire on Ogra," Teka said to me. "We're not sure how yours will do, so you sit in the back. Keep the Kereseth boys in line."

Sifa had escorted Eijeh to a landing seat already. He was strapped in and staring at the floor. I sighed, and made my way down to the main deck. Akos and I sat across from Eijeh, and I pulled the straps across my chest and lap. Akos fumbled with his own, but I didn't help him—he knew how to do it, he just needed to practice.

I watched Teka and Sifa as they prepared for landing, poking buttons and flicking switches. It seemed routine for Teka. That was reassuring, at least. I didn't want to free-fall through a hostile atmosphere with a captain who was panicking.

"Here we go!" Teka shouted, and with only that warning, all the lights in the ship switched off. The engine stopped its whirring and humming. Dark atmosphere struck the nav window like a wave of Pithar rain, and for a few long moments I couldn't see anything, couldn't feel anything. I wanted to scream.

Ogra's gravity caught us, and it was worse, much worse than feeling nothing. My stomach and my body felt suddenly separate, one floating up and the other pulling hard to the ground. The craft shuddered, metal plates squeaking against their screws, the steps to the nav deck rattling. My teeth clacked together. It was still too dark to see anything, even the currentshadows that twisted around my arms.

Next to me, Akos let out a litany of curses under his breath, in three languages. I couldn't speak. My flesh weighed too heavily on my bones.

A slamming sound, then, and the engine whirred again. Before the lights turned on, though, the planet lit up beneath us. It was still dark—neither sun nor currentstream could possibly penetrate Ogra's atmosphere—but it was dotted with light, veined with it. The ship's control panel glowed, and the horrible, heavy falling sensation disappeared as the ship moved forward instead of down, down, down.

And then, hot and sharp and strong: pain.

CHAPTER 10 | AKOS

CYRA WAS SCREAMING.

Akos's hands were shaking from the landing, but still undoing the straps that held him in place, almost without his permission. Right when Akos was free he launched himself from his seat and slid to his knees in front of Cyra. The shadows had pulled away from her body in a dark cloud, the same way they had when Vas forced her to touch him, down in the amphitheater's prison where she had almost lost her life. Her hands were buried in her hair, clenched. She looked up at him, and a strange smile twisted her face.

He put his hands on hers. The shadows looked like smoke, in the air, but they pulled back into Cyra's body like dozens of strings yanked at once.

Cyra's odd smile was gone, and she was staring at their joined hands.

"What will happen when you let go?" she said quietly.

"You'll be just fine," he said. "You'll learn to control it. You can do that now, remember?"

She let out an airy laugh.

"I can hang on as long as you like," he said.

Her eyes hardened. When she spoke, it was with gritted teeth. "Let go."

Akos couldn't help but think back to something he'd read in one of the books Cyra had put in his room on the sojourn ship. He'd had to read it through a translator, because it was written in Shotet, and it had been called *Tenets of Shotet Culture and Belief*.

It said: *The most marked characteristic of the Shotet people is directly translated as "armored," but outsiders might call it "mettle." It refers not to courageous acts in difficult situations—though the Shotet certainly hold valor in high regard—but to an inherent quality that cannot be learned or imitated; it is in the blood as surely as their revelatory language. Mettle is bearing up again and again under assaults. It is perseverance, acceptance of risk, and the unwillingness to surrender.*

That paragraph had never made more sense to him than it did right now.

Akos obeyed. At first, when the currentshadows reappeared, they formed the smoky cloud around her body again, but Cyra set her jaw.

"Can't meet the Ograns with a death cloud around me," she said.

Her eyes held his as she breathed deeply. The shadows began to worm their way beneath her skin, traveling down her fingers, wriggling up her throat. She screamed again, right into her teeth, half a dozen izits from his face. But then the breath hissed out, same as it had come in, and she straightened. The cloud was gone.

"They're back to how they were before," he said to her. "Like they were when I met you."

"Yeah," she said. "It's this planet. My gift is stronger here."

"You've been here before?"

She shook her head. "No. But I can feel it."

"Do you need a painkiller?" he said.

Another headshake. "Not yet. I have to readjust sometime. May as well be now."

Teka was talking on the nav deck, in Othyrian. "Ship ID Renegade Transport, Captain Surukta requesting permission to land."

"Captain Surukta, permission granted to landing area thirty-two. Congratulations on your safe arrival," a voice responded over the intercom.

Teka snorted as she switched off the communicator. "I bet that's standard practice, congratulating people on surviving."

"I've been here before," Sifa said, wry. "It is indeed standard practice."

Teka guided them to landing area 32, somewhere between the veins of light that had greeted them once they passed the atmosphere. Akos felt a bump as they touched down, and then they were there. On a new planet. On Ogra.

Ogra was a mystery to most of the galaxy. It had become the subject of a lot of rumors, from as silly as "Ograns live in holes underground" to as dangerous as "Ograns are shielding their own atmosphere so we won't find out they're making deadly weapons." So when Akos stepped out of the ship, he didn't know what would greet him, if anything. For all he knew, Ogra was barren.

His hold on Cyra's hand loosened as he paused at the bottom of the steps to stare. They were in a city of sorts, but it was like no city he'd ever seen. Small buildings, glowing with green and blue lights of all shapes and sizes, rose up all around them, dark shapes against a dark sky. Growing around and between them were trees without leaves to absorb the sun—their branches twisted around pillars, folding whole towers into their arms. The trees were tall, too, taller than anything else around, and the contrast of the clean lines of buildings and the organic curves of growing things was strange to him.

The glowing, though—that was even stranger. Faint dots that he recognized as insects wove through the air; panels of light showed dim impressions of the insides of houses; and in the narrow channels of water that replaced some of the streets, there were streaks of color, like poured dye, and the flash of movement as some creature made its way along.

"Welcome to Ogra," an accented voice said from someplace up ahead. Akos could only see the man by the white orb that hovered around his face. As he spoke—in competent Shotet, no less—the orb attached to his chest, right under his chin, and lit his face from beneath. He was middle-aged, lined, with stark white hair that curled around his ears.

"If you'll form a short line, we can note your presence here and then escort you to the Shotet sector," he said. "We have only an hour before the storms begin."

The storms? Akos raised an eyebrow at Cyra, and she shrugged. She didn't seem to know any more than he did.

Teka was first in line, reporting her surname with a brisk tone that read as businesslike.

"Surukta," the man repeated as he typed her name into the small device in his hand. "I knew your mother. I was sad to hear of her passing."

Teka mumbled her way through something, maybe gratitude, though it didn't sound like it. Then it was Cyra's turn.

"Cyra," she said. "Noavek."

The man paused with his fingers over the keys. He looked menacing with that white light glowing under his face, casting shadows that filled his eye sockets and the deepest creases of his face. She stared back, letting him look her over, from silverskin to armored wrist to worn boots.

But he didn't say anything, just typed her name into his device and waved her past. She kept her hand in Akos's, her arm stretched out behind her until he, too, was waved along.

Teka tripped over to them, her eyes wide and shining.

"Amazing, right?" she said, smiling. "I always wanted to see it."

"You've never come before?" Cyra said. "Not even to see your mother?"

"No, I was never allowed to visit her." There was an edge to her voice. "It wasn't safe. The exile colony has been here for over two generations, though, ever since the Noaveks came into power."

"And the Ograns just . . . let you stay here?" Akos said.

"They say anyone who can survive this planet has a right to be here," Teka said.

"It doesn't look as dangerous as I was expecting," Cyra said. "Everyone always talks about how hard it is to survive here, but it seems peaceful enough."

"Don't let it fool you," Teka said. "Everything here is ready to attack or defend—the plants, the animals, even the planet itself.

They can't eat sun, so they eat each other instead—or you."

"The plants are carnivorous?" Akos said.

"From what I know." She shrugged. "Or they eat the current. Which probably explains why they've been able to survive here—if there's anything Ogra has a lot of, it's the current." She smiled, with some mischief. "And as if the constant threat of being devoured wasn't enough . . . well, let's just say he's not talking about a little Awakening shower when he says 'storms.'"

"Cryptic, aren't you?" Cyra said, frowning.

"Yes!" She grinned. "It's nice to have the upper hand for once. Come on."

Teka led them to one of the canals. They had to go down some steps to get to the water's edge. They were cracked from the tree roots, and uneven. Akos reached down to run his hand over the persistent roots, which were covered in a fine, dark fuzz.

There were *plants* here. He hadn't thought about foreign plant species on Pitha, mostly because there were no plants to be found on Pitha, at least not where he could reach them. But Ogra was thick with trees. He wondered, with a thrill of excitement, what you could make with the plants here.

A boat waited at the edge of the canal, long and narrow, with room for only four people across each row of benches. Akos guessed by its glint that it was made of metal. It was dark except for the glow of the water beneath it, a streak of rosy pink.

"What's that light?" he asked Teka.

But Teka wasn't the one who answered, it was the woman stationed at the front of the boat, her dark eyes lined with white paint. At first he thought maybe there was a practical reason for the paint, but the longer he looked at her, the more it seemed just decorative, like the black lines people smudged near their eye-lashes at home. Here, white just showed up better.

"There are many strains of bacteria that live in Ogra's waters," she said. "They light up in different colors. Let them remind you that only our darkest water is safe to drink."

Even the water could defend itself on Ogra.

Akos followed Teka down the unsteady plank that connected shore to boat, and stepped on one bench to get to another. Cyra settled herself next to him, and he put his hand on her wrist, where the armor ended. He squeezed, and leaned over the edge of the boat to look at the water. The streaks of pink were moving, lazy, with the current of the water.

He tried not to think about Sifa and Eijeh settling in behind them, Sifa's eyes watchful so his own didn't have to be. But the boat dipped with their weight, and his stomach sank, too. He couldn't avoid Eijeh on Ogra like he had on the ship. They were going to be stuck together, the Thuvhesits among Shotet among Ograns.

The woman at the front sat, taking into her hands huge oars that dangled on either side of the vessel. With a sharp yank she drove them forward, her face showing no effort. She was *strong*.

"A useful currentgift," Cyra commented.

"It comes in handy every now and then. Most of the time I am called upon to open stubborn jars," the woman said, as she found a rhythm in her rowing. The ship cut through the water like a hot knife through butter. "Don't put your hands in the water, by the way."

"Why not?" Cyra said.

She just laughed.

Akos kept looking over the side, at the changing colors beneath the water's surface. The pink glow clung to the shallows, near the edge of the canal. Where it was deeper, there were specks of blue, wisps of purple, and wells of deep red.

"There," the Ogran woman said, and he followed the tilt of her head to a massive shape in the canal. At first he thought it was just more of the bacteria, finding the current. But as they slid past it, he saw it was a creature, twice as wide as their narrow boat and twice again as long. It had a bulbous head—or he assumed it was a head—and at least a dozen tentacles that tapered to feathery ends. He was able to see it only because of how the bacteria clung to it, like paint streaking its smooth sides.

It turned, tentacles twisting together like rope, and on its flank he saw a mouth as big as his own torso, framed all around by sharp, narrow teeth. He stiffened.

"The undersides of these boats are made of a current-shielding material we call 'soju,'" the Ogran woman said. "The animal—a galansk—is drawn to the current, to devour it. If you put your hand in the water, it would be drawn to you. But it can't sense us in this boat."

And true to her word, with the next pull of her oars, the galansk turned again, and dove deep, becoming just a faint glow under the surface of the water. A moment later it was gone.

"You mine this metal here?" Teka asked the woman.

"No, no. There is nothing on this planet that is not current-rich," the woman said. "We import soju from Essander."

"Why do you live on a planet so determined to kill you?" he said.

The Ogran woman smiled at him. "I could ask the Shotet the same question."

"I'm not Shotet," he said.

"Are you not?" she said with a shrug, and continued to row.

His back ached by the time they got to their destination, from the stress of the landing followed by sitting on the uncomfortable bench in the boat. The Ogran woman steered them toward the edge of the canal, where there were stone steps overrun with the same velvet-soft wood he had touched earlier. Next to the steps was the yawn of a tunnel.

"We must go underground to avoid the storms," she said. "You can explore the Shotet sector another time."

The storms. She said it reverently, but not fondly—it was something she feared, this woman with the strength of half a dozen people, and that made Akos fear it, too.

He climbed out of the boat on unsteady legs, relieved to find solid ground. He reached back to help Cyra, his mouth drawn into a thin line.

"I thought the Shotet were fierce," he said. "But the people here must be downright lethal."

"A different kind of ferocity, perhaps," she said. "They don't hesitate, but they fight without finesse. It's a kind of . . . clumsy courage. And a kind of madness, too, to live in a place like this."

Akos knew, listening to her, that she had spent more time observing the Ograns than she would ever admit to—that she didn't even realize there was anything to admit to, because she assumed all other people were as inquisitive as she was. She had likely watched every piece of footage of Ogran combat she could get her hands on, and half a dozen other subjects, besides. All those files were stored in her quarters on the sojourn ship, her little den of knowledge.

They walked into the tunnel, led at first by the Ogran woman's whistling alone. But ten paces in, Akos saw light. Some of the stones in the walls of the tunnel were glowing. They were small, smaller than his fist, and set at random into the walls and ceiling.

The woman whistled louder, and the stones grew brighter. Akos pursed his lips, hiding his face as he tried a whistle of his own. The light in the stones near him went white, with the warmth of sunlight. Was this as close to sunlight as Ogra ever got?

He glanced at Cyra. She winced, the currentshadows lively across the back of her neck, but she was smiling at him.

"What?" he said.

"You're excited," she said. "This planet is probably going to kill us, and you love it."

"Well," he said, feeling defensive, "it's fascinating, that's all."

"I know," she said. "It's just, I don't expect other people to love the odd and dangerous things I love."

She draped her arm around his waist, her touch light, so he didn't feel her weight. He leaned into her, slinging his own arm over her shoulders. Her skin went blank again at his touch.

Then he heard it—the low rumble, like the planet itself was growling, and at this point, he wouldn't have been surprised to hear that it was.

"Come along, ice-dwellers," the Ogran woman sang, her voice ringing.

She reached down and stuck her pinkie through something—a metal loop in the dark floor. With a flick of her wrist, a trapdoor pulled up from the ground, scattering dust. Akos spotted narrow stairs that disappeared into nothingness.

Well, he thought, *time to summon some Shotet mettle.*

CHAPTER 11 | CYRA

THE LAST TIME I had walked into a crowd, it was to pretend to kill my own brother, and they had thirsted for my blood.

And before that, he had carved my skin from my head to the tune of hundreds of cheers. I reached up to touch the silverskin that covered me from throat to jaw to skull.

No, I did not have pleasant memories of crowds, and I was not likely to form them here, with only Ograns and Shotet exiles waiting for me.

We had walked down the dark stairs, feeling our way with the soles of our shoes and the brushes of our fingers, and turned a sharp corner, and here we were: in a dim waiting space with creaky wood floors, and the glow of Ogran clothing, most of which adorned Shotet bodies, though I only knew because of the language they spoke.

Ogran clothing—which even the Shotet wore, here—had no real distinct style, some of it tight and some flowing, some ornate and some simple, but the embrace of that ever-present *glow* was there, in bracelets and anklets and necklaces, shoelaces and belts and buttons. One man I passed even had stripes of red light—faint, but still, light—stitched into the back of his jacket. It gave everyone an eerie look, lit from beneath by their garments, their faces difficult to see. Those with fair skin, like Akos's, almost gave off their own light—not an advantage on a planet as hostile as this.

There were benches for sitting, and high tables for standing around. Some held glasses with a clear substance that scattered light inside them. I watched a bottle passed through a group of people, bobbing along like their hands were waves. Children sat in a circle near my feet, playing a game with quick hand motions passed in a round. Two boys, a few seasons younger than me, play-fought near one of the massive room's wooden pillars. This was a space for gathering and, I sensed, not much else; this was not where the Shotet lived, or worked, or ate, but just a space to wait out the storms. The Ogran woman had remained vague about what "the storms" actually were. Not surprising. Ograns seemed to trade in vague language and weighty looks.

Teka melded into the crowd right away, throwing her arms around the nearest exile she recognized. That was when people began to take notice of us—Teka, with her pale skin and even paler hair, required no introduction. Akos was a head taller than most people in the room, and drew eyes naturally.

And then there was me. Glinting silverskin and currentshadows crawling all over my body.

I tried not to tense as some people went quiet at the sight of me, and others muttered, or *pointed*—who had taught them manners?

I was used to this sort of reaction, I reminded myself. I was Cyra Noavek. Guards at the manor backed away from me instinctively, women held their children near at the sight of me. I drew myself up straighter, taller, and shook my head when Akos reached for me, to help me with my pain. No, better to let them see me as I was. Better to get this over with.

I pretended I was not breathing harder.

"Hey." Teka pinched the elbow of my oddly sized mechanic's jumpsuit and tugged. "Come on, we should introduce ourselves to the leadership."

"You don't know them already?" I said, as Akos searched behind him—for his mother and brother, I assumed, though he had been avoiding them since we landed.

I tried to imagine how I would have acted if my mother had returned to my life after I had accepted that I would never see her again. In my mind, it was a happy reunion, and we fell into our old rhythms of care and understanding. It certainly wasn't that simple for Akos, with the history of betrayal and subterfuge that existed between him and Sifa, but even without that, perhaps it was never simple. Perhaps I would have avoided Ylira just as he avoided his mother.

Or maybe it was just that she spoke in riddles, and it was exhausting.

Once Akos had rounded up his family, we all followed Teka deeper into the room. I tried to keep myself from marching, though that was my instinct—scare them on purpose, so I didn't have to watch them grow frightened by accident.

"So we're right near the village of Galo," Teka said. "It's mostly full of Shotet exiles now, but there are still some Ograns who live here. Merchants, mostly. My mother said we'd integrated pretty well—oh!"

Teka threw her arms around a pale-haired man with a mug in hand, then shook hands with a woman with a shaved head, who tapped Teka's eye patch in gentle mocking.

"I'm saving my fancy one for a special occasion," Teka replied. "Do you know where Ettrek is? I have to introduce him to—ah."

A man had stepped forward, tall, though not as tall as Akos, with long dark hair drawn up into a knot. I couldn't decide, in this light, if he was my age or ten seasons older. The rumble in his voice didn't do much to help.

"Ah, here she is," the man said. "Ryzek's Scourge turned Ryzek's Executioner."

He put an arm around me, turning as if to draw me into a group of people all holding glasses of whatever-it-was. I pulled away from him so quickly he might not have had the chance to feel my currentgift.

Pain darted across my cheek, and followed my next swallow down my throat. "Call me that again and I will—"

"What? Hurt me?" The man smirked. "It would be interesting to see you try. Then we would see if you are as good at fighting as they say."

"Regardless of whether I am a good fighter or not," I snapped, "I am not Ryzek's 'Executioner.'"

"So humble!" an older woman across from me said, tipping some of her drink into her mouth. "We all saw what you did on the news feed, Miss Noavek. There's no need to be shy about it."

"I am neither shy nor *humble*," I said, feeling my mouth twist into my sourest smile. My head was *pounding*. "I just don't believe everything I see. You should have learned that lesson well enough, exile."

I almost laughed, seeing all their eyebrows pop up in unison. Akos touched my shoulder, the part covered with fabric, and bent closer to my ear.

"Slow down on making enemies," he said. "There's plenty of time for that later."

I stifled a laugh. He had a point, though.

At first, all I saw next was a broad smile in the dark, and then Jorek collided with Akos. Akos looked too confused to return the embrace—actually, he didn't seem particularly affectionate, as a rule, I had noticed—but he managed to give Jorek a good-natured slap on the shoulder as he pulled away.

"Took you long enough to get here," Jorek said. "I was beginning to think you guys got kidnapped by the chancellor."

"No," Akos said. "Actually, we abandoned her in an escape pod."

"Really?" Jorek's eyebrows popped up. "That's sort of a shame. I liked her."

"You *liked* her?" I said.

"Miss Noavek," Jorek said, bobbing his head to me. He turned back to Akos. "Yeah, she was a little scary, and apparently I gravitate toward that quality in friends."

My cheeks warmed as he looked from Akos to me and back again, pointedly. Jorek thought of me as a friend?

"How's your mom?" Akos said to him. "Is she here?"

Jorek had stayed behind after our little mission to ensure that his mother made it through the chaos of Voa.

"Safe and sound, but no, she's not here," Jorek said. "She said if she ever manages to land on Ogra, she's never going to try to take off again. No, she's keeping an eye on things for us in Voa. Moved in with her brother and his children."

"Good," Akos said. He scratched the back of his neck, and his fingertips scraped along the thin chain he wore, the one with the ring Ara Kuzar had given him hanging from the end of it. He didn't wear it out of affection, as Ara and Jorek had undoubtedly hoped he would, but as a burden. A reminder.

Teka had disappeared for a moment, but she returned now with a sturdy woman at her side. She was not tall or short, really, and her hair was pulled back into a tight braid. The smile she gave me was warm enough, though like the others, she didn't even glance in Akos's direction. Her attention was solely mine.

"Miss Noavek," the woman said, offering your hand. "I am Aza. I sit on our council here."

I glanced at Akos, asking a silent question. He rested his hand on the bare skin where my neck met my shoulder, extinguishing my currentshadows. I knew without trying that I was not capable of controlling my gift right now, as I had learned to in the renegade hideout in Voa. Not in Ogra's currentgift-enhancing atmosphere, with days of limited sleep behind me. It was taking all the energy I had just to keep it contained, so it wouldn't explode out of me as it had when we first landed.

I took the woman's hand, and shook it. Akos may not have commanded her attention before, but his ability to extinguish my gift certainly did. In fact, everyone around us looked at him— specifically, at the hand he kept on my skin.

"Call me Cyra, please," I said to Aza.

Aza's gaze was curious, and sharp. When I dropped her hand, Akos dropped his, and my currentshadows returned. His cheeks were bright with color, and it was spreading to his neck.

"And you are?" Aza asked him.

"Akos Kereseth," he said, a little too quietly. I wasn't used to the meek side of him, but now that we weren't constantly surrounded by the people who had kidnapped him or killed his father or otherwise tormented him—well. Perhaps this was what he was like, under somewhat more normal circumstances.

"Kereseth," Aza repeated. "It's funny—for the duration of this exile colony's existence, we have never had a fated person pass through our doors. And now we have two."

"Four, actually," I said. "Akos's older brother Eijeh is . . . somewhere. And his mother, Sifa. They're both oracles."

I cast a glance around for both of them. Sifa emerged from the shadows behind me, almost as if summoned by her name alone. Eijeh was a few paces behind her.

"Oracles. *Two* oracles," Aza said. She was finally startled, it seemed.

"Aza," Sifa said, nodding. She wore a smile intended, I was sure, to be inscrutable. I almost rolled my eyes.

"Thank you for sheltering us," Sifa said. "All of you. We have walked a hard road to get here."

"Of course," Aza said stiffly. "The storms will be over soon, and we will be able to find a place for you to rest." Aza stepped closer. "But I must ask, Oracle . . . should we be concerned?"

Sifa smiled. "Why do you ask?"

"Hosting two oracles at once seems like . . ." Aza frowned. "Not a good sign for the future."

"The answer to your question is yes. Now is indeed the time for concern," Sifa said softly. "But that would be the case whether I was here or not."

She tilted her head, and another Ogran woman—this one fair-skinned, dotted with freckles, and wearing bracelets that lit up a gentle white—stepped forward. The bracelets helped me to see her face when she gestured to me, whispering in Ettrek's ear.

"Miss Noavek," the Ogran woman said then, when her whispering was finished. Her eyes—as dark as my own—followed the currentshadows that now cradled my throat like a choking hand, and felt much the same. "My name is Yssa, and I have just heard from someone in our communications tower. We have received a call for you, from Assembly Headquarters."

"For me?" I raised my eyebrows. "Surely you're mistaken."

"The recording was broadcast on the Assembly-wide news feed a few hours ago. That is as quickly as we can receive them on Ogra. Unfortunately, this one has a time limit," she said. "The message is from Isae Benesit. If you wish to respond, you must be prepared to act immediately."

"What?" I demanded. I felt a buzzing in my chest, like the hum of the current but stronger, more visceral. "I have to respond *immediately*?"

"Yes," Yssa said. "Or you will not get back to her in time. Our communications delay is regrettable, but there is no way to bypass it. We can record you from here and send the footage up to the next satellite, which departs our atmosphere in just minutes. Otherwise we must wait another hour. Come with me, please."

I reached for Akos's hand. He gave it, and held on tight, and we followed Yssa through the crowd.

Yssa had the message cued to a screen on the far wall. It was as large as I was with my arms outstretched. She had me stand on a mark on the floor, shooed away everyone who was standing around me—including Akos—and turned on a light that cast my face in yellow. This was for the camera that would record my message, I assumed.

I had been instructed in matters of diplomacy by my mother, but only as a child. After her death, neither my father nor my brother had bothered to continue that part of my education. They had assumed—reasonably—that I would never need to know those things, weaponized girl that I was. I tried to remember what she had told me. *Stand up straight. Speak clearly. Don't be afraid to think about your answer—the pause feels longer to you than it does to them.* That was all I could remember. It would have to be enough.

Isae Benesit appeared on the screen before me, larger now than she had ever been in life. Her face was uncovered—the disguise was unnecessary now that her sister had been killed, I assumed, and the two could no longer be confused for each other. The scars stood out from her skin, prominent but not garish. Though the rest of her face was painted with makeup, the scars had been left alone. At her insistence, I assumed.

Her black hair shone, pulled back from her face, and she wore a high-collared dress—I assumed, I could only see to her waist—made of a thick, black material that looked almost liquid. An off-center button shone gold against her throat. And there was a gold band around her forehead. A crown, of sorts, though the least ornamental one I had ever seen. This was not a chancellor who wanted to be associated with the abundance and wealth of Othyr. This chancellor led Osoc, Shissa, and most important, Hessa. The very heart of Thuvhe.

She appeared to have taken great pains not to appear pretty or delicate. She was striking, eyes lined in careful black, skin left to its usual olive tone without embellishment other than powder to limit its shine.

I, meanwhile, hadn't had a proper bath in over a week, and I was wearing an ill-fitting jumpsuit.

Wonderful.

"This is Isae Benesit, Fated Chancellor of Thuvhe, speaking on behalf of the nation-planet of Thuvhe," she began. The room went quiet around me. I squeezed my hands into fists at my sides. Pain raced through my body, sparking in my feet and spreading through my legs and around my abdomen.

I blinked tears away, and forced myself to focus, and stand as still as I could.

"This message is addressed to the successor of the so-called throne of Shotet," she continued. "As Ryzek Noavek has been confirmed dead, by blood succession laws obeyed by the Shotet people themselves, it must be delivered to Cyra Noavek before the common break of day, measured on this day at 6:13 a.m."

"The past few seasons have brought with them several acts of Shotet aggression: In one invasion, our falling oracle was killed, and our rising oracle was kidnapped. And just a few days ago, my sister, Orieve Benesit, was kidnapped and murdered in a public forum."

She had practiced this statement. She had to have, because she didn't so much as stumble over the words, though her eyes glittered with malice. Perhaps that was just my imagination.

"The escalation of these aggressive acts has become impossible to ignore. It must be met with strength." She cleared her throat— quietly, just a brief moment of humanity. "What I will read to you now are the terms of Shotet surrender to Thuvhe.

"Item one: Shotet will disband its standing army and surrender all weapons to the Thuvhesit state.

"Item two: Shotet will surrender its sojourn ship to the Assembly of Nine Planets, and forgo the sojourn in favor of settlement in and around the area known as Voa, immediately north of the southern seas.

"Item three: Shotet will permit Thuvhesit and Assembly troops to occupy Shotet until such time as Shotet has been restored to order and peaceful cooperation with Assembly and Thuvhesit authority.

"Item four: Shotet will desist in referring to itself as a sovereign nation, and will instead acknowledge its belonging to the nation of Thuvhe.

"Item five: Shotet will pay reparations to all public facilities and families affected by Shotet aggression of the past one hundred seasons, on the planet of Thuvhe and abroad, in an amount to be determined at a later date by a committee of Assembly and Thuvhesit authorities.

"Item six: All Shotet identifying as 'exiles' of the Noavek regime will return to Thuvhe and settle at a location distinct from Voa, where they will be pardoned and granted full Thuvhesit citizenship."

I felt like my entire body was curling into a fist, one finger at a time, squeezing blood from every knuckle. I hardly noticed the pain of my currentgift, though the shadows raced along my skin, at their deepest, densest black.

"You will respond to this message accepting these terms, or I will issue a declaration of war, at which point the blood of your own people will be on your hands," Isae continued. "A response must be received by the common daybreak, measured on this day at 6:13 a.m., or your life will be assumed forfeit, and we will proceed to the next member of your family line. Transmission complete."

Isae's face disappeared from the screen. Everything was silent around me. I closed my eyes and fought for control of my body. *Now is not the time*, I told it, as it raged with pain. *Now is not the time to take up space in my head.*

I tried again to think of my mother's lessons, but I could only think of her. The tilt of her neck, the cold smile she wore when she wanted someone to wither from the inside out. The way she used her quiet, rich voice to get exactly what she wanted. I could try to imitate her, but it wouldn't work for me. I already knew that I was no Ylira Noavek.

The only persona I had ever been able to adopt was that of Ryzek's Scourge, and I desperately didn't want to be that, not again, never again.

"Are you ready to respond, Miss Noavek? You have only a few minutes," Yssa said.

I was not ready to respond, not ready to act as the leader of a divided country that had never showed me anything but disdain. Around me now were the critical eyes of people who had been exiled because of the cruelty of my own father and my own brother. I was aware of the insult it must have been to them, to see me treated like their leader when I was really part of the same family that had tortured and excluded them.

But someone had to do this, and right now, the task fell to me. I would have to do my best.

I straightened. Cleared my throat. And nodded.

Yssa nodded back. I focused on the sights ahead of me, recording my image and voice to send it along to Isae.

"This is Cyra Noavek, acting sovereign of the rightful nation of Shotet," I said, and though my voice shook, the words were right. The yellow light burned against my face, and I stared straight ahead. I would not flinch at my currentshadows, I would not—

I flinched. It didn't matter, I told myself. I was in pain. Flinching was what I did.

"Shotet rejects your terms of surrender, as living under them would be worse than the bloodshed to which you referred," I continued. "Ryzek Noavek is dead, and the crimes he committed against Thuvhe, whether directly or indirectly, are not representative of his people."

I had run out of formal language.

"I think you know that," I said instead. "You have walked among us and met our resistance effort face-to-face."

I stopped. Thought about what I wanted to say.

"The nation of Shotet respectfully requests a cessation of hostilities until such a time as we can meet and discuss a treaty between our two nations," I said. "War is not what we want. But make no mistake, we *are* a nation, divided though we are between Ogra and Urek, and will be treated as such. Transmission complete."

I didn't realize, until I was finished, that I had just revealed the location of the exile colony—formerly secret to all but the Ograns—to Isae Benesit. It was too late to change that, though.

Before anyone could speak, I held up a hand to get Yssa's attention.

"Can I record another message? This one is to be delivered immediately to Voa satellites."

Yssa hesitated.

"Please," I added. It couldn't hurt.

"Okay," she said. "But it must be brief."

"The briefest," I said.

I waited for her signal to begin. This message I could do without thinking, without rehearsing. When Yssa nodded, I took a breath, and said:

"People of Voa. This is Cyra Noavek. Thuvhe has declared war on Shotet. Hostiles incoming. Evacuate to the sojourn ship immediately. I repeat, evacuate to the sojourn ship immediately. Transmission complete."

With that, I bent at the waist, bracing myself on my knees, and struggled to breathe. I was in so much pain my legs felt like they would give out at any moment. Akos rushed forward, clutching first at my shoulders, and then at my hands. I braced myself against him, my head slotted next to his, my forehead against his shoulder.

"You did well," he said quietly. "You did well, I have you, I have you."

When I glanced over his shoulder, I saw tentative smiles, heard murmurs that almost seemed . . . approving. Was Akos right? Had I really done well? I couldn't believe that was true.

War was coming. And no matter what Akos said, no matter what anyone said from now on, *I* was the one who had urged it forward.

CHAPTER 12 | CISI

"This Cyra Noavek," Ast says as he turns a smooth stone in his left hand. I had noticed that Ast was always moving, whether bouncing his knees or chewing on the pliable edge of his comb or fidgeting with something between his fingers. "There any chance she'll agree to the terms?"

I laugh. The idea of Cyra Noavek, who'd kept fighting in the arena even after her own brother *peeled skin from her head*, handing over her country to Thuvhe without so much as an argument is downright ridiculous.

"Well it's not like I've met her," Ast says, defensive.

"Sorry, I didn't mean to laugh at you," I say, "it's just, she'd fight with a wall if it got in her way."

"I don't anticipate her surrender, no." Isae gives her response like she's sitting far away instead of right across the room. She's at a little table next to the window. We're on the side of the Assembly satellite facing away from the sun, so the window shows stars and space and currentstream, instead of an image of Thuvhe. It makes Isae look smaller and younger than she usually does. "They aren't built for surrender, the Shotet. The Assembly Leader was right—they're like . . . an infestation. You think they're small, so they'll be easy to deal with, but they just keep coming and coming. . . ."

I go cold at the word *infestation*. That's not a way to talk about people, even if they are on the other side of a war. That's not the way *Isae* talks about people, either, not even when she's angry.

She straightens up, and clasps her hands in her lap.

"I need to decide my next move," she says. "Assuming the war declaration will go out as planned."

Ast runs the pad of his thumb over the stone. It's from his home planet, some brim rock that has a number instead of a name, with air you can't breathe without a gasper, the slang term for whatever the actual device is called. He spent most of his life with a bulky thing strapped to his face just so he could survive, he told me. *You gotta make whatever time you've got worth it*, he said to me, like he'd said it dozens of times before, like it wasn't closer to a manifesto than casual conversation.

"I think you need to strike hard," he says, after a few circles of his thumb. "The Shotet don't respect anything less. Hit 'em hard or you may as well not hit 'em at all."

Isae's head lowers like she's disappointed, only I know it's not that, it's just that she's bearing a lot of weight. She's fighting her own war, as well as the war the Assembly planets want, as well as the one against the grief that surges up inside her right where I can see it, making her say and do things she wouldn't usually say or do.

"I could hit the center of Voa," she says. "That's where most of the Noavek supporters live."

The center of Voa was where we walked to get to the amphi-theater. Where I got a cup of tea from one of the vendors, and his eyes crinkled at the corners when he passed it to me. She can't just—*hit* the center of Voa.

"You'd take out Ryzek's lackeys as well as make a statement," Ast points out. "It's a good idea."

"That's not a military target," I say.

Ast shakes his head. "There aren't any Shotet civilians, not really. They all know how to kill. Isae and I know that better than most."

The attack that took his father was the same one that gave Isae her scars, I've learned. And the same one that claimed her parents' and friends' lives. Their ship, the ship that had housed Isae most of her life, was boarded by Shotet sojourners who interpreted "scav-enging" as "theft and murder." It made both of them biased in the same way, as well as tying them together in a way I couldn't quite grasp.

"What weapon will you use?" he says. "A foot army wouldn't be good strategy against the Shotet, given the skill level of their average citizen."

"They aren't *citizens* of Shotet," Isae says tautly. "They are in active rebellion against my rightful governance."

Ast replies quietly, "I know."

Isae chews on a knuckle, her teeth digging hard into the skin. I want to tug her hand away from her mouth. "I still have to con-firm with the Pithar leadership, but it's their technology we'll be using. They call it an anticurrent blast. It's . . . effective. I could aim it at the amphitheater where Ori was killed, and the destruction would radiate outward from there. It would level the building completely."

My breaths come shallow. This is why I came here, to stop Isae from doing something she'll regret, to make sure Thuvhe stays on the right path. So I have to calm her down. I have to stop both of them while they're still building momentum. I push my gift forward in a rolling wave, hitting them both at once. Ast flinches at it, like he always seems to, but Isae doesn't seem to notice it. I imagine the currentgift water lifting the weight from her body away so she floats, then dragging at her limbs, gentle, as it pulls back to me.

"There are laws against striking at civilian targets unnecessarily," I say softly.

Isae looks at me lazily, like she's half-asleep. Her lower lip is streaked red.

"There's a soldier encampment outside Voa," I suggest.

"Where we don't even know anyone will *be*," Ast argues. "Voa's in a state of total upheaval. The soldiers have probably gone into the city to keep order. Attack the encampment and you risk just slicing and dicing at some tents and buildings."

Isae is still chewing that knuckle. A flash of red shows me it's bleeding now. She's got that same wild energy she had before she killed Ryzek, only now there's no focus to go along with it. Ast offers her a place to put her destructive energy, but at what cost? Civilian lives? Old men and women, children, dissenters, renegades, the sick and needy?

Not to mention the cost to her, as the person who orders that kind of destruction.

Come on, think.

"Killing people isn't the only way to be effective," I say. "The Shotet have a few things they hold dear. Their language——" I choke as Ast's irritation with me flares to life, and my currentgift responds, keeping me from continuing.

"Yeah, sure, let's go after abstractions instead of concrete targets," Ast says. "That'll work."

I push my gift forward again, another wave. What Isae needs right now is a little bit of calm and peace. And no matter how tied Ast and Isae are to each other, he can't give her that.

I can.

"Shh, Ast," Isae says, holding up a hand. "Cee, go on."

I wait for the tight feeling in my throat to work itself loose. It takes Ast calming down for it to happen, and not just his calm, but his shame at keeping me from talking. It's not until his expression is well and properly cowed that I can speak again.

"Their language is dear to them," I say, "as well as the oracles—which are out of the question—and the sojourn."

"The sojourn." Isae nods. "You're right." Her eyes are alight. "We could hit the ship. They just got back, so there's probably just a skeleton crew aboard—loss of life will be minimal, but the symbolic victory would be enormous."

It's not my solution, but it's not Ast's, either. I guess that's better than nothing.

Ast frowns, his eyes fixed as ever on an uncertain point at middle distance. He hasn't moved in a while, so the flying beetle that guides him with its clicking and chirping is just perched on his shoulder, its antennae shifting in the same incremental way his mechanical eyes do.

"It's a little soft," he says.

"It's better to regret being too soft than being too hard," Isae says, in a clipped voice that says the discussion is over. "I'll contact General Then. Make sure we have surveillance images of the ship that aren't from half a season ago."

She smiles at me, the expression a little too fierce for my comfort. It means the Isae who killed Ryzek is still in there somewhere, waiting to strike again. I shouldn't be so alarmed by it, really. This is what attracted me to her to begin with, after all—she's capable, decisive. She didn't need anybody to take care of her, least of all me. She'd never admit to needing it now.

But the thing about falling for somebody is, you *want* to take care of them. So that's what I'm going to do.

We eat dinner together, Ast, Isae, and me. Since Ast doesn't respond well to my currentgift, I have to learn how to deal with him the way everybody else does—trial and error. So this time I try to ask him about growing up on the ship with Isae, and it seems to set him at ease. He tells me about trying to teach Isae how to fix engines, which is what his dad did, and all she wanted to do was pry bolts loose. She tried to get him to join in on her etiquette lessons once, and he made her laugh so hard she snorted tea up her nose.

"It came out my *eye*," she says as she laughs.

Slowly but surely, I decide: I'll pry my way between them. Not to get in the way, but to make sure she does the right thing, the level-headed thing. Her message to General Then sounded steady enough, and she's laughing now, as she tells stories from her past, but I'm still worried. After you've watched someone kill a man with a kitchen knife, there's a lot more to worry about.

Ast leaves once the plates are cleared, and I get ready to go, too, sure she's tired out from the day's decisions. But she catches my hand as I rise from my chair, and says, "Would you mind staying awhile?"

"Of course," I say.

She loses all her ease like she's shedding clothes, pacing the length of the windows and then turning to walk back. I try to help her, but just as it did when she was on her way to Ryzek's cell on the renegade ship, my currentgift fails me. She tugs her hair, agitated, so it curls tighter around her ears.

"My gift comes with its challenges, too," she says to me after a few laps around the room. For a long time I thought her gift was simple, just seeing other people's memories at a touch. But it's more than that. She lives with the past always tugging at her, trying to carry her away on its tide. "Since Ori—" She stops, swallows, starts again. "I've been getting stuck in memories. Which is fine when they're good ones, like with Ast, but they're not always good, and they come into my dreams—"

She flinches, and shakes her head.

"We could talk about something lighter," I say. "Until you fall asleep."

"I'm not sure. . . . I don't think it'll work." She's still shaking her head. "I wondered if . . . it's silly, but—"

"Whatever will help you," I say.

"I wondered if you could let me into your memories," she says. "If I used my currentgift to see them, maybe I could get some peace, for a little while."

"Oh." I hesitate. I don't have that many good memories to

choose from. The ones from my childhood are tinged with sadness, because they're all building up to Eijeh and Akos being taken, or my father dying. The ones from after, where I'm trying to pull Mom back from constant distraction, aren't great, either. It wasn't until I reunited with Ori that things lightened up more often, and that was partly because I was getting to know *Isae*. . . .

"I'm sorry, I shouldn't have asked, it's an invasion of privacy," Isae says.

"No! No, it's not that," I say. "I was just thinking that a lot of my good memories involve you and Ori, and I wasn't sure if that would be uncomfortable."

"Oh." She pauses. "No, that's . . . fine."

I move to her bed, and sit on the edge of it, where the blanket is still smooth and tucked under the mattress. I pat the space next to me, and she sits down, angled so she can look me in the eye.

"Give me a tick," I say.

"A 'tick.'" She smiles. "That's one of my favorite Hessan words."

I close my eyes, then, so I can remember. It's not just about thinking of when I met her, or when I felt like I was really her friend—it's about the details. What the air smelled like, how cold it was, what I was wearing. And that's not so easy. I was in school, so I was always wearing my uniform the first few times we spent together, a thick robe that covered my clothes so they wouldn't get plant dust and bark and stems all over them. . . .

"Go ahead," I say, as I remember the smell of peeling skin from a saltfruit, green and tangy.

She's used her currentgift on me before, when we were getting to know each other better, so I know to expect her hand on my face. Her fingers are cold and a little clammy, but they warm up fast on my cheek, and anchor at my jaw. Then we're moving together into the past.

I stood behind a rope barrier with a crowd pressing against my back. I didn't mind it then because it meant warmth, shelter against the wind and snow. I still had to curl my hands into fists inside my mittens to keep my fingers warm, but I didn't feel that chill, that deep chill that makes your teeth feel brittle.

We stood there for a long time before the ship appeared above us, lowering without swerving to the landing pad. The ship was small and humble, a Hessa transport. The people around me gasped when they recognized it, the battered metal, the heat vents that keep the engine from freezing. To me it seemed like a message: I am one of you, just a simple Thuvhesit. *It was a manipulation.*

The Hessa ship landed, and the door opened, and a woman in black stepped out. Her face was covered, of course, from nose on down. But she wasn't wearing goggles, like the rest of us were, so I could see her dark eyes, with their narrow slope, eyelashes pressed up into the skin above them.

At the sight of her, everybody cheered. Not me, though, I was trying to figure out if I was seeing things. Those were Ori's eyes, but I hadn't seen her in years, and she was . . . well, she was Ori.

A tick later, another woman stepped out behind the first—the chancellor's sister, I assumed, only I could have sworn I was seeing double. She was the same—same height, same coat, same face covering. Same eyes that scanned the crowd without feeling.

The women walked shoulder to shoulder toward the building. They didn't stop to grasp hands. They lifted gloved hands to wave; their eyes crinkled in smiles that we couldn't see. One's gait was smooth, like she was rolling over the ground on wheels. The other's was buoyant, making her head bob up and down as she moved. When they passed me, I couldn't help it; I pulled my goggles down so I could see their faces better, see for myself if this was Ori or not.

One set of eyes found mine. Her steps faltered, just a little. And then they were gone.

Later that day, I heard a knock.

I lived in the dormitory just next to the hospital, connected to it by a covered bridge. Sometimes I leaned my forehead against the glass and stared down at the iceflower fields from there. I could only see smudges of color from up here, where the buildings of Osoc dangled in the sky like chandeliers.

My rooms were small and packed tight with objects. Fabric, mostly. Paper—and as a result, books—was a luxury on a planet without many trees, but we spun fabric out of iceflower stems, and treated it with purity petal essence to make it soft. We dyed it all kinds of colors, muted and bright, dark and light. Anything but gray, which was what we saw all the time. I hung fabric across shelves, to hide what was on them; I draped it on the walls to cover up where they peeled. Mostly my room was a kitchen; I had little burners here and there with something stewing on them, and the air was full of steam or smoke, depending on the day. They weren't clean rooms, but they were warm.

They weren't fit for the company I got that day, though. I wiped my hands on an apron and opened the door, sweat wetting my brow. A very tall, thick man stood right in front of me, looking gruff.

"Their Highnesses of the family Benesit request the honor of your hospitality," the man said. He wasn't a Thuvhesit; I could tell by how he left his shirt buttons open at the throat. He was wearing pale gray, which

meant he must be from the Assembly, and his formal tone confirmed it.

"Uh," I said, because it was all I could manage. Then my currentgift kicked in, and his posture relaxed, so I didn't feel as nervous. "Of course. They are welcome here, as are you."

The man gave me a little smile.

"Thank you, ma'am, but my job is to stay outside the door," he said.

He checked my apartment to make sure it was safe, roaming through each room with his eyes on all my stuff. Even poked his head into the bathroom to make sure nobody was crouched in my shower with a knife, or so I assumed. Then he stepped out, nodded to someone out of sight, and there they were. Two tall, lean women in black dresses buttoned up to the throat, hooded, with fabric covering their faces. I stepped back to let them in, but I didn't greet them. All I could do was stare at them.

Then one of them stepped past me to close the door, and smiled at me. I could tell by how her cheek creased.

"Cisi," she said, and then I knew, I really knew, it was her.

"Ori," I said, and we collided in a tight hug, squeezing little laughs out of each other.

Over her shoulder, I saw her sister walking through my little apartment, trailing her fingers over everything she passed. She paused by the shelf where I kept pictures of my family behind a gauzy hanging so I didn't have to look at them if I thought it might hurt too bad.

I pulled away from Ori, who fumbled to pull her hood and face covering down. She looked just like I thought she would——the same, but sharper, older. Her black hair was mussed from the hood, and straight as straw, pulled into a knot at the back of her neck. Her mouth, already tilted up at the corners, curled into a deeper smile.

"I can't believe . . ." I can't believe you're the chancellor's sister, I can't believe you're here, *was what I meant to say, but I couldn't.*

"I'm so sorry." *She looked down.* "If there had been another way . . ."

How could you lie to me all our lives? *I thought, because I knew I couldn't say it. I couldn't say anything at all, in fact.*

I put my hand on her elbow and guided her into the room, toward the cushions I had piled around a burner and a sturdy pot with tea steeping in it. I was studying the effects of cold-steeped iceflower against the warm kind.

"Where did you go?" *I said.*

"The Assembly ship," *she said.* "Isae was there . . . recovering."

She looked to her sister, then, so I knew the chancellor's name was Isae. She perched on the only chair in the room, close to her sister. Her hands were folded in her lap for a tick or two before she rolled her eyes and tugged the face covering away from her mouth and nose. The scars that bisected her face were wicked, and fresh, judging by their bright red color.

They weren't beautiful. Scars rarely were.

"Recovering from this, is what she means." *Isae waved a hand in front of her face.*

I tried a smile. "That must have been difficult."

Isae snorted.

"So you're the oldest Kereseth, then," *she said.* "You're the talk of the system, these days. The Kereseths—oracle, traitor, and . . . well, the one who ought to be careful around knives. 'The first child of the family Kereseth will succumb to the blade,' isn't that your fate?"

I choked. My brother is not a traitor. I'll be as careless around knives as I damn well please. Get out of my apartment. Who the hell do you think you are? *I couldn't say any of those things, though.*

"Isae!" *Ori said, chastising.*

"I suppose I shouldn't bring up unpleasant subjects uninvited," she said, "but it's the reality of who you are, and who I am, and who my sister is. And I like to face reality."

"You're being rude," Ori said.

"It's fine," I said, my tongue finally loosening. "I've experienced worse."

Isae laughed, like she knew what I was trying to say. Maybe she did. She must have been educated by the Assembly, at least for a little time, and they, better than most, must have known how to say two things at once.

"They would have loved you at the Assembly ship," she said in a low voice.

"Good memories, I said, not ones where you're angry with me!" Isae pulls me out of memory and into the Assembly ship again, and though she's scolding me, she's also laughing.

"I'm sorry, it's hard to control!" I say with a giggle.

"I was horrible to you." Isae's eyes sparkle a little when she looks at me next. They're a nice color, dark brown with a little warmth to it, like rich earth. "How did you ever become my friend?"

"Come back in and I'll show you," I say.

The smell of spice came to me first. My hands were buried in it, plunged into a wad of dough the size of my head. A cloud of flour puffed up around my face as I slammed the dough down on the counter. I didn't visit home often, but it was the Deadening time, and I had never missed the Blooming in Hessa, so I was there for a few days.

Sitting at the table behind me was Isae Benesit. She had refused to go to the temple with Ori, who wanted to ask the oracle—Mom—about something. So Ori dropped her off here like she was a kid that needed to be *watched, even though she knew we didn't like each other much.*

Isae had a full cup of tea in front of her. As far as I could tell she hadn't even touched it since I had made it an hour before.

"So," she said, after I had folded the dough over itself and slammed it down again. "Do you come home often?"

"No," I said, and I was surprised by how sharp the answer came out. Normally my gift didn't let me talk that way to people.

"Any particular reason?"

I paused. I wasn't sure I'd be able to answer her question. Most people didn't really want to hear about my troubles, even if they asked, which meant I literally couldn't talk about them. Grief had a way of doing that, making people uncomfortable.

"Too many shadows in this house," I said, inching toward the subject slowly.

"Ah," Isae said. And then—to my surprise—she said, "Want to tell me about them?"

I laughed. "You want to hear about them?"

She shrugged. "We don't seem to be good at talking about the more casual stuff, and I don't have the time for that anyway. So. Yeah. I want to hear about them."

I nodded, and slapped the dough ball down on the counter. I licked some of the raw dough off my fingers before washing them in the sink and wiping them dry on a cloth. Then I led her to the living room. The whole house smelled yeasty and spiced from the bread. My pants were still marked with flour fingerprints.

I pointed to a part of the living room floor that looked just like every other part of the floor, worn and wooden.

"There," I said. "That's where his body fell."

Isae didn't ask me who I was talking about. She knew the story—

everyone in Thuvhe knew the story. Instead, she crouched next to the spot where my father died, and ran her fingers over the rough grain.

I just stood there, frozen. And then I started to talk.

"I sat with his body for hours before I cleaned it up," I said. "Part of me expected . . . I don't know. For him to wake up, maybe. Or for me to wake up from the nightmare." I let out a little sound. Something small and pained. "Then I had to deal with it. Wrap up his body. Find a bucket and fill it with warm water. Get a bunch of old rags. Imagine standing there at the linen closet trying to figure out how many rags you need to clean up your father's blood."

I choked, but not from my currentgift this time—on tears. I hadn't cried around another person since my currentgift developed. I had thought it was just out of the question for me now, like asking people rude questions or laughing when someone took a spill on an icy road.

Isae began to mouth a prayer. Only it wasn't one of comfort or even the one a person said when someone died. It was a blessing, for a sacred place.

Isae thought the place where my father died was sacred.

I knelt next to her, wanting to hear her voice as it shaped the words. Her hand wrapped around mine, and it was more than strange, touching someone who I didn't even know, didn't even like. But she squeezed tight, so I wouldn't let go, and finished up the prayer quietly.

I still didn't let go.

"I've never been able to tell someone that before," I said. "It makes people too uncomfortable."

"Takes more than that to make me uncomfortable," she said.

Her cool fingers sweep over my cheekbone, catching tears. She tucks a curl behind my ear.

"Your definition of a good memory needs work," she says,

softly, the very gentlest of jokes.

"I hadn't cried in seasons, unless I was alone," I say. "No one was ever there to comfort me, not even my mother. All the tragedies of my life, they're too hard for most people to handle. But you could handle it. You could handle whatever I told you."

Her hand is still behind my ear.

Then it's in my hair, twisting the curls around her fingers.

And I kiss her. Once: soft, brief.

Again, harder, with her kissing me back.

Again, like we can't stand to be apart.

My rough hands find the back of her neck, and we're pressed together, fitted together, tangled together.

We bury ourselves as deep in this little pocket of happiness as we can get.

CHAPTER 13 | AKOS

THE EXILES FIT THEM into temporary housing all stacked on top of each other, the beds dug right into the wall in metal-lined slots. It wasn't a permanent arrangement, but it would do for a few days—that's what the exile who showed them their beds had said, anyway.

Cyra took the topmost bed—they weren't wide enough to fit two people, so there was no chance of sharing—because she was a good climber, and Teka, equally nimble, took the second highest. Sifa and Eijeh took the lower two beds in the stack, so Akos found himself right in the middle. Between two Thuvhesits and two Shotet. It was like fate had given up on subtlety and had decided to just start poking at him.

Even though there was a sheet of metal separating him from Teka's bed, he still heard the slide of sheets as she tossed and turned all night. He woke to the woman who slept in the next column over dropping to a half crouch below him. There was something about the way she moved, the way her legs bent, that he recognized.

"Must be losing my touch if I can rouse you," the woman said, roughly, as she pulled on a pair of pants. She glanced up at him.

"I know you from somewhere," he said, swinging his legs over the edge of his bed and dropping to the floor. He curled his toes against the cold of the ground.

"I was there when you earned your armor," she said. "One of your observers. You're Kereseth."

Earning armor required three witnesses. It had taken him a long time to get Vakrez Noavek, the general, to agree to summon them for him. Vakrez had sneered at the idea that someone who wasn't Shotet-born could kill an Armored One. It had been Malan, his husband, who talked him into it. *If he fails, so what?* he had said, nodding to Akos. *You prove a Thuvhesit isn't fit to wear our armor. And if he succeeds, it reflects well on your training. Either way, the gain is yours.*

He had winked at Akos then. Akos had the feeling Malan got his way with Vakrez more often than not.

"Good to see you've found your footing," the woman said. "That business with the Armored One was a bit unorthodox."

She nodded to his wrist, where he'd marked the loss of the animal as surely as he would have marked any other life. A strange thing, to the huddle of Shotet who had granted him armor. He had put a hash through the mark like Cyra told him to, though.

He didn't cover up the marks when the woman looked them over, like he might have around his family. But he did run the tip of his finger across the line that belonged to Vas Kuzar. He hadn't decided yet whether he thought of it as a triumph or a crime.

"Enough chatter!" Teka growled from the above bunk. She threw her pillow, hitting the woman in the head with it.

◁≪≫▷

Akos had gotten spare clothes from an exile about his size the
night before, so he got dressed and splashed water on his face to
wake himself up. Cool water ran down the back of his neck and
followed his spine. He didn't bother to dry it. Ograns kept their
buildings warm.

When he stepped outside to go to the mess, though, he realized that for the first time in a long time, nobody was telling
him where he could and couldn't go, or chasing him so he had to
hide. He decided to keep walking. He went past the mess hall,
an old warehouse the Shotet had repurposed, and toward the
Shotet-Ogran village of Galo.

The Shotet had done such a good job of adapting that he
couldn't tell them apart from Ograns most of the time, even
though Teka had said this village was full of exiles. He caught a
few Shotet words passing by one of the market stalls, an old Shotet
man bickering over the cost of an Ogran fruit that looked like a
brain and glowed, faintly, with some kind of dust. And the fabric
one of the women was shaking out of her window was stitched
with a map of Voa.

The permanent structures were bent into each other, some
walls warped from age. Some of the doors opened into each other,
warring for dominance in front of the shops. Alleys only as wide
as his shoulders led to still more shops buried behind the first row.

There were hardly any signs—you had to figure things out
by poking your head inside. Half the objects they were selling
weren't familiar to him anyway, but he got the sense Ograns liked
their things small and intricate, if at all.

He felt jumpy, like someone was going to catch him walking

around and punish him for it. *You're not a prisoner anymore*, he kept telling himself. *You can go wherever you want.* But it was hard to really believe it.

Then he caught a scent on the air that reminded him so much of jealousy dust he couldn't help himself. He ducked into one of the alleys, turning sideways so he wouldn't scrape his shirt on the damp stone, and inched closer. Vapor huffed from a window up ahead, and when he peeked between the bars, he saw an older woman bent over a stove, stirring something in an iron pot. Hanging all above her were bundles of plants, tied off with string, and from floor to ceiling, wherever there was room for a shelf, were jars marked in Shotet characters. The cluttered space held knives and measuring cups and spoons and gloves and pots full to bursting.

The woman turned, and Akos tried to slip out of sight, but he wasn't quick enough. Her eyes trapped his, and they were as bright blue as Teka's. She had a beak of a nose, and her skin was almost as fair as his own. She whistled at him between her teeth.

"Well, come in then, you may as well help stir," she said.

He bent under the doorframe. He felt too big for her narrow shop—was it a shop?—and too big for his own body. She came up to his chest, and she was slim, her arms muscled despite her age. There was no place for the feeble here, he thought. He would have asked Cyra what became of the feeble-bodied who dared to defy the Noaveks, but he didn't want the answer.

He took the spoon from her.

"Clockwise. Scrape the bottom. Not too fast," she said, and he did his best. He didn't like the sound the metal spoon made against the bottom of the pot, but there was nothing for it. There wasn't a wooden spoon in sight. Trees probably tried to kill you if you cut them down, here.

"What's your name?" she said gruffly. She had moved on to a countertop only as wide as her hips, and was chopping leaves he didn't recognize. But dangling right in front of his nose was a bundle of sendes leaves. Where had she gotten them? Could they grow on Ogra? Surely not.

"Akos," he said. "How did you get sendes leaves here?"

"Imports," she said. "What, you think it's cold enough to grow an iceflower here?"

"I don't think the warmth is really the greatest obstacle," he said. "No sun, now that's a problem."

She grunted in what sounded like agreement.

"They don't risk flying in new shipments often," she said. "You're not interested in my name?"

"No, I—"

She laughed. "I'm Zenka. Don't get so twitchy about it, I'm not about to scold a person for caring more about the plants than they do about me. That would be downright hypocritical. Slow down, you'll beat the poor things half to death at the rate you're going."

Akos looked at his hand. He'd picked up the pace of stirring faster than he meant to.

He slowed his hand. Clearly he was out of practice.

"You ever get hushflowers here?" he said.

"Not much good they do me," she said. "Don't know how to handle them, and they're not to be trifled with."

He laughed. "Yeah. I know. My town had a fence around them to keep people from hurting themselves."

"Your town," she said. "Where's that, then?"

He realized, too late, that he might not want to run his mouth about being Thuvhesit in unfamiliar company. But it had been so long since he'd met a person who didn't already know who he was.

"Hessa," he answered, since he couldn't see a way around it. "Not my town anymore, I guess."

"If it ever was," she said. "Your name's Akos, after all. That's a Shotet name."

"I've heard," he said.

"So you know about iceflowers, then," she said.

"My dad was a farmer. My mom taught me a few things, too," he said. "I don't know anything about what grows on Ogra, though."

"Ogran plants are ferocious. They live on other plants, or meat, or current, or all three," she said. "So if you aren't careful, they'll bite your arm clean off, or shrivel you from the inside out. Harvesting here is more like hunting, with the added benefit of nearly poisoning yourself every time you take a step into the forest." She was smiling a little. "But they can be useful, if you can get them. They need to be cooked, usually. Takes away some of their potency."

"What do you make with them?"

"Been working on a medicine that will suppress the current, for those whose currentgifts are too strong for them here," she said. "A lot of Shotet find it unlivable. I could use the help, if you're interested in chopping and peeling and grating."

He smiled a little. "Maybe. Not sure what else I'll have to be doing while I'm here."

"You don't intend to stay long."

She meant that he didn't intend to stay on Ogra long, but Akos
heard it, first, as bigger than that. How long would he live, before
he met his fate? A day, a season, ten seasons? He felt like a deep-sea
creature on a hook, being drawn toward the surface. He couldn't
help but go where the line pulled him, and death waited above the
water. But there was nothing he could do about it.

"My intentions," he said, "don't really matter anymore."

The mess hall was too quiet when Akos got to it, his fingertips
stained green from some Ogran stem he had cracked open for
Zenka. Too quiet, and too busy, everyone rushing around but not
really going anywhere. He was scanning the room for Cyra when
Jorek came up to him, his skinny arms bared by his shirt—which,
judging by the frayed edges near his shoulders, he had cut the
sleeves off of himself. Maybe with his teeth.

"There you are," Jorek said. "Where'd you go? Everyone's losing their minds."

Right away, Akos felt so tired he might collapse right there
on the mess hall floor, on top of a discarded bread crust. "What's
going on?"

"The Ogran satellite brought down a bundle of news a few
minutes ago. They're beaming it to the screens here as soon as
they can. But apparently it's a doozy," Jorek said. "They wouldn't
say much, but they hunted down Cyra, and I don't think it's just
because Isae Benesit thinks she's our sovereign."

Akos spotted Cyra across the room, from the shine of silverskin on her head, which was bent toward Aza, one of the exile
leaders. She was scowling, which he knew didn't mean she was
mad, even though that's how it looked. When she was mad, she

was a statue. When she was laughing, she was scared out of her mind. And when she was scowling . . . well, he didn't quite know.

He was making his way over to her when the screens—there were four in the room, suspended from the middle in a cluster, like a chandelier—lit up and started playing footage. At first it was just the standard news feed, and then it switched over to a shot of a man's face. He was fair-skinned, with a deeply lined face and a stern brow. He was thin, and narrow through the shoulder, but he didn't look fragile—the opposite, really. He looked like he was using every bit of himself for muscle and energy, with nothing to spare. Most peculiar, though, was the dusting of freckles across his nose, too youthful to belong to such a stern and aged face.

Everyone in the mess hall went still.

"I am Lazmet Noavek," he said, "and I am the rightful sovereign of Shotet."

CHAPTER 14 | CYRA

MY FATHER'S FACE IS a spark.

And all my memories are kindling.

A thousand moments of his eyes skimming right over me as he scanned a room. And his taut, wiry arm with its rows and rows of kill marks. And the vein that pulsed in the center of his forehead when someone displeased him. Those were the images I had of him, sealed away in my mind, but the worst ones were not those.

I never saw him in his worst moments, because I was never invited into the room—a favor, I now knew, though at the time it had felt like exclusion. Ryzek had been invited, though. When he was young, he had attended executions, and interrogations, and brutal training that treated soldiers of Shotet as disposable. And when he was older, he was forced to participate, to learn the art of pain the way others learned music or language, and to build a reputation for himself every bit as terrifying as my father's.

So my worst memories of Lazmet were actually memories of Ryzek, or my mother, finally dismissed from his presence. My mother's hands trembling slightly as she removed her necklace, or undid the buttons of her gown. Ryzek clamping both hands over his mouth so no one would hear him sob—though of course I knew what to listen for—or screaming at Vas for no reason, screaming himself hoarse.

Now Lazmet Noavek himself stared at me from the screen above my head, and I forced myself to straighten. He was looking at a sight, of course, not at me, but it felt like the first time he had ever made eye contact with me, and I wanted to bear up under his scrutiny. He was the worst of Ryzek bound in sinew and bone, but I still wanted his approval, my father's approval.

Maybe not your father, a voice in my head said.

"I am Lazmet Noavek, and I am the rightful sovereign of Shotet," he said. He looked thinner than he had the last time I saw him, and more lined, but he was otherwise unchanged. He had begun shaving his head when his hair thinned, and his skull was smooth except for the bones that protruded on either side at sharp angles. The defined muscle that wrapped around his bones, and the armor that he wore even now, could not quite disguise how narrow he was through the shoulders. He was tanned and weather-beaten—not brown like I was; he had the look of someone fair who has been scorched by a harsh sun for many seasons. His face was rough with the start of a beard.

Only Ryzek and Vas had been there when he supposedly died, out on a sojourn. They had been on a separate mission, and a secret one: finding and capturing an oracle. Ever since my father learned my brother's fate—*the first child of the family Noavek will fall to the family Benesit*—they had both been searching for a way out of it. Every sojourn was a new chance to hunt down an oracle. On this particular sojourn, they had been attacked by local armed forces and, outnumbered, Lazmet had fallen, forcing Ryzek and Vas to flee. There had been no body, but no reason to suspect Ryzek hadn't told the truth. Until now.

I wondered if they had even been attacked at all. Where had Lazmet been all these seasons? He couldn't have been in hiding. He would never have surrendered his power willingly. He must have been imprisoned somewhere. But how had he gotten out? And why had he returned now?

Lazmet cleared his throat, and it sounded like rocks tumbling down the face of a cliff. "Whatever you have previously heard from the woman-child who murdered both my wife and my son should be disregarded, as she is not the leader of Shotet based on our laws of succession."

Eyes shifted to me from all angles, then flicked away again. I told myself I didn't care. But I remembered my shadow-streaked hand clamping on my mother's arm, to push her away, and shuddered. I had not killed Ryzek, but I couldn't claim to be innocent of my mother's death.

I could never claim to be innocent again.

"I speak for the people of Shotet, a people who have for hundreds of seasons been scorned, insulted, and disparaged by the nation-planets of the Assembly. A people who have, despite that constant scorn, become strong. We have met every possible criteria for inclusion in the Assembly. We settled on a planet, and still we were disregarded. We formed a mighty army, and still we were disregarded. We were given a fated family, spoken into being by all the oracles in the solar system, and *still we were disregarded*. We will be disregarded no longer."

Despite my fear of him, I felt something surge within me. Pride in my people, my culture, my language, and yes, *my nation*, which I had never stopped believing in, though I had disagreed with the methods my family had used to establish it. I was buoyed by his words even as I was afraid of what they meant, and when I looked around, I felt certain I was not the only one. These people were exiles, enemies of the Noaveks, but they were still Shotet.

"We reject the terms of Chancellor Benesit's peace," he said. "There can be no peace between us while there is no respect. Therefore the most efficient course of action is to work against peace. I submit this message as a declaration of war against the nation of Thuvhe, led by Chancellor Isae Benesit. We will meet again in battle, Miss Benesit. Transmission complete."

The screens all switched to another piece of footage, something from the high peaks of Trella, where fog swirled so high it turned into clouds.

All around me the mess hall was oddly quiet.

We were at war.

"Cyra." Akos's voice was a comfort. So familiar, its rumble. What were the first words he had said to me? Oh, yes—they had been explaining his gift. *I interrupt the current*, he had said. *No matter what it does.*

If my life was a different kind of current—and it was, in a certain sense, a flow of energy across space, brief and temporary—he had certainly interrupted it. And I was better for it. But now the question I had held in my mind ever since he first kissed me, about whether it was his fate tying him to me or not, felt more urgent than before.

"That was my father," I said, with something between a hiccup and a giggle.

"Pleasant man," he said. "A little too soft-spoken, though, don't you think?"

The joke eased me back into the present. When before everything had been quiet, now it was roaring with conversation. Teka was having a heated argument with Ettrek, which I knew because her finger was in his face, almost jabbing him in the nose when she gestured. Aza was with a few other grave-looking people, her face half-covered with her hand.

"What happens now?" Akos said to me softly.

"You think I know?" I said, shaking my head. "I don't even know if you and I count as exiles. Or if Lazmet counts exiles as Shotet."

"Maybe we're on our own, you and me."

He said it with a glint of hope in his eyes. If I was not an exile, if I was not even Shotet, then staying with me was not a sign of his inevitable betrayal. The family Noavek had so long been synonymous with "Shotet" in his mind that the sudden paring down of everything I was appealed to him. But I could not be made smaller, and moreover, I didn't want to be.

"I am always a Shotet," I said.

He looked taken aback at first, tilting away from me. But his rejoinder came quickly, and it was sharp: "Then why do you doubt me when I tell you I am always a Thuvhesit?"

It wasn't the same. How could I explain that it wasn't the same? "Now is not the time for this debate!"

"Cyra," he said again, and he touched my arm, his touch light as ever. "Now is the *only* time for this debate. How can we talk about where we're going now, what we're doing now, if we haven't talked about who—and what—we *are* now?"

He had a point. Akos had a way of getting to the heart of things—he was, in that way, more of a knife than I was, though I was the sharper-tongued of the two of us. His soft gray eyes focused on mine like there were not over one hundred people crowded around us.

Unfortunately, we didn't possess the gift of focus in equal measure. I couldn't think in all the chatter. I jerked my head toward the door, and Akos nodded, following me out of the mess hall and into the quiet stone street beyond. Over his shoulder I saw the village, faint dots of light dancing all over it, in all different colors. It looked almost cozy, not something I had thought a place like Ogra could be.

"You asked who we are now," I said, looking up at him. "I think we need to move even further back and ask, are we a 'we'?"

"What do you mean?" he asked, with sudden intensity.

"What I mean is," I said, "are we together, or am I just some kind of . . . *warden* again, only it's fate keeping you prisoner this time, instead of my brother?"

"Don't make it sound simple when it isn't," he said. "That's not fair."

"Fair?" I laughed. "What, in your entire life so far, has made you think anything will be 'fair'?" I stepped wider, so I felt like I was rooted to the ground, the way I might have if we had been about to spar. "Just tell me—tell me if I'm something you're choosing, or not. Just tell me."

Just get it over with, I thought, because I already knew the answer. I was ready to hear it—even eager, because I had been bracing myself since our first kiss for this rejection. It was the inevitable by-product of what I was. Monstrous, and bound to destroy whoever was in my path, particularly if they were as kind as Akos.

"I," he said, slowly, "am a Thuvhesit, Cyra. I would never oppose my country, my home, if I felt like I had a choice."

I closed my eyes. It hurt worse—much worse—than I was expecting it to.

He went on, "But my mother used to say, 'Suffer the fate, for all else is delusion.' There's no point in fighting something that is inevitable."

I forced my eyes open. "I don't want to be something you 'suffer.'"

"That's not what I meant," he said, reaching for me. I backed up. For once, the pain that wrapped around every limb was not a curse to me—though not a gift, never a gift—but another set of armor.

"You're the one thing that makes my life bearable," he said, and the sudden tension in him, suffusing every muscle, reminded me of how he had braced himself every time Vas came around. It was the way he looked when he was guarding himself against pain. "You're this bright spot of light. You're—Cyra, before I knew you, I thought about . . ."

I raised my eyebrows.

He drew a sharp breath. His gray eyes looked glassy.

"Before I knew you," he began again, "I didn't intend to live past rescuing my brother. I didn't want to serve the Noavek family. I didn't want to give my life to them. But when it's you . . . it seems like whatever the end is, it might be worthwhile."

Maybe, to another person, this might have sounded kind. Or at least realistic. A person couldn't avoid fate. That was the whole point. Fate was the place at which all possible life paths converged—and when the oracles said "all," they meant *all*. So was it really so bad, being something good in the fate Akos dreaded?

Maybe not. To another person.

Unfortunately, I was not another person.

"What you're telling me," I said, "is that if you're going to have your head chopped off anyway, it's at least nice to have your head on a very soft chopping block."

"That's . . ." He made a frustrated noise. "That's the worst possible way to interpret what I said!"

"Yeah? Well, it's my way," I snapped. "I don't want to be the gift someone gets when they've already lost. I don't want to be a happy inevitability. I want to be chosen. I want to be *wanted*."

"You think I don't want you? Haven't I made that clear? I still chose you over my family, Cyra, and it wasn't because of fate!" He was mad now, practically spitting at me. Good. I wanted to fight. Fighting was something I could do, something I had trained myself to do whenever things got difficult. It was what kept me safe—not avoidance, because when had I ever been able to avoid the things that hurt me? No, it wasn't pretending I wouldn't get knocked down that protected me, but the knowledge that I would get back up as many times as I had to.

"How do you know?" I demanded. "It's not saying yes if you don't feel like you have a choice!"

"This isn't about me, this is about your own insecurity." He spoke fiercely, hotly, against my face. We were too close together but neither of us moved back. "You don't think anyone could possibly want you, so therefore, I must not be able to really want you. You're taking something good away from yourself because you don't think you deserve it."

"It's *because* no one has ever wanted me that I feel this way!" I was almost yelling. There were people milling around, and they stopped at my sudden increase in volume, but I didn't care. He was knocking me down, again and again, every time that he didn't say what I wanted him to say—that he chose me, that he wanted this, that he knew it, that fate was irrelevant.

All I wanted was for him to lie, and for me to believe it. But I didn't have to be an oracle to see that of all the possible futures that existed, there wasn't a single one where that outcome was possible. I would never believe a lie. And Akos would never tell me one.

"I am in love with you," I said. "But for once in my life, I want someone to choose me. And you don't. You can't."

I felt the mood change, as we stepped back, Akos looking suddenly bereft, like he had had his arms full and someone had come along and taken away everything he was carrying. I felt the same way. Empty-handed.

"I can't change the way things are," he said. "You can't blame me for that."

"I know." He was right, and that was why there was no point in arguing anymore. I had begun the conversation with a demand for honesty, but honesty didn't need to come from him—it needed to come from me. His fate was a reality, and as long as he had his fate, he couldn't care about me the way I needed him to. And I only knew that I needed him to because he had encouraged me to try to value myself more highly. So we were tangled in a web together, cause and effect and choice and fate all intermingling.

"So you're going to stay here, because your fate is with me," I said hollowly. "And I'm going to stay here, to help them figure out how to handle my father. And you and I . . ."

"Will be what we are," he said. So quiet.

"Right." My eyes burned. "Well, I need to talk to them about Lazmet. Can you find Teka and make sure she's all right?"

He nodded. I nodded. We both walked back into the mess hall, where everyone was still gathered around the screens, which now showed the wavy blur of heat above the sands of Tepes.

CHAPTER 15 | CYRA

THE PROBLEM WITH OGRA, I decided, was that it was *dark*.

Well, that was obvious.

But it was a different kind of dark than other places, where you could turn on a lamp and see everything in a room. Here, no matter what lights you attached to your clothes or fixed to a wall, the darkness crept in, devouring.

So though everyone in the storm shelter—the most trusted and capable among the exiles, Jorek had told me—wore something that glowed, and though lanterns hung from long chains, like vines, from the ceiling, I still felt like I was surrounded by shadows.

It was thanks to Jorek that I was invited to this meeting at all. Though I had acted as something of a leader when called upon to do so, I had not earned a place among them, not really. But I knew more about the family Noavek than all the people in this room put together, so here I stood, at Jorek's shoulder, too stung by what Akos and I had said to each other to pay much attention to the exiles' bickering.

I had told him I loved him. *Loved him.* What had I been thinking?

Jorek elbowed me. He had embraced the bright adornments of Ogran clothing with enthusiasm, the lines of his jacket traced in bright fabric panels two fingers wide. The afterimage of the green bars lingered for a few moments after I looked away from him, and across the room, at Sifa and Eijeh Kereseth.

They were oracles, after all. A group of fate-faithful Shotet couldn't help but hunger for whatever scraps of vague wisdom they could offer, if any.

"Sorry," I said, and cleared my throat. "What did you say?"

Aza raised an eyebrow at me. Whatever I had missed had been important, it seemed.

"I asked you if you could offer us any guidance as to whether your father will come after us here, on Ogra, or not," she said.

"Oh." It was my supposed expertise on my father that had won me my place here, and now was the time to put it to use. I shook my head. "He knows better than to fight a war with two fronts, particularly when the targets are so far apart. I'm sure he doesn't view you as worthy of his attention, so he'll focus on Thuvhe."

I winced, half out of pain and half at my own clumsy phrasing. *Slow down on making enemies*, Akos's whisper from earlier reminded me, his lips brushing my ear. Such a short while ago, but everything was different now.

"Lovely," Aza said, sharp. "Thank you for that insight, Miss Noavek."

"We need to kill him." The words launched from my mouth without warning, sounding desperate and small. Everyone looked at me, and I was thankful to the currentshadows staining my skin and the relentless Ogran darkness for disguising my blush.

"We do," I added, as an afterthought. "He's a greater danger to Shotet than the chancellor of Thuvhe ever will be."

"Forgive me for saying so," a wry voice spoke from somewhere near Aza, coming from a man with a shadowed face and a somewhat pointed beard. "But are you really telling us that we should focus our attention on just one man instead of the *declaration of war* that has just come our way?"

"Just one man?" I said, anger rising fast and hot within me. "Does the chancellor of Thuvhe go after a person's family for multiple generations to punish them for disloyalty? Does the chancellor of Thuvhe collect eyeballs in jars? No. Thuvhe can wait. Lazmet needs to be handled *now*."

"How dare you," the bearded man said, stepping toward me fast, "even *speak* of the horrors committed by your father in such a cavalier fashion? How dare you even *stand* here——"

I moved forward to meet him in the space between us, now clear of people. I was ready, ready to fight, ready to scream. I had seen my father come back from the dead and I didn't know what to do with all that I felt about it except punch this man right in his perfectly shaped facial fuzz.

"This is unproductive," spoke a cool, clear voice from my right. It belonged, of course, to our resident oracle. Sifa came to stand between me and my would-be opponent, her hands tucked into her sleeves.

"Behave like an adult, please," she said to the man. And to me: "You, too, Miss Noavek."

My instinct was to snap back at her—I hated to be patronized—but I knew that would only make me look more impetuous, so I denied myself the impulse.

"Can you guide us, Oracle?" Aza said to Sifa.

"I am not yet sure," Sifa said. "Things are changing quickly."

"Maybe you could just tell us whether we should focus our energy on Lazmet Noavek or on Thuvhe," Aza pressed.

Sifa glanced at me.

"Thuvhe is the greater threat to you," she said.

"And we should just trust you?" I said. "Without knowing what your aim is?"

"You will speak to the oracle with respect," Aza scolded.

"The oracle's job is to work for the best future for our planet," I said. "But whose best future is that, exactly? Thuvhe's, or Shotet's? And if it's Shotet's, then is it the best path for the Shotet exiles, or the Noavek loyalists?"

"Are you suggesting I have given preferential treatment to Thuvhe thus far?" Sifa scowled at me. "Trust me, Miss Noavek, I could have buried the fates of your family, and told the other oracles to deny them as well, if I had thought it would result in the best future for our planet. But I didn't. Instead, I allowed your family to use their new 'fate-favored' status to justify seizing control of Shotet government. My lack of intervention is why your family ever came into power in the first place, because it was what needed to be done, so do not think to accuse me of favoritism!"

Well. She had a point.

"If you all ignore my father now," I said, "you will regret it. You will."

"Is that a *threat*, Miss Noavek?" the bearded man demanded.

"No!" Nothing was coming out right. "It's an inevitability. You asked me here to tell you about my family—well, I just did.

Thuvhe may destroy Shotet lives, but Lazmet will destroy Shotet's soul."

I could almost feel them rolling their eyes at me. Perhaps I ought to have chosen less dramatic words, but I had meant them. It was difficult to explain to a person who feared for his life that death was not the worst he could encounter. Lazmet Noavek was.

CHAPTER 16 | AKOS

"ARE YOU *STILL* SLEEPING?" Jorek said. His face was right next to Akos's somehow, even though Akos's bed—or really, his hole in the wall—was high off the ground. Jorek had to be standing on the edge of another bunk.

Akos wasn't still sleeping, and he hadn't been since the general clamor of everybody getting up and going to the mess hall woke him up. He just hadn't gotten up yet. Getting up meant splashing water on his face and neck, combing his hair flat, changing his clothes, eating, all things he just . . . didn't care to do just then.

"And if I am?" he said, rubbing his face with his palm. "Am I neglecting some duty I don't know about?"

"No," Jorek said, frowning. "I guess not. But Cyra was arguing with exiles all morning, and I thought you'd be with her, since you two are basically welded to each other."

Akos felt guilty at that. Pretty much the only duty he did still have was to keep Cyra away from pain, and he wasn't doing such a good job at that lately, even though her currentgift was worse here.

"Well, I can't get up if you're blocking my way, can I?" he said.

Jorek flashed a smile and hopped down from his perch on one of the lower bunks. Akos put his legs over the side of the bed and dropped heavily on both feet. "They still don't want to go after Lazmet?" he said.

"*We* still think Thuvhe is a far greater threat than Lazmet, and we should focus our energies there," Jorek said. "Plus, we don't even know how to get to him. Or where he is. Or how to get through the wall of soldiers he's undoubtedly surrounded himself with."

"Well, we could probably find him by looking for the wall of soldiers," Akos said. "Don't see that every day."

Jorek winced, looking at him. "You're looking a little rough, there, Kereseth."

Akos grunted, and stuck his feet in his shoes. *Wash face, comb hair, eat breakfast*, he told himself. He went to one of the sinks that stood right in the middle of everything and stuck his head under the faucet.

He braced himself on the edge of the sink and sighed into his reflection. He did look bad. Paler than usual, dark circles, faded bruises from the fight with Vas at the corner of his eye and jaw. His freckles standing out like little pockmarks all over his nose. He dragged his fingers through his hair a couple of times just to make it flat, then touched the bruise on his jaw.

Vas's fist was swinging, split knuckles coming at him——

His stomach sucked in hard, like he was about to puke.

"You okay?" Jorek asked him.

"I'm fine," he said. "Gonna go make Cyra some painkiller."

"All right," Jorek said, but his brow was furrowed with concern.

He tapped the doorframe to Zenka's shop. She was bent over a table, digging what looked like a mix between a spoon and a knife into the pulpy flesh of an Ogran fruit. At each new dig, the fruit flickered with light, like a faltering lantern.

"Don't be so dramatic," Zenka said to it. "You had a good long life."

"You can't blame it for trying to survive," he said to her.

She didn't startle, just glanced up at him and arched an eyebrow. "It's already lost that fight. This is a liek—when it's still on the vine, it heats at a touch. Burns most of those who try to harvest it right through their gloves. So if it's here now, that means its harvest was well-earned."

"And we all accept the fates we earn?" he said.

"What kind of a question is that? You sound like some kind of Ogran mystic." She rolled her eyes, which told him how she felt about Ogran mystics.

"Or like my mom," he said. "The oracle. Maybe I'm turning into her."

"Ah, we all become our parents, eventually," Zenka said, stabbing the fruit again. "What do you want, Thuvhe?"

"I want a space to brew a painkiller," he said. "And . . . access to ingredients."

"Do you also want the moon in a jar?"

"Does Ogra have a moon?"

"Yes, and it's almost small enough to put in a jar, to be honest." She put the fruit down, and the tool she was using to scoop its flesh.

"I'm willing to work for the privilege of using your space," he added. "In case that wasn't clear."

"All right," she said. "But if you prove yourself to be lazy or useless, I reserve the right to revoke that privilege at any time."

"Agreed," he said.

She set him the task of grinding the tooth of a particularly ferocious flower into a powder. "In its powder form," she said, "it can help with circulation." Akos had a hard time focusing on the task in front of him, but his hands were capable enough, from seasons of practice.

Later that day she cupped some seeds in her hands to show him how they glowed, and what color. Hunching over her in the little shop, peeking between her fingers, made him feel like a kid again, and he ached so badly he had to pause for breath.

The only real marker of time on Ogra was the waning of the bioluminescence that supplied Ogra's only natural light, or the storms that battered the walls in the evening. He didn't know how long he spent crushing teeth before Zenka told him he could start on the painkiller. Then she stood at his shoulder, watching, as he measured out ingredients. He had brought some of his own hushflower, but the supply was getting low. Zenka dug some out of her storeroom and shook the jar at him.

"I thought you said you didn't have hushflower," he said.

"No, I said I didn't know how to use it," she said. "Besides, you don't go around admitting to strangers that you have a dangerous poison on hand."

"Fair enough," he said, and he got to work.

CHAPTER 17 | AKOS

HE STARTED GOING TO Zenka's shop in the mornings, before most of the others woke up. Cyra's bed was always empty by then, the blankets rumpled near the foot of the bed, like she'd kicked them off in her sleep. If she slept at all—Akos wasn't sure she could rest much, with her currentgift acting up the way it was. He made her painkillers, but they weren't as good as they had been in Voa. He was having trouble focusing.

Zenka was always brewing when he got there. She wasn't much for chatter—she just told him what to stir, or slice, or peel, and then she'd choose an Ogran ingredient to tell him about. One day it was the pulpy flesh of a fruit that grew only in the warmest months. It looked harmless enough, but when it detected something that channeled the current—like a person—it sprouted barbs. Another day she showed him how to peel the wings off a dead beetle without provoking it to squirt poison posthumously.

Often the work he did was more practical. He spent a couple of mornings in a row painting the outside of woven baskets with something that would keep their contents fresh, and those went to Ogran harvesters so they could eat lunch at midday. Akos still wasn't sure how anyone knew what midday was, in this place, where the sun never shone.

Akos expected to feel the absence of the sun at one point or another, and from time to time he did note it, the same way he noted the temperature of the air. But he didn't suffer for the lack of it any more than he suffered from the heat. It was just another thing that pricked at his mind, drawing out new questions.

Zenka was silent for the most part, unless she was telling him what to do. But one day, she asked him the question he'd been waiting for her to ask since he first met her:

"How did you come to be among the Shotet, if you grew up in Hessa?"

Akos nearly sliced through his own finger as he said— schooling his features so they stayed neutral—"I was an enemy of Ryzek Noavek. A captive."

At that, Zenka laughed a little.

"That doesn't say much, does it? We are all enemies of the family Noavek here. Kidnapped, imprisoned, mutilated, tortured. A colony of the bereaved." Her teeth clicked like she was snarling. "It makes you more Shotet than not, to have made an enemy of a Noavek."

"I try to understand," he said, "why you all insist that being Shotet is something other than it is. I was born in Thuvhe; I'm Thuvhesit. How is it not that simple?" He paused. "And if you say something about the revelatory tongue, I will mangle these urestae."

"It's always more complicated than that, Shotet or not," Zenka said, with a strange softness in her voice he hadn't heard before.

"You think being Thuvhesit is only about being born on one side of an imaginary line on the ground or another?"

"No, but—"

"We didn't always have a planet," she said. "The current-stream was home, more than a piece of rock. Or our ship. But as a people, we are maybe more closely tied than most to our identity, because we have always had to struggle against disappearing completely. We fight for you, for your belonging, because we fight for our existence. We will surrender the one only when we surrender the other."

Akos stood still. He felt like he was standing inside her words, for a tick. Isae had said something similar not a few weeks ago, had touched his face and told him that he belonged to her, to Thuvhe. But her claim to him had been shaken by Ori's death. The same could not be said of the Shotet. They had claimed him without knowing him, without needing him to even accept it. All they had needed were however many drops of Shotet blood he had in his veins.

He drew a sharp breath.

"Come," she said. "Let me show you something."

She led him out of the shop—which she left open, with everything boiling just as it was—and into the room next door. The door was on a swinging hinge, so it hit Akos in the butt after he walked in, startling him. The room beyond was Zenka's living space, clearly, since it looked just like the shop, with all its clutter and jars of ingredients and bundles of herbs hanging from the low ceiling. There was a bed in one corner with the sheets rumpled, and a desk along the far wall with a book open on it.

Zenka picked the book up and held it out to him. It was so

stuffed with pages it didn't close right; it fell open in Akos's palms. On the page in front of him was a sketch of a plant, roots to flower. Next to it, in her tight little script, were Shotet characters he couldn't read. There hadn't been time to learn more of them.

"What is it?" he said.

"This is my journal," she said. "I keep track of all the plants I find—I've been doing it since I was young. Sometimes you can dry them and fix them to the pages, but most of the time I sketch. I did it for every sojourn we went on, so I have plants from every planet in there. That's a softwillow—they grow sparsely on the peaks of Trella. They aren't much good for medicines, but their tufts smell sweet, so they're good for stuffing in your shoes."

Akos smiled, and turned one of the thick, sturdy pages. On the next page was an Ogran plant he recognized—it produced a bulbous fruit that looked like a person with puffed cheeks, and its main roots grew straight down, deep, much bigger than the plant itself.

"That one's a voma," she said. "Its juice is the most powerful strengthening agent I've ever encountered—even better than harva or sendes from your country. You should keep one of these journals. The two planets you've been to are widely regarded as having the most interesting plant life in the system. You should keep track. Here."

She took the book from him and set it down, then hunted in a pile of books next to the desk. When she didn't find what she was looking for, she crouched next to the bed and pulled out another box of books. She found a red one, about the size of his hand, from heel to fingertip, and offered it to him.

It was a simple thing, but he felt a thrill of fear as he took it from her and ran his fingers down the cover. For a long time he had not dared to own much of anything, because it might be taken away. And this—every page was a place he might go, a thing he might see. It should have been exciting, all the new possibilities, the complete freedom. But it was overwhelming.

"Blank," she said. "Fill it. It'll give you something to do other than mope."

"I'm not moping," he said, frowning.

Zenka laughed. "Then maybe you mope so often you've forgotten what not moping is like. But you're especially downtrodden today."

He opened his mouth to explain, and she held up a hand.

"I'm not asking," she said. "Just observing."

He touched a hand flat to the cover of the empty journal. He wanted to fill it—or really, he wanted to want to. Wanted to remember having goals in life, the way he had before he was kidnapped. Or even after—he'd wanted to save Eijeh, to get home, to help Cyra. But the space that had been filled with fire, the space that knew desire and drive and perseverance, was empty now, the flame gone out.

When Akos wasn't toiling away in Zenka's shop, he was with Jorek. At meals, mostly, because it seemed like Jorek was always at meals—not eating, necessarily, but holding court. Sometimes he was there for hours at a time, telling stories and prompting other people to tell them, drumming with spoons, shouting teasing insults at whoever had just come in. After a couple days, though, Akos realized that wedged between the jokes and the drumming and the stories were other conversations, about Ogra, or Voa, or the Assembly. This was how Jorek gleaned information—by making himself available for people to talk to.

It was easy to be with him, though, because he didn't ask for anything, even Akos's attention. He seemed to know that his constant chatter was soothing, even if Akos didn't give anything back. He kept waiting for Jorek to run out of patience for his "moping," as Zenka called it, but it hadn't happened yet.

"Well, Kereseth, you gave me a great idea," Jorek said, sliding his tray into place next to Akos.

"Not sure how that's possible," Akos said. "I haven't had a great idea in seasons."

"Normally I'd argue with you, but you're the one who wanted to hoist Cyra Noavek out of a packed amphitheater with nothing but a rope and some hope—" He paused, so that the full effect of the rhyme could be felt—Akos groaned—and then continued, "So I believe that you're not an idea man. But you did spark one!"

"Do tell."

"You said we should look for a wall of soldiers to figure out where Lazmet is," Jorek said. "So I sent a message to my mother, who observed a larger-than-usual concentration of soldiers around Noavek manor. And she figured maybe we should get someone we know in there, just in case we need that intel." He raised his eyebrows once, twice, three times. "Guess who's going to Voa?"

Akos felt the weight in his stomach get, if possible, even heavier.

"You're leaving?" he said.

"Yeah." Jorek's expression softened a little. "With my name, I was maybe the only exile who had an 'in' with Vakrez Noavek."

"Sure." Akos nodded. "And you'll be with your mom in Voa, too."

"There is that." Jorek elbowed him. "I'll be back, though. This war thing can't last forever, can it?"

Akos didn't point out that the reason wars didn't last forever was because too many people ended up dead.

"It's a good idea," Akos said. "When do you go?"

Jorek shrugged. "A week or so. Gotta wait for an Ogran transport. Do you know they export dead bugs to Othyr? This place is weird."

Zenka had told Akos that Ogra's primary export was extracts of various poisons and excretions to Othyr. Some were for medicinal purposes, but most were for various Othyrian vanities—skin cream, cosmetics, spa treatments. Zenka rolled her eyes at it.

"The oracle's coming," Jorek said in a low voice. "It's too late for you to bolt, sorry."

Akos sighed.

"You've been avoiding me," Sifa said matter-of-factly, as she plunked herself down in the seat across from his.

His first instinct was to deny it, but that never worked with his mom. Once she decided she knew something, there was no point in arguing with her about it, even if she was wrong. *Being an oracle doesn't mean you know everything*, he sometimes wanted to tell her. But that was something a child said.

"That's because you're spending all your time with Eijeh doling out prophetic wisdom to the exiles," he said. "And I've heard about all I can take from him. And prophecy. And wisdom in general."

Jorek snorted into his food.

"The exiles may have given us a little apartment to use as a makeshift temple, but they are too awed to consult us as often as I expected, so we are far from busy. As for Eijeh, well . . . I convinced him to begin again with me, as if we had just met," she said, stirring the grainy mush in her bowl. If it was possible to stir a spoon thoughtfully, she was doing it. "You might try doing the same."

"I'm no good at games of pretend," Akos snapped.

"Nor am I," she said. "Though I guess I have the added benefit of having seen possible futures in which he and I really hadn't met. Where he was taken from me sooner, or had his memory entirely erased instead of just altered."

There wasn't much of her that wasn't oracle, he'd realized. Her currentgift had taken her over, and it was now the whole of her, inescapably. It was hard not to blame her for it, even though he had no idea what it was like to have a gift so intrusive, so constant, that it changed the way you saw every part of your existence. His was the opposite. Sometimes he forgot his currentgift was even there.

"Please don't go," Sifa said, putting her hand on his.

"What?" he said. "I wasn't going to——"

And then Eijeh set his plate down next to Sifa. All he had on it was fruit. Akos remembered Eijeh stuffing his face with everything he could find in the kitchen, getting up to cut himself two slices of bread right when dinner was over. A lot had changed.

Sifa's hand tightened.

"I'm going to need your help in a moment," she said.

And then at the same time, both her and Eijeh's eyes went unfocused at once.

Not long after, they both started screaming.

CHAPTER 18 | EIJEH

IT IS STILL STRANGE, not feeling the other heartbeat, but we are adjusting. If anything, it's easier now with just the one body to contend with.

Still, when we wake in the middle of the night in a hole in an Ogran wall, there is a kind of loneliness.

And when we see him, this Akos, we are never sure whether he is an enemy or a brother. There are parts of us that reflect on hazy memories of chasing him through fields, or laughing with him across a dinner table, and others that see him as a catalyst for trouble, a factor of unpredictability in a plan that must remain predictable.

He did, in fact, bring about our ruination, inspiring Cyra's betrayal, facilitating her escape, driving her toward renegades and exiles alike. But he did it for us as much as he did it to destroy us, and we are always holding those two opposing forces in tension. We are getting better at holding things in tension—two histories, two names, two minds. "We" are becoming more of an "I."

We are watching him, the oracle's hand covering his, a plate of fruit in front of us to appease one appetite, when it happens.

A sudden jerk, like a hook caught around a rib and pulling, inexorably. But it is not the rib cage of this body that is pulled, it is our combined being, the Eijeh and the Ryzek, the Shotet and the Thuvhesit, the very *all* of us.

And then we are a ship. Not a small transport vessel or a passenger floater but a warship, long and narrow, sleek at the top and bottom but craggy on the side like the face of a cliff. We descend through a dense layer of clouds—white, and cold, and vaporous. When we break through the cloud layer, much of the land beneath us is also pale, a distant stark white shifting into beige and gold and brown as the land warms along the equator.

Then we are not a ship but a child, small, standing near the edge of a packed-clay rooftop. We scream for a father as the dark shape descends, casting a shadow over the city. A city of patchwork, part of us recognizes, the city of Voa. "Is it the sojourn ship?" we ask our father, as he comes to stand beside us.

"No," our father says, and we are gone again.

We are not a child but a maintenance worker, dressed in coveralls that are patched at the knees. We have both hands buried in an instrument panel, a tool between our teeth as we feel for the right part. Pressure around our abdomen and thighs tells us we are in a harness, and we dangle from the anchor higher up on a metal face. We are on the sojourn ship, part of us helpfully suggests, making repairs.

A shadow falls over us, and we tilt our head back to see the smooth underside of a ship. Its name is painted across its bottom in a language we do not recognize and cannot read, but we know this ship is not Shotet.

We are a woman with a scarf wrapped tightly around her neck, bunched beneath her chin, and we are running toward the sojourn ship with a child's hand clasped in ours. We carry a heavy sack over one shoulder; it is soft with clothing, but the corner of a book pierces our side with every other footstep. "Come on," we say to the child. "We'll be safe on the sojourn ship, come on."

We are a younger woman with a screen in hand, standing at the loading bay doors as a crush of people fight to make their way inside the ship. We cling to a handle on the wall to stay steady as people push and push and push. We shout to a young man behind us: "How many have evacuated so far?"

"A few hundred!" the man shouts back.

We look up at the big, dark ship. A set of doors opens on its underbelly, and another. A huge section of metal pulls apart, showing an open hatch right above us. The ship has come to hover right over the sojourn ship, which is perched on a metal island across the sea from Voa so that we can repair it and improve it in time for the next sojourn.

"Are they deploying ships?" we demand, though we know the man behind us has no answer.

Something falls from the rectangle, something big and heavy and glinting in the sun.

And then brilliant, blinding light.

⊰⊱

We are the child on the rooftop again, watching as light so white, so scorching, envelops the sojourn ship and radiates out like rays from the sun. But the rays are curled, like roots, like veins, like the dark fingers that cradled the traitor Cyra Noavek's face as she killed our sovereign.

The brightness sprawls across the ocean, sending water scattering away so it swells, huge, toward the shores of Voa. The brightness burns through clouds, reaching as high as the atmosphere, or so it seems. It is a wall of light that collapses all at once, like two hands clapping together.

And then wind—wind so strong it roars in our ears and makes them ring, wind so strong it knocks us, not just over, but a few feet forward, slamming into the clay of the roof. It rushes over us, and we lose consciousness.

We are hundreds
of slowing hearts.

CHAPTER 19 | CYRA

I STOOD WITH THE Shotet exiles around the screens in the mess hall, all of us pressed together. Enemies, friends, lovers, strangers, we were shoulder to shoulder, watching as the sojourn ship was ripped to shreds.

It was a hundred things, the sojourn ship. Our history. Our freedom. A sacred vessel. A workplace. A symbol. A project. An escape.

A home.

As I watched the footage play again and again, I thought of clearing my mother's closet of all her clothes and shoes, too small and dainty for me to wear myself, for the most part. I had found secrets tucked away in her pockets and shoeboxes: love letters from my father, when he was a gentler man; labels from bottles of pain medication and wrappers from the drugs she took to escape; another woman's lip paint, smeared on a scarf, from an affair. The story of her imperfect life, told in stains and scraps of paper.

And I had filled that space with my own story, my splattered stove, the suits of armor that glinted when the lights I strung over my bed struck them, and the rows upon rows of footage from other worlds, dancing and fighting and building and fixing. They were not just objects, but escapes when pain made it hard for me to stay in my own body. My comforts in despair.

It had also been the place where I fell in love.

And now it was gone.

The fourth time the footage played, I felt fingers against mine. I pulled away instinctively, not wanting to transfer my currentgift to someone else, but the hand found mine, insistent. I turned to see Teka at my side, her eye welling up with tears. Maybe she wanted my pain, or maybe she wanted to offer me comfort; either way, I held on to her, keeping most of my currentgift to myself, as much of it as I could.

Her grip lasted only for a moment or two, but it was enough.

We stood and watched the footage play again, and we did not look away.

Later, I pressed my face to my pillow and sobbed.

Akos climbed into my bunk and curled his body around mine, and I allowed it.

"I told them to evacuate," I said. "I'm the reason there were so many people on that ship—"

"You tried to help," Akos said. "All you did was try to help."

It wasn't reassuring. What a person *tried* to do didn't matter—what mattered was the result. And the deaths of hundreds were the result here. That loss was my responsibility.

In a fair world I would have marked every single life on my

arm, to carry them around forever. But I did not have enough skin
for that.

Akos held me tighter, so I could feel his heartbeat against my
spine, as I began to sob again.

I fell asleep with the press of wet fabric against my face.

"CONFIRMED, CODE 05032011. PROCEED."

Some moments you put into a little file in your mind because you know they're important, and what Isae Benesit says to signal the attack on Voa is one of those. She says it clearly, every consonant crisp, and she doesn't hesitate. When she's done she pushes back from the desk where she was speaking to General Then, stands up, and walks away, brushing off Ast's outstretched hand.

It doesn't take long for the attack to start. For the anticurrent blast Pitha loaned us to fly toward Thuvhe on a special ship designed for just this purpose. The crew of the ship is Pithar, but it's General Then, the commander of Thuvhe's armed forces, who actually presses the button, per Thuvhesit law.

I imagine the hatch doors opening at his touch, and the weapon—long and narrow, with squared edges—falling, falling, falling. There's poetry in it, in that poetry can be raw, and cruel, and strange, like this.

Isae, Ast, and I watch it from her quarters. The Assembly ship is facing the sun, then, so the walls are opaque, and they show an image of Shissa in the swirling snow. The little flakes get stuck to the sights that captured the footage, every now and then, so the image is blurry most of the time, white blobs right up against the dark night sky. Between them, though, I see the buildings hanging from the clouds like drops of rain suspended in time. Shissa isn't home, but it's where I went to school, where I found a life away from my mom and her constant prophecies, so I still love it there.

Shissa is what I'm looking at when the news footage comes up on the screens, and I see only a flash of the sojourn ship's destruction before closing my eyes against it. Isae stifles a sharp sound.

"What is it?" Ast says. No robotic guide beetle can help him with something on a screen, after all.

"There were people around it, did you see?" Isae says. "Why were there people around it?"

I turn up the volume on the news feed just in time to hear: *"Initial reports suggest there were a few hundred Shotet around the craft, attempting to evacuate the city—"*

I turn the screen off.

"A few . . ." Isae gasps. "A few *hundred*—"

Ast shakes his head. "Stop that, Isae. Casualties were still minimal."

"Minimal," I say, and it's all I can manage. General Then's estimates said casualties would be around three dozen. Not *hundreds.*

"Yeah," Ast says, eyeballing me. "Minimal. Compared to what could have been. That's why you suggested the sojourn ship, remember?"

There's a flow of words in my mind—*hundreds, men, women, children, old, young, middle-aged, kind, cruel, desperate, people people people*—but I stop it, like two hands clapping around an insect to kill it. I am better at this than I should be, after too many tragedies poisoned my memories. It's how I survive.

I don't answer Ast. I am tired of the way he prods at me. I pull back on my gift as hard as I can, hoping that if Isae feels less comfortable, she'll call him off.

She's facing the swirls of snow, arms folded. The Shissa buildings in the footage light up green, purple, pink. They remind me of the baubles they sold at the Hessa market when the planting started, for people to hang in their windows for luck.

Isae's shoulders shake. Shudder, really. She slaps a hand against the glass to steady herself.

Ast and I both stand, eager to comfort even though I'm sure he doesn't know how any more than I do.

Isae is hunched, turning so I can see the side of her face.

She's *laughing*.

"All those . . . people . . ." She gasps, wrapping her free arm around her stomach. "Bowled right over!"

Ast's face goes slack with horror, but I know what this is.

"Isae," I say. "Take a deep breath."

"All those . . ." Isae bends at the knees. Her hand squeaks against the glass as it slides down.

I walk to the bathroom and run cold water over a washcloth to soak it all the way through. I carry it back to her, dripping all over the floor. She is crouched next to the window, laughing, sobbing.

I put the wet cloth on the back of her neck, and run a hand over her back. Ast finally seems to catch on—a bit late, I think, but he seems dense that way—and he urges Pazha forward with a whistle, so its clicking guides him to us. He crouches near us, silent but present. It's the closest he and I have ever been to each other. Sharing air.

"All those people," she whimpers.

I watch Ast's reaction as I unfurl my currentgift like a banner and drape it over all three of us. For once, he doesn't object.

"I miss her," she whispers later, as we sit together by the window and watch the currentstream.

I take her hand, and press it to my cheek.

I show her a memory of Ori asleep at our kitchen table, slumped over a detailed sketch of an iceflower. There was ink smeared on her cheek. My father sipped his tea, smiling fondly down at her, and my mother clicked her tongue, though her eyes still smiled.

My father bent to ease his arms around her, and carried Ori to the living room. I watched her long legs bounce up and down with his footsteps.

"Well," my mother said to me. "We do call it 'Ori's room,' after all."

Isae and I drift gently out of the memory, her hand still pressed between my cheek and my palm, and she smiles at me.

I'm holding her together, I think.

And, *What happens when I can't anymore?*

Kyerta. Noun. In Ogran:
"That which has been crushed into a new shape"

CHAPTER 21 | CISI

THE DESCENT TO OGRA almost kills me.

It took some doing—and some careful use of my current-gift—but I convinced Isae to let me go to the Shotet exiles to start peace talks. *We can work together to unseat Lazmet. The exiles are not our enemies. Their goals are aligned with ours.* It took a while for my words to take root, and even now, she's still skeptical, but she did agree to let me suss out the situation, at least.

Seven days after the attack on Voa, she secures me a spot on a transport carrying food to Ogra. I squeeze into a seat between a massive crate of fruit engineered in an Othyr lab and a refrigerator packed with bird meat from Trella. The crew is Trellan—a language I don't speak—so I can't join in when they joke with each other. And Trellan is spoken in a monotone, so I can't even pretend I'm listening to music. They smile at me every now and then, so I know they don't mind me, but that's no surprise. No one minds me, even if they haven't quite figured out why.

Then the ship's captain, who is thick through the legs and shoulders, with a tuft of chest hair poking out the top of his shirt, tells me in broken Othyrian, "Buckle! Now!"

It's lucky, maybe, that no one told me what to expect, because I might have made them turn back.

All the lights on the ship go off at the same time, and then I'm screaming and it's dark and I'm screaming. I can't breathe and I'm sure, then, that the ship is running out of air and I'm going to die here in a pile of meat. I'm clinging so hard to the straps covering my chest that my hands go numb, or maybe that's from terror. The last thing I think is that I never even got to speak to Mom again.

Then the lights come back on, and gravity catches me, and the crew are all staring at me like I sprouted a third eye. They laugh, and I try to join them, but really I'm just focused on breathing.

It's not long before we're standing on Ogran soil.

An Ogran woman named Yssa—"Ee-sah," she says to me, slowly, when I don't get it the first time around—takes me to the exiles in a little boat that cuts like a knife through the light-streaked water. She speaks Othyrian like she's counting beans, dropping words one by one, but it's the only language we have in common, so we trade nonsense until we reach solid ground again.

She walks me through the uneven streets of a village where Shotet and Ograns live side by side. Yssa points things out to me—a stall of polished stones she likes, the place where she buys her groceries, the tiny carved dolls that gave her nightmares as a child. She doesn't explain how they know what "night" is here, and when she gestures, the glowing bracelets around her wrist clatter together.

"Which one is your brother?" she asks me.

"Very tall, fair-skinned, like you," I say. "He came with Cyra Noavek."

"Oh! The heavy one," she says.

"Heavy?" I say, confused. "No, he's thin."

"No, no. Not heavy in body. He carries a weight," she says. "I don't know the word."

"Oh." I've never thought of my brother that way. The tall, deadly man who fought his way out of a Shissa hospital and into an amphitheater prison didn't seem weighed down by anything—if anything, he seemed faster and lighter than everyone around him. But maybe I just can't really see him. There is a special kind of sight that comes with not knowing someone your whole life, and Yssa has it.

"I will take you to where they gather," Yssa says. "He may be there, and he may not."

"That's fine, thank you," I say.

She leads me to an old warehouse with cracks climbing up the outer walls. There's a sign fixed above the door with some characters on it I can't read. They look Shotet.

We walk in, and it definitely feels like a Shotet place, in all the ways I've been taught to expect. All the tables have been pushed back against the walls, and people are either sitting at them or perched on top of them, in a kind of ring.

As we walk in, people are pounding on the tables in a rolling rhythm, so loud it's all I can focus on at first. Then I look at what's happening in the middle.

Cyra Noavek, her hair in a long tail behind her, is throwing her body at a giant of a man. She is graceful and strong, like a knife thrown by a skilled hand. The large man—and he must be large, to make a woman of her stature look so dainty—catches her, wrestles her over his shoulder, and hurls her away.

I gasp as she topples to the floor, which is covered with mats, but still looks hard enough to hurt. But she's already rolling over like her body is made of rubber, grinning, a ferocity in her eyes I recognize. It's the way she looked at Ryzek Noavek before he peeled the skin from her skull. And it's the way Isae looked right before she committed murder.

With a yell, she throws herself at him again, and the crowd roars.

It goes on this way for a while, with Cyra building speed and determination before my eyes. It's the speed that seems to unsettle her opponent—he doesn't know where to look, or how to block what she throws his way, though it doesn't do much damage. She tries to tackle him, and he catches her, trapping her, only for her to twist her body around him like a necklace. She locks her legs around his neck, and he chokes.

He taps one of her legs with one hand, and she releases him, sliding to the ground. The crowd roars, and she moves to the side to chug water from a spout near the windowsill.

"They do this all the time now," Yssa says. "I am not sure what the goal is. Do they intend to fight the Thuvhesits one-on-one?"

Cyra spots me across the room. The spark in her eyes dies.

She comes toward me, and when she's closer I see bruises and scratches up and down her bare arms, probably from other fights. Yssa edges closer to me, putting a shoulder in front of me.

"I was asked to ensure Miss Kereseth's safety among you," Yssa says to her. "Please don't make that task difficult for me."

Cyra stops right around spitting distance, and for a tick, I think that's what she's going to do: spit at me. Instead she demands, "What are you doing here?" She holds up a hand. "Don't pull that currentgift shit on me; I've got no use for ease right now."

It's so automatic I didn't even realize I was doing it. I pull back as much as I can. Her currentshadows have buried themselves under her skin again, and they cover her in dark webs. She grits her teeth.

"I'm here to——" I pause. I don't want to give myself away. "I'm here to see my family, all right?"

"You're not welcome," she says. "Or did the declaration of war escape your attention?"

I wish——not for the first time——that I could turn my own gift on myself, set myself at ease, just for a little while. But I can't soothe away the lump in my throat or ease off the weight of guilt. I helped Isae pick her target. Before I got here I felt confident that I did something good, considering the options I had——I talked her down from hitting Voa head-on, didn't I? I had saved quite a few lives with nothing but a clever tongue and my currentgift.

But right now I'm standing among people who lost something. Friends, family. A place that was special to them, maybe even sacred. So how can I feel like I did something good? How can I think that these people are any different from my own, any more worthy of violence or loss?

I can't. I don't.

But I'll do what I have to, just like anybody.

"Just tell me where to find Akos," I say.

"Akos." She snorts. "You mean my faithful servant, determined to die for me?" Her eyes close for a tick. "Yeah, I know where to find him. It's just down the road."

CHAPTER 22 | CYRA

EVERYTHING HURT, BUT I no longer cared.

Well, I *did*, because no one wanted to be in pain. It was a survival instinct. But insofar as my rational mind was capable of overcoming my physical state, I embraced the pain, I let it throw me into frantic motion. I was sweat-soaked and exhausted and ready for more. Anything to make it easier to be this burning, writhing thing I had become.

I didn't want to take Cisi Kereseth to the quiet place Akos had claimed as his own in the wake of the attack, the old woman's shop off an alley in Galo. There was too much of *him* there, in the bubbling pots and tap of the knife against the cutting board.

As Cisi, Yssa, and I exited the cafeteria, a young woman, with densely curled hair cut short, spat on the ground near my feet.

Oruzo, she called me.

The literal translation was "a mirror image," but the real sense of the word was that one person had become another, or was so similar to them as to be indistinguishable. So, after the attack on Voa, many of the exiles had taken to calling me "Oruzo"—successor to Ryzek, to Lazmet, to the Noavek family. It was a way to blame me for all the lives lost in the failed evacuation, because of my foolishness. If I hadn't sent that message to them, telling them to flee—

But time could not run backward.

I walked too fast for Yssa and Cisi to keep up, so that I wouldn't have to speak to them. Cisi had gone to be with *that woman*, the one who had destroyed my home, and I would not forget.

Akos was hunched over a pot when I reached the shop, dipping a finger in whatever he was brewing—likely a painkiller, as his perceived duty to me was his only motivator these days. He sucked the fingertip, tasting what he had made, and swore, loudly, in Thuvhesit.

"Wrong again?" the old woman asked him. She was sitting on a stool, peeling whatever-it-was into a bowl at her feet.

"The only thing I'm good for and I can't even get it right," he snapped.

He looked up at me, and flushed bright red.

"Oh," he said. "Hi."

"I'm here to—" I paused. "Your sister is here."

I stepped aside to reveal her. They stood at that distance from each other for a few long, quiet moments. He turned off the burner, and crossed the room, folding her into a hug. She squeezed him back.

"What are you doing here?" he asked her softly.

"I'm here to open peace talks with the exiles," she said.

I snorted. Not only was her mission ridiculous—how could we have peace talks with a nation that had *destroyed the sojourn ship?*—but she had also lied to me about it.

"I'm sorry I lied to you," she added over her shoulder to me. "I thought you were going to hit me, so I reached for the most convenient excuse to be here."

"Cyra would never hit you," Akos said.

The way he said it, without hesitation or doubt, made my chest ache. He was the only one who had ever thought so well of me.

"If you are all going to stand around chatting, do it somewhere else," the old woman said, getting to her feet. "My shop is too small and my fuse too short for such nonsense."

"I'm sorry for the waste of your ingredients, Zenka," Akos said to her.

"I learn a great deal from your failed attempts, as well as your successful ones," Zenka said to him, not unkindly. "Now go."

Her lined face turned to me, and she gave me a look of appraisal.

"Miss Noavek," she said as I retreated into the alley, by way of greeting.

I nodded back, and slipped away.

There was no room to walk side by side in the alley, so we filed down it one by one, with Yssa in the lead and Akos bringing up the rear. Over Yssa's shoulder, I saw Sifa and Eijeh waiting for us in the hard-packed street beyond the alley. Sifa pretended to be interested in the little glowing fish at the stall nearest to her, kept in tall cylinders full of water, but I wasn't fooled. She was waiting for us.

Eijeh looked nervously over his shoulder. His hair was curling behind his ears now, grown out enough to show its natural texture. There was a slim ribbon sewed into the shoulders of his shirt, and it glowed a faint blue. Most people here adopted some elements of Ogran dress, so they would be visible in the dark. Not me, though.

I knew I had no place here, at this impromptu Kereseth reunion—which was probably orchestrated by the oracles, if Sifa and Eijeh's presence meant what I thought it did. I moved to leave, meaning to disappear into the constant night, but Akos knew me too well. I felt the shock of his hand, pressing against the small of my back. It was brief, but it sent a shiver through me.

Do that again, I thought.

Never do that again, I also thought.

"Sorry," he said, in low Shotet. "But—would you stay?"

Behind him, Cisi and Sifa embraced, Sifa's hand running over Cisi's curls with a tenderness I remembered from my own mother.

Akos's gray eyes—set now in a face more sallow than it had any right to be—begged me to stay. I had distracted myself from him in the week since the attack, refusing most of the comfort he offered, unless it was in the form of a painkiller. I couldn't let myself stay close to him now, knowing that he was only here because of his own fatalism. He made me weak, though. He always had.

"Fine," I said.

"I hoped you would come," Sifa was saying to Cisi, whose eyes were on Eijeh. He held himself at a distance from the others, plucking at his cuticles. His posture and gestures were still like those of my late brother. It was . . . disconcerting.

"Eijeh thought it was likely," she continued. "He's only a

beginner, but his intuition is strong. So we came to facilitate a particular path."

"Ah, you're admitting to it this time?" I said, my arms crossed to disguise the clench of my hands.

Akos's fingertips touched one of my elbows, sending the pain away. I didn't let myself look at him.

"Yes," Sifa said. Her hair was in a pile of curls on top of her head, a hatpin stuck through the middle of it so it stayed in place. The little jewels at the end of the pin glowed pale pink. "Come. We're wanted elsewhere."

"Probably," Eijeh qualified.

"Probably," Sifa repeated.

"You're not making me want to spend more time with oracles," I said.

Akos's lips twitched into a smile.

"And what a shame that is," Eijeh replied drily. "Our loss, I'm sure."

I stared at him. I had never heard Eijeh Kereseth make a joke before, particularly not at *my* expense.

There was no time to retort, because I turned and saw a menacing sight: the outline of an Ogran transport vessel. Its edges were lined with white tubes of light, but the persistent dark flattened them, making the whole thing look like the face of a beast, hanging in the air. Tucked-back wings became ears, a vent beneath the forward fuselage was a mouth, and the tail was a single horn.

An Ogran in a flight suit came toward us. His skin was dark brown, but his eyes were iridescent, like the scales of a fish. They caught all the light around them and tossed it back, silvery-bright.

A manifestation of his currentgift, I was certain, though what it did was as yet a mystery.

Somewhere to my right, Yssa uttered what sounded like an Ogran curse word under her breath.

CHAPTER 23 | AKOS

Akos tried to get a sense of the Ogran ship in the dark, but it was difficult. When they first landed on Ogra, he thought the sky was always the same, but that wasn't the case—sometimes it was velvet black, sometimes worn black, sometimes almost blue. And now, with the sky at its darkest, the ship all but disappeared, but for the light they had used to mark its shape.

Yssa stepped forward. "Pary. Hello."

She didn't sound cold, exactly, just as she never really sounded warm. But something had changed in her. She knew this person.

"Yssa," the Ogran said. "I'm surprised to find you here."

"I was sent to be an ambassador from our people to the Shotet," she said. There was definitely something off about the two of them, Akos decided. There was too much familiarity in the way they spoke to each other. Ex-lovers, maybe? "And you're surprised to find me among them?"

"I meant here, with . . . two oracles of Thuvhe," the man called Pary said. "But maybe that was foolish of me."

Akos felt Cyra shift under his hand, getting restless. Sure

enough, she was already opening her mouth.

"State your business, would you?" she said. "We've got a family reunion happening here."

"Miss Noavek. You are just as anticipated," Pary said with a wide smile. "My business is that of the oracle of Ogra. You have—all of you—been summoned by her, and I am tasked with taking you to her immediately. She is on the other side of Ogra, on the edge of the wilderness, so we must fly there to make it on time."

Of course, Akos thought, with no small amount of scorn. His mom and Eijeh had come into the village—where they almost never went—for just this reason. He hated the feeling of it, all the threads of fate coming together and tangling in a knot. The only other times in his life he had felt it happen, his dad had ended up killed, or he had killed Vas—

Vas, his face shining with sweat, a bruise at the corner of his eye from who knows what—

"And if we don't want to go?" Cyra said.

"That would be unwise," Pary said. "According to Ogran law, the oracles' summons must be obeyed. And as a Shotet exile, you are obligated to obey our highest laws, unless you want to compromise your own refugee status."

Cyra glanced at Akos.

"Oracles," he said with a shrug, because there wasn't much more to say.

The inside of the Ogran ship was downright startling.

It was alive in a way Akos had never seen, didn't think a ship could be. The structure was metal, but there were plants growing everywhere, some behind glass, some out in the open. He recognized a couple of them from what Zenka had taught him, though he'd only seen them shriveled or sketched or chopped up. One of the plants behind glass looked like a perfect globe until its thick, jagged petals peeled apart, revealing the same teeth he had learned to grind into a powder. It snapped at him as he walked by.

Cisi went to one of the others—a flowered vine that twisted around one of the ship's support beams—like she was pulled there by a magnet. A dark green tendril reached for her finger and wrapped around it, gentle. Akos rushed to her side and flicked it to make it back off.

"Apparently they start off friendly and turn fierce," he said to her. "But if you ignore them they don't usually do anything."

"Do all the plants here try to kill you?" Cisi said.

"Almost all," he said. "Some try to befriend you so you'll defend them against other plants."

"You'll notice there are almost no animal species on Ogra," Pary said as he walked past them. "That is because the plants are so highly developed. There is a wide variety of insect species, for the propagation of plant life, but we are the only warm-blooded beasts that walk this planet."

Pary settled into the captain's chair. There was no copilot or first officer that Akos could see, just Pary and a stretch of buttons and switches and levers. Yssa took the seat beside him, though. The forward fuselage was big enough to fit all of them, on bench seats with protective straps. Given what Akos knew about the planet's tendency to fight back against everything, everywhere, he thought they needed more than some *straps* to protect them, but nobody had asked him.

"Did the oracle say *why* she wanted us dragged to her?" Cyra said, while she was strapping herself in. She finished her own buckles and then reached over—unconsciously, it seemed like—to help Cisi with hers. Akos took the seat on her other side, at the end of the bench.

"It's not for me to ask," Pary said.

"The oracle is not very . . ." Yssa paused, searching out the word in Othyrian. She asked in Shotet, "How do you say, 'forthright'?"

Akos repeated the word in Othyrian, for Cisi.

"It is not an oracle's job to answer questions like those," Sifa said. "We have only one job, and that is to protect this galaxy. Sorting through the inconsequential information that other people find essential is not up to us."

"Oh, you mean inconsequential information like 'You, my youngest son, you're going to get kidnapped tomorrow'?" Cyra snapped. "Or 'Isae Benesit is about to murder your brother, Cyra, so you may want to make your peace with him'?"

Akos grabbed a handful of his own leg to steady himself. He wanted to tell Cyra not to use his pain as a weapon against his own mom; he wanted to tell his mom that Cyra had a point. But he felt so heavy with the hopelessness of it that he gave up before he started.

"You demand to know things from the Ogran oracle that you will find out within the day," Sifa snapped. "You're angry that you aren't told what you want to know exactly when you want to know it. What a frustrating existence you must find this, that it doesn't meet your every need for you instantaneously!"

Cyra laughed. "As a matter of fact, I *do* find it frustrating."

She had been this way since the sojourn ship attack, Akos

thought. Primed for a fight, no matter what form it came in, no matter who it was with. Cyra was always prickly, and he liked that about her. But this was different. Like she kept throwing herself at a wall in the hope that one of these days, it might finally break her apart.

"Quiet on deck!" Pary announced. "Can't focus with all of you arguing."

Yssa joined in the dance of readying the ship, and the way they did it together, Pary and Yssa, made Akos think they had done it a hundred times before. Their arms crossed, fair and freckled against dark and unblemished, and stretched past each other without getting in each other's way. The choreography of familiarity.

The ship lurched and shuddered as it rose from the ground. The engines roared, and the vines and plants twitched and fluttered like the wind was blowing. Akos watched the flowered vine curl more tightly around its support beam; the plant behind glass curled into itself and glowed orange in warning.

"We'll be flying above the storms, to avoid their damage," Pary said as the ship flew up and forward. "It will be rough."

Akos couldn't help his own curiosity. They'd been hiding from "the storms" whenever the alarm went off since they arrived on Ogra—almost every day, it felt like. But he'd yet to hear a good description of what the storms *were*, exactly.

The ship's flight wasn't as smooth as a Shotet ship's. It jerked and shivered, and from what Akos could tell, it was slow. But they got up high enough that he could see the little glowing patches of villages, and then the big, bright splotch of Ogra's capital city, Pokgo, where the buildings were tall enough to make a jagged horizon.

Their ship turned as it climbed, away from Ogran civilization and toward the stretch of dark that made up the southern forests. There were plenty of glowing things there, as there were everywhere else, but they were covered by dense greenery, so from a distance it was difficult to see anything but void.

The ship jerked up, which made Akos grab blindly for Cyra's hand. He didn't mean to squeeze hard, but judging by her laugh, that's what he was doing. The clear view they'd had of Ogra's surface was gone, replaced by the dense swirl of clouds. And then, up ahead, color and light coalescing, just like they had when the sojourn ship passed through the currentstream.

A blue line of lightning cut through the cloud layer and stretched down. The ship jostled Akos's head from side to side so hard he could hear his own teeth clattering together. Another flash, this one yellow, seemed to happen right next to them. Pary and Yssa were shouting things at each other in Ogran. Akos heard retching as someone—Eijeh, probably, he'd always had motion sickness—threw up.

Akos watched as Ogra took the glowing colors the rest of the planet boasted so proudly and hurled them right back, brutal and relentless. As Pary promised, they moved right over the storm, which jostled them all but didn't down the ship. The acrid smell of vomit, combined with the constant shuddering of his head, made him want to be sick himself, but he tried to keep it down. Even Cyra, who usually loved things that made other people scared out of their minds, looked like she had had enough, her teeth gritted even though he was taking care of her currentgift.

It took a long time for Pary to announce that they were landing. Next to him, Cyra heaved a sigh of relief. Akos noted the shift of the ship toward the ground, aiming at some dense forest that looked the same to him as everywhere else.

But as they came closer, the trees seemed almost to part, making way for a cluster of buildings. They were lit from beneath by pools of glowing water—saturated by the same bacteria that made the canals around Galo light up, Akos assumed. Otherwise they were small wooden buildings with high, peaked roofs, connected by paths that looked bright against the otherwise gloomy backdrop. Spots of light moved erratically everywhere, tracing the paths of flying insects.

The ship touched down just inside a stone wall, on a landing pad.

They were at the temple of Ogra.

CHAPTER 24 | CYRA

I BENT TO TOUCH the path beneath our feet. It was smooth, flat stone—white, a color uncommon to Ogra. This place was packed with glowing things, in the gardens, and pools, and flitting around in the air.

Pary led us toward one of the larger buildings. We had landed at the bottom of a hill, so it would be a climb to get anywhere, and I assumed the oracle resided at the top. The air tasted sweet after the stale panic inside the transport vessel—I never wanted to travel during an Ogran storm again—and I gulped it down, keeping pace with Pary, with the others behind me.

As we passed through one of the gardens—most of the plants were held away from us by a mesh fence that had a current running through it, I noted—Yssa spoke from behind me, with a tone of controlled fear. "Pary."

I turned back to see a large beetle, almost as long as my palm, crawling on Akos's cheek. Its wings had bright blue markings, and its antennae were bright, searching. There was another one on his throat, and a third on his arm.

"Stay still," Yssa told him. "Everyone else step back from him."

"Shit," Pary said.

"I take it these insects are poisonous," Akos said. His Adam's apple bobbed with a particularly hard swallow.

"Very," Yssa said. "We keep them here because they are very bright when they fly."

"And they avoid anything that is a particularly strong conduit for the current," Pary added. "Like . . . people. *Most* people."

Akos's eyes closed.

Frowning a little, I stepped forward. Pary grabbed my arm to stop me, but he couldn't stand to touch me; his grip slipped, and I kept walking. Inching closer, and closer, until I was *right* in front of Akos, his warm breath against my temple. I lifted a hand to hover over the beetle on his face, and, for the first time, thought of my currentgift as something that might protect instead of injure.

A single black tendril unfurled from my fingers—obeying me, *obeying me*—and jabbed the beetle in the back. The light inside it flaring to life, it darted away from him, and the others went with it. Akos's eyes opened. We stared at each other, not touching, but close enough that I could see the freckles on his eyelids.

"Okay?" I said.

He nodded.

"Stay close to me, then," I said. "But don't touch my skin, or you'll turn us both into poisonous insect magnets."

As I turned around, I made eye contact with Sifa. She was giving me an odd look, almost like I had just struck her. I felt Akos behind me, staying close. He pinched my shirt between two fingers, right over the middle of my back.

"Well," Eijeh said. "That was exciting."

It was the sort of thing Ryzek might have said.

"Shut up," I replied, automatically.

There were beautiful, expansive rooms on the hill. Grand spaces, the furniture covered with protective cloths, the planks of the wood floors stained in different patterns, the tiles painted with geometric designs in sedate greens and muted pinks. The warm Ogran air flowed easily through each space we walked through, most of the walls built to fold back. But Pary didn't take us to any of them.

Instead, he brought us to the series of buildings where we would stay overnight. "She wants to see each of you separately, so it will take some time," he said. "This is a peaceful place, so take advantage of the opportunity to rest."

"Who gets to go first?" I said.

"The oracle's esteemed colleague, Sifa Kereseth, of course," Pary said, inclining his head to Akos's mother.

"I am honored," Sifa said, and they walked away together, leaving me, Akos, Eijeh, Cisi, and Yssa.

"Anything we should know?" I said to Yssa. "You used to live here, I assume? You seem to know as much about it as Pary does."

"Yes. Pary and I both worked here, once, before I was sent to be an ambassador," she said. She switched into Shotet. "I'm afraid I have nothing useful to say except that the oracle is far more than she initially seems, and if she wants to see each of you separately, that is because she has something distinct to say to each of you."

Akos repeated this in Thuvhesit to Cisi, on a slight delay. I had never seen Cisi look quite this way—not frightened, exactly, but tense, like she was bracing herself.

I didn't often think of Cisi's fate, but I thought of it then. *The first child of the family Kereseth will succumb to the blade.*

The little buildings where Pary had told us we could stay were arranged in a circle around a garden, and all the walls were open, so it was easy to track who came and went. Sifa didn't return from the oracle, but Pary came to collect Eijeh, who was increasingly making me feel like I was in the presence of Ryzek again.

Akos joined me in the garden, after ensuring there were no killer beetles flying around. Still, he stayed close to me, closer than he normally would.

"What do you think she'll say?" I asked him.

He sighed, and I felt it against my hair. "I don't know. I've given up trying to know what oracles are going to say to me."

I laughed. "I bet you're tired of them."

"I am." He stepped closer, so his chest was against my back and his nose was in my hair, tilted down so I could feel his breaths against the nape of my neck. It would have been simple to move away. He wasn't holding me there; he was hardly touching me, in fact.

But so help me, I didn't want to move.

"I'm tired of everything," he said. "I'm tired all the time."

He sighed again, heavily.

"Mostly," he said, "I'm tired of not being near you."

I found myself relaxing, shifting back so I was pressed against him, a wall of heat all the way down my spine. He rested his hands on my hips, his fingers creeping under the hem of my shirt just enough to dull my pain. *Let the damn poison beetles come*, I thought, as I felt a kiss on my neck, right behind my ear.

This was inviting further pain, and I knew it. His fate wouldn't let him choose me, and even if that wasn't the case, I suspected the deep well of his grief wouldn't let him choose anything at all. But I was sick of doing what was good for me.

He kissed where my neck met my shoulder, lingering, his tongue tasting my skin, which was likely salty from sweat. I reached up and buried my fingers in his hair, holding him against me for a moment, and then twisting my neck so our mouths collided. Our teeth clacked together, and normally we would have drawn back and laughed, but neither of us was in a laughing mood. I pulled at his hair, and his hands tightened around my hips so hard it was just on the good side of painful.

I had buried myself in rage since the destruction of the sojourn ship, and since the illusions between him and me fell away. Now I buried myself in wanting him instead, twisting into him, grabbing his body wherever my hands found purchase. *Want me*, I told him, with each clutch of my fingers. *Choose me. Want me.*

I leaned back for just a moment, just to look at him. The straight line of his nose, and its scattered freckles. His skin was the color of sandstone, and the powder people used to keep their skin from shining, and the envelopes my mother had used to send letters. His eyes were insistent on mine, their color exactly like a storm rolling in over Voa, carrying in them the same apprehension, like even now he was afraid I might stop. I understood. I was afraid I might stop, too. So I pressed into him again, before I could.

We stumbled together toward one of the rooms, stumbled out

of our shoes. I yanked a curtain across the space exposed to the courtyard, but really, I didn't care if anyone saw, I didn't care if we were interrupted, I just wanted to take and take and take whatever he would give, knowing that this might be the last time I let myself.

CHAPTER 25 | CISI

THE HALL OF PROPHECY, where I go to meet the Ogran oracle, is big and grand, like its name suggests. It's about what I expect, since that's what the hall in Hessa Temple is like, and I used to go visit Mom at work all the time.

The Ogran space isn't as colorful as Hessa's, though. The walls are paneled with dark wood. Carved and etched into the wood are elegant designs that take the shape of what I assume are Ogran plants. They look almost like they're writhing and snapping right in front of me.

There are windows near the ceiling, untinted, that must be lit from outside, because they glow with a light that's not natural to Ogra itself. The room itself is narrow and long, with sculptures about an armspan away from each other. Some of them are as carefully shaped as the carvings on the walls, and others are hard and grotesque, but all have a kind of menace to them. Most things on Ogra do.

The oracle herself stands in front of one of the sculptures—one of the taller ones, made of metal plates that arc toward the ceiling and twist around each other. They're all polished on one side and raw on the other, and fastened to each other with big bolts the size of my fist. The oracle's hands are folded in front of her. Her oracle robes are a deep, rich blue, and she's barefoot. Stouter than Mom, and smaller. She glances at me, and offers me a smile.

"Cisi Kereseth," she says. "My name is Vara. Come, look at this."

I smile back, and stand next to her, looking up at the sculpture. I only do it out of politeness. I'm no good at looking at art.

"This sculpture was constructed about thirty seasons ago, when the city of Pokgo began to expand. People were angry that we were losing some of what they called 'Ogran humility.' The traditional Ogran belief is that our planet humbles us—reminds us that there are some things we cannot overcome." Vara shrugs. "Some things we should not try to control."

She gives me a pointed look. I'm not sure what to make of it. My instinct is to calm her. I try water, the most useful of my textures, but I can tell it doesn't do much to her. What makes Ograns comfortable, I wonder? Wind, the warmth of a fire, the softness of a blanket? I sift through a few in my mind before finding one I think seems right—the feeling of cool glass under your palm.

Vara raises an eyebrow.

"I have often wondered what that felt like," she says. "It is a heady thing, to be touched by your gift. It is all too easy to succumb to its influence."

"I'm sorry," I say. "I don't mean to—"

Vara rolls her eyes. "Come on, girl. You can fool people who don't know you that well, but I, along with every other oracle in my generation, have been seeing visions of you from birth. I know that your control is far more advanced than most who can influence their own gifts. I also know that you are trying to do good, when you use it against people. So let's talk about Isae Benesit, Cisi."

The way she lays it all bare makes me feel jumpy, and all the words I could say to defend myself get stuck in my throat. I nod, because that's all I can do to show her that I heard what she said.

"Do you truly care about her?" she asks. "Or are you just manipulating her to accomplish your own aims?"

"*My* aims——" I choke out.

"Yes, I know——you are only doing what you think is best. But the fact is, you are making decisions about the future of this galaxy unilaterally, so they *are* your aims, and no one else's."

I don't like to think of what I'm doing with Isae as manipulation. It's not that simple. If only Vara knew how much Isae worried me, sometimes. How easy it was for her to kill Ryzek, and order an attack on innocents in Voa. How wild her eyes are when she lets herself disappear into anger, and how settled she seems when I draw her back. She needs me.

Which gets me back to Vara's original question——of whether I really care about her.

"I do care for her," I say. "I love her. But I worry for her. In a fair world, she would have space to feel her grief, but we don't really have the time to let her work out what she's going through on her own, not with a war going on."

Vara purses her wrinkled lips.

"Perhaps you are right," she says. "In that case, I must tell you to be careful of the one I've seen in some of your futures——the mechanic's boy. Ast."

"He senses currentgifts, doesn't he," I say. "He always seems to know when I'm using mine, even if I'm being really careful."

"It seems that way," Vara says. "And he's getting more and more suspicious of you. And more and more angry that Isae is *not* suspicious, I think."

I nod. "Thank you for the warning."

"Be careful, girl," Vara says, catching my hand and squeezing it tightly. A little too tightly. Her pupils are big—most Ograns' are, since there's so little light everywhere—but I can see a slim green ring around them that makes up her irises.

"And don't trust the Othyrians." She squeezes still harder. "Don't let her agree to it. Whatever you do."

I'm not sure what she means, but I know she wants me to nod, so I do.

CHAPTER 26 | AKOS

IT WAS LATE THAT night that the oracle finally asked for him—or rather, *them*, because she wanted to see him and Cyra at the same time.

Earlier, they had fallen asleep tangled up in each other, with light from the plants in the garden casting a soft glow through the curtain Cyra had drawn. The silverskin on one side of her head had been cool against his chest, where she insisted on laying to listen to his heartbeat.

He didn't know what had come over him, in the garden, pulling her close when he knew it was selfish, that he couldn't give her what she wanted, at her own insistence. He ought to listen to her, maybe even break things off with her completely, because there was no ridding him of his fate and no way of convincing either of them that things would be the same if he didn't have death in service to her family to look forward to.

But the longing for her had pierced right through the haze that had settled over his mind the past few weeks, and he was too relieved at feeling *something* that he hadn't had the heart to suppress it. And he'd gone on wanting her, even while they struggled closer and closer. Like there just wasn't enough of her and never would be.

He couldn't take her hand as they walked—it would only attract the beetles, and he wasn't eager to have one of them perched on his face again—but he stayed close, so he could almost feel her. Her currentshadows were moving faster, darting across her throat and disappearing under her collar, and he wished he could do more for her than the mediocre painkiller he had given her before they left.

Pary led them to the top of the hill, but not to the large hall lit bright from within—down, to the lower level of the place, where the ceilings sloped too close to the top of his head for comfort, and the floorboards creaked with every step. He had to bend to pass through a doorway, and found himself in what looked like a kitchen. A woman not much older than his own mother stood there, her hands buried in a pile of dough. Her arms were freckled, and her hair was gray and curly, cut short around her head.

She smiled up at them when they walked in, with all the warmth he'd learned not to expect from oracles, who always seemed disconnected and harsh to him, even the falling oracle of Thuvhe, before his death.

"Cyra, Akos, welcome," she said. "Please, sit."

She gestured to the bench across the table from her. Akos did as she said, but Cyra stayed on her feet, arms crossed.

"Would you feel more comfortable with busy hands?" she asked Akos. "I know you have an affinity for making elixirs. There is plenty here to chop."

"No," he said, his face flushing with warmth. "Thank you."

"Do you have a name?" Cyra asked, blunt as ever. "Or should we just call you 'Oracle'?"

"Ah, forgive my rudeness. My name is Vara," she said. "I sometimes forget that the people I know do not know me, in turn. Is there anything I can do to make you less hostile, my dear?" She nodded to Cyra. "Or are you content to remain this way?"

A faint crease appeared in Cyra's cheek, the way it did when she was suppressing a smile.

"Fine, I'll sit," she conceded. "But don't read too much into it."

"I wouldn't dare," Vara said as Cyra perched on the edge of the bench next to Akos. Even sitting down, the two of them were taller than Vara, who was short and thick through the middle. There was something familiar about her.

"Are you related to Yssa in some way?" he asked.

"Well spotted, darling, yes. She is my daughter. A rather . . . late-in-life entanglement it was," she said. "She gets her father's frame. Tall and long-limbed. The rest was mine." She broke a piece off the dough and popped it in her mouth.

"Now," she said as she swallowed, "I'm sure you are wondering why I didn't put on my traditional Ogran robes and meet you in the Hall of Prophecy like a proper oracle."

"It crossed my mind," Akos said.

"I would expect no less from the son of an oracle," Vara said, still with that kind smile. "Well, really, let's keep this between us, but I hate that hall. It makes me feel short. So do the robes! They were made for the last oracle, and he was much bigger than me. Besides—I thought, given the nature of what I have to discuss with you both, you might appreciate the more comfortable surroundings."

Akos felt like he'd been dunked in cold water, suddenly. *Given the nature of what I have to discuss with you.*

"So it's not good news," Cyra said, wry. Leaning on sarcasm almost always meant she was scared out of her mind. The tightening of her hands around the edge of the bench suggested the same thing.

Vara sighed. "Oh, the truth rarely is, dear girl. What I have for you today is something we call 'kyerta'—do either of you know the word?"

Cyra and Akos both shook their heads.

"Of course not. Who speaks Ogran but Ograns?" Vara's laugh was like a thin trickle of water. "You see, we think of oracles as delivering the future only, and that's most of what we do, yes." She grabbed a fat metal cylinder from a shelf behind her, and used it to roll the dough flat. "But it's the past that brings about the future—often it stays hidden, shaping our lives in ways we do not understand. But sometimes it must force its way into the present in order to change what's coming."

She broke the dough into three large pieces, and rolled them between her hands until they were long and thin, like tails. Then she began to braid them.

"Kyerta," she said, "is a revelation that causes your world to shift on its axis. It is a profound truth that, once you know it, inevitably alters your future, though it has already occurred and should, therefore, change nothing."

She finished the braided dough, and set it aside with a sigh. Dusting off her hands, she sat down across from them and leaned into her arms.

"In your case, this kyerta comes in the form of your names," she said. "You have lived your lives as Akos Kereseth and Cyra Noavek, when in fact, you are Akos Noavek and Cyra Kereseth."

She sat back from the table.

Akos struggled to breathe.

Cyra let out a peal of laughter.

CHAPTER 27 | CYRA

I CLAPPED MY HAND over my mouth to stop the sound, a horrible, forced laugh without any mirth in it.

Cyra Kereseth.

It wasn't the first time I'd ever thought the name. I had day-dreamed about it once or twice, leaving the name Noavek behind and taking on Akos's name, someday in an ideal future where we got married. It was customary for the lower-status person in a marriage to change their name, in Shotet, but we could make an exception, to rid me of the label I hated. The name Cyra Kereseth had become, to me, a symbol of freedom, as well as a sugar-sweet unreality.

But Vara didn't mean that my name was Cyra Kereseth through some hypothetical, far-off marriage. She meant that my name was Cyra Kereseth *now*.

The hard part was not believing I wasn't Cyra Noavek. I had suspected it since my brother told me I didn't share his blood, maybe even since my blood didn't work in the gene lock that he had used to keep his rooms secure. But believing I belonged to the same family that had raised Akos to a soft heart and a knowledge of iceflowers—that was another thing entirely.

I didn't dare look at Akos. I wasn't sure what I would see when I did.

I took my hand away from my face.

"What?" I said, stifling another giggle. *"What?"*

"Sifa would tell the story better," Vara said. "But unfortunately that task now falls to me, because it is Ogra's future that hangs in the balance. When you were born, Akos, to Ylira and Lazmet Noavek, Sifa saw only dark paths ahead of you. And likewise, Cyra, born to Sifa herself, and Aoseh Kereseth, only dark paths ahead of you. She despaired for both of you.

"And then something happened that had not happened in quite some time—a new possibility presented itself. If she crossed your paths—if she switched your places—new possibilities opened up, and a few—very few, mind you, but a few—did not lead to doom. So she reached out to Ylira Noavek, a woman she had never met before and would never again meet, to present the solution to her. It was very fortunate, for her, that Lazmet had not yet been to see his child. It was likewise fortunate that the bloodlines in both your families are so richly varied that virtually any combination of features and skin shades wouldn't raise eyebrows.

"They met just past the Divide, the feathergrass that separates Shotet from Thuvhe, and they traded their children, so that both might have a chance to avoid their darkest paths," Vara said, with a tone of finality. Her fingers were dusted with brown flour, her nails bitten down to stubs. "Lazmet was told that he had been misinformed about the sex of his child. The messenger who had delivered the news was executed, but Lazmet accepted you as his,

Cyra, and all proceeded as Sifa had hoped."

I was caught in my imagining of the moment, my swaddled, infant form passed into Ylira Noavek's hands, with feathergrass swaying in the background. I drew myself out of the fiction, suddenly furious.

"So you're telling me," I said, slumping forward over the table to point a finger at her. "You're telling me that my *mother* handed me over to be raised by a bunch of monsters, and I'm, what? Supposed to be *grateful*, because it was for my own good?"

"It's not up to me to tell you how to feel," Vara said, her dark eyes soft. "Only to tell you what happened."

I felt like a pot boiling over, all anger and hysteria bubbling up inside me, irrepressible. I wanted to shake the soft look from her eyes, or laugh in her face; I wanted to *move*, above all else, to escape the pain that now raced through every izit of my skin, covering me in dark patches.

When I finally dared to glance at Akos, I saw him stone-faced and completely still. It was unnerving.

"I'm sure I don't have to point out to you that there is one bright spot in all this," Vara said. "Your fates."

"Our fates," I repeated, feeling stupid. "What about them?"

"There is a reason the fates don't name names," Vara said. "*The second child of the family Noavek will cross the Divide. The third child of the family Kereseth will die in service to the family Noavek.* My dear girl, *you* are the third child of the family Kereseth. And I suspect your fate has already been fulfilled."

I made a big show of putting two fingers against the side of my throat to check for a pulse. "Silly me, thinking I hadn't *died in service*——"

I cut myself off.

But that wasn't true, was it?

My brother had tried to make me torture Akos, there in the underground prison where he had captured us and forced us to our knees. I had drawn all my currentgift into myself, trusting in my strength to keep me alive. But that strength had faltered—just for a moment, just enough to be considered a death. My heart had stopped, and then started again. I had come back.

I had died for the family Noavek—I had died for Akos.

I stared at him, wonderingly. The fate he had dreaded, the fate he had allowed to define him since he first heard it spoken by my brother's lips . . . it was *mine*.

And it was done.

CHAPTER 28 | AKOS

ALL THE THINGS THAT he was—
   Fated traitor, Kereseth, *Thuvhesit*—
   Had been stripped away.

He hadn't said a word since the oracle invited them to share a cup of tea with her, and Cyra declined. The truth was, he'd lost all his words. He didn't even know which language he ought to speak in. The categories he'd used to define them—Thuvhesit, the language of his home and his people; Othyr, the language of off-worlders; Shotet, the language of his enemies—didn't apply anymore.

   Cyra seemed to know that he couldn't speak. Maybe she didn't understand it, and how could she? She had lit up like a piece of kindling when Vara told them the truth; she was emotionally elastic, could throw herself out of rage just as fast as she threw herself into it. But even though she didn't understand him, she didn't pester him, either.

   All she had done was touch him, tentative, on the shoulder, as she said, "I know. I didn't want to share blood with them, either."

And that was it, wasn't it. She shared a history with the Noaveks, and he shared blood. He was hard-pressed to figure out which one was worse.

He didn't sleep. Just walked the paths around the temple, not even bothering to avoid the dangerous plants that were growing everywhere, or the beetles that could kill him with a bite. He didn't recognize most of the growing things, but some of them he did, and he looked for them just to give himself something else to think about, for just a little while.

The beetles came and went, except for one—a small one that perched on his hand, twitching its light-up wings and wiggling its antennae. He sat on a rock in one of the gardens to stare down at it.

It reminded him, for some reason, of the Armored One he had killed for its skin. He had been out there in the fields outside of Voa, where the Armored Ones wandered, keeping to themselves for the most part. It had taken him a while to realize they weren't going to attack him. It was the current that enraged them, not him; he was a relief to them, just like he was to Cyra.

Maybe this beetle was the same, avoiding those who channeled the current because the energy was too harsh for it to stand. The pattern on its back was like spilled ink, taking no particular shape. It lit up blue-green, when it did light up, a soothing color.

After some time the prickle of the little clinging legs didn't bother him, and neither did the threat of its substantial pincers. It was a little monster, just like him. It couldn't help how it was born.

The oracle's revelation was like a crumpled piece of paper that just kept unfolding more and more. First it showed him the things he wasn't anymore. And then it showed him the things he was: a Shotet. A *Noavek*.

The man who had taken everything from him—father, family, safety, and home—had been his brother.

And the man who had made Ryzek—Lazmet. He was Akos's father. Still alive, still so alarming to Cyra—unshakable, unfaltering Cyra—that she had panicked at the sight of his face alone.

"What do I do now?" he asked the beetle on his hand.

"Surely that thing won't respond to you," Pary's voice said from behind him. "I don't claim to understand other people's currentgifts, though."

Akos whipped around fast. The beetle on his hand still didn't stir, thankfully.

"Don't come much closer," he said. "Killer beetles, and all."

"They seem to like you," Pary said. "Whatever you are is a very strange thing."

Akos nodded. That wasn't up for debate.

Pary stood in front of him—at a safe distance—with his hands in his pockets. "She must have told you something difficult."

Akos wasn't sure *difficult* was the right word for it. The beetle crawled from his thumb to his sleeve, pincers clicking audibly. Hopefully that wasn't what it did before it attacked. Akos didn't think it was going to attack him, though.

"There are a lot of people across the solar system who think oracles are elitist, you know," Pary said. "Only giving fates—and therefore importance—to certain families. It seems like an unnecessary display of favoritism to people who don't understand how fates work, how they do not allow an oracle to choose anything at all. But those who have fates know better."

Pary's eyes glinted with the glow of a flower in the garden, reflecting orange.

"A fate is a cage," he said. "Freed from that cage, you can choose, do, go . . . whatever, wherever you'd like. You can, in some ways, finally know who you are."

Akos had been too busy thinking about who he was related to to think about fates, though he knew that was where Cyra's mind had gone. Maybe he ought to be happy that he wasn't fated to die anymore, but he'd been hanging on to that so hard that it was hard to adjust. It was like he'd been carrying a weight around for so long he forgot what it was like to be without it, and now he felt too light, like he might float away.

And his true fate? *The second child of the family Noavek will cross the Divide.*

Well, he'd already done that, crossed the stretch of feather-grass that separated Thuvhe from Shotet. He'd done it more than once. So his fate had been fulfilled, and now, Pary was right. He could choose whatever. Do whatever.

Go.

Wherever he wanted, wherever he *needed* to go.

A decision was just coming together in his mind when he heard the scream, high and grating. A wail joined it, and then a low shout. Three voices raised in acknowledgment of pain. Three oracles.

By now, he knew what it meant: there had been another attack.

The beetle fled from his wrist as he ran up the hill to the room where his brother slept. He ripped the sheer curtains aside to see Eijeh sitting up in bed, his fingers knotted in his curly hair as he moaned. It had been a long time since Akos had seen Eijeh so rumpled, his shirt twisted around his torso and half his face marked by the crease of a pillowcase.

Akos hesitated at the edge of the room. Why had he come here, instead of going to his mom's room? He'd lost the parts of Eijeh he'd been so determined to save, and now he knew that what was left of Eijeh wasn't even related to him anyway, so what kept drawing him back?

Eijeh lifted his head, eyes locking on Akos's face.

"Our father," Eijeh said. "He's attacking them."

"Eijeh," Akos said. "You're confused—our father is—"

"Lazmet," Eijeh said, rocking back and forth, still clutching his head. "Shissa. He attacked Shissa."

"How many dead?" Akos touched Eijeh's shoulder, and his brother—his brother?—pulled away.

"No, don't, I need to see—"

"How many?" Akos demanded, even though deep down he knew it didn't matter whether it was a handful or dozens or—

"Hundreds," Eijeh said. "It's raining glass."

Then Eijeh burst into tears, and Akos sat on the edge of the bed.

No, it didn't matter that it was hundreds. His path forward remained the same.

CHAPTER 29 | EIJEH

"YOU HAVE TO FIND ways to ground yourself," Sifa said to us. "Or the visions will take over. You'll get stuck in all the possibilities and you won't be able to live a life."

We answered, "Would it be so bad? To live a thousand different lives instead of your own?"

She narrowed her eyes at us, this woman who was our mother, an oracle, and a stranger all at once. We had ordered the death of her husband; we had suffered the loss of that man ourselves. How odd it was, to be responsible for so much pain, and to have suffered as a direct result of that responsibility, all at once. As our identities melded more and more, we felt more profoundly the contradictions inherent in our being. But there was nothing to be done about it; the contradictions existed, and had to be embraced.

"Whatever made you, made you for a purpose," she said. "And it wasn't to become a vessel for other people's experiences; it was to have your own."

We shrugged, and that's when the images came.

⧼⧽

We are in the body of a man—short, stocky, and standing before a cart full of books. The smell of dust and pages is in the air, and shelves tower above him. He places a heavy volume on a tray that sticks out from the shelf, and keys in a code on a device he carries. The tray zooms off to the shelf where the book is supposed to go—a story above his head, and to the left.

He sighs, and walks to the end of the aisle to look out the window. The city—which we recognize as Shissa, in Thuvhe—is full of buildings that hover so far above the ground that the iceflower fields beneath it look like mere patches of color amid the snow. The buildings appear to be hanging from the clouds themselves. Across the way is a tiered diamond-shaped structure of glass that glows green at night, lit from within. To its left, a curved mammoth lit up soft white, like the land beneath it.

It is a beautiful place. We know it.

We are not a man anymore. We are a woman, short and shivering in a stiff vest of Shotet armor.

"Why does anyone live in this damn country?" she says to the man next to her. His teeth are chattering audibly.

"Iceflowers," the man said with a shrug.

She flexes her hands in an attempt to bring feeling back to her fingers.

"Shh," he says.

Up ahead, a Shotet soldier has her ear pressed to a door. She closes her eyes for a moment, then pulls back, and motions the others forward. They slam a metal cylinder into the door, several times, to force it open. The lock pops off and clatters to the cement floor. Beyond the door is a control room of sorts, like the nav deck of a transport vessel.

A scream pierces the air. We rush forward.

We are standing at a window, one hand pressed to cold glass, the other pulling a curtain back. Above us is the city of Shissa, a cluster of giants that drape over us always. It has been our colorful comfort in the night ever since we were a child. The sky without buildings in it seems bare and empty, so we do not like to travel.

Since we have been staring at them, the buildings do not move, not even in the strongest wind. That is thanks to the Pithar technology that holds them upright, controlled by small towers on the ground, near the iceflower fields. We don't understand how it works. We are a field worker. The boots—with hooks on the bottom, to catch on ice sheets—are still on our feet from the day's labor, our shoulders still sore from hauling equipment.

As we watch, the hospital—a bright red cube right above us—*shifts*.

Shudders.

And drops.

It falls, pulling a gasp from our lungs. Like something dropped into a bucket of water, it seems to move slowly, though that can't be true. It sends snowflakes up in a faint white streak as it drops. And then it collides with the ground.

We are a child in a hospital bed. Our body is short and slim. Our hair sticks to the back of our neck—it is hot in here. The rails are up on the side of the bed, like we're some kind of *kid*, and can't be trusted not to roll off in our sleep.

The bed jerks beneath us, and we startle, grabbing the rails.

Only it's not the bed that's moving—it's the *floor*. It's falling out from beneath us. The city slides away, just outside the windows, and we cling to the rails, teeth gritted—

And then we're screaming—

The Shotet woman—we—tugs at the straps of her armor as we run. We fastened them too tight, and they're digging into our sides, keeping us from moving as fast as we'd like.

The sound as the building falls is nothing like we have ever heard. The crunching, smashing—the screaming, wailing, gasping—the rush of air around it—it is deafening. We clap our hands over our ears and keep running, toward the transport vessel, toward safety.

We see a dark shape flinging itself off the hospital roof.

Our knees are buried in the snow. The man from before is next to us, shouting something we can't hear. Our cheeks are hot. Startled, we realize that the Shotet woman's face is wet with tears.

This is the retribution Lazmet Noavek ordered. But it feels more like horror.

"Come on!" the other soldier is saying. "We have to go!"

But how can we go, when all those people need help?

How can we go on, when so many are lost?

How can we go on?

CHAPTER 30 | CYRA

THAT EVENING, AKOS LEFT to walk the gardens, and I found myself alone. The humid Ogran air had made my cheeks damp, and I wanted to wash my face. I stumbled to the bathroom, stinging and aching, and leaned my forehead against the tile wall as I turned on the faucet. My fingers always hurt worse than the rest of my body, the currentshadows coalescing in my extremities, like they were itching to escape.

I splashed my face with water, and dried it with the front of my shirt. *Cyra Kereseth*, I thought, trying out the name. It felt false, like I was trying to put on someone else's clothing. But being in this place, where the blankets were still thrown back from where Akos and I had lain tangled together, felt just as wrong. I had been someone else when we rested here, with my ear against his chest.

Suddenly I needed to get out, to move. I walked to Pary's ship, on the far side of the hill, away from the gardens, so I wouldn't run into Akos. The ship's hatch opened at the touch of a button, the interior lights on, guiding me to a seat near all the restrained plants of Ogra.

I was sitting there, in front of the plant that looked like a giant mouth, my head in my hands, when the hatch opened again. I lifted my head, sure it would be Akos, that we could finally talk about what we had heard. But it wasn't.

It was Sifa.

She didn't close the hatch, so I could still hear the buzz of insects and the whisper of wind while she stood, staring at me. I stared back. The pain that surged through me at the sight of her, at the thought of what she had surrendered me to as a child, was startling. I stayed still to keep it contained. No flinching, no shaking, no moaning. Nothing that invited comfort. I didn't want her to see that she could hurt me.

"You spoke to Vara," she said to me at last.

I sat up, and pushed my braid over one shoulder.

"Yeah, thanks for that, by the way," I said, twitching a little at a currentshadow racing across my face. "Nothing like the news of your own abandonment coming from a stranger."

"You have to know—" she began, and then I was on my feet, boots planted on the grate floor, a line of guiding light between my feet.

"Yes, please, tell me what I *have to know*," I snapped. "Is it how you felt dumping your own daughter into a family of monsters? Or lying to your son for his entire life? Is it how you did it for the good of Thuvhe, or Shotet, or the goddamn current? Because yes, that's really all I want to know—how hard this was *for you*."

I felt huge, suddenly, like a wall of muscle. She wasn't frail— she had a certain wiry strength to her—but she was not built like me, solid through the hips and shoulders. I could have knocked her down with a punch, and part of me wanted to try. Maybe it was the part of me that was Noavek, the part that wouldn't have existed if she had kept me safe instead of trading me away.

Sifa stayed by the hatch, silhouetted by the lights on the little runway behind her. Her hair was piled on one side of her head, scraggly, like she hadn't combed through it in days. She looked so tired. I didn't care.

"What did you see?" I said. "What did you see in our futures that made you trade us? What could possibly have been so bad that it was better to hand me over to the Noaveks than to let me suffer it?"

She closed her eyes, face tightening, and I felt cold creeping down my spine.

"I am not going to tell you that," she said, opening her eyes. "I would rather you hate me than know what I saw become of you, of Akos. I chose the best path for you, the one that had the greatest potential."

"You don't have the right," I said in a low voice, "to decide my path for me."

"I would do it again," she said.

I was thinking about that punch again.

"Get away from me," I said.

"Cyra—"

"No," I said. "Maybe you could determine what happened between us when I was an infant, but you have lost that power."

I stood. As I moved toward the hatch, to pass her, her posture changed. She slumped oddly against the doorway, head angled down, hair spilling around her face.

And then raised her voice in a harrowing scream.

Another vision, then. Something horrible.

At first I stood before her, simply listening, her voice scraping at the insides of my head. And then I crouched before her as she slid down the wall to the ground, unwilling to offer comfort, but unwilling to leave without knowing what she saw.

It took some time for her to go quiet. The scream stopped with a sound like a gag. I had learned that asking Sifa direct questions rarely resulted in anything productive, so I didn't speak. My currentshadows burning across my belly, I waited, hunched there in the dark. Behind me, the mouth-plant snapped its brittle jaws.

It took so long for her to speak that my legs went numb.

"There's been an attack on Shissa," she said, breathless. "Courtesy of Lazmet Noavek."

My first thought—though it shamed me a moment later—was: *So?*

Thuvhe had struck us first. Alarming though it was to think of an armed force at my father's command, this was a war, and both sides suffered in a war.

But I had not forgotten how I felt when the sojourn ship broke apart over Voa. Wherever Akos was, he was about to feel the same thing. Despite my anger at our enemies, I couldn't wish this on someone I loved.

I left Sifa there, the woman who had given me blood and then given me away. I had no comfort to give her and no desire to give it. I sprinted down the white stone path to the gardens to find him. But that place was empty, the beetles buzzing undisturbed. So I ran, instead, to the room where we had slept. The bed was empty.

I went from room to room, searching out Cisi's bed—empty. But in the room that would have been Sifa's, I found Yssa instead.

Her red hair clung wetly to her cheeks, as if she had just bathed.

"I'm sorry," she said.

"For what, the attack?" I said. It was a strange thing to apologize to me for.

"Attack?" she said. She didn't know yet, then. "What attack?"

I shook my head. "In a moment. What are you sorry for, Yssa?" I said, impatient. "I need to find Akos, now."

"That's just it," she replied. "He's gone."

I felt like I might burst into flames, like one of the lethal vines in Ogra's forests, exploding at a careless touch.

"Pary left just a moment ago with Cisi and Akos. They intend to depart Ogra on the same vessel that Jorek Kuzar will be on, headed back to Voa, at the break of day," Yssa said.

"They didn't leave word," I said. I wasn't asking.

"I wish I knew more. Pary didn't tell me anything. I know you must be confused—" she said.

But I wasn't confused. Perhaps if I had been normal, if I had grown up with any other name, I would have been.

Akos had been released of his fate, and of his obligation to me. And so he had left, gone home. Why would he feel the need to leave a message of farewell, or simply of explanation, to Ryzek's Scourge? That would be too considerate. Too much for a person like me to possibly expect.

I sat, heavy, on the trunk that stood at the foot of Sifa's bed. My currentshadows ran thick across my skin.

He was gone.

And I was alone again.

Oruzo. Noun. In Shotet: "A reflection, as in a mirror"

CHAPTER 31 | CYRA

SWEAT RAN INTO THE corner of my mouth. I licked the salt taste away and burst into a run. It was a risk, but I thought I could surprise him with strength he wasn't ready for.

My opponent was tall and lean. Ettrek, the one who had called me "Ryzek's Scourge" in the storm sanctuary when I first arrived, and insisted on the name whenever he saw me. But right now, he was just an arrangement of limbs, a particular density of meat. I threw my body at his, driving my elbows low, toward his gut.

The school of the mind—elmetahak—would not approve of my risk taking. *A risk should only be taken when there is no other option available*, the teachings said. In this case, they were correct. I had miscalculated.

Ettrek's arm slammed like a girder against my chest and shoulder, knocking me flat on my back. All around me the crowd roared their pleasure.

"Bleed, oruzo!" someone in the crowd jeered.

I heard, in their shouts, a memory. Of kneeling on a platform with a knife against my throat. My brother poised above me with rage and fear intermingled in his eyes. My people calling me "traitor," my people crooning for my blood. The silverskin on my head prickled.

They still crooned for my blood, even here, on Ogra. To them, I was still a Noavek, still better dead than alive.

I looked up at the wall, at Ettrek, about to bend down to deliver the final blow. I knew him. He called me "ally," he fought me for sport, but deep in the heart of him, he still wanted me to hurt.

So I slid a hand behind his head, as tenderly as a lover, and drew him closer. *Hurt me more*, the movement said. *Go ahead.* He jerked back like my touch was poison—and it was—and he fell back, off balance. I crawled on top of him, pinned him, made to elbow him in the face—but I stopped before striking him, my eyebrows raised.

"Yeah, yeah, I concede," Ettrek said, and the crowd booed. They were tired of watching me win. Tired of watching *Noaveks* win.

That Lazmet's blood didn't run in my veins, that I might not technically even be *Shotet*, didn't matter to them.

Did it matter to me?

Later, when the leaders of the Shotet exiles asked me to represent my people to the Ogran leadership—not knowing, of course, that I was not the true inheritor of my brother's throne—I thought of how I had felt, with my back flat on the ground, with those people cheering for my pain and defeat.

They hated me. They did not accept me. They didn't want me to represent them.

"The more traditional of the two Ogran leaders values law very highly, and you are the legal heir to the sovereignty," the exile leader, Aza, said to me with a hint of desperation.

Teka added, "We need your help, Cyra."

I looked at her—her pale hair limp from Ogran humidity, a dark circle beneath her remaining eye betraying her fatigue—and suddenly, Shotet was not the nameless crowd that had surrounded me more than once. Shotet was her. And Jorek. And even Yma. People who had been trampled by the powerful, just as I had. People who needed this small thing in order to fight back.

And I owed it to them. I had told people to evacuate. I had let slip that the exiles were on Ogra. I carried the Noavek legacy, even if I didn't carry their blood. I owed this at the very least, for what I had done.

"Fine," I said.

"I look ridiculous," I said to my reflection. Or, really, I said it to Teka, who stood behind me with her arms folded, sucking a dimple into her cheek.

I wore a floor-length jacket with sharp shoulders, buttoned tight across my chest and falling straight to the floor. Every seam was stitched with glowing thread, though, which made me feel more like an Ogran spacecraft than a person. The collar—made entirely of luminous fabric—lit my face from beneath, making my currentshadows especially nightmarish when they flowed across my skin.

Which was constantly. What little control I had retained when we first landed on Ogra was gone, as if Akos had taken it with him when he left.

"Aza wanted to make sure you looked the part of a sovereign, even if you're not really one. And now you do," Teka said. "Besides, everyone here looks ridiculous, so you fit right in."

She gestured to herself. She was dressed like me, except her jacket was gray—to complement her coloring, the Ogran seam-stress had said—and fell to her knees instead of her ankles. She wore pants to match it, and her pale hair was pulled back into a sleek knot. My own was in a thick, bumpy braid over one shoul-der, on the side opposite the silverskin.

We were about to attend a meeting with representatives of Ogra in Pokgo, Ogra's capital city. They had invited us to discuss the "request"—more like a demand—issued by the government of Thuvhe that the Ograns no longer give shelter to Shotet exiles, in the wake of the attack on Shissa.

I felt ill. The only reason Thuvhe had known to make that demand of Ogra was because I had told Isae we were here. My currentshadows were dense and quick, and this restrictive cloth-ing wasn't helping. I couldn't deny that it emphasized the length of my body in a nice way, though.

"You're going bare-faced?" I said to Teka, turning away from the mirror. "You could at least smudge something on your eye, you know."

"Every time I try I just end up looking stupid," she said.

"I could give it a try," I said. "My mother taught me when I was young."

"Just don't zing me with your currentgift," Teka said, a little grouchy.

I had found a little black pencil to trace my lash line in one of the shops in Galo. I had tried to barter with the clever Ogran woman who ran it, but she had pretended not to understand my accent, so I eventually gave up on the game and bought it for its full price. I removed its cap and stood in front of Teka, bending so our faces were on the same level. I couldn't brace myself against her, so I braced my hands against each other, to steady them.

"We could talk about it, you know," Teka said. "Him leaving like that? Not so much as a good-bye? We could talk about it, if you . . . you know. Needed to."

Not so much as a good-bye. He had decided I wasn't worth that basic decency.

I clenched my jaw.

"No," I said, "we can't."

If I talked about it, I would want to scream, and this coat was too tight around my ribs for that. It was the same reason I now avoided Eijeh and Sifa—always together, these days, and consulting with exiles about the future almost hourly. I couldn't bear the feeling.

In light, short strokes, with pauses as my currentgift swelled and receded like a tide, I lined Teka's eyelid with black, using the other end of the pencil to smudge it. When I first met her, she would have stabbed me rather than let me get this close to her, so though she would deny it if I asked, I knew she was softening toward me, as I had already softened toward her.

A soft heart was a gift, whether given easily or with great reluctance. I would never take it for granted again.

She opened her eye. Its blue looked even more brilliant with the black to frame it. She wore what she called her "fancy eye patch" on the other eye—it was clean and black, and held to her face with ribbon instead of a stretchy band.

"There," I said. "Almost painless."

She looked at herself in the mirror. "Almost," she agreed. But she left the pencil in place, so I knew she liked it.

I tried not to think about Akos, or dream about him, or imagine conversations we might have had about what I was experiencing. I was already barely containing my rage at Thuvhe; I didn't need something to stoke the flames further.

On the flight to Pokgo, however, I allowed myself just a moment of weakness before reprimanding myself.

As the ship glided between tall buildings—built higher than any of the ones in Voa, so tall they might have scraped the bottom of the Shissa ones that fell—I pictured the look of wonder his face would have worn if he had seen it.

And I would have said something like, *Ograns allowed a certain percentage of trees to be preserved when they built Pokgo, which is why it still looks like a forest below us.*

He would have smiled, amused as always by the knowledge I kept filed away.

But not amused enough by me to give me a damn explanation before—

Stop, I told myself, blinking tears from my eyes. There was pain in my knees, hips, elbows, and shoulders, pain in all the spaces between my bones. I couldn't indulge this.

There was work to be done.

The ship docked at a building near the center of Pokgo, where all the buildings were so close together I could peer into strangers' offices and living spaces and see how they decorated them. Ograns favored excess, so most of them were packed with objects of personal significance or fine craftsmanship. Everyone seemed to have the same decorative boxes, made of polished wood with little patterns carved into them.

When the hatch opened, I shuddered a little, because the wind that blew in was strong and it was clear we were higher up than I had realized, given the drop in temperature. Someone on the docking station guided a motorized walkway to the hatch. It had neither handrails nor some kind of visible fail-safe to keep a person on top of it. Our Ogran captain, a thick man with a substantial gut, walked right across it with the grace of a dancer. Yssa followed, and I was close behind her, forcing my eyes up and focused on the open doorway that was my destination.

If Akos had been here, I would have held his hand, my arm stretched out behind me like a banner.

But Akos was not here, so I made it across alone.

Ograns were ruled by a pair of people, one a woman and the other sema, the word in Shotet for neither woman nor man. There were two major political factions on Ogra, I knew, one amenable to change and the other not. Each one presented a viable candidate every ten seasons, and they ruled together, by compromise or by bargaining. It seemed impossible to me that such a thing could work, but apparently it wasn't, because the system had lasted two hundred seasons so far.

The sema leader introduced themselves as "Rokha," and had close-cut hair the color of Urek sand, a dusting of freckles on their skin, and delicate, pursed lips. The woman—"Lusha," she had called herself, as she gripped my arm in greeting—was taller, thicker, and several shades darker-skinned than I was. The pencil smeared above her lashes had a faint shimmer to it, lighting her eyes from above, and it suited her.

"You are Cyra Noavek," Rokha said to me, as we all stood in a group before the meeting was called to order. Lusha was talking to Yssa and Aza behind me—I could tell because her hearty laugh kept filling my head with a mirth I couldn't feel.

"Allegedly," I said, because I couldn't help myself.

Rokha laughed.

"You're taller than I thought," they said. "I suppose anyone looks short beside Ryzek Noavek."

"Looked," I corrected them. To me it was just a grammatical error, a courtesy to someone who didn't speak Shotet as a native. But their face tightened in recognition of the insensitivity.

"My apologies," they said. "You lost him so recently."

"I wouldn't say I lost anything," I said.

Rokha raised an eyebrow. The freckles on their eyelids made me think of Akos, and a web of currentshadows spread over my eye socket, making me wince.

"I can't tell if you are joking or not," Rokha said.

"That should please you. Ograns love mystery, don't they?" I replied sourly, and Rokha squinted at me, as if puzzled, as Lusha called the meeting to order.

"Let us speak plainly," Lusha said, and Rokha snorted.

Lusha wrinkled her nose at them, like a child might at a sibling. She was the more traditional of the two Ogran leaders, I knew, so she had a tendency to pontificate and stand on ceremony. I suppressed a laugh as Rokha winked at me across the low table. We sat on stools around it. The heavy fabric that covered me from throat to ankle pooled around me, glinting with the luminous thread that held it together.

"Okay," Aza said. "Then—plainly speaking—we are surprised that Ogra would even consider expelling us when we have co-existed comfortably for so long on this planet."

"We would not consider it if the pressure were merely coming from Thuvhe," Lusha said with a sigh. "But Thuvhe is backed by the Assembly, and they are seeking powerful alliances. Our intelligence reports the chancellor is on her way to Othyr at this very moment."

I glanced at Teka. She looked as troubled as I felt, her mouth drawn down toward her chin. If Thuvhe made an alliance with Othyr, this war was effectively over. No one would stand against Othyr, not without a cause greater than "keeping Shotet from being obliterated."

As far as I knew, Othyr had always been the wealthiest and most powerful planet in the galaxy. It had been, at one time, rich with natural resources, but as our race advanced, they turned to more intellectual pursuits than mining or farming. Now they developed technology and conducted research. Nearly every advance that had been made in the field of medicine, space travel, food technology, or personal conveniences had come out of Othyr. If a planet were to cut itself off from Othyr, it would lose access to the things we had all—Shotet included—come to rely on. A leader would be mad to risk it.

"Why is the Assembly backing Thuvhe instead of maintaining neutrality, as they have in the past? Suddenly this is no longer a 'civil dispute,' as they've been insisting for over ten seasons?" Teka said.

"They sense that we are vulnerable," Aza replied. "They undoubtedly see this as a cleanup effort. Get rid of Shotet trash. Blast it into space."

I relished the anger in Aza's voice, so similar to my own.

"That may be a slight exaggeration," Lusha chastened. "The Assembly would surely not engage in a conflict unless they thought—"

"Then tell me why—" Aza's voice shook as she interrupted Lusha. "Tell me why an attack against innocents fleeing to the sojourn ship in Voa was not considered a war crime, when an attack against innocents in Shissa was. Is that not because Thuvhesit children are considered innocent, and Shotet children are not? Is it not because Thuvhesit people are considered productive, and the Shotet are characterized as brutal scavengers?"

"I thought you didn't support Lazmet Noavek's actions against Thuvhe," Rokha said, voice hard. "You issued a statement condemning the attack immediately upon hearing about it, after all."

"And I stand by that statement. Lazmet Noavek has recruited himself an army composed of supporters of his late son. His actions against Shissa had nothing to do with us, and we certainly would not have done something so cruel," Aza said. "But that doesn't mean that Thuvhe doesn't deserve some kind of retribution for what they did to us."

I didn't have to be an expert in these kinds of meetings to know this one wasn't going well. The preferred communication style for an Ogran was like a hammer hitting a nail, and it was the same for Shotet. In fact, our cultures had more in common than not—we valued resilience, we occupied planets that defied us, we revered the oracles. . . .

If I could make them see how connected we were, maybe they would agree to help us.

"Why do they hate us?" I said, head tilted. I pitched my voice high, so it would sound like I was genuinely confused.

"What do you mean, *why*?" Aza scowled at me. "They have always hated us! Their hatred is without basis, without foundation—!"

"No hatred is mindless, not according to the mind of the one who hates," Teka said, nodding at me. "They hate us because they think we are backward. We follow the currentstream, we honor the oracles."

"And the oracles, by naming the Noavek family's fates, have affirmed Shotet's place in the galaxy," I said. "But the Assembly didn't listen. The Assembly didn't grant us sovereignty. They want to limit the oracles' power, not magnify it by honoring the fates. And so they hate us, for revering the very people from whom they want to wrest power."

"That is a bold claim," Lusha said. "Treasonous, some might say, to suggest that the Assembly wants to strip the oracles of their power."

"The only treason I acknowledge," I said, "is treason against the oracles. And I have never once committed that crime. The same cannot be said of our governing body."

Aza said, "Two seasons ago, Ogra was on the verge of war because the Assembly wanted to release the fates of the fated families to the public, was it not? I read the transcript. You yourself, Lusha, seemed particularly angry about their choice."

"I didn't see a reason to break our traditions," Lusha said stiffly.

"That act," Teka said, "of needlessly declaring all the fates to the general public, resulted in the kidnapping of an oracle of our planet, and culminated in the very war that we're in right now. The Assembly sowed the seeds for this war by defying the oracles. And now they want to crush us because of it?"

I didn't know if she was making any headway. I wasn't good at reading faces. Nevertheless, she persisted:

"The Assembly is threatened by any planet that is fate-faithful," Teka said. "It started with us, but don't think it will end with us. Tepes, Zold, Essander, Ogra—all the fate-faithful planets are at risk. If they can call us backward and orchestrate a war to get rid of us, they can do it to you. We all have to stand together if we want to keep their power limited, as it should be."

I tried to read Rokha and Lusha's body language—I was not so poor at that—but it was difficult without understanding Ogran culture better. Rokha's hands were folded neatly on the table in front of them. Lusha's arms were crossed. Surely not a good sign, in any culture.

I cleared my throat. "I have an idea, before we even get that far."

Everyone turned toward me, Teka with her mouth puckered.

"I have met Isae Benesit, Chancellor of Thuvhe. She spent days with Shotet renegades when she was in Voa. She *just* sent someone to Ogra to talk about an alliance. She knows that we are not the same as Lazmet Noavek." I lifted my shoulder. "It's not Shotet that's the problem for her; it's the current regime. And we are in agreement on that point."

"First you say it's the Assembly waging this war, and then it's just Isae Benesit?" Lusha demanded. "Which is it?"

"It's both," I said. "The Assembly is using Isae Benesit for a reason—they want to follow the law. They won't attack without

cause. So if Thuvhe won't attack us, the Assembly has no inter-
mediary through which to wage war. The conflict dissipates.
Appease Isae, and we appease the Assembly. Unseating Lazmet
would appease Isae."

"Let me guess," Teka said. "Your proposed solution is to kill
him."

I wasn't sure how to answer, so I didn't try.

"You Noaveks," she said. "Always eager to draw blood."

"I refuse to choose a complicated solution just because it leaves
my hands clean," I snapped. "I have been urging you all to take
Lazmet Noavek seriously since his face first appeared on screens
across the galaxy. He is powerful and he holds half of Shotet in his
fist. If he is dead, we can reclaim our people and negotiate a peace.
Until he is dead, peace will be impossible."

I was sitting like my mother, I realized. Back straight, hands
folded, legs crossed at the ankles. Perhaps she was not my mother
by blood, but I carried more of her in me than I carried of the oracle who had traded me for the sake of fate. I had not ceased to be
a Noavek. It was not often a comfort, but in this situation, where
strength was required, I did not disparage it.

Rokha bobbed their head a few times.

"I think there is a solution here that suits all of us," they said.
"Miss Noavek, since this is your idea, we will arrange for you to
propose your solution to Chancellor Benesit herself, on a secure
feed. In the meantime, we will open discussions—Shotet and
Ogra both—with Tepes, Zold, and Essander. Just to explore our
options. Lusha?"

"*Discussions*, only," Lusha said, jabbing the table in front of her
with one finger. "Covert ones. We don't want the Assembly to

think we are planning some kind of rebellion."

"We can send our envoys on delivery vessels as they exit the planet's atmosphere," Aza said. "The Assembly hardly pays attention to Ogra to begin with—they won't be checking your flight ledgers."

"Fair," Lusha said. "We are agreed, then. Miss Noavek, we will arrange for you to speak to the Chancellor of Thuvhe within a week."

I felt my pulse in my fingertips. I needed time, more time than I could ask for, more time than they could give me. And even with time, could I really plan to assassinate my own father—could I even do it successfully, given what had happened when I made the attempt on Ryzek's life?

If you can't do it, no one can, I reminded myself. *If you can't do it, we're done for anyway, so you may as well try.*

When I stood, it was on steady feet, and with steady hands. But I felt anything but steady.

CHAPTER 32 | CYRA

TEKA AND I RETURNED to the small apartment to which
Aza had assigned us. It was a single room, with a stove half as
wide as the one I had used on the sojourn ship—I thought of
its permanent splatters with a sharp pang that made me hesitate with my jacket buttons—and a bathroom we couldn't both
stand in at the same time. Still, there was a little desk where I
read late at night, when Teka turned away from the light. She
kept tools and wires and computer parts in a box in the corner,
and built little things in her spare time, little remote control
vehicles with wheels, or a hanging ornament that sparked when
the wind blew.

She stripped off her jacket as soon as we were through the
door, and tossed it on the bed, its sleeves inside out. I was more
careful with mine, undoing each metal button with both hands.
The luminous thread was stitched around each buttonhole, keeping it from tearing—a finely made thing, it was, and one I hoped
I would get to keep.

Teka was over at my desk, touching her fingers to the page I had left open with a notebook beside it.

"'The family Kereseth is one of the oldest of the fated families—arguably the first, though they have never expressed much interest in debating that point. Their fates rarely, if ever, guide them toward leadership positions, but rather to sacrifice or, more mysterious still, seemingly unremarkable destinies.'" Teka frowned. "Are you translating this from Ogran yourself?"

I shrugged. "I like languages."

"Do you *speak* Ogran?"

"I'm trying to learn it," I said. "Some scholars say it's more poetic than most languages—has more rhyming or near-rhyming sounds. I prefer Shotet for poetry, personally, because I don't enjoy rhymes, but . . ."

She was staring at me.

". . . I do enjoy the challenge of it. What?"

"You're odd," she said.

"You just built a little machine that makes chirping sounds," I said. "And when I asked you what it was for, you said 'chirping sounds.' And I'm the one who's odd?"

Teka smiled a little. "Fair."

Her gaze returned to the book. I knew she was about to ask me why I was translating the section about the Kereseth family, and maybe she knew that I knew, too, because she never actually asked the question.

"It's not what you think. I'm not looking into them because of *him*," I said. "It's . . ."

I hadn't told anyone what Vara said to me. My Kereseth blood seemed like a secret that ought to be kept. After all, it was the Noavek name that made me useful to the exiles now. Without it, they might dispose of me.

But I had committed worse crimes in front of Teka than having the wrong name, and she was still here. In the past, the idea of trusting another person would have terrified me. But I didn't feel that fear now.

"The oracle told me something," I said.

And I told Teka the story.

"Okay, so you're telling me it doesn't bother you *at all* that Akos ended up being attracted to someone who shares genes with a person he believed to be his sister. And mother." Teka was flopped on the floor, cracking the shells of some kind of Ogran nut—roasted to get rid of its poisonous qualities, of course—with her fingernails.

"I'll say it one more time," I said. "He and I. Are not. Related. At all! In any way!"

I was leaned up against the side of the bed, my arms draped over my bent knees.

"Whatever," Teka said. "Well, at least you aren't actually planning to commit patricide, then. Since Lazmet isn't actually your father."

"You're really fixating on the blood-relationship thing," I said. "Just because we aren't technically related doesn't mean he's not my father. And I say that as someone who would *really* like for him not to be my father."

"Fine, fine." She sighed. "We should probably start planning this whole assassination thing, if you have less than a week before you're talking to Isae."

"We?" I raised my eyebrows. "I'm the one who volunteered for this stupid mission, not you."

"You're obviously going to need my help. For one thing, can you even fly yourself back to Thuvhe?"

"I can fly a ship."

"Through Ogra's atmosphere? I don't think so."

"Okay," I said, "so I need a pilot. And a ship."

"And you need to find out where Lazmet is. And get in, unseen. And figure out how you're going to kill him. And then how you're going to get out afterward." She sat up, and popped the flesh of the nut, stripped of its shell, into her mouth. Tucking it into her cheek, she said, "Face it, you need help. And you're not going to get many volunteers yourself. You may have observed, the exiles aren't exactly wild about you."

"Oh really," I said flatly. "I hadn't noticed."

"Well, they're stupid that way," Teka said, flapping her hand at me. "I'll get you the people you need. They like me."

"Can't imagine why."

She threw the broken shell at me, hitting me in the cheek. I felt better than I had in a long time.

Later that night, after hours of talking ourselves in circles about the assassination plan, Teka fell asleep fully clothed in her bed. I cleaned up the shells—which now covered the floor—and sat at the book of fated families to resume my translation.

The sight of the word *Kereseth*, written in Ogran, sparked heat behind my eyes. I picked up my pen, pausing every few seconds to wipe tears from my eyes or snot from my nose.

I had pretended, with Teka, that I was translating this section of the book to learn more about my own family, that it had nothing to do with Akos.

But the unfortunate truth was that I was still in love with him.

CHAPTER 33 | AKOS

A FEW SEASONS AGO, he'd been dragged into the city of Voa by soldiers of Ryzek Noavek, badly beaten, with his scared brother at his heels. The warm, dusty air had choked him. He hadn't been used to crowds, or the loud laughs of people gathered around food stalls, or all the weapons, tapped casually in the middle of conversation, like they didn't matter.

Now he walked with his palm balanced on the knife sheathed at his waist, without thinking much of it. He had tied a cloth around his nose and mouth, and cropped his hair close to his head, to keep from being recognized by the wrong people. But it didn't seem likely he would be. Most of the people he passed were too focused on getting where they were going to give him more than a quick glance.

There weren't crowds in the streets anymore. Those who were walking did it with heads down, their bags tucked close to their sides. Soldiers dressed in armor stamped with the Noavek seal walked the streets, even the poorer ones at the edge of the city where Akos had gotten off the small transport vessel that had carried him here. Half the little shops were boarded up, or had their doors chained shut. There had obviously been some looting and vandalism in the wake of Ryzek's death—not surprising—but things seemed under control now. Too much control, with Lazmet sitting on the throne.

Akos was getting to know his way around Voa, at least the part of Voa that Ara—Jorek's mother—and Jorek lived in. If the city was arranged in concentric circles around Noavek manor, Ara and Jorek lived with Ara's brother in one of the middle rings, the perfect place to disappear. The apartments were crowded together, each one a different style, with a door in a different place, forming a maze. Akos had stumbled into two courtyards that morning when he left, and had to backtrack to where he started each time.

Ara had sent him to the market to search out flour for her baking, and he'd come up empty. The market had a news feed in one of the stalls, so he'd gone to see if there was any word about Ogra.

He'd left Ogra without saying anything to Cyra, knowing it would make her hate him—that was the point. If she hated him, she wouldn't look for him. She would assume he had gone back to Thuvhe, and leave him be.

Akos had to keep forcing his attention back to the path he was walking instead of what was around him. He passed by a line of people so long he couldn't see what they were waiting for until two blocks later, when he saw a run-down office with the Shotet character for "medicine" above it. A health clinic. Down an adjacent alley, two kids fought over a bottle of something Akos didn't recognize.

A lot of people had been hurt in the attack, and basic supplies like antiseptic or silverskin were limited. Loved ones were always waiting at health clinics, lately, in the hope they might inch closer to what they needed. Still others bought black market "cures" that either didn't do anything or made things worse. Ara and her family had, fortunately, been untouched by the blast.

Akos spotted the wall of graffiti he used as a landmark. The colors were bright, most of the symbols still unintelligible to him, though he recognized the one for Noavek, standing out in the center. He tapped on the wooden door just past it, looking left and right to make sure he was alone. He could still hear the scuffling of the kids in the alley behind him.

Ara's brother's house was packed with junk, like a lot of Shotet houses were, all the furniture pieced together from other things. The drawer handles in the kitchen were made of floater parts, and the knobs on the oven were claw grips from the toy robots Shotet children battled with.

Sitting at the low table on the other side of the room were Ara Kuzar, a bright blue shawl around her shoulders, and Jorek. He had let a full beard grow in on his face, patchy in places, and he wore armor with the seal of Noavek under his shoulder. He looked worn, but he still gave Akos a smile when he walked in.

"I'm sorry, Mrs. Kuzar—no flour," Akos said to Ara. "No news from Ogra, either. I think the Noavek propaganda machine is going strong."

"This affectation of calling me 'Mrs. Kuzar' was cute at first," Ara said wryly. "But it's getting downright alarming. Sit. You need to eat something."

"Sorry," he mumbled, sitting across from Jorek. He pulled the scarf down around his neck, and ran a hand over his shorn hair, still surprised at how short it was. It was prickly in the back. "How's the manor?"

"Boring," Jorek said. "I saw the side of Lazmet's head today. Most of the upper-level guards are stationed near Ryzek's secure rooms—you know, the ones Cyra's blood couldn't get us into. But he walked through the back door today."

Akos logged that information away, along with everything else he'd heard about Lazmet since getting to Voa, which wasn't much. He was a myth in people's minds more than a man, so what they knew sounded like legends and folk tales instead of facts.

"At least I don't have to fight in Thuvhe or anything," Jorek said. "Not that I would. That attack was . . ." He shook his head. "Sorry. Don't mean to bring it up."

Akos tucked a hand into his pocket and took out a strip of dried hushflower petal. He was chewing them more than he should these days. He would run out soon. But the tension in his jaw and shoulders was giving him headaches, and he needed to be able to think, if he wanted to face what was next.

He was here, in Voa, to kill Lazmet Noavek. And it wouldn't be easy.

"There's something I need to talk to you about," Akos said.

"I was wondering when you'd get to the point," Jorek said.

Ara set a plate down in front of Akos. There wasn't much on it—a roll, probably a little stale by now, some dried meat, some pickled saltfruit. She brushed the crumbs off her fingers and sat down next to her son.

"What Jorek means is, we like having you here, but we know you don't do things without a good reason," Ara said, flicking the side of her son's nose to chastise him. "And crossing the galaxy is no small thing."

Jorek rubbed his nose.

"Not everyone can wait things out on Ogra. Some of us have to get our hands dirty," Akos said.

"But those who can stay safe, should," Ara said.

Akos shook his head. "I had to get my hands dirty, too. Call it . . . fate."

"I call it a choice," Jorek said. "And a dumb one."

"Like leaving your girlfriend—and your mother and brother—without a word of explanation," Ara said, and she clicked her tongue.

"My mother and brother don't need me to leave word to know where I am. And this is how things are between Cyra and me," Akos said, defensive. "She plotted for weeks to send *me* away without telling me about it. How is this different?"

"It is not particularly different," Ara said. "But that doesn't make it right, either time."

"Don't scold him, Mom," Jorek said. "He was basically born scolding himself."

"Scold me all you like," Akos said. "Especially because I'm about to ask for something you won't like."

Jorek's arm snaked across the table, and he stole some meat from Akos's plate.

"I want you to let me into the back gate of Noavek manor," Akos said.

Jorek choked on the meat he was now chewing, prompting Ara to thump him on the back with her fist.

"What are you going to do once you're inside?" Ara said, narrowing her eyes.

"It's better if you don't know," Akos said.

"Akos. Trust me. Even you, pupil of Cyra Noavek, are out of your depth with Lazmet," Jorek said, after he had swallowed his bite. "There isn't a single shred of decency in him. I don't think he even has the capacity for it. If he finds you, he'll turn you into a goddamn stew."

"He won't kill me," Akos said.

"Why, because of your stunning good looks?" Jorek snorted.

"Because I'm his son," Akos said.

Ara and Jorek stared at him in silence.

Akos pushed his plate across the table, toward Jorek.

"Want my roll?" he said.

CHAPTER 34 | AKOS

AKOS RID HIMSELF OF the heavy robe he had worn to get there, tossing it in an alley. It would only slow him down past this point, and he was cloaked by night, anyway.

He kept his footsteps as quiet as he could as he crept along the high wall behind Noavek manor. He still remembered staring out at this wall when he was a prisoner, teaching Cyra to make pain-killers. It had been his way out: Go through the hidden hallways. Get to Eijeh. Leave through the back gate, using the code Cyra had showed him without meaning to.

He could have pried open the locking mechanism himself and shoved his fingers inside, disrupting the current, but the risk of getting caught was too high. The guard changed too often. So instead he stood by the back door and waited for Jorek to open it.

It had taken a lot of arguing to get Jorek to agree to this. Not just with Jorek, but with Ara. They suspected, of course, what Akos was here to do, and they didn't want him to take the risk. They thought it was bravado, or stupidity, or downright instability.

Eventually, it was the reminder of what Akos had done for

Jorek that got him to agree. The ring that hung around his neck, and the precise mark on his arm. Jorek had owed him a favor. A big one.

The heavy door opened a crack, showing a sliver of a man—boots, armor, patchy facial hair, and a bright, dark eye.

Jorek jerked his head to the side, beckoning, and Akos opened the door just wide enough to slip through. Once it closed behind him with a click, he knew he couldn't go back. So, even though he halfway thought he'd lost his mind, he kept going forward.

As agreed, Jorek got him to the kitchen. Akos found the edge of the wall panel that would let him into the manor's hidden passageways, and pulled it back. The familiar musty smell washed over him, sending him into memory. Terrified and desperately hopeful, with the toe of Eijeh's shoe catching on his heel. And then, that little pool of heat in his gut as he followed a painted Cyra to the Sojourn Festival, the one that told him he liked her, no matter how hard he pretended otherwise.

Liked her, then loved her. Then left her.

Jorek pulled him into a hug, quick and firm, before leaving Akos alone in the dark passageway.

He stopped at the corners where the walls split, feeling for the symbols he had learned from Cyra. An X for a dead end. A circle with an up arrow for stairs going up, and a circle with a down arrow for stairs going down. A number for which floor he was on.

He had gone this way when he went to free Eijeh. All he had to do was get to that part of the house again, and then he'd be near the gene-locked rooms that had confounded the renegades when they came here to kill Ryzek. Cyra's blood hadn't opened the locks, but Akos's would, if Vara wasn't screwing with them both.

Akos got to the exit he'd taken when he got Eijeh out. He knew he was tripping the same sensors that had made his escape attempt fail on that fateful day, but it didn't really matter; he wasn't trying to go unnoticed here. He left the panel open behind him and walked past the door that had once been Eijeh's with a little shiver.

Even in the dark, this part of the house was grand. Dark wood, almost black, on the floor and the walls. Light fixtures packed with fenzu, sedate now as they slept through the night. Decorative vases and sculptures, made of warm metal or polished stone with veins of color running through it, or etched glass. He couldn't imagine running through these halls as a kid, skimming the wood paneling with his fingers. He probably wouldn't have been allowed to run, or touch walls, or fall on his brother laughing, or any of the things that had made his young years rich and warm.

He got to the secure door that he was pretty sure led to Ryzek's old bedroom, and held up his hand over the locking mechanism. His fingers were trembling.

He stuck his hand in the lock, wincing as it pierced his finger, drawing blood.

A click, and then the door opened.

If there had been any doubt in his mind that he was a Noavek, it was gone now.

CHAPTER 35 | CYRA

IT WAS, PERHAPS, NOT the best idea for Teka to approach me during breakfast, before my brain had booted up.

I was hunkered down over my bowl of grains and fruit, watching Eijeh. He sat two tables away, facing me, with his own plate of food in front of him. But there was something odd about him. He was poking at the grains with his spoon, picking out the darker ones and putting them in a line along the edge of his tray. When I first saw Eijeh a few seasons ago, snuffling in the Weapons Hall before my brother, he had been filled out and tall; he had looked sturdy, though not overweight. But this Eijeh was pecking at breakfast, and there were still hollows in his cheeks.

"Uh," Teka said. "Why are you staring so hard at Kereseth?"

She stood in front of me, partially blocking my view of the new oracle. I didn't look away, though, still watching Eijeh jab at his bowl.

"My mother told me, once, that she used to scold Ryzek for being a picky eater," I said. "He ate fruit, but little else. And no matter what she put in front of him, he found something to pick at. She hoped he would grow out of it, but . . ." I shrugged. "I don't think he ever really did."

"Okay," Teka said. "Did an Ogran give you some xofra venom? I've heard it addles the mind."

"No. It's nothing, never mind," I said. I looked up at her. "You know, when you stand like that, you look even shorter."

"Shut up," Teka said. "I found you some volunteers. Come on over."

I sighed, and picked up my bowl. My boots were still untied, so the laces flapped with each footstep. Teka led me to a table in the corner, where two other people sat: Yssa, and the man I had fought weeks ago, with the knot of hair on top of his head. Ettrek.

"Hey there, Scourge," he said to me. He had the kind of face that didn't give away his age, skin smooth but not layered with the pudge of youth, dark eyes glittering with mischief.

I didn't like him.

"No," I said to Teka. "I'm not working with this idiot."

"My name is pronounced 'Ettrek,'" he said, grinning.

"Listen, it's not like you have a deep pool of applicants, here," Teka said to me. "Ettrek knows people in Voa who can get us whatever supplies we need, as well as give us a place to land."

"And you?" I said to Yssa. "You're Ogran. Why do you want to get mixed up in all this?"

"I am a good pilot," Yssa said. "As to why I want to be involved, well. I have lived among people affected by Lazmet Noavek for several seasons now, and if there is something I can do to help defeat him at last, I will do it."

I looked them over. Teka, her blond hair made frizzy by the

Ogran humidity. Yssa had glowing bracelets up to one elbow, and she had lined her eyes in luminous pencil, so they glowed oddly. Ettrek waggled his dark eyebrows at me. Was this the crew I would march back into Voa with, triumphant?

Well. It was the best I was going to get.

"Fine," I said. "When do we leave?"

"I'll check the launch schedule, but it had better be sometime this week," Teka said. "It'll take a few days to get to Urek. Once we're through the atmosphere, I can send a message to Jorek in Voa, and get a better sense of the situation. And Ettrek can reach out to his contacts. But we can't do any of that from here."

"All right," I said.

"Hold on," Ettrek said. "What qualifies you to be in charge of this mission, anyway?"

"I'm better than you," I said. "At everything."

Teka rolled her eyes. "She knows the target, Trek. You want to charge into Voa to kill a man you don't understand or know at all?"

Ettrek shrugged. "Guess not."

"Everybody take this week to do what you need to get done," Teka said. "I'll start getting the ship ready now. I might need a new gravity compressor, and I know we need food."

"And," I said, thinking of what Isae had used to kill my brother, "maybe some new kitchen knives."

Teka wrinkled her nose, likely remembering the same thing. "Definitely."

"Anyway, we might not be coming back, so . . ." I shrugged. "Say your good-byes."

"You're just bursting with optimism, aren't you," Ettrek said.

"Did you expect the person leading your assassination mission to be cheerful?" I said. "If so, I think you're in the wrong field." I set my half-finished bowl of breakfast down, and drew the knife at my hip instead. I leaned across the table and pointed the blade at him. "And by the way, if you call me 'Scourge' again, I will cut that stupid knot right off the top of your head."

Ettrek licked his lips, considering my knife.

"Okay," he finally said. "Cyra."

CHAPTER 36 | CISI

I WATCH OUR DESCENT through Othyr's puffy clouds like I'm even farther away than I am, drifting through space and looking down at the entire planet at once. I've felt like this since Akos and I parted ways, halfway between Ogra and Thuvhe. He didn't want to come with me back to Assembly Headquarters, and I didn't much blame him, so I'd hitched myself to the next Assembly freighter at some moon outpost and let him take the autonav back home. Truth be told, I am jealous of him, puttering around our warm kitchen, stoking the burnstones in our courtyard stove.

Ast comes to stand next to me, arms folded.

We're on a big Assembly craft, the nice, sleek kind they save for chancellors and regents and sovereigns. You can't see any of the ship's guts—they're all hidden behind panels made of a pale metal that looks almost white. I tripped earlier and when I smacked my hand against a wall to steady myself, I left a handprint. *Whose job is it to polish all the walls?* I wonder.

Ast and I are both dressed up, or as "up" as Isae could get us to go. I wear a dress with long sleeves—so I look Thuvhesit, I figure, because Othyrians aren't as determined to button everything up to the throat as we are—in a soft gray. Ast is in trousers and a shirt with a collar. The guide bot whizzes around his head, clicking so he can hear its location.

"Isae's doing it again," he says. "Go fix her."

"I can't stop her all the time," I say. "It's wearing me out."

Since the attack on Shissa, Isae's been going over every single person who died in the attack on her screen. She keeps spitting facts at me, too. *Shep Uldoth, thirty-four. He was a father of two, Cisi. His wife died, too, so now the kids are orphans.* As much as I told her she couldn't dwell on the lives lost forever, she didn't pull herself away. She said she liked the anger going through the names gave her. It reminded her of what she had to do.

I'm pretty sure she's just tired of grieving for Ori, and needs something else to focus on, but I don't say so.

"I don't really care if you're worn out," Ast says coolly. "You don't think this is wearing *her* out? It's more important that she be rested than you, you know."

I want to curse him out, but my currentgift stops me. So I just ignore him until he storms off.

The ship passes through the cloud layer, and I can't keep myself from stepping closer to the glass. I've never been to Othyr before.

Most of the planet's surface is covered with cities. There are a couple of big parks that cultivate the planet's wildlife—feeble, most of it, which was why Othyrians hadn't much bothered with it—but the rest is glass and metal and stone. Glass walkways stretch this way and that, connecting the buildings, and sleek little floaters, much nicer than the ones we flew in Thuvhe, dart in and out of metal tubes that control traffic.

So it's hard to explain to myself, given all that synthetic chaos, why Othyr is pretty. Maybe it comes down to the big blue sky, the sunlight gleaming on the buildings in gold, green, blue, and orange. Maybe it's the neat little parks that show all different colored flowers and trees, the best-looking plants from every other planet but this one. But there is something nice in how busy it is, a kind of cheerful productivity.

I clasp my hands in front of me as I walk down the hall, so I don't brush any of the walls. Isae is sitting in a waiting room, perched on the edge of a gray sofa. A view of Othyr shows through the floor-to-ceiling window, but she's not even glancing at it. Her eyes are fixed on the portable screen in her hands.

"Arthe Semenes. Fifty years old. She was visiting her kid in the hospital after surgery. Both of them are dead now." She shakes her head. "A hospital, Cisi. Why did they have to target a hospital?"

"Because Lazmet Noavek is evil," I say. "We knew that before, and we know it now, and we'll never forget it."

I am filling the room with calming water. Letting it lap up against her ankles, tap against her toes.

"He's not the only one who made it happen," she says. "Every Shotet who went along with him and didn't stop it is to blame."

"We're landing," I say. She's not wrong, but the heat she says it with makes me nervous. I imagine wading up to my waist, dragging my fingers through the soft weight of water.

"When's the meeting?"

"It's over dinner," I say. "They don't like strict business meetings here, apparently."

"Wouldn't want to let a person focus on the issues at hand," she says. "Gotta dazzle them into doing whatever you say instead."

"Exactly," I say. She sounds more like herself already. She gets up, sets the screen down, and crosses the little room to stand in front of me.

"Did Ast yell at you again?" she says, brushing her fingers over my face. "He seemed upset when he left. I don't know why he takes it out on you."

I shrug. It's the best I can manage.

"I'll talk to him again," she promises. "I trust you, and so should he, even if he doesn't like your currentgift. It's not like I don't know when you're using it."

I smile. She doesn't, of course, always know when I'm using it. But it's good that she thinks so.

CHAPTER 37 | AKOS

THE ROOM BEYOND THE gene lock smelled like fruit. Akos let the door close behind him, breathing the acid sweetness. This wasn't Ryzek's bedroom—it was an office. And the desk had some kind of peel on it, green and puckered, the source of the smell. Beside it was a dormant screen on top of a stack of paper. Books were stacked here and there, with titles he mostly couldn't read, unless they were in Othyrian. Those were all about history.

The rug under his feet was thick and dense. Comfortable to stand on. There were footprints pressed into it, back and forth, like somebody had been pacing not too long ago. Growing in a pot in the corner was a little tree, its trunk the same dark color as the floorboards. A tree native to the band of forests north of Voa, its leaves robust and healthy.

Akos felt a squeeze in his head, like he was getting a headache, and ignored it. He moved instead toward the map that hung on the wall behind the desk, a map of the solar system. Their planet was marked "Urek" instead of "Thuvhe," so he knew it was a Shotet-drawn map. The lines were careful, precise, and faded to light sketch marks at the edges, marking the boundaries of where the Shotet had gone. They were wider than Akos expected. Somehow it had never really struck him that before the Shotet became scavengers and warriors, they had been explorers.

He felt the squeeze in his head again, and paused. He had heard something. A shift, maybe, someone walking in another room, on another floor.

No, not a shift—a breath. An exhale.

Akos drew his blade and whipped around, arm extended. Leaning against the wall behind him was a tall, thin, weathered man.

Lazmet Noavek.

"My currentgift doesn't work on you," Lazmet said.

Akos's mouth went dry.

"No currentgifts work on me," he forced himself to say. The first words he'd ever said to *his father.*

Lazmet pulled away from the wall. He was holding a current-blade of his own. As Akos watched, he balanced it on his palm and spun it, catching it by the handle. So Ryzek had learned that little habit from his father, then.

"Is that how you got in here?" Lazmet said.

Akos shook his head. Lazmet stepped closer, and Akos shifted to the side, keeping distance between them. He felt like he was in the arena again, fighting another man to the death. Only he was much less prepared for this fight than he'd been for the one with Vas, or Suzao.

He never should have come here. He knew that now. Just looking at Lazmet in person, empty behind the eyes, calm and faintly amused . . . there was something not right about him.

Something Akos didn't understand.

"Then I admit to some confusion, because I'm the only person who can access these rooms," Lazmet said. "So I know that while someone might have let you into the manor, they could not have let you in here."

"My blood got me in," Akos said.

Lazmet's eyes narrowed. He came closer. Akos had run out of space behind him, so he shifted again, knife still outstretched. Lazmet eyed the blade curiously—he probably wasn't used to seeing a currentblade without the black tails binding it to a person's hand.

"I began to suspect, when my youngest child grew older, that she was not actually mine," Lazmet said quietly. "I thought maybe her mother had been unfaithful to me, but I see now that isn't the case. She was just the wrong child entirely."

Akos didn't understand how he wasn't more shocked. More *startled*, at least.

"What is your name?" Lazmet asked him, spinning his current-blade.

"Akos," Akos said.

"That is a fine Shotet name," Lazmet said. "I assume my wife chose it for you."

"I wouldn't know," Akos said. "I never knew her."

Lazmet came closer still, and then lunged. Akos was ready for it, had expected it since he saw the man against the wall. But he wasn't ready for how fast Lazmet was, grabbing him and twisting so hard Akos had no choice but to release the blade. Akos's training kicked in, and he feinted, pretending at weakness while swinging a fist at Lazmet's side. Lazmet grunted, his grip still hard around Akos's wrist, and Akos kicked him hard in the knee.

Lazmet let go of him then, stumbling a little. But not enough. He surged up and forward, slamming Akos into the wall with the currentblade at his throat. Akos froze. He was pretty sure Lazmet wouldn't kill him, at least not until he heard an explanation, but that was no guarantee that he wouldn't carve Akos up in the meantime.

"It's a shame you didn't know her. She was quite a woman," Lazmet said casually. He lifted his free hand and ran his fingertip down the side of Akos's nose, onto his cheekbone.

"You look like me," Lazmet said. "Tall, but not broad enough, with these accursed *freckles*. What color are your eyes?"

"Gray," Akos said, and he felt compelled to add "sir" to the end, though he wasn't sure why. Maybe it had to do with the knife at his throat and the substantial strength of the man pressing him to the wall. It seemed to hum in Lazmet's bones like a piece of the current itself.

"That would be my mother's side of the family," Lazmet said. "My uncle wrote love poems about my aunt's stormy eyes. My mother killed them both. But I'm sure you've heard that story already. I understand it's a popular one in Shotet."

"I've heard it mentioned." Akos fought to keep his voice steady.

Lazmet released him, but didn't go far, so Akos couldn't make a dive for the weapon on the floor.

"Do you know if my son is dead?" Lazmet said. He quirked his eyebrows. "I suppose I mean my *other* son."

"Yes, he's dead," Akos said. "His body is in space."

"A decent enough burial, I suppose." Lazmet spun his blade again. "And did you come to kill me? It would be in the grand tradition of our family, you see. My mother killed her siblings. My supposed daughter killed her brother. My firstborn son lacked the stomach for killing me, in the end—he was content to trap me in a cell for several seasons instead. But you wear some marks, so perhaps you are not so weak-willed."

Akos clapped his hand around his wrist, to cover up the kill marks there. It was an instinct that seemed to confuse Lazmet, who tilted his head at the sight.

Akos wasn't sure what the answer was anymore. He knew Lazmet needed to die, based on the way Cyra reacted to the sight of him alone, and everything he'd heard since then. But he hadn't been sure, deep down, if he could do it or not. He still wasn't sure. Regardless, he wasn't about to admit that to Lazmet.

"No," Akos said. "I didn't come to kill you."

"Then why did you come?" Lazmet said. "You took great risks to do so. I assume you have a reason."

"You're—you're the last blood relative I have left," Akos said.

"Is that a reason? It's a stupid one, if it is," Lazmet said. "What is blood, exactly? Just a substance, like water or stardust."

"It's more than that to me," Akos said. "It's—this language. It's fate."

"Ah!" Lazmet smiled. His smile had a wickedness to it. "So now you know that little Cyra's painfully boring fate actually belongs to you. 'The second child of the family Noavek will cross the Divide.'" His eyebrow arched. "And you, I assume, as a born Shotet, have never been across the stretch of feathergrass that separates us from our Thuvhesit enemies."

Lazmet was analyzing him, making assumptions. They were incorrect, but Akos saw no need to correct him. Not yet, anyway.

The less Lazmet knew about him, the better.

Lazmet went on: "You speak with the diction of someone who is low status. Perhaps you think I will send you to Thuvhe with my army, for some higher purpose. That I will elevate you beyond your grasp."

Akos kept his expression neutral, though the idea of marching into Thuvhe and waging war just to attain a higher social status sickened him.

"Whether I help you with that or not depends, I suppose, on whether you are worth anything to me or not," Lazmet said. "I know that you can kill, which is encouraging. You can't imagine how difficult it was to train Ryzek to take lives. He threw up after the first time. Disgusting. And my wife forbade me from attempting the same with Cyra, though I hear she had a greater capacity for it, in the end."

Akos blinked at him. What did you say to a man who was deciding whether your life was worth living right to your face?

"You seem to have some meager fighting skill. You're bold, though unwise at best, and stupid at worst." Lazmet tapped the tip of his blade against his chin. "Your currentgift intrigues me, but it is . . . troubling, in some respects. Tell me about your marks, boy."

The part of Akos that had been stalled, like a bad motor, started rumbling again.

"You think you'll know something useful about me based on who I've killed and how?" Akos said. "What about you—what if I judged your worth based on the fact that your weak-willed son managed to trap you somewhere for seasons?"

Lazmet's eyes narrowed.

"My son was coached by his mother into winning the loyalty of some strategically placed soldiers," Lazmet said. "The ability to win hearts is not one I have ever possessed, I will admit that now. They kept my imprisonment secret, and guarded me faithfully— from a distance, so I couldn't use my gift against them. But the chaos in Voa following my son's murder resulted in a loss of power in some sectors, and I took my opportunity to escape. All my former guards are now dead. I have their eyeballs in a jar to remind me of my own weakness. It was my own failure that resulted in my captivity, not my son's success." He stepped back. "Now tell me the names you wear on your arm, boy."

"No," Akos said.

"I am getting bored with you," Lazmet said. "And trust me, you don't want me to be bored. Even without my currentgift, it would be simple for me to kill you."

"The last life I took was Vas Kuzar's," Akos said.

Lazmet nodded. "Impressive," he said. "You know, of course, that I can look up his death in the arena records and find out the name you used?" He stepped closer again, and brought his knife up between them. "You must also have realized that waiting for you outside this door are many guards. You will not leave this house alive, if you try to leave it. And given how you entered this room, in the dead of night, with a knife, I am hardly going to allow you any freedom within these walls. Which means you will be imprisoned here, and I will have ample time to find out everything I need to know about you."

"I realize all those things," Akos said. "But I didn't fight Vas in the arena. I fought him in the chaos while your son died. There's no record of his death anywhere."

Lazmet smiled. "And you have more than one mark on your arm. How encouraging, to realize that you are not a complete idiot. Congratulations, Akos Noavek. You are not boring."

Lazmet lurched forward and opened the door before Akos could move an izit. Armored guards filled the small office.

"Take him to a secure room," Lazmet said. "Don't hurt him for sport. He's my blood."

Akos went quietly, Lazmet's hollow expression following him all the way down the hall.

CHAPTER 38 | CYRA

I HAD TO LEAVE the relative safety of Shotet-exile-occupied Galo and return to Pokgo for the conversation with Isae Benesit. The one I had promised the Ogran leaders I would have, in exchange for them delaying our deportation. The immediate future of Shotet, in other words, was resting on my shoulders.

Not that I felt any pressure, or anything.

In Pokgo, in the forest just outside the city limits, was a high tower built into the trunk of a massive tree, the only place where a person could broadcast off-planet. On the journey, I pestered Lusha's assistant for information about why that was possible, why at that location and nowhere else, and all he knew was that there was a "soft spot" in Ogra's atmosphere there.

"That a scientific term?" I asked. "'Soft spot'?"

"Obviously not," the man retorted. "Do I look like an atmospheric scientist to you?"

"You *look* like a person with a brain who lives on this planet," I said. "How is it you aren't curious?"

He didn't have an answer to that, so I got up and walked the

perimeter of the ship, pausing at each plant behind glass to scru-
tinize it. There was the rippled, brain-like fruit that hung heavy
from sturdy vines; the cluster of beakish purple leaves that had
two rows of teeth just past their edges; the tiny, starburst-shaped
fungi that glowed purple and stuck to your skin if you touched
it, leeching nutrients from your body. I wondered if, deep in the
jungles here, there were plants that had not yet been discovered—
how many possibilities were there on this unexplored planet,
packed to the brim with the grotesque and the fierce alike?

We reached the tower within the day, the ship touching down
on a landing pad cradled between two huge branches. I stood just
outside the ship, staring at the wide tree with the tower built into
its hollowed trunk. I had never seen a plant so large in my life—it
was as large in circumference as the taller buildings in Voa, but
those had been constructed by our hands, not the buzz of natural
life that some said came from the current.

I crossed the platform that led from the landing pad to the
tower. It swayed a little under my weight, two wires the only
things keeping me from toppling over the side. My mouth grew
drier with each step, but I forced myself to keep moving. Lusha's
assistant gave me a knowing smile as he checked in with the guard
by the door.

In order to get into the broadcasting room, I had to submit to
a brief search—the guard seemed unwilling to touch me, and I
didn't reassure her—and climb several flights of stairs. At the top
of the steps, I paused to dab my hairline—now moist with sweat—
with the inside of a sleeve, and followed Lusha's assistant in.

The broadcast room was abuzz with people—standing at mon-
itors, bent over panels of switches and buttons, plucking pieces of

fuzz from the round rug in the middle of the room. Fixed sights, like eyeballs attached to stalks, hung upside down from the ceiling right in the center of the space. The rug was dark and didn't have a pattern—I assumed it was there to dampen the sound, as any reflective surface might have echoed. This was the top floor of the tower, so its windows looked out over the top of the tree, where the huge leaves—bigger than I was—flapped against the glass. They were dark purple, almost black, and trapped in mossy vines.

"Ah, there you are," a long-haired sema with what looked like a wad of cloud in hand said to me. It was the sort of thing a person said to someone they already knew, but I didn't know them, so I stared quizzically until they offered an explanation.

"Wasn't sure whether you knew how to paint your face or not," they said, in Othyrian. "Looks like all you need is some dust so you don't shine. Good."

They brought the white puffy thing down on my face, and pale dust erupted in a cloud around me, making me sneeze. They held up a mirror so I could see that the powder had made my face matte and even.

"Thank you," I said.

"Stand on the X," they said. "They're hailing the Assembly ship now."

"Good," I said, though I wasn't sure I believed it was good at all. I was about to talk to a woman who thought I was complicit in the murder of her twin sister, after all. And I was going to ask her to cooperate? Compromise?

This was not going to go well.

Still, I made my way to the little X on the rug marked with iridescent tape, and looked up at the sights. Someone near the wall tapped a button a few times to lower them, so the sights were at my eye level. A screen lowered in front of me, to show me Isae Benesit, when she appeared. For now, the screen was a blank white, waiting to be filled with an image.

Soon enough, Lusha's assistant was announcing that they had made the connection with Othyr, and were about to broadcast. He counted down in Othyrian, and then Isae Benesit's scarred face flickered to life in front of me. Pain coursed through my hands, intensifying in my knuckles, which felt like they were breaking. I blinked away tears.

For a moment, she just stared at me, and I stared back.

She looked . . . unwell. She was thinner than she had been when I last saw her, and the skin under her eyes had purpled, even through the layer of makeup she was surely wearing to cover it. Beyond those obvious signs, though, there was something . . . *off*. There was a wildness to her gaze that hadn't been there the last time she looked at me, like she was about to fly apart.

This was the woman who had killed hundreds of my people—a shell of a woman, with flight in her eyes.

"Chancellor Benesit," I said finally, my jaw tense.

"Miss Noavek," she replied, in a clipped, formal voice that didn't quite belong to her. "I suppose I shouldn't say 'sovereign,' since your own people can't agree on one, can they?"

I decided not to tell her that even the exiles didn't want me as a leader—that they called me oruzo, "successor"; that they blamed me for all the people *she* had killed; that I was only standing here to correct some of my own mistakes. But I felt those truths pulsing inside me like another heart. I was no sovereign.

I said, "My people are divided, as you would know if you

regarded us with any decency at all. As for my legitimacy, I am one of two viable heirs to the sovereignty. You may feel free to deal with the other one, if you'd prefer it."

She looked at me for a moment, almost as if she was considering it. But her resignation was evident on her face. Much as she hated me, I was the only supposed Noavek who offered either of our nations hope for peace.

Bolstered by that confidence, I straightened.

Isae cleared her throat, and said, "I agreed to this call because I was assured you had a worthwhile offer for me to consider. I suggest you make it before I decide this is not worth my time."

"I'm not here to beg at your feet," I snapped. "If you'd rather continue down your path of rampant destruction, there's really nothing I can say to stop you, so—"

"*My* path of rampant destruction," she said, with a mirthless laugh. And then another, longer peal of laughter. "Hundreds of *my people*—"

"Were killed by my father and his loyalists," I said loudly. "Not by me. Not by any of the people here."

"And in his place, you would have done . . . what?" she snapped. "You forget, I've met you, Cyra Noavek. I know your talent for *diplomacy*."

"I would have selected a military target, in accordance with our galaxy's laws," I said. "Of course, I would also have waited to negotiate reasonable peace terms instead of hitting hundreds of fleeing refugees with advanced Pithar weaponry—"

"I didn't know there were refugees on board," she said, her voice suddenly hushed.

I had thought, once, that Isae reminded me of shale, hard and jagged. And she was shale now, too, easily broken into fragments. A shudder went through her before she went on, as if that broken moment hadn't happened at all.

"I offered you terms of surrender, as you recall," she said. "You refused them."

"What you offered," I said, my voice trembling with rage, "was insulting and disrespectful, and you knew full well we would not accept it."

I stared into the sight instead of at her image on the screen, though I could see her stony expression just beyond its eye.

"Your offer, Miss Noavek," she said finally.

"What I want is for you to drop this *request* for the Ograns to kick us off their planet, which would force seasons-old enemies of Lazmet Noavek to return to a war zone," I snapped. "And in return, I will kill him."

"Why am I not surprised that the solution you propose involves murder," she said drily.

"The originality of your insults is truly stunning," I said. "Without Lazmet to lead them, his faction of soldiers will be easily subdued—by us. The exiles will seize control of Shotet, and we can negotiate a peace instead of killing each other."

She closed her eyes. She had gone to great lengths to look older than she was, I noticed, just as I had. She wore a jacket cut in the traditional Hessan style, black and buttoned diagonally across her chest, finishing at the side of her throat. Her hair was pulled back tight, throwing the angles of her face into sharp relief. The scars, too, gave her a maturity that most people at our age didn't have. They said she had survived something, endured something she never should have had to. But despite all those things, she was young. She was young, and wanted all this to stop.

Even if she never understood what she had done to me, to my people, at least we both had that: we wanted this to stop.

"I have to take action," she said, opening her eyes. "My advisers, my people, my allies demand it."

"Then just give me time," I said. "A few weeks."

She shook her head.

"The Shissa hospital *fell from the sky*," she said. "People who needed help, people who——" She choked, and stopped.

"I didn't do that," I said, firm. "We didn't do that."

I realized, too late, that maybe now wasn't the time to insist on my own innocence. Maybe I could have gone further with some sympathy.

But she destroyed the sojourn ship. She attacked us. She deserves wrath.

But maybe I would do better with mercy.

"One week," she said. "That gives you three days after you've made the journey from Ogra to Thuvhe."

"One week," I repeated. "To get from Ogra to Urek, plan an assassination, and carry it out. Are you mad?"

"No," she replied simply. "That's my offer, Miss Noavek. I suggest you take it."

And if I had been softer, kinder, perhaps her offer would have been more generous. But I was who I was.

"Fine," I said. "I'll send you a message when it's done."

And I walked right out of frame.

CHAPTER 39 | CISI

OTHYRIANS HAVE SOFT HANDS. That's the first thing I notice.

Soft hands, and soft bodies. The woman who greets us at the elegant apartments where we'll be staying for this short visit carries more weight around her hips and thighs than most Thuvhesit women. Something about it appeals to me. I wonder what it would feel like, to touch a body with so much give.

Judging by the look she gives me, she's wondering something similar about me. I don't look like a Hessa girl, really—most people from Hessa work the iceflower farms or do some other kind of hard labor, so they're muscled and lean. I'm built more like the people in Shissa, where I went to school, narrow with a store of flesh around the waist. *For the colder months*, people sometimes joked.

Most of those people are dead now.

The Othyrian tells us, in an unctuous voice, where we'll go for dinner and what our "attire" should be like. I very nearly exchange a Look with Ast at that, and then I remember he can't see it——and likely wouldn't want to share a moment like that with me anyway.

Still, I do put on my formal gown for dinner. The one formal thing I own. It's in the Hessan style, which means it looks almost like a military uniform on top, buttoning across my heart from shoulder to ribs. It's tailored tight to my body, down to my waist, and then flows in a softer skirt to the floor. The color is crimson. Hushflower red, for luck.

In the hallway, Ast fusses with the buttons on his cuffs. They're small and made of glass, slippery. I don't think much about it when I take his wrist in mine and do them up for him. I'm surprised he lets me, though.

"She told me I'm being too rough on you," he says to me, his voice hard. The beetle he uses to guide him flies a fast circle around my head and shoulders, close enough to skim my clothes with its little legs, clicking all the while.

"Did she," I say, flat, grabbing his other wrist.

"The thing is—" He seizes my hand, suddenly, and holds me fast. Too hard. Leaning close so I can smell something sharp on his breath. "I don't think I am, Cisi. I think you're too clever, too motivated, and too—*sweet*."

I finish up with his buttons, and walk away without responding. There's not much to say, really.

Isae waits near the doors where the Othyrian woman said she'd meet us. Isae turns, and the sight of her hits me hard, like I've run right into it. Her eyelids are traced with perfect black lines, her lips stained a faint pink. Her hair is pulled back tight, and shines like polished glass. She is dressed in the Osoc style, a body-skimming under layer—dark blue—with loose fabric draped over it, giving hints of her hip's curves when it presses here or there.

"Wow," I say to her.

She rolls her eyes a little, doing a quick slashing gesture with one of her fingers to point out the scars that cross her face. I notice them, of course, every time I look at her, but to me, they don't detract from her beauty. They are just distinct, like a birthmark or a dusting of freckles. I lean in to touch my lips to the one above her eyebrow.

"Still wow," I say.

"And you," she says, glancing at Ast. "Ast, you have never looked more uncomfortable."

"Then I look how I feel," he says stiffly.

The doors slide open in front of us, and standing just beyond them is the Othyrian woman from earlier. I don't remember her name. Most Othyrian names have at least three syllables, which means I forget them right away.

We follow her to a floater that hovers near the edge of the balcony. It's different from the ones back home—more like an enclosed platform than an actual vehicle. We stand together inside it, and the woman—Cardenzia? Something with a "zia," I think— pilots us, by which I mean she presses a button and we zoom toward a preprogrammed destination. The floater doesn't shake or jolt at all, just glides over manicured parks and past gleaming buildings. It lifts us through a layer of wispy clouds, then pauses by a loading dock—I'm not sure what else to call it, though I've never seen a loading dock so fancy in my life. It's also enclosed, since we're high up, and the floors are reflective black tile, as if heavy spacecraft don't have to land on top of them all the time.

Cardenzia, as I've now decided to call her, leads us across the empty dock to a maze of wide hallways, lined with portraits of former Othyrian leaders, or framed flags of all the Othyrian provinces. Doormen wearing black gloves open a set of gilded double doors for us at the end of one such hallway.

I thought I was ready for more Othyrian extravagance, but I have to stop and stare in awe in the next room. Someone cultivated a garden inside this place. Above us, the sunset-light glows through skylights, casting orange-tinted streaks on the dark leaves of vines that wrap around chair legs and creep across the edges of the table. Trees stand in a line on one side of the room, their leaves dark purple and blue, with lighter veins running through them. Strings of light hang from the ceiling—their actual "strings" are near invisible, creating the illusion of glowing orbs that hang like falling raindrops in midair all over the room.

A woman comes over to greet us. I know by the circlet of gold atop her head that she is a ruler of Othyr, and her name falls right out of my head, like my manners. A man follows her, wearing a similar circlet, and another man behind him. All three have even skin and perfect hair and white teeth. The men have facial hair that looks like it was drawn on with a fine-tipped pen.

"Welcome to Othyr!" the woman says, smiling that white, white smile. "Chancellor Benesit, it is a pleasure to meet you at last. Is this your first time visiting our beautiful planet?"

"Yes, it is," Isae replies. "Thank you for hosting us, Councilwoman Harth. These are my advisers, Cisi Kereseth and Ast."

"Ast, no surname?" Councilwoman Harth says.

"No need for surnames in the brim," Ast replies. "Not like we're keeping track of dynasties or anything, Your Grace."

"The brim!" one of the men bellows. "How charming. This must be quite different for you, then."

"Plates are plates, whether they're shiny or not," Ast replies. It's the most I've ever liked him.

"My name is Councilman Sharva," the shorter of the two men says. His hair is black, his mustache curled at the ends. He has a big nose, perfectly straight and narrow through the bridge. "And this is Councilman Chezel. The three of us are in charge of interplanetary cooperation and aid." They want us to use their surnames, then. I guess that's what makes this a business meeting instead of a casual get-together. He continues, "And you, Cisi—are you also from the brim?"

A woman wearing the same black gloves as the men who opened the doors earlier passes out small glasses of something I don't recognize. It smells sharp and tangy. I wait for the Othyrians to drink before I do, so I can see how they manage it. They take dainty sips from the glasses, which are only large enough to be pinched between two fingers. They are etched with swirling designs.

"No," I say. "I'm from Hessa, on Thuvhe."

"Kereseth, was it?" Councilwoman Harth addresses me. "Where have I heard that name before?"

"My family line is fated," I say. "And my mother is the sitting oracle of Thuvhe."

Everybody goes quiet. Even the woman with the tray of glasses—empty now—pauses to look at me before leaving the room. I know Othyrians don't revere the oracles, but I didn't know being related to one was such a scandal.

"Oh," Harth says, lips pursed. "You must have had a very . . . interesting upbringing."

I smile, even though my heartbeat is picking up speed. I won't panic. If anyone can make these people love the daughter of an oracle, it's me.

"Speaking to my mother is a little like trying to grab hold of a fish," I say. "I love her dearly, of course, but I am always relieved to talk with people who are not allergic to specificity."

Chezel laughs, at least, and I send them all a feeling as fine as the softest fabric, gliding over them. I'd be surprised if it didn't work. Othyrians irritate me, but they're not complicated— they're not guarded against people like me, people with gentle voices and titles like "adviser."

"So you are not a fanatic, then," Chezel says. "That is a relief. I was not looking forward to hearing discussion of how we ought to elevate the oracles' position instead of overseeing them."

I want to tell him to eat shit. I want to tell him that having my entire community find out I was destined to get sliced or stabbed someday was a nightmare, that the Assembly's policy of "transparency" was the reason my brothers got kidnapped and my father, killed. But my currentgift won't let me, and I don't really try to force it. They want me to be docile and sweet, so that's what I'll be.

And if Ast glares at me the whole time, well, that's just another thing to ignore.

"You just appeared as if from nowhere, my dear," Harth says to Isae. "Where did your family stash you away?"

"On a pirate ship," Isae says. Harth laughs a tinkling laugh.

Chezel comes toward me, and I see the strategy. Sharva is angled toward Ast, Harth is tackling Isae, and Chezel is on me— they are splitting us up so we can't help each other. For what purpose, I don't know.

"What do you think of Othyr so far?" Chezel asks me.

I sip my drink.

"It's . . . well constructed," I say.

"Whatever do you mean?"

"It's designed to dazzle, and it does," I say. "I come from a place where beauty is harder to see. My eyes are trained to search for it, but here, I guess I can give my eyes a rest."

"I have never been to Thuvhe, I confess," Chezel says. "Is it as cold as they say?"

"Colder than that," I say. "Especially in Hessa, where I am from."

"Ah, Hessa," he says. "'The very heart of Thuvhe.' Is that not what they call it?"

He says the phrase—"the very heart of Thuvhe"—in labored, but accurate, Thuvhesit.

I smile. "But you must know the rest of the quote?"

He shakes his head.

"'Hessa is a land of ill-mannered, poorly groomed, inarticulate dirt-lovers who spit on their hands to wash them,'" I say. "'Yet it is the very heart of Thuvhe.'"

Chezel pauses for a tick, then lets out a loud guffaw. In the pause, I angle my head toward Isae to catch some of her conversation with Harth. Harth is offering condolences for the attack against Shissa. Asking for details.

"Do you find that to be accurate?" Chezel asks me.

"Oh, I don't know," I say airily. "Sometimes we use water to wash our hands, in the warmer months."

Chezel laughs again. I try again to hear what Harth is saying to Isae. But her voice is too quiet, more like a murmur. I'm working so hard to pay attention to her that I keep forgetting about my gift, and I can feel the tension in the room rising like a temperature nobody else can feel but me.

"I meant," Chezel says, voice a little harder now, "do you find Hessa to be a backward place? You are the child of an oracle, after all."

"I'm not sure I understand the connection," I say with some effort. If he gets more antagonistic I won't be able to talk at all, I'll just stand here with my mouth opening and closing like a fish.

"Simply that oracles are a relic of the past, not a reflection of our present," he says. "People on Othyr make their own destinies. Their importance is determined by their industry, not their possession of a fate."

"None of your fellow councilors are from fated families?" I say.

One of his eyes twitches at the corner.

"On the contrary, our elected representative is Councilwoman Harth's cousin. Her segment of the Harth family was not 'favored by fate,' as they say," he says. "That man's fate is not a guarantee of his worth, or his fitness, but traditions do take some time to die."

I nod. I understand now. Councilwoman Harth wants to be in power, but power was given to her cousin instead. She blames it on his fate—and maybe she's right, or maybe he really was the one for the job, I'll never know. But either way, she's jealous, and it sounds like Chezel is, too.

"That must have been difficult for Councilwoman Harth," I say. "As one who seeks to influence, to have that position granted to another in her family."

"There is still time for everyone to get what they deserve," Chezel says.

A bell rings on the far side of the room, signaling us to go to the table for dinner. The gilded plates have place cards on top of them. Isae and I have Harth between us, but Isae plucks Harth's card from its place and swaps it for mine, with a smile. She reaches for my hand, folding our fingers together. It is a clear signal that we're together, but it's also an excuse to change the seating, I'm sure. I play along, my smile shy and my gaze lowered.

We sit, leaves framing our shoulders and lights dancing above our heads. A line of servants emerge from a hidden door on the far side of the room, covered with ivy, and carry plates to us. It's like a dance, all their movements synchronized. I wonder if they have to practice it.

"I forgot to ask, Chancellor, if you or your advisers would like to take advantage of Othyr's excellent doctors while you are here. We offer complimentary health screenings to our distinguished guests," Harth says, as if I am a window between them instead of a body.

"Subpar as Thuvhe's doctors may be," Isae says, voice hard, "we'll pass, thanks."

Her accent is starting to leak into her trained voice, which I know she hates. I split my focus, sending water toward her, and wrapping the others in finery. I have to press hard to feel the tension in the room give, but give it does. Ast glances at me.

"I don't know if Isae—oh, I mean Chancellor Benesit—" I pause, letting myself blush. A nice show for the Othyrians. "I don't know if Chancellor Benesit told you, Councilwoman Harth, but I was in school to be a chemist before I was Her Highness's adviser. I am reasonably good at preparing iceflowers for medicine."

"Are you," Harth says, sounding bored. "How fascinating."

"My research was in the area of breaking down iceflowers to

their basic compounds," I say, layering a heavy, rich fabric over Harth in particular. She appears to need more of my currentgift. "Which I am certain would be useful to Othyr, since it relies on us so heavily for its most potent ingredients."

"Yes," Isae says. "I assume you have still been unsuccessful in cultivating iceflowers here on Othyr?"

"We have, in fact," Harth says. "It seems they will only grow on your planet. It's very strange."

"Ah, well, Thuvhe is an odd little place, always changing," I say. "We are so flattered that you have taken an interest in us."

Isae glances at me sidelong, like she's not sure what I'm angling at. I let my comment dangle, awkward, between Harth and me.

"Of course," Harth says. "We only wish to offer our support."

"What do you mean when you say 'support'?" Ast asks, and for once, I'm glad he's here. He can ask the questions my current-gift won't let me ask.

"Sorry," he says, propping his elbows up on the edge of the table. "I'm no good with manners, or whatever—when I want to know something, I just ask it."

"An admirable quality, Ast," Harth says. It's probably a dig at me, and it stings. "Our intention was actually to ask Chancellor Benesit what Thuvhe needs in this struggle against Shotet. We have a great deal of resources at our disposal."

Ast looks at Isae, and shrugs.

"Weapons," he says.

"Ast." Isae says his name like a warning. "We haven't agreed that's necessary yet."

"I mean, go ahead and dither all you want, Isae," he says. "But eventually we're gonna need to fight back. Pitha gave us one anticurrent blast, and we could use another one, to start. Better ships, too, probably, since Thuvhe's are out of date and slow . . . and can't even carry the damn weapon."

Harth laughs. Chezel and Sharva join in.

"Well," Chezel says. "Those requests don't sound too difficult to grant, do they, Councilwoman?"

"No," she replies with a smile. "We will be happy to give you what you need, provided Chancellor Benesit agrees."

"While I'd prefer it if my advisers would handle things with more delicacy," Isae says, sharp, "Thuvhe does need to protect itself. It would be helpful to have another long-distance weapon to use against Shotet, to keep from having to fight a war on land or in the sky—as a last resort, you understand. Their combat skills are quite advanced, as we all know. And none of our ships are equipped to make use of such a weapon."

"Then it is settled," Chezel says, picking up his glass.

My throat feels tight. I strain against it, fighting to make a sound, any sound. Finally, the only thing I can think to do is to knock my fist against the table. I squeeze Isae's hand, tightly, hard enough to crack her knuckles.

"Wait a moment," Isae says. "Cisi's currentgift unfortunately prevents her from speaking freely in some situations, and she clearly has something to say."

"Thank you," I manage. "I am—curious about something."

"What's that, dear?" Harth says. I don't like her tone. It makes me feel about an izit tall.

"My father told me not to trust any deal where one person gains more than the other," I say. I raise my eyebrow. I can't quite ask the question, but I feel like I've gotten close enough.

"That is a good point," Isae says quietly. "What will Othyr expect in return for its generosity?"

"Is the defeat of a galaxy-wide pest not enough of a reward?" Harth says.

I shake my head.

"There's no precedent for this level of cooperation between us," Isae says. "We maintain a neutral relationship because we depend on each other for the good of both Othyrians and Thuvhesits, but—"

"But we often find ourselves on different sides of particular issues, yes," Harth says.

"Most notably," Sharva says, speaking for the first time. His voice is a rumble, but thin, no richness to it. "Most notably, in the decision to release the fates of the favored lines to the public."

"Yes," Isae says tersely. "A decision that affected my planet disproportionately, as we are possessed of not one, but *three* favored families."

"Nonetheless, Othyr stands behind its decision," Sharva says. "And wishes to press for even greater oversight of the oracles moving forward."

Ast sits back. His face is unreadable. But he doesn't seem uncomfortable, to me. I guess I always just assumed he didn't like me because of my currentgift, but maybe it's my oracle mother, too. Maybe he's on Othyr's side in this whole thing.

"And you want Thuvhe's support," I say. "In exchange for weapons."

It's clear to me now, what the oracle Vara meant. *Don't trust the Othyrians. Don't let her agree to it, whatever you do.* This has to be the "it" she was talking about—a promise of support.

"We would hope that giving Thuvhe support now would encourage you to rethink your position on the oracles," Sharva clarifies. "We know that Thuvhe is not an overly fate-faithful nation-planet; that it, too, wishes to embrace the future of this galaxy, and set it up for success rather than failure."

"What kind of oversight of the oracles are you talking about?" Isae says.

"We simply want to be aware of what the oracles discuss, and what plans they are making given the future they see unfolding," Harth says. "They make decisions on a regular basis that affect all of us. We wish to know what those decisions are. We wish to have access to the information that they possess."

I feel . . . quiet. Not unlike the way I feel when Akos holds my hand, like all the current has gone still around me. In the past few weeks, I saw my own mom manipulate Akos into killing someone, just because she wanted the man gone. I saw her let my oldest friend die when she probably could have prevented it. She says those actions were for the greater good. But what if we don't agree on what that "greater good" is? Should she get to decide without anybody looking over her shoulder?

Even the warning the oracle Vara gave me is manipulation. What future is Vara trying for? Is she working for my best interest, or Thuvhe's, or Ogra's, or the oracles'? *Don't let her agree to it.* Should I listen, or no?

I chew on the inside of my cheek.

"Who will be able to access this information? Anyone who wants it?" Isae asks. "The wide release of the fates didn't turn out well for many on my planet."

"It will be limited, of course, to the Assembly," Harth says.

"We do not want to endanger the public."

Isae's head bobs, slowly.

"I'd like some time to talk this over with my advisers," Isae says. "If you don't mind."

"Of course," Harth says. "Let us eat, and move to lighter topics. We can talk in the morning, when you have made your decision."

Isae inclines her head, agreeing.

CHAPTER 40 | CISI

"Not sure why we even need to talk about this," Ast says gruffly.

We are in Isae's temporary quarters on Othyr. He stands against a wall of light—a window so wide and clean it doesn't seem to be there at all. The sun is setting behind Othyr's glass buildings, the light refracting a dozen times over so the whole city sparkles orange. Right when we got here Ast unbuttoned his cuffs, so now they flap around his wrists whenever he gestures.

I sigh, and rub my temples with both hands. For all that Ast pretends to be a low-class mechanic from the brim, he's not a fool—he knows this isn't some simple exchange, Othyrian aid in exchange for a promise. It's a tipping point for what kind of nation we're going to be. Enemies of Othyr . . . or enemies of the oracles.

And then there's the issue of the weapons.

"I just promised Cyra Noavek time before we pushed Ogra for Shotet deportation," Isae says. "And now you want me to pursue an aggressive response instead of a diplomatic one. That's why we need to talk about it."

"Diplomacy." Ast snorts. "Did Shotet go for a diplomatic solution in Shissa?"

The room is already so tense I can't talk. I feel it like the humid air in a greenhouse, filling my mouth. I try to counter it with a clumsy press of my currentgift, sending the feeling of water everywhere like an overturned bucket. Ast's mouth twists with disgust, and I pull back a little.

"Setting aside the issue of weaponry for a moment," I say gently, "there is also the issue of oracle oversight."

"I don't give a shit if Othyr wants to keep an eye on the oracles," Ast says. "Why do you?"

"That's the problem—that *Othyr* will keep an eye on them, and not anyone else," Isae says. "You don't know these people like I do. Othyr exerts an extraordinary amount of control over the Assembly. If the information gleaned from oracle oversight is only released to the Assembly, it is essentially giving *Othyr* control over the fates instead of the oracles, which is only trading one problem for another."

"You're being indecisive," Ast says. "You've been like this since we were kids. You don't want to do something unless you can practically guarantee its outcome."

I open my mouth, but nothing comes out. Not a word, not a sound. Isae is too focused on Ast to notice me struggling. *Don't let her*, Vara's voice says in my mind. *What the hell am I supposed to do to stop her?* I ask her, in my head. *I can't even talk!*

"I asked you to come here because I thought you would keep me honest," she says to Ast. "But you have to acknowledge that you don't have experience with all this."

"It's because I don't have experience that I can make it clear for you," he says, moving closer.

Water, water, I think. I remember sinking to the bottom of the warm pool in the temple when Mom taught me to swim, how pleasant the light pressure of water around my head had been. A gentle squeeze.

"I don't know politics, it's true," he says, more quietly now. "But I know Shotet, Isae. We both do."

He touches the tips of his fingers to the screwdriver he keeps at his side instead of a knife.

"They took my family from me," he said, "and they took your family from you. They promised a peaceful scavenge, and then resorted to murder and theft. That is who they are."

He holds out his hands, palms up, and she places hers on top of them, letting him squeeze her fingers, gently.

"You promised to give Noavek a week before acting. You didn't promise what action you would take," he says. He's created a kind of bubble around them, and I am not inside it. "If she can't kill Lazmet Noavek, you will have to act, and deportation of Shotet exiles won't be enough. Remember the names? The names you've been reciting?"

Isae blinks tears from her eyes.

"So many people," she says.

"Yes," he says. "Too many people. It can't happen again, Isae. You can't let it."

My face is hot with anger. He is preying on her grief, her sorrow for the loss Thuvhe suffered as well as the loss she herself suffered. She hasn't been right since Ori's death. She's drowning in hurt. And he is taking advantage of that.

"We need stronger weapons," he says. "We can't engage in a land war with the Shotet, because we'll die. I know supporting Othyr might lead to something you don't like. But you won't even get the chance to fight that battle if you don't win this one."

She's nodding at Ast when I slip out of the room. I have to do something about this. And if my currentgift won't let me talk, I'll have to do it another way.

Making contact with Ogra isn't difficult. It's just a matter of finding Cardenzia. I wait until evening settles into night before seeking her out. I touch her arm, gentle, as I explain that my mom is on Ogra visiting the Ogran oracle, and I want to make sure she's all right. I keep my smile wide and I use my currentgift to wrap her in fine fabric, the kind that slides over your skin.

I must be getting stronger with all this practice, because she relaxes right away under its influence, and leads me to the communication tower. Her secure code gets me access to the satellite, and I gush my gratitude—with another touch of cloth.

I sit in the broadcasting chair, which is metal with a rigid back, to keep people from fidgeting while they send their messages. The room is full of technicians, but it doesn't matter. They don't speak Thuvhesit. Othyrians learn more common languages, like Pithar or Trellan, not our silky, windswept tongue.

"This message is for Cyra Noavek," I say to the sight capturing my face and voice. "Isae Benesit is considering aggressive action. Othyr intends to make a play against the oracles, and they have requested Thuvhe's support in exchange for weapons. She's— she's grieving. She's desperate. We all are. And at the heart of her,

I don't think she'll ever believe the word of a Shotet."

I look down.

"You can't fail," I say. "Kill Lazmet Noavek. Don't fail. Transmission complete."

I tap the screen in front of me to begin compressing the recording into the smallest possible data file. The Ogran satellite ship delivers data to Ogra's surface once a day, so Cyra will receive it by tomorrow, if she's going to see it at all.

"What was that?"

It's Ast.

I use the hard back of the chair to steady my hands when I get to my feet. I don't know how much of my message he heard.

I brush off my skirt and turn toward him. He's disheveled, like he ran here, the beetle buzzing in a quick circle around his head before it coasts around the perimeter of the room, and flies a tight circle around my body.

His eyes are unfocused and stationary, as always, but his brow is furrowed.

"Because it sounded like you were giving *our enemies* confidential information about Thuvhe's negotiations with Othyr," he said. His voice trembles with rage. I need to be careful.

"You . . ." I begin, but I can't go any further. He is too angry. My currentgift is too strong. I struggle against it, working the muscles of my throat, my mouth. In my head is a string of silent curses. Why this gift, why now, why—

"Cancel that message!" he shouts to one of the technicians. "It contains classified information that should not be shared."

One of the technicians looks from Ast to me.

"I'm sorry, but whatever this is," she says, "I don't want to be in the middle of it."

With the tap of a screen and the press of a button, my message, my last, desperate call to Cyra, is gone.

I try to think of a currentgift texture I haven't used against him before. Blankets and sweaters have never worked on him. Finery is a waste of time. Water doesn't affect him. I wish I knew more about the brim, or about the ship he grew up on, so I could suss out what's calming to him.

"You try to control her with that evil power you call a gift," he says. "And now you betray her to the very people she is fighting?"

You try to control her, too, I want to say.

She could fight them without blowing up their city, I want to say.

He speaks a command to the beetle in a language I don't know, and it lands on my shoulder, letting out its high-pitched whistle. He follows the sound, grabbing my upper arm. I jerk back, but he's too strong.

"Hey," one of the technicians says. "Let go of her, or I'll have to call security."

Ast releases me, and I stumble out of the room and into the hallway, shaken. I half walk, half run back to Isae's room, which is right next to mine. I am about to knock when I see that her light is already off—she's asleep.

I want to get to her before Ast does. Find a way to explain what I did that makes Ast seem irrational and paranoid. If I talk to her first, maybe I can destabilize whatever argument he has, maybe—

I need to think this through. I go to my room instead, so I can splash water on my face, careful to lock my door behind me.

I go to the little bathroom attached to my room and stick my head in the sink. I drink straight from the faucet, and water runs into my ear. When my throat is soothed, I reach blindly for the towel and press it to my face. I think I hear something. Clicking.

When I drag the towel down, Ast is standing behind me.

"Do you know what the children of mechanics learn to do?" he says in a low voice. "Pick locks."

My currentgift stifles me. It doesn't care that I'm in danger; it doesn't care for my survival. It just strangles me, keeping me from screaming. I grab for the glass near the sink so I can break it, make a noise. While I lunge for it, he lunges for me. Something glints silver in his fist.

He's strong. His hand is big enough to hold both of my wrists. His hands fumble over me, then find my shoulders. I drop the glass and it doesn't break. He lifts me to my toes, and I bite, finding the flesh of his arm. I bite down as hard as I can, so hard he groans and his skin tears.

A hot pain spreads through my side. My shirt clings, wet, to my rib cage. In the mirror I see fierce red spreading down my body the same way it spread around my father's head. It's the color of hushflowers, the color of Blooming gowns and the glass dome of Hessa Temple. Red, the color of Thuvhe.

He stabbed me.

This is it. *The first child of the family Kereseth will succumb to the blade.*

This is my fate, at last.

He drops me, moaning over his arm, which bleeds in a half circle from where I bit him. I fall heavy on the floor. I haven't made a sound. No one will come get me if I don't make a sound. I reach for the fallen glass as Ast tries to stanch the flow of blood from his arm.

I'm going to pass out. But not yet. I raise the glass, and using all the strength I have left, I slam it against the stone floor as hard as I can. It shatters.

Ogra. Noun. In Ogran: "The living dark"

CHAPTER 41 | AKOS

No one brought him food.

The cell was lavish, as far as cells went. A soft bed with a heavy blanket. A tub in the bathroom as well as a shower. A thick rug on the hardwood floor. It was essentially just a bedroom with a sophisticated lock, one that Akos was sure he could dismantle if he had enough time, but then he would have an entire household of soldiers to contend with.

He drank water from the faucet, when he had to, but no food came his way, and he wasn't stupid enough to think it wasn't on purpose. If Lazmet had wanted him fed, he would have been fed. They were starving away his currentgift.

In the morning, after he woke, the door finally opened. Akos was standing by the window, thinking about how bad it would hurt if he jumped out and made a run for it. Not a smart decision, he knew—he'd break both legs and get caught by a dozen guards even if he did manage to run away.

A tall man with a scarred face, and a short, white-haired woman walked into the room. The man was Vakrez Noavek, the commander of the Shotet military, who had seen to Akos's education as a soldier. The woman looked familiar to Akos, but he didn't remember her name.

"I don't understand," Vakrez said, squinting at Akos.

"Oh, do catch on, Vakrez," the woman said, with humor in her voice. "Only Noaveks are that tall and yet that thin. Like drawn hot glass. He's Lazmet's son, obviously."

"Hello, Commander," Akos said to Vakrez, his head bobbing.

"I'm going to tell him your name and where you came from, you know," Vakrez said to him. "So what was the point of the evasion in the first place?"

"It bought me time," Akos said.

"So you two know each other," the woman said, sitting in a chair by the fireplace. Akos had thought about climbing out the chimney, but after investigating, ruled out the possibility. It was too narrow for him to fit.

"He was a soldier. Not a very good one," Vakrez said with a grunt.

The woman raised an eyebrow. "My name is Yma Zetsyvis, boy. I don't think we've been formally introduced."

Akos frowned at her. He knew her. Her husband, and her daughter, had both been subject to Cyra's currentgift before they died, and she had been glued to Ryzek's side after that.

"What are you doing here?" he asked. "I thought you were both loyal to Ryzek. And now, what, you just . . . switch to his father before his body is even cold?"

"I am loyal to my family," Vakrez said.

"Why?" Akos said. "Didn't Lazmet's mother kill your mother?" He paused. "Why are you even still alive? I thought she killed everyone, including his cousins."

"He's useful," Yma said, brushing a lock of white hair over one shoulder. "So he lives. That's the Noavek way. It is why I am alive as surely as it is why *you* are alive, boy."

Vakrez scowled at her.

"What use do you have to a man like Lazmet Noavek, sir?" Akos couldn't help but add the honorific. He was used to seeing Vakrez Noavek as this armored, authoritative thing. Someone to be feared.

"I read hearts," Vakrez said, looking uncomfortable. "Loyalties. Other things. It's hard to explain."

"And you?" Akos said to Yma.

"He reads hearts, and I rip them apart." Yma examined her fingernails. "We've been sent to assess you, if we can."

"Hold out a hand, boy," Vakrez said. "I have other work to do today."

Akos's guts grumbled with hunger, but he couldn't feel the hum-buzz of the current, so he knew his gift hadn't failed yet. He held out a hand, and Vakrez grabbed him around the wrist, yanking him closer. He stared up into Akos's eyes, squinting, squeezing. His skin was warm and rough.

"Nothing," Vakrez said. "He'll need more starving time. Maybe a beating or two, if Lazmet is impatient."

"I told him it was too soon," Yma said. "He didn't listen, of course."

"He only listens to people he respects," Vakrez said. "And he only respects himself."

Yma stood, straightening her skirts. She wore light gray, a pillar of pale against the dark wood of Noavek manor. He wasn't sure what to make of her, the way her bright eyes lingered on him, the way she pursed her lips as she looked him over. Like she wanted to say something but couldn't figure out what it was.

"Get some rest, boy," she said. "You may need it."

He had not eaten in days.

Vakrez had visited every so often, to see if Akos's currentgift had failed yet. But it was still clinging to him, even now, when he was too weak to do much more than sit next to the fire until it dwindled, and then stoke the flames again.

That was where he was when Yma came to his room again. She wore blue as pale as her eyes, draped artfully around her slim body. The combined effect of her pale hair, pale skin, and pale clothing made her almost glow in the dark. He hadn't gotten up to turn on the lights, so only the fire lit the room.

She sat in the chair beside him, folding her hands in her lap. She had seemed confident when she was here with Vakrez before, but now she rocked back and forth a little, tangling her fingers in her lap. She didn't look at him when she started to speak.

"He took me from my home when I developed my current-gift," she said. There was no question that the "he" she was talking about was Lazmet.

"I had a sister, and one living parent. My mother," she went on. "I was low status. A nobody. He gave me clothes, and food, and vaccinations—for those things alone I would not have refused him, but you also don't refuse Lazmet Noavek, or you end up . . ."

She shivered slightly.

"Because he forced me to distance myself from my family,

though, I was protected when they turned against him, so to speak. My sister Zosita taught languages, you see, in secret." Yma laughed, softly. "Imagine that. Becoming an enemy of the state just because you *teach* something."

Akos squinted at her.

"I'm not good with faces," he said, "but do I *know* you somehow? Other than seeing you at Ryzek's side, I mean."

"You know my niece, Teka," Yma said, still without looking at him.

"Ah," he said.

"I'm surprised, frankly, that Miss Noavek didn't tell you about me. She's more trustworthy than I gave her credit for, I suppose. She found me out the night before she felled her brother. I'm the one who poisoned Ryzek before their confrontation in the amphitheater."

"Cyra 'found you out'?" Akos said. "As a spy, you mean."

"Of a sort," Yma said. "I am uniquely positioned in that I can bend a person's heart toward me, if I stay close to them, and do my work subtly, slowly. That's why Ryzek kept me around even when my entire family was against him. But it is much more difficult with Lazmet. His heart is . . . uniquely disconnected from everyone, everything. Hard as I try, I can't get him to budge an izit in any direction."

She turned toward him at last. He noticed that her lips were peeling, like she had gnawed on them one too many times. The skin around her fingernails, too, was raw. She was wearing thin, trying to keep Lazmet in her grasp, that much was clear.

"You seem decent," she said. "Your affection for Miss Noavek notwithstanding. But I don't put my trust in other people. I wouldn't put it in you, if I wasn't desperate."

She reached somewhere in the folds of fabric wrapped around her, and took out a small drawstring bag, the kind fancy people used to carry Assembly chips—the general system currency, which people of Shotet rarely used. She handed it to him, and when he opened it, his mouth filled up with saliva.

She had brought him dried meat. And bread.

"We have to strike the right balance," she said. "You can't appear to be in vigorous health, or he'll suspect someone. But you need your currentgift to work. And it's in shambles right now."

It took all of Akos's willpower not to stuff the entire wad of dried meat in his mouth at once.

"I'll teach you about him, when I come in here. I'll teach you how to pretend with him that what I'm doing to your heart is working," she said. "I'm good at pretend, these days."

"Why are you doing this?" he said.

"You are the only person I have ever met that he can't control with his currentgift," she said. "Which means you are the only person who can kill him."

Her eyes were wide. She seized his arm before he could lift the first mouthful to his lips.

"I need your word that you will be committed to this. No half measures," she said. "You will do as I say, exactly as I say, even if what I tell you to do horrifies you."

Akos was too desperate for food to really think it through, and besides, he didn't have many options.

"Yes," he said.

"Your word," she said, still not releasing him.

"I give you my word," he said. "I'll do whatever I have to do, to kill him."

She took her hand away.

"Good," she said, and she returned to staring at the fire while he stuffed his face.

CHAPTER 42 | CYRA

THOSE WHO SOLD THEIR goods on carts along the main thoroughfare of Galo were packing up for the day. I stopped to watch the woman who sold sculptures of blown glass—small enough to sit on a palm—wrap them in fabric and set them in a box, lovingly. The storms would come soon, but I would not see another storm on Ogra.

I moved along, toward the ship park where Teka had left her transport vessel for safekeeping and repair. I passed a man waving smoked meat in my face, and sema selling seedlings that snapped and bit at whatever came near them. I would miss the bustle of this place, so like the streets of Voa, but without the feeling of dread I got there.

I had passed the last of the carts—piled with baskets of roasted nuts of all varieties, including some from other planets—when I saw a man crouched in the middle of the street, clutching at his own head. His shirt pulled taut across his shoulders, showing the bones of his spine. I didn't recognize him as Eijeh until I had already drawn closer. I recoiled at the recognition, bringing my hand back from his shoulder before I touched it.

"Hey," I said, instead. "*Kereseth*. What is it?"

He twitched at his name, but didn't answer, so I took hold of his shoulder, and jostled it a little.

"Eijeh," I said.

The name was still difficult for me to say, the only vowel-consonant pattern in Thuvhesit that I still struggled with. Though part of me knew Eijeh Kereseth was indeed my brother, I was equally certain that we could never be siblings to each other, because I couldn't even say his name.

He lifted his head, his eyes swimming with tears. That, at least, was a familiar sight. Eijeh had always been prone to tears, unlike his brother.

"What is it?" I asked him. "Are you ill?"

"No," he forced out. "No, we got lost. In the future. I knew I would—I knew it was the worst outcome, but I had to see, I had to know—"

"Come on," I said. "I'll take you to your mother. I'm sure she can help."

I couldn't touch him—not on Ogra, where my currentgift was stronger—but I grabbed a fistful of his shirt, using it to yank him up. He lurched to his feet, wiping his eyes with the back of his hand.

"You know," I said, "my mother used to tell me that those who go looking for pain—"

"Find it every time, I know," he said.

I frowned.

That was something only Ryzek would know.

Surely it had been in one of the memories Ryzek gave Eijeh.

As he wiped his eyes, I saw that his fingernails were bitten down to the beds, and his cuticles were chewed beyond repair. Also a habit of my brother's. Could he have learned a habit from memories?

I pinched his sleeve, and tugged him toward the temporary lodging I knew the Ograns had given him and Sifa. It was nicer than the one I shared with Teka, because it housed *oracles*, and it was right in the middle of town. I knew it by the flag—stitched with a red flower—that hung in the window, over the street.

There was a narrow, creaky door between two shops that led up to the place. It had been painted so many times that in the places where the paint peeled, it showed different colors—orange, red, green. The top layer was dark blue. I pushed through it and pulled Eijeh up the narrow steps to the apartment above.

I would have knocked, but the door was already open a crack. Sifa sat inside the living room—decorated with hanging fabrics, some thick and comfortable, others thin and gauzy. Her legs were crossed, her feet bare, her eyes closed. The very picture of a mystic.

My mother.

I hadn't spoken to her since the morning after I met with Vara. I had avoided her, in fact, pretending that knowing my origins had no impact whatsoever on who I was now. My mother was still Ylira Noavek, my father still Lazmet Noavek, my brother still Ryzek Noavek. Acknowledging the truth of my origins meant admitting they had power over me. And I could not admit that.

I wouldn't.

I rapped on the door, pushing it open. Sifa turned.

"What happened?" she said, coming to her feet. She was looking at Eijeh's tear-streaked face.

"I didn't—I didn't do what you told me," he said, wiping his eyes again. "I didn't ground myself. It was—"

Before they could get lost in their oracle oddities, as they always seemed to when they were together, I interrupted him.

"Are you Ryzek?" I said to Eijeh.

Eijeh and Sifa both stared at me, blank.

"When you first woke, you said 'we.' '*We*' got lost in the future," I said.

"I don't know what you're talking about," he said.

"Oh?" I stepped toward him. "So that wasn't my delusional, egocentric brother referring to himself in the royal 'we'?"

Eijeh started to shake his head.

"It's not my brother who's biting your nails, picking at your food, spinning your blade, remembering our mother?" I said.

I knew my voice was loud, maybe loud enough to hear through the walls, but I didn't care. I had seen my brother's body. I had shoved it into space. I had scrubbed his blood from the floor. I had buried my anger, my grief, my pity.

My currentshadows were now flowing down my arms, winding around my fingers, and slipping between the seams of my shirt.

"Ryzek?" I said.

"Not exactly," he replied.

"What, then?"

"We are a *we*," he said. "Some of us is Eijeh, and some of us is Ryzek."

"You've been . . ." I struggled to find the way to phrase it.

". . . partly Ryzek this entire time, and you said nothing?"

"After getting murdered?" he retorted. "Keep your current-gift away from me." The shadows were beneath my skin and on top of it, both, stretching toward him, itching to be shared. "And you wonder why people don't like you?"

"I have never once wondered that," I said. "And you——" I turned to Sifa. "You don't look surprised, as usual. You've known this whole time that a spy might be among us——"

"He has no interest in spying," Sifa said. "He just wants to be left alone."

"Not a cycle ago, he murdered Orieve Benesit to keep Ryzek in power," I said in a low voice. "And now you tell me he wants to be left alone?"

"As long as Ryzek's body existed, we were trapped where we were," Eijeh—Ryzek—whatever—replied, leaning close. "Without it we are free. Or we would be, if not for these damn visions."

"Those damn visions." I laughed. "You—Ryzek—tortured Eijeh by trading memories with him in order to *get* those visions, if I recall correctly. And now you hate them?" I laughed again. "That seems fitting."

"The visions are a curse," he said, looking uncomfortable. "They keep throwing us into other people's lives, other people's pain——"

My mind felt like an overstuffed toy, all the contents bursting the seams. It had never occurred to me that Ryzek—in whatever form he now found himself—might not want the power he held. But when I thought of the Ryzek I had known, the one who covered my ears in dark hallways, and carried me on his back through

Shotet crowds on the way to the sojourn ship, it didn't seem so strange.

But that wasn't right. Neither Ryzek Noavek nor Eijeh Kereseth deserved to be free from the consequences of what they had done.

"Well, now it's not just the visions throwing you into other people's pain," I said. "Because you're coming with me to Urek."

"No, we're not."

I leaned in close, so close we were sharing breath, and lifted both hands, holding them over Eijeh's face. My currentshadows were so dense now that I had no trouble displaying my power in all its horror, the dark tendrils weaving over my skin and under it, staining me and enfolding me. Pain shrieked through every izit of me, but having a goal had always helped me to think through pain.

"Come with me," I said in a harsh whisper. "Or I will kill you, right now, with my bare hands. You may have some of Ryzek's learned skill, but you are still in the body of Eijeh Kereseth, and he is no match for me in a footrace or a fight or even a goddamn contest of wills."

"Threats," he gritted out. "I would say they are beneath you, but they never have been, have they?"

"I prefer to think of them as promises," I said, smiling, all teeth.

"Why do you even want us to go?"

"I am doing something that requires expertise in the habits of Lazmet Noavek," I said, "and your mind is a treasure trove."

He opened his mouth to object, and Sifa spoke over him.

"He will go," she said. "And so will I. Our time here is done."

I wanted to argue, but my logical side couldn't quite manage it. It wouldn't hurt to have not one, but two oracles on board to help with our assassination plan. Even if one contained my evil brother and the other was the biological mother who abandoned me.

It was ridiculous.

But so was much of the galaxy.

CHAPTER 43 | AKOS

"THE MOST IMMINENT OF our problems is Vakrez," Yma said.

Akos lay on the floor by the fireplace, his guts grumbling. He had gotten faint earlier while walking back from the bathroom and, rather than getting up when Yma came in, had just flopped onto his back. She shoved another satchel of food into his hand, and he took it, not half as eager as he'd been the last time she came. He'd discovered that half a meal was almost worse than no meal at all.

Still, he ate it, this time pacing himself so he could savor every bite.

"You have no control over your currentgift?"

"No," Akos said. "I never really thought about it as something that could be controlled."

"It's possible," Yma said. "I was with Ryzek when he ordered your currentgift starved away. He wasn't sure that it would work, but it's always worth a try, if you want to disable someone's gift."

"It worked," Akos said. "That was the first time I felt Cyra's currentgift."

The thought brought a sharp, hot sensation to his throat. He swallowed it down.

"Well," Yma said. "That it was possible to turn yours off then suggests that you may be able to have more mastery over your gift now."

"Oh?" He rolled his head to the side. "And how's that?"

"I told you that my family was low status. Well, what the Noaveks seem to understand that others in the galaxy do not is that low-status people have just as much value. We have long histories, recorded lineages, recipes . . . and secrets." She rearranged her skirt as she crossed her legs the other way. The fire crackled.

"We have passed along some exercises that help a person learn to control their currentgift," she said. "For some, those exercises obviously don't work, but I can teach them to you, if you promise to practice. That way you can turn off your currentgift to let Vakrez read your heart, and turn it back on to resist Lazmet's control, when the time comes."

"What exactly does Lazmet want?" Akos said. "What did he tell you to do to me?"

"He calls me the Heart Bender," she said. "What I do is too abstract for words. But I can shift a person's loyalties, over time. I take the raw feeling that's there—your love for your family, or your friends, or your lover—and change it so it leads you to a different destination, so to speak."

"That," Akos said, closing his eyes, "is horrifying."

"He wants me to bend your heart toward him," she said. "Get up. You're wasting my time, and there isn't much of it to spare."

"Can't," Akos said. "Head hurts."

"I don't care if your head hurts!"

"You try half starving for days!" he snapped.

"I have," she bit out. "Not everyone grew up wealthy, Mr. Kereseth. Some of us are familiar with the weakness and aches that come from hunger. Now get. Up."

Akos couldn't say much to that. He sat up, darkness washing over his vision, and turned toward her.

"Better," she said. "We have to talk about your game of pretend. The next time you stand before him, he will expect to see some kind of shift. You must behave as if that's the case."

"How do I do that?"

"Pretend your resolve is weakening," she said. "It shouldn't be too difficult. Let him get something out of you. Some kind of information he wants, that doesn't compromise your mission. Tell me your mission."

"Why?" Akos furrowed his brow. "You know my goddamn mission."

"You should be telling yourself your mission every single moment of every day, so you don't cost us everything! Tell me your mission!"

"Kill him," Akos said. "My mission is to kill him."

"Is your mission to be loyal to your family, your friends, your nation?"

Akos glared at her. "No. It isn't."

"Good! Now, the exercise."

She directed Akos to a chair and told him to close his eyes. "Come up with an image for your currentgift," she said. "Yours separates you from the current, so you could think of it as a wall, or a plate of armor, something like that."

Akos had never much thought about the power that lived in his skin, mostly because it seemed less like the presence of power than the absence of it. But he tried to think of it as armor, the way she said. He remembered the first time he had dropped armor over his head—the weaker, synthetic kind, when he was first sent to train at the soldier camp. The weight had surprised him, but it had been comforting, in a way.

"Think of the details in what it looks like. What is it made of? Is your armor made of different plates stitched together, or is it one solid piece? What color is it?"

He felt stupid, picturing imaginary armor, picking colors like he was decorating a house instead of trying to pull off an assassination plot. But he did what she said, calling the armor dark blue because that was the color of his earned Shotet armor, and plated for the same reason. He thought of his real armor's scrapes and dings, the signs that he'd put it to good use. And Cyra's nimble fingers as she pulled the straps taut for the first time.

"What does it feel like? Is it smooth, or rough? Is it hard, or flexible? Is it cold, or warm?"

Akos wrinkled his nose at Yma, but didn't open his eyes. Smooth, hard, warm as the kutyah fur he had once worn to protect himself from the cold. The thought of that old coat, with his name written on the tag so he wouldn't mix it up with Cisi's, made him feel achy.

"Hold the most vivid imagining of your currentgift that you can. I'm going to put a hand on you in three . . . two . . . one."

Her cool fingers pressed to his wrist. He tried to think of his Shotet armor again, but it was hard, with his memories all jumbled, Cisi trying to stuff her long arms into a child's coat, Cyra holding his shoulder steady as she yanked at the armor straps.

"You're not focused," Yma said. "We don't have time to work on this, so you'll have to practice on your own. Try different images, and try a modicum of self-discipline."

"I'm disciplined," he snapped, opening his eyes.

"It's easy to be disciplined when you're well fed and healthy," she retorted. "Now you need to learn it when your brain is barely functioning. Try it again."

He did, this time imagining his coat of kutyah fur, in Thuvhe, which was another kind of armor against the cold. He felt its tickle against the back of his neck where the coat ended and his hat began. He tried this image twice more before Yma checked the delicate watch she wore around her wrist, and announced that she had to go.

"Practice," she told him. "Vakrez will come to you later, and you need to be able to pretend."

"I need to master this by *later today*?" he demanded.

"Why do you have this expectation that life will make concessions for you?" She scowled. "We are not promised ease, comfort, or fairness. Only pain and death."

With that, she left.

Her speeches are almost as encouraging as yours, he said, to the Cyra in his mind.

He tried to practice what Yma had taught him. He did. It was just that he couldn't get his mind to focus on one thing for more than a couple minutes at a time. So it wasn't long before he wavered.

He walked the periphery of the room, pausing to peer out the slats in the window coverings, which were the same dark wood as the floor. They were elegant bars for a prisoner, he thought.

He hadn't done much thinking about his dad, not since his death. Every time thoughts of him did come up, they were an intrusion, and he shifted his focus back to the greater mission of rescuing Eijeh as he had promised. But in this place, hungry and confused, he couldn't do much to keep them out. The way Aoseh had gestured—big and unwieldy, knocking things off the table or smacking Eijeh in the head by mistake. Or how he had smelled like burnt leaves and oil from the machinery in the iceflower fields. The one time he had shouted at Akos for a bad score on a test, then broke down into tears when he realized he had made his youngest son cry.

Aoseh had been big and messy with his emotions, and Akos had always known his dad loved him. He had wondered more than once, though, why he and Aoseh didn't seem to be anything alike. Akos held everything close, even things that didn't need to be secret. That instinct toward restraint, he realized, made him more like the Noaveks.

And Cyra—bursting at the seams with energy, opinions, even anger—was more like his dad.

Maybe that was why it had been so hard not to love her.

Vakrez came in, and Akos wasn't sure how long the commander had been there before he cleared his throat. Akos stood blinking at him for a few ticks, then sat heavily on the edge of the bed. He had meant to brainstorm a better image for his current-gift. He hadn't done it. Now Vakrez would find out that Akos was getting his strength back, and he would be suspicious.

Shit, Akos thought. Yma had suggested armor, a wall—a protective barrier between Akos and the world. None of those things had felt right, when she said them, but what else was there?

"Are you all right, Kereseth?" Vakrez asked him.

"How's your husband? Malan," Akos said. He had to buy some time.

"He's . . . fine," Vakrez said, narrowing his eyes. "Why?"

"Always liked him," Akos said with a shrug. Could ice be a protective barrier? He knew ice well enough. But it was something to be wary of, at home, not something that protected you.

"He's nicer than I am," Vakrez said with a grunt. "Everybody likes him."

"Does he know you're here?" What about a metal casing, like an escape pod or a floater? No, he didn't really know those as well.

"He is, and he told me to be kinder to you." Vakrez smirked. "Said it might help you open up more. Very strategic."

"I didn't think you needed me to *open up*," Akos said darkly. "You pretty much just get to dig around in my heart no matter what I say about it, don't you?"

"I suppose. But if you are not intentionally obfuscating your emotions, it is easier to interpret them." Vakrez beckoned to him. "Stick out your arm, let's get this over with."

Akos rolled up his sleeve, exposing the blue marks he had stained into his skin with Shotet ritual. The second one had a line through the top of it, and noted the loss of the Armored One he had killed in pursuit of higher status.

He found himself returning to that place. To the fields just beyond the feathergrass, where the wildflowers were fragile and mushy, and the Armored Ones roamed, avoiding anything that transmitted too much current. The one he had killed had been relieved to find him. He had been a respite from the current.

Akos had felt a kind of kinship with it then, and he found that kinship again now. Imagining himself monstrous, with too many legs and a hard, plated side. His eyes, dark and glittering, hidden under an overhang of rigid exoskeleton.

Then, with a shock of violence, he imagined that exoskeleton riven in two. And he felt it, the second the current rang through him again, buzzing in his bones. Vakrez nodded to himself, his eyes closed, and Akos focused on keeping the wound open, so to speak.

"Yma told me she would use her gift to encourage you to dwell on your devotion to your father—Kereseth, that is, not Noavek," Vakrez said. "I see she's been successful."

Akos blinked at him. Had Yma done something to him when she was there, to make him think of Aoseh? Or was it just a coincidence, that he had? Either way, it was lucky.

"You don't seem well," Vakrez said.

"That's what happens when your biological father imprisons you in his house and starves you for days," Akos snapped.

"I suppose you're right." Vakrez pursed his lips.

"Why do you do what he says?"

"Everyone does what he says," Vakrez said.

"No, some people stop being cowards and *leave*," Akos said. "But you're just . . . staying. Hurting people."

Vakrez cleared his throat. "I'll tell him about your progress."

"Will that be before or after you prostrate yourself before him and kiss his feet?" Akos said.

To his surprise, Vakrez didn't say anything. Just turned and left.

Lazmet was seated at a table by the fire when Akos was escorted to his quarters again. The room looked like the one Akos had unlocked when he first came to this place: dark wood panels, reflecting shifting fenzu light, soft fabrics in dark colors, books stacked on almost every surface. A comfortable place.

Lazmet was eating. Roasted deadbird, spiced with charred feathergrass, with fried fenzu shells on the side. Akos's gut rumbled. It wouldn't be so difficult to snatch some of the food off the table and shove it in his mouth, would it? It would be worth it, to taste something that wasn't pickled or dried or bland. It had been so long. . . .

"That's a bit childish, don't you think?" he managed to say, after swallowing a mouthful of saliva. "Taunting me with food when you're starving me?"

Akos knew this man wasn't really his dad. Not in the way Aoseh Kereseth had been, teaching him how to button up his coat, or how to fly a floater, or how to stitch up a boot when the sole came loose. Aoseh had called him "Smallest Child" before he knew that Akos would end up being the biggest, and he had died knowing he couldn't keep Akos from being kidnapped, but trying—fighting—anyway.

And Lazmet just looked at him like he wanted to take him apart and put him back together again. Like he was something you dissected in a science class to see how it worked.

"I wanted to see how you would react to the presence of food,"

Lazmet said, shrugging. "Whether you were animal or man."

"You've brought Yma Zetsyvis in with the specific purpose of altering what I am, whatever I am," Akos said. "What does it matter what the 'before' is, when you're controlling the 'after'?"

"I'm a curious man."

"You're a sadist."

"A sadist *delights* in suffering," Lazmet said, lifting a finger. His feet were bare, his toes buried in the soft rug. "I do not delight. I am a student. I find satisfaction in learning, not pain for the sake of pain."

He covered his plate with the napkin that lay across his lap, and stepped away from the table. It was easier for Akos to deny himself the impulse to lunge at the plate when he couldn't see it anymore.

Yma had told Akos to pretend his resolve was weakening. That was the goal of this meeting—to prove to Lazmet that his methods were working, but not to be too obvious about it, so Lazmet became suspicious.

Yma had helped him find his way again. He had been aimless since Ryzek died—and since his hope for Eijeh's restoration died, too. He had not had a side, a mission, a plan. But Yma had helped him find his way back to the same pinhole focus that he had directed at his brother since his arrival in Shotet. He would kill Lazmet. Nothing else mattered.

He had betrayed Thuvhe. He had abandoned Cyra. He had lost his name, his fate, his identity. He had nothing to return to, when this was over. So he had to make it count.

"So you are a Thuvhesit, I hear," Lazmet said. "I always thought the revelatory tongue was a legend. Or at the very least, an exaggeration."

"No," Akos said. "I find words in it that I didn't even know existed."

"I'd always wondered," Lazmet said. "If you don't have a word for a thing, can you still know what it is? Is it something that lives in you that goes unarticulated, or does it disappear from your awareness entirely?" He picked up his glass, which contained something purple and dark, and sipped from it. "You may be one of the only people who can possibly know, but you don't seem to have the capacity to answer."

"You think I'm stupid," Akos said.

"I think you've programmed yourself to survive, and you have little energy for anything else," Lazmet said. "If you had not had to fight to live, perhaps you could have become a more interesting person, but here we are."

The only reason I care about being "interesting" to you, Akos thought, *is because I'm pretty sure you'll kill me if I'm not.*

"There's a word in Ogran. Kyerta," Akos said. "It's . . . a life-changing truth. It's what brought me here. The knowledge that you and I were related."

"Related," Lazmet said. "Because I had sex with a woman, and she handed you off to an oracle? Everyone in the damn galaxy has parents, boy. It's hardly a unique achievement."

"Then why did you care what color my eyes were?" Akos said. "Why did you have me brought here to speak to me again?"

Lazmet didn't answer.

"Why did you bother," Akos said, stepping toward him, "to

turn Ryzek into a murderer?"

"The word 'murderer' is reserved for people we don't like," Lazmet said. "Anyone else, and they're a warrior, a soldier, a freedom fighter. I trained my son to fight for his people."

"Why?" Akos said, tilting his head. "What do you care for his people, for your people?"

"We are better than them," Lazmet said, slamming his glass down on the table beside his chair. He stood. "We learned the reaches of this galaxy when they hadn't even come up with names for themselves. We know what is valuable, what is fascinating, what is important, and they throw it away. We are stronger, more resilient, more resourceful—and they have somehow managed to keep us low since they became aware of us. We will not remain low. They do not deserve to be above us."

"You think of the Shotet as *you*," Akos said. "I see."

"You have your ideals, I am sure—you have that shine in your eyes." Lazmet sneered a little. "And I have something else."

"And that's . . . what?" Akos said. "Cruelty? Curiosity?"

"I want," Lazmet said. "I want, and I will take whatever I can get my hands on. Even if it's you."

Lazmet came toward him. He hadn't noticed before that he was taller than his father. Not by a lot, because Lazmet towered over most people, but by enough that it was noticeable.

Akos imagined himself as the Armored One, and eviscerated himself, for the tenth time that day. He had been practicing since Vakrez left the day before. He had barely slept, in order to practice. He had learned to suppress his currentgift quickly, and to bring it back just as quickly. It required all of his energy, but he was improving.

He felt the pressure of Lazmet's currentgift against his mind, and gave in to it. It was strange, the sensation like someone wiggling a wire into his head and touching it, lightly, to the part of his brain that controlled his movements. His fingers twitched, then tapped together, without him telling them to. Lazmet's mouth twitched as he registered the movement, and Akos felt the imaginary wire retract.

"Vakrez has given fascinating reports on the state of your insides, Akos," Lazmet said. "I have never seen him puzzle quite so much over someone. He says you are making progress in the right direction."

"Eat shit," Akos said.

Lazmet smiled a little.

"You should sit," he said. "I'm sure you're tired."

Lazmet crossed into the sitting room. It was a simple room, with a soft rug by a fireplace, and bookshelves packed with books in all languages. Lazmet sat in the armchair next to the fire, and buried his toes in the plush of the carpet. Akos followed, hesitant, and stood by the fire. He *was* tired, but he wanted to take his little rebellions where he could get them. Instead of sitting, he braced himself on the mantel, and stared into the flames. Someone had dusted them with some kind of powder that turned them blue, just at the edges.

"You grew up with an oracle," Lazmet said. "Do you know that I spent much of my adult life trying to find an oracle?"

"Did you try looking in a temple?" Akos said.

Lazmet laughed a little. "You realize, of course, that it's not simply a matter of going where they are. Capturing someone who knows you are coming is nearly impossible. Which is why I confess

I am confused as to why your mother left you and your brother to be stolen away. She must have known you would be taken."

"I'm sure she did," Akos said bitterly. "She must also have believed it was necessary."

"That is cruel," Lazmet said. "You must be angry."

Akos wasn't sure how to answer. He wasn't Cyra, digging in her claws wherever she could, though he definitely understood the impulse.

"You know, I'm not sure I understand your strategy here," he said eventually. "And there is one, so don't disrespect me by pretending there isn't."

Lazmet sighed. "You're being boring again. But maybe you're right—I do have something I want from you. And something I'm willing to trade."

He crossed the room again, going to the table where he had covered up his meal. The smell still lingered in the air, juicy meat and rich sauce, with the feathergrass burned just to the point where its hallucinogenic qualities disappeared and only its spicy flavor remained.

Lazmet moved to the next seat at the table, and lifted a metal dome that had been covering the place setting there. Revealing another roasted deadbird. Another side of fried fenzu shells. And a diced saltfruit.

"This meal is yours," Lazmet said. "If you will tell me how you got into this manor."

"What?" Akos had fixated on the food. The rest of the room went dark around him. His stomach was beginning to *ache*.

"Someone must have helped you get into this house," Lazmet said, patiently. "None of our outer locks were disabled or tampered with, and you could not possibly have scaled the wall without someone noticing. So tell me who it was that let you in, and you may eat this meal."

Jorek. Long, skinny arms and patchy facial hair. He had taken the ring that Akos wore around his neck before they left his uncle's home, for safekeeping. He had offered his arm to his mother to stabilize her on the cobblestone. *Jorek is a good man*, he reminded himself. *He didn't even want to let you into the manor. You manipulated him into doing it.* He couldn't possibly give Jorek's name to Lazmet in exchange for a meal.

Tell me your mission.

No, he thought, to the Yma that lived in his head. *Not this. I won't do this.*

Yma had told him to look for an opportunity to give Lazmet information. To show him something was changing. To keep him from getting bored. Well, this was it—served on a plate.

"I don't believe you." Akos closed his eyes. "I think you'll take the food away the second I tell you what you want to know."

"I won't," Lazmet said. He stepped away from the plate. "Here, I'll even back away. Trust me in this simple thing, Akos. I do not delight in pain. I want to see what you will do, and it doesn't serve me to withhold something from you once you've done as I asked. Surely you see the logic in that."

Akos's eyes pricked with tears. He was so hungry. He was so tired. He needed to do as Yma said.

Is your mission to be loyal to your family, your friends, your nation?

No.

That was not his mission.

"Kuzar," he choked out. "Jorek Kuzar."

Lazmet nodded. He walked away from the table and took his seat in the armchair, leaving Akos to his meal.

The feathergrass had turned sour in his stomach. It kept coming back up in burps, the flavor rising in the back of his throat. Reminding him.

Akos touched the hollow of his throat, where the ring of Ara's family had once pressed. He wouldn't see it again. That didn't bother him so much—he never felt like he had earned it in the first place. Killing a man wasn't something that should get you welcomed into a family, he knew. But the thought of how Ara would look at him, if he ever got out of here . . .

He pressed his hand over his mouth as another burp came up.

There came a tap at the wall panel next to the fireplace. It slid back to let Yma in. She looked more casual than usual, her white hair tied back, dressed in dark training clothes and soft shoes. Her eerie blue eyes fixed on him.

"Tell me," he said, voice wavering.

"You did what was necessary," she said.

"*Tell me* what happened," he snapped.

She sighed. "Jorek has been arrested," she said.

Akos tasted bile, and bolted toward the bathroom. He had just made it to the toilet when he started heaving, throwing up everything he had eaten in Lazmet's sitting room. He waited out the stomach spasms with his forehead against the seat, tears leaking out of the corners of his eyes.

Something cool pressed to the back of his neck. Yma drew him back and pressed the flusher. She took the wet cloth from his neck and used it to wipe his face, kneeling beside him. Her usually passive face looked weary now, the lines in her forehead and around her eyes more apparent than usual. It wasn't a bad thing.

"The night my husband, Uzul, and I decided that I would turn him in to Ryzek, thus prematurely ending his life for the good of our cause, I sobbed so hard I pulled a muscle in my abdomen. It hurt to stand up straight for a week," she said. "He had only months to live, you see, but those months . . ."

She closed her eyes.

"I wanted those months," she said, a few ticks later.

She dabbed at the corner of Akos's mouth.

"I loved him," she added simply, and she tossed the cloth into the sink.

He expected her to get up, now that she had cleaned his face, but she didn't. Yma sat down on the floor, right next to the toilet, her shoulder leaning into the seat. After a tick she put a hand on his shoulder, and the weight, and her silent presence, were comfort enough.

CHAPTER 44 | CYRA

MY LAST VIEW OF Ogra from above was one of glittering light.

Then Yssa ordered us to ready ourselves. Sifa and Ettrek sat closest to the exit hatch. Yssa and Teka were on the nav deck, and I was with Eijeh—Ryzek—whoever he was now—closest to them. I glanced at Eijeh to make sure that he had strapped himself in properly, and the straps were crossed over his chest, right over the sternum, where they should be. Launching through Ogra's atmosphere required a sharp burst of energy, followed by a quick shutdown, to break through the dense layer of shadow from beneath. Yssa guided the ship down to the right elevation, angled us appropriately, and punched the button on the nav panel.

We shot forward, the sudden force making my body slam into the straps that held me in. I gritted my teeth against the pressure. Yssa switched off the ship's power, and we were swallowed by a darkness so complete, we may as well have disappeared.

And then everything—the darkness, the pressure, the terror,

and even some of my pain—fell away at once as Yssa turned the ship's power back on, and we drifted among the stars.

I had thought that Teka, who last flew me across the galaxy, was a good pilot, but Yssa was an artist. Her long fingers danced over the nav center, making small adjustments to Teka's settings, and she guided us with unprecedented smoothness toward the currentstream, so we could travel alongside it. It was a cool yellow now, touched with green, a sign that more time had passed than I realized since I first landed on Ogra.

"You don't mind Yssa poking around at your nav center?" I said to Teka, nudging her with my shoulder. We were on the nav deck—it was safe to walk around now that we were through the atmosphere—looking out at the depthless darkness in our path.

I sometimes referred to it as "nothingness," like most people did, but most of the time, I didn't think of it that way. Space was not a finite container, but that didn't mean it was empty. Asteroids, stars, planets, the currentstream; space debris, ships, fragmented moons, undiscovered worlds; this was a place of endless possibility and unfathomable freedom. It was not nothing; it was *everything*.

"What? Oh, no, I definitely want to smack her pokey little hands away," Teka said, narrowing her eye at Yssa, who was still busy with the controls. "But the ship likes her, so I'm keeping my mouth shut."

I laughed a little.

It took me a few moments to realize the source of my sudden relief: my currentshadows, which had burrowed under my skin again when we landed on Ogra, now coasted on top of it. Their ache and sting were still present, but so diminished that I was nearly giddy with it. To one who is in pain all the time, even minor differences can be miracles, of a sort.

"We just got pinged by an Assembly patrol," Yssa announced.

Teka and I exchanged an alarmed look.

"They say they have an old warrant on a craft matching this description," Yssa said, reading from the nav screen.

"Warrant for what? Being Shotet?" Ettrek asked.

"Could be for drugging and spacing Isae Benesit when we didn't want to go with her to Assembly Headquarters," Teka suggested.

"You did *what* to Isae Benesit?" Yssa said.

"She had just murdered my brother in the hold, what else was I supposed to do?" I said.

"Oh, I don't know . . . give her a medal!" Ettrek said, waving his arms.

I glanced at Eijeh. He was eyeing Ettrek like he was about to reach out and smack him.

It was getting easier to think of Eijeh as two people in one body—or one new, blended person—since I saw so much of my brother, yet so little of him at once. It was Ryzek's pride that made him chafe against Ettrek cheering his murder, but it was Eijeh's passivity that tempered his reaction. They had, together, become something . . . else. New, but not necessarily better.

Time would tell.

"Tell them the Ograns lent us this craft and we don't know about the original crew," Teka said to Yssa. "Should be convincing if you record your image on the sights. You don't sound Shotet at all."

"Okay," Yssa said. "The rest of you get out of range."

We stood back while Yssa activated the sights in the nav screen to record her message, in fitful Othyrian. She was a talented liar, for an Ogran.

It would take days to get from Ogra to Urek. I spent most of my time leaning over the table in the galley, drawing a map of Noavek manor, floor by floor. I went through the servants' passages in my memory, again and again, feeling in the dark for notches and circles and false panels. I told myself it would be useful for the mission ahead of us, as well as a good way to avoid Sifa, but those weren't the only reasons I did it. I felt like re-creating the place on paper was a way of purging myself of it, room by room. When I was done with this, that place would no longer exist to me.

At least, that was the theory.

When I was finished, I ordered Eijeh—I had taken to referring to him by that name, because that was the body he was in, and he hadn't yet objected—into the galley. The others had been confused by my inclusion of Eijeh in our little group, but I just told them I wanted to bring the oracles along, and no one asked any further questions.

He stepped into the room with a wariness to his expression that made me think, unexpectedly, of Akos. Ignoring the sharp feeling that brought to my throat, I pointed at the drawings of Noavek manor, labeled by floor in my jagged, unsteady handwriting.

"I want you to check these for accuracy," I said. "It's difficult to re-create a place from memory."

"Maybe you want to spend your days wading through memories of Noavek manor," Eijeh said, sounding more like Ryzek in that moment, "but we do not."

"I do not give a shit what you want," I snapped. "This is the problem you have, the problem you've always had. You think you have hurt worse than anyone else in the galaxy. Well, no one cares about your story of woe! There is a *war* going on. Now check! The damn! Drawings!"

He stared at me for a few moments, then stepped toward the table and bent over the drawings. He surveyed the first one briefly, then reached for the pen I had left at the edge of the table, and started redrawing the lines around the trophy room.

"I don't know Lazmet nearly as well as you do," I said, when I had calmed somewhat. "Is there anything you can recall about him that might help us get to him? Strange habits, particular proclivities . . . ?"

Eijeh was silent for a while, stepping to the right to look at the next drawing. I wondered if I would have to bully him into answering my question the way I had bullied him into checking my maps, but then he spoke.

"He reads mostly history," he said, in a strange, soft voice I had not heard from him before. "He's obsessed with texture—all his rugs and clothes have to be soft. I heard him scolding one of the staff for starching his shirts too much once. She made them too stiff." He gulped, and scratched out one of the doorways I had marked, drawing it on the other side of a bedroom. "And he loves fruit. He used to have one of his transports smuggle in a particular variety from Trella—altos arva. It's often boiled down and used in smaller quantities as a sweetener, because most people can't handle how sweet it is raw. The rest of this looks fine."

He set the pen down, and straightened.

"You know you're only going to get one chance at him, right?" Eijeh said. "Because once he knows you're there—once he knows what you're trying to do—"

"He'll control me with his currentgift," I said. "I know."

Eijeh nodded. "Am I allowed to leave now, or are you going to threaten me with death again?"

I flapped my hand at the door. A plan was beginning to come together in my mind. I leaned back against the counter and stared at the drawings, hoping for inspiration.

We had to wait to get in touch with Jorek until we were in receiving range of Thuvhe, which was four days into the journey.

By the time we reached it, I was tired of the smell of the recycled water—chemical, from the purification process—and the canned food we had been reheating on the galley's little stove, and the itchy fabric that covered my sleep pallet. I was also tired of the memories I had here, of lying clutched together with Akos on blankets, and bumping hands at the galley counter as we both reached for bowls, and trading sly looks over Teka's head whenever she stood between us.

It was the first time I had considered—and only for a moment—that the destruction of the sojourn ship might have had a positive side. At least I wouldn't be able to return to my memories of him there.

I felt sick at even the momentary deviation in my thoughts.

There was nothing positive about the obliteration of my home, and the loss of life that had accompanied it. I was just going mad, trapped in this ship.

I was combing through my wet hair with my fingers when I heard thundering footsteps down the hall outside, and stuck my head out of the bathroom to see who it was. Teka was tripping toward me, barefoot and paler than usual.

"What?" I said.

"Jorek," she said. "Jorek's been arrested."

"How?" I said. "Wasn't he working as a guard at the manor? He's a Kuzar!"

"I talked to his mother." Teka came into the bathroom and started pacing, heedless of the puddles of water I had left while drying off. She left small footprints in her wake. "Ara said last week, they were contacted by *Akos*."

I felt his name as a kick to the stomach.

"What?" I said. Akos was in Thuvhe. Akos was at home, outside of Hessa, pretending the war didn't exist. He was—

"He persuaded Jorek to let him into Noavek manor. Jorek didn't want to, but he owed Akos a favor." Teka paced even faster.

"And what did he intend to *do* in Noavek manor?" I demanded. "Does she know?"

"She suspects the obvious," Teka said. "That he went to do the same thing we're about to do."

I stepped back. Leaned against the wall.

I hated this. The moment the anger squirmed away. It was easier to boil with rage that Akos had abandoned me without a word, easier to let that act confirm what I suspected about myself, that no one could stand me for long. But knowing that he had left me like that for a *reason* . . .

Teka went on: "A week after Akos got to the manor, Jorek was arrested. Ara thinks—"

"Akos wouldn't have given Jorek's name," I said distantly, shaking my head. "Something must have happened."

"Everyone has a limit," Teka said. "It doesn't mean Akos meant to—"

"No," I said. "You don't know him like I do. He just—wouldn't."

"Fine, whatever," Teka said, throwing up her hands. "But Jorek is probably going to be executed, because you and I both know Lazmet Noavek doesn't just have people arrested and let them go!"

"I know, I know." I shook my head. The thought of Akos in Noavek manor again made me feel like screaming. He couldn't be there.

"Does she know if Akos is dead?" I asked quietly.

"One of her sources says no," Teka said. "Says he's being kept prisoner, but nobody knows why—what good can he do Lazmet?"

It was a measure of exactly how much I feared my father that I didn't feel much relief. Lazmet's reasons for wanting people alive were worse than his reasons for wanting them dead. I had watched the work he did on my brother, the slow work of destroying and rebuilding him. The way he ensured his own future, his own legacy, by constructing his son in his own image. Now that Ryzek was gone, would he do the same to Akos?

How much harm had he already done?

"I don't know," I said. "But whatever it is, it's not good."

Teka stopped pacing.

We stood facing each other, the almost certain loss of two friends between us.

I expected to feel the acute pain of grief, but there was nothing. The black hole in my chest had devoured every last feeling in my body, leaving me empty, just a sack of skin held up by bone and muscle.

"Well," Teka said. "Let's go kill your dad, then."

CHAPTER 45 | CYRA

FROM THE MOMENT UREK entered our view, a globe of swirling white, I felt like a countdown began. We had three days. Three days to finish planning an assassination and carry it out. Three days to end this war before it destroyed Thuvhe and Shotet both.

I had never seen the skies above Voa so empty. In the distance there was a government patrol vessel, painted with the seal of the family Noavek. It was one of the newer ones, all diagonal lines, like it was perpetually diving. It gleamed in the hazy light of day.

It was the only ship in sight.

"Don't worry," Teka said, likely noticing that the rest of us had gone silent. "We're cloaked. We look like a patrol ship to them."

At that very moment, a red light flashed on the nav panel. Yssa looked back at Teka with eyebrows raised. It was a call, probably from the patrol vessel.

"Patch them through," Teka said, unbuckling herself and moving to stand at Yssa's shoulder.

"*This is patrol ship XA774. Please identify yourself.*"

"Patrol ship XA993. What are you doing afloat, XA774?" Teka said, without faltering for even a moment. "I don't see you listed on the updated schedule."

She was pantomiming for Yssa, pointing out the spot where Ettrek's people had told us to land, urging her to move fast.

"At what time was your schedule issued, 993?"

"1440," Teka replied.

"You're out of date. This one was issued at 1500 hours."

"Ah," Teka said. "Our mistake. We'll make our way back to our docking station."

She slapped a hand over the switch to turn off our communicator. "Go!"

Yssa pressed hard on the accelerator with the heel of her hand, and we zoomed toward the landing spot. Teka was nearly knocked off her feet by the sudden movement, so she clung to the back of Yssa's chair as we lost altitude. Yssa lowered the ship to the patch of empty rooftop on the outer rim of Voa that Ettrek's contacts had indicated.

"Is there really a patrol ship XA993?" I asked.

Teka grinned. "No. They only go up to 950."

Right after we touched down, before Yssa could even turn off the engine, a group of people rushed toward the ship, carrying a huge stretch of fabric between them. I watched through the nav window as they threw the fabric over the ship, drawing it taut with long cords. As the hatch opened behind me, they completely covered the nav window.

Ettrek deboarded first, greeting a man with black hair long enough to brush his shoulders with a clasped hand. When I moved closer, I realized they had to be brothers, maybe even twins.

"Wow, you weren't kidding," the brother said. "Cyra fucking Noavek is with you."

"How did you know my middle name?" I said.

He smiled, and offered me a hand. "My name is Zyt. Short for something so long I don't even remember it myself. I'm Ettrek's older brother."

"You probably don't want to shake my hand," I said. "You're welcome to shake Teka's twice, though."

"Don't volunteer me for extra handshakes," Teka said. "Hi. Teka Surukta."

"Here are some oracles," I said, gesturing behind me to Eijeh and Sifa. Zyt raised his eyebrows.

We did the rest of the introductions under the cover of the cloth they had thrown on top of our ship, which looked sturdy and likely served as good camouflage. Then Zyt led us to the rooftop access door, and down several flights of stairs. The stairwell had no windows, and smelled like garbage, but I was glad it gave us shelter.

I moved away from my brother—and I wasn't even sure which of them I meant—to skip ahead a few steps.

"What's it like out there?" I asked Zyt, falling into step beside him.

"Well, at first there was a lot of looting," Zyt said. A lock of hair fell against his cheek. "Good for business. But then Lazmet took power, and that pretty much scared sense into everyone. He imposed a curfew, started rounding people up and arresting them, stuff like that. Bad for business."

"What business are you in, exactly?" I said.

"Smuggling," Zyt said. His eyelids fell heavy over his eyes, narrowing them somewhat, and he had a mouth given to smiles. He gave me one then. "Mostly medicine, but we smuggle whatever's lucrative—supplies, weapons, whatever."

"Ever smuggle fruit?" I said.

"Fruit?" Zyt raised his eyebrows.

"Yeah, I need to get my hands on some altos arva. It's Trellan," I said. "And since imports from Trella are illegal . . ."

"Smuggling is the only option. I see." Zyt tapped his chin with a finger. There was a bruise under his nail. "I'll find out."

If we had altos arva, we could use it to get into Noavek manor undetected, pretending that Lazmet's customary shipment of it had arrived early. The guards likely wouldn't dare to risk Lazmet not getting what he wanted. They would let us right in.

"Hey," Zyt said, "you should probably cover up your head. That silverskin's . . . conspicuous."

"Right."

I had been prepared to obscure my face once we arrived in Voa, so I wore a long black coat with a hood. It was made of a light, tough material called marshite, imported, like most waterproof fabrics, from Pitha. I put the hood up, and Zyt opened the door at the bottom of the stairs to the bright light of day.

The wind made the folds of my coat snap and billow as I walked. The streets of Voa were emptier than I had ever seen them before, full of scurrying men and women folded inward, eyes down. It had never been easier to disappear among them.

"It's not far," he said. "Are all your people keeping step?"

I looked over my shoulder. Everyone had their hoods up, so it was difficult to tell who was a smuggler and who wasn't. I counted a bright streak of hair—Teka—and the bump of a knot atop a

head—Ettrek—the bridge of a freckled nose—Yssa—and a lop-
ing gait—Sifa—and turned back.

"Looks like it," I said.

Zyt led us down two streets before approaching a small, ram-
shackle apartment building. A light above us flickered as he turned
the key in the lock. The apartment beyond—on the ground
level—was cramped and messy. There were tables and cabinets
and chairs leaned up against the walls in the hallway.

I stood aside as the others filed in, counting Teka, Ettrek, and
Yssa before I realized I had forgotten to check for Eijeh. Just as I
felt the beginnings of panic, I saw him jogging toward the door.

"What kept you?" I snapped.

"Untied shoe," he said.

"You know that you can just walk with an untied shoe for a
street or two, right? It's not actually life-threatening."

Eijeh just rolled his eyes, and closed the door behind him.

The apartment wasn't much. One room served as living room,
dining room, and bedroom, the floor spread with slim mattresses,
one of which had a hole with stuffing coming out of it. There was
a bathroom, but the shower was just a pipe protruding from the
ceiling, and there was no sink. Still, Zyt was heating water for tea
when I went into the kitchen.

"We'll rest here tonight," Zyt said when I poked my head in.

"Need help?" I said.

"Not unless you're skilled in the dangerous art of chopping
hushflower."

I raised an eyebrow at him.

"Oh really? Full of surprises, you are. Come chop it, then."

It was crowded, with two people in the kitchen, but I took a place at the cutting board, and he stood at the stove. He handed me the fresh hushflower—contained in a jar—and the gloves I would need to prepare them without poisoning myself, and pointed me toward the knife drawer.

I set the hushflower on the cutting board, upside down, and pressed the flat of my knife to the place where the petals joined to split them apart. Then I sliced the dark red streak down the center of one of the petals, and it lay flat, as if by magic.

"Nice," Zyt said. "How did you learn?"

I paused. I was tempted to call Akos a friend, but it seemed too simple for what he had been to me, too small a word.

"Ah. Forget I asked," Zyt said, and he reached for a jar of something else, high up on the slanted shelves.

"Is this your place?" I asked. "Or someone else's?"

"It was my mother's, before she died. Chills and spills took her. That was before we had figured out how to smuggle medicine." Zyt bent his head over the pot of water he had set on the only burner, and tapped the jar he held to dust the water with powdered fenzu shell.

I kept chopping the hushflower. It was my family's fault that his mother had not had access to medicine—Lazmet had begun the practice of hoarding donated medicine from Othyr, and Ryzek had only continued it. I had gotten the expensive inoculation when I was a child.

"I was in love with him, the one who taught me how to prepare hushflower," I said. I wasn't sure why I was telling him this, except that he had shared some pain with me, and I wanted to do the same. The exchange of suffering didn't have to be even—but it was a kind of currency, his sorrow for mine. A way toward trust. "He left me. No explanation."

Zyt made an exaggerated disgusted noise in the back of his throat, and I smiled.

"What an idiot," he said.

"Not really," I said. "But it's nice of you to say."

We drank tea and ate warm bread for dinner. It was not the best meal I had ever had, but it wasn't the worst. The other smugglers kept to themselves, except for Zyt, who sat beside Ettrek and told stories from their childhood for hours. They had us all laughing before long at Ettrek's sad attempts to prank his older brother, and Zyt's savage retaliations.

Then everyone found somewhere to sleep—not an easy task, in a room this small—and one by one, we drifted off. I had never been good at sleeping, particularly in places with which I was unfamiliar, so I soon found myself slipping out the back door to sit on the back step, facing the alley.

"Saw you get up." Teka sat next to me on the step. "You're not much for sleeping, are you?"

"Waste of time," I declared.

Teka nodded. "It took me a long time to sleep again after . . ." She waved a hand over her eye patch. "Kind of a horrible memory."

"Kind of," I said with a short laugh. "I'm not sure what's worse." I paused, thinking of her mother's public execution. "I didn't mean—sorry."

"You don't have to be so careful around me," Teka said, looking at me from the corner of her eye. "When I didn't like you, it was because I made too many assumptions. After I let them go . . . well, I'm here on your crazy mission, aren't I?"

I grinned.

"Yeah," I said. "You are."

"I am, so when I bring something up, I don't want you to take it too personally," she said, guarded. "Akos."

"Yeah?" I frowned. "What about him?"

"Honestly?" She sighed. "I'm a little worried that when push comes to shove, you'll prioritize saving him over killing Lazmet, now that you know he's here, and alive. I've been worried about it since I told you about him."

I sat for a moment, listening to the night air. It was loud in this part of the city, despite the curfew and the aura of depression that had settled over all of Voa. People argued and laughed and played music in their apartments at all hours, or so it seemed. Even in the alley I saw the glow of lanterns still lit, defiant against the night.

"You're worried I'll do what I did last time, when I didn't kill Ryzek," I said.

"Yes," Teka said, unflinching. "I am."

"It's different this time," I said. "There's . . . more, this time."

"More?"

"More that I care about," I said. "Before, all I had, the only good thing I had, was him. And now, that's not true anymore."

She smiled, and I bumped her with my shoulder.

Then I heard something behind me. A squeak. The pressure of a foot against an old floorboard. Turning, I saw a dark shape in the living room, the silhouette of a man—a soldier, judging by the bulk of him—holding out a currentblade. Beneath it, the space where Eijeh had been, a bump under a blanket, was empty.

Eijeh was gone. And someone else was here.

I turned, and stood, and ran, and roared, all at once. As the shape bent, blade upraised, I stepped on someone's leg and shoved, hard, at the intruder. My hands met armor with a *crack*. I gritted my teeth against the pain of impact, and bent at the waist to dodge the swinging blade.

Someone had told the Shotet police to come here.

I drove my elbow low, under the bottom edge of the armored vest, and hit the man in the groin. He groaned, and I made a grab for his weapon. Out of the corner of my eye, I saw Teka's hair swinging as she leapt at the person behind the first. The smugglers, as well as Ettrek, Sifa, and Yssa, were now awake, and scrambling.

The pain of my currentgift disappeared in my adrenaline, but I didn't forget it. As I wrenched the blade from the man's hand, I gave in to the desire to share my pain with him, and currentshadows crept around his wrist, merging with the ones that wrapped around his currentblade. I watched the two combine, and bury themselves in his flesh, now a richer and darker black.

He screamed.

I kept going. I lunged at the next woman in uniform I saw, grabbing her face instead of her throat, pressing currentshadows toward her until she choked on my pain, until it filled her open, gasping mouth. I brought her head down to meet my knee, raised high enough for the two to collide, with as tall as I was.

I was not afraid of their numbers. I wasn't afraid of anyone, not anymore. It was what made me a Noavek—not that I was so powerful I couldn't be threatened, but that I had already survived enough horrors, enough pain, to be accustomed to the inevitability of both. But I *was* powerful—that much I knew.

I kept going, grabbing the next man I could get my hands on. They had made a mistake in invading us through that narrow hallway, because it created a funnel through which only one of them could charge at a time. So I took them on one at a time, until there were no more. Behind me was silence. I assumed the others had left.

I turned to make for the back door. I didn't know how many of the police I had killed and how many I had simply disabled, but either way, I needed to flee. When I turned back toward the living room, though, I saw Zyt, Sifa, Ettrek, Yssa, and Teka waiting for me, each of them looking a little surprised.

"Go!" I shouted.

And we all ran.

"Well, your crew don't waste any time fleeing, do they, Zyt?" Teka huffed, leaning against the wall.

We had decided, mid-stride, to make our way for the half-destroyed building where the renegades had made their camp, when I was last on Voa. It was the only other safe place we knew. Teka had taken the lead, navigating winding streets apparently from memory. The edges of the city were fraying like the cuffs of a shirt, more damaged and broken than closer to the center. There was graffiti scrawled on the side of every building: simple characters written in black, in some places, and in others, sprawling murals of characters as tall as a man, filled in with colors as bright as the currentstream. The graffiti covered up the cracks in the buildings, the boards where windows had been, the dirt that dusted each wall with brown. But I was most transfixed by a simple statement, written neatly beneath one windowsill: *Noaveks Own Us.*

"What do you expect?" Zyt replied. "They're smugglers, they're not particularly ambitious."

"We don't need them anyway," Ettrek said. "Zyt is the one with the contacts."

"Yes, the contacts for the smuggling of . . . fruit, apparently?" Zyt raised an eyebrow at me.

"Yes," I said, offering no further explanation.

"Now might be a good time to explain what you need a bunch of fruit for," Zyt said.

"It *might* be a good time," I countered. "But how can we be sure?"

I took a vial of painkiller from the pack at my side and tipped it into my throat. It was one of Akos's "subpar" batches—and he wasn't wrong to call them that, they weren't nearly as effective as most of his painkillers—but it was better than nothing.

The plants growing between the cracks in the broken floor had spread much farther in the time we had been away from this place. Vines were beginning to creep up the walls, and everywhere I looked, there were splashes of color from wildflowers. *The kind that turn to mush*, I thought, and it was an Akos thought, not one of my own.

Suddenly I needed to be alone. I slipped away, into the stairwell where I had first showed Akos that I could control my currentgift. My back against one of the stone walls, I slid to the ground and let the tears come.

Later, Teka found a bottle of fermented fruit juice in the cabinets of someone who had lived in this place before it was destroyed, and we all took a glass together to steady ourselves before we tried for more sleep.

Sifa offered a toast, translating to Shotet from Thuvhesit: "To what we have done, what we are doing, and what we will do."

And I drank.

CHAPTER 46 | AKOS

HIS OTHER MEMORIES OF grief involved time slipping away. Oil beading on water. The sudden lack of presence in his own life, the self-protective drifting.

He wished he had that now.

Now, he felt every tick and every hour. Vakrez had come by that morning to a dead-eyed stare, closed his fingers over the pulse in Akos's wrist, and left. Vakrez's hands were cold and clammy and then gone.

A few days passed before he was summoned to Lazmet's side again. This time he was brought to the Weapons Hall, the place where he had first learned his fate. Of course, it wasn't really his fate, but he had carried it around for seasons anyway. *Don't trust your heart*, that fate had told him, and he'd hated it for that reason.

Now, he thought it maybe had a point.

Lazmet was staring at the wall of weapons, tapping his chin. It was like he was picking out a cheese, Akos thought, and he wondered if he was about to experience some kind of new horror, in which his own father systematically broke his bones or carved out pieces of his flesh. It seemed like the kind of thing Lazmet might do. Out of curiosity.

It wasn't until she moved out of the shadows that he saw Yma was there. There was a warning in her stare, when she gave it to him. And then her mask was back on, that enigmatic smile, the elegant posture. Knowing what he now knew about her, he recognized that she would never be comfortable this way, in a gown, in a manor, playing games with royalty.

"Thank you for your report, Yma," Lazmet said. "You can go."

Yma inclined her head, though Lazmet wasn't looking, still spellbound by the wall of weapons. She brushed Akos's arm on her way out, the brief touch giving some kind of comfort. And a reminder.

"Come here," Lazmet said to him. "I want to show you something."

Akos was supposed to be acting like he was slipping into Lazmet's control, piece by piece, so he climbed the steps to the dais. The room had an eerie green cast to it, light glowing through the row of jars on shelves up higher than Akos's head. White orbs floated in the jars, suspended in green liquid. Preservative.

They were eyes. Akos tried not to think about it.

"We're not a culture that keeps mementos. After all, that would suggest we trust in some kind of permanence, and the Shotet have always known that objects, places . . . they can be lost in an instant." Lazmet gestured to the wall of weapons. "Weapons, though, we allow ourselves to pass down. They're still useful, you see. So you can trace the history of our family here, on this wall."

He reached for a hatchet on the far left. The blade was rusty from disuse, the metal handle still cloudy with fingerprints.

"We're an old Shotet family, but not old money," Lazmet said, touching his finger to the hatchet blade. "My grandfather killed his way to prominence in our society. This hatchet was his handiwork. He was a weapons maker. Not particularly talented. What he lacked in artistry he made up for in brutality, when he served in the Shotet army."

He put the hatchet away, moving along to a staff. At each end of it were the mechanisms Akos recognized from currentblade handles. When Lazmet held it, dark tendrils of current wrapped around first one end of the staff, and then the other.

"My wife's design," Lazmet said, with a smile that almost seemed fond. "She was not a talented fighter, but she was theatrical. She knew how to be beautiful, and charming, and intimidating, all at the same time. It's a shame her life was claimed by someone so . . . unworthy of it."

Akos schooled his features to stay blank.

"I brought you here to eat," Lazmet said. "On your . . . restricted diet . . . I recognize I can't completely deny you food. So I thought we might have dinner."

There was a table on the dais, pushed up against the far wall. It didn't seem big enough for the kind of grand dinners that Lazmet probably had, but it was long, about the width of Akos's armspan, and had a seat at either end. Akos thought this was probably all a part of Lazmet's strategy, forcing him to eat in the greenish light under jars of eyeballs, in full view of all the weapons the Noavek family had used to bleed their way to the top of Shotet society. He was meant to be unsettled by this.

"I'm not really in a position to refuse dinner," Akos said.

"No, you certainly aren't," Lazmet said, smirking as he put the staff back in its place. Near the edge of the wall of weapons was a bell, built into the wall. He rang it, and gestured to the table for Akos to sit down. Akos did, his head swimming. The food Yma had given him was just enough that he felt his hunger all the time. He drank glass after glass of water just to give his body the impression that it was full of something.

The fenzu that usually swarmed in the globular chandelier were half-dead and needed to be replaced. Akos could see the husks of their bodies collected at the bottom of each glass globe, little prickly legs up in the air.

"Vakrez tells me you are too consumed with self-hatred for him to get a meaningful reading," Lazmet said. "Yma assures me that you are progressing. That a vulnerable heart is easier to bend."

Akos didn't answer. Sometimes he wondered if Yma was playing a game with him. Indulging his desire to kill his father while worming her way in to do her actual work. He had no way of knowing that she was on his side, not really, except her word.

A wall panel behind Lazmet pulled back, and three servants filed into the Weapons Hall, carrying plates covered with protective domes of gleaming metal. They set one plate in front of Lazmet, one in front of Akos, and a third in the center of the table, then backed away. Akos didn't see if they left or if they simply fell into the shadows.

"I am familiar with how guilty people think, though I myself find guilt to be a worthless emotion," Lazmet said. "Why feel bad for a thing you did with full conviction, after all?" He hadn't sat down yet. He snapped his fingers, and one of the servants came forward with a cup made of etched glass. She poured something into it, something dark purple and thick, and Lazmet drank.

"I know that you are thinking there may still be time to undo what you have done to your friend," Lazmet said. "It's a last effort to maintain the part of your identity that I most need you to let go of. You are someone who thinks in extremes, and you have placed me, my family, perhaps all of Shotet, in an untouchable, unreachable place inside you that you have labeled 'bad.'"

He reached across the table to the dome in the center, and lifted it. The plate was empty but for a jar, a smaller version of the ones lining the walls. It, too, held greenish preservative. And bobbing inside it were two white globes.

Akos tasted bile and roasted deadbird. He could have looked away. He already knew what was in the jar. He didn't need to keep looking—

One of the globes turned, showing a dark iris.

"I take one eye if I intend to let someone live," Lazmet said. "I take both if they are executed, as Jorek Kuzar was at midnight last night."

Akos swallowed reflexively, and forced himself to close his eyes. If he kept looking, he would vomit. And he would not give Lazmet the satisfaction of seeing him vomit.

"The truth," Lazmet said softly, "is that you cannot undo what you have done. It's too late. You will never be able to return to the people you once counted as friends. So you may as well let go, Akos."

There was horror somewhere at the edge of his mind, so close he could touch it without difficulty, if he dared. He breathed, and drew away from it. Not now, not yet.

What is your mission?

Akos opened his eyes, staring up at the man whose blood and

bone and flesh had conspired to create him.

To kill Lazmet Noavek, came the answer, clearer now than ever before.

Lazmet sat down across from him, and uncovered his plate, offering the dome to the servant behind him. On his plate was a roll, a piece of cooked meat, and a whole fruit, its peel still on. Lazmet frowned at it.

"I didn't think this shipment would come for another week yet," he said, picking up the fruit. Akos recognized the peel from when he had broken into Lazmet's office.

A green glimmer caught his eye just over Lazmet's shoulder. The wall panel had slid back, silent, and a dark head was jutting out of the opening. The head lifted, showing a sliver of silverskin, and a pair of sharp, dark eyes.

Behind Lazmet, Cyra raised a currentblade about the length of her forearm, and made to stab him in the back. Akos didn't stir an izit.

Lazmet, however, lifted a hand, as if signaling for another glass of whatever it was he was drinking. And Cyra's hand stopped, right in the middle of her downward swing.

"Cyra," Lazmet said. "How kind of you to remember my favorite fruit."

CHAPTER 47 | CYRA

MY FATHER HAD NEVER used his currentgift on me. That would have required him to acknowledge my existence, which he had preferred not to do. So I had not realized how strange it would feel, to be the target of his unique power. I felt him wriggling around in my head, an uncomfortable pressure in the primary central cortex of my brain, which triggered movement. I assumed that was the area he manipulated, anyway. It could also have been my cerebellum.

Not the time for a debate over anatomy, I scolded myself.

Regardless of where he focused his currentgift, it was working. My fingers, hand, and arm were completely stiff, holding the blade halfway between where I had raised it and where I had intended to shove it. The rest of my body also seemed to be incapable of movement—not that it was numb, exactly, but it was like a pile of kindling that refused to take a spark. Everything felt the same, but I couldn't get it to move.

He seemed to want me to respond, though, because what small movement I *was* able to channel was in my mouth and jaw.

"No problem," I said, feeling oddly clearheaded though I knew that I was about to die. My last chance to kill him had been a moment ago, and now it was gone. Lazmet's control over my body was absolute as of the moment he became aware of my presence.

Except, I thought, *if Akos touches him.*

I tried to make eye contact with Akos, to somehow communicate what I wanted him to do, but I couldn't move.

The wriggling in my brain went deeper, and I felt utter revulsion. My fingers pulled apart around the knife handle, and the blade clattered to the floor. Lazmet stood, faced me, and picked it up, examining the handle.

"Not a finely made knife," Lazmet said.

"It would have done the job," I said.

"Any fool with a hammer can smash in a skull, little daughter," he said. I had forgotten how tall he was. Though I stood taller than most women, he still towered over me, as Ryzek had. And with his pale skin tinted green by the light through the jars of preservative, he looked like a rotting corpse. "I thought you more refined, based on upbringing alone."

"My access was limited," I said. "Trust me, I would have wrapped my mother's blade in silk and crammed it in your eye socket if I had had unlimited resources."

He released me halfway, so my arm fell to my side, and my posture straightened. I regained the use of my eyes, so I could blink and look at Akos, who sat motionless at his place at the table.

He had only been here for two weeks, if the information we had gotten from Ara was correct, but he had changed. He had always been lean, but his face was now gaunt, and if he had stood, I was sure the slight paunch that had made his waist soft was now gone. The bones in his wrists stood out like little rocks under the skin. He was paler than pale, as green in this light as my father was, and unkempt, like he had not bothered to bathe in several days.

I ached with hunger, with sympathy, and yes, with longing, even still, as I looked at him. Knowing that he hadn't abandoned me just to return home and wait out the war had made it more difficult to be angry with him. Coming here had been stupid, but it had at least been for a greater purpose.

I stared at him, trying to get some kind of acknowledgment that I was standing right in front of him, and he stared back, but without recognition. He almost looked the way Eijeh had, after Ryzek had traded his first memory with him—like he didn't know who I was, or where he was. Like someone had broken him and put him back together incorrectly.

"There is a saying from a Shotet cleric that seems apt, given the situation," Lazmet said. He spun the knife on his palm, and caught it by the blade, offering it back to me, handle first. I gritted my teeth as the wriggling in my brain began again, and my hand extended, my fingers closing around the handle. "Only use a blade if you're prepared to die by it."

I shuddered, hard, as I realized what he was about to do. I fought the *thing* in my brain with every ounce of my strength as my hands both clasped the handle, turning the blade to face my own stomach. He had left my mouth free so that he could hear me scream, I was sure of it.

"Akos!" I yelled. "Touch him!"

"My son's currentgift is not active at the moment," Lazmet said. "But he is, of course, welcome to try."

Akos had not moved. I watched as he swallowed, hard, and fixed his gaze on me.

"No," he said quietly. "There's no point."

My hands pulled closer, and the tip of the blade touched my stomach—and somehow I had always known this was how death would find me, at the hands of my own family, and at the end of my own knife—

But though this felt familiar, and even expected, I refused to accept it.

It hadn't occurred to me until then that though Lazmet controlled my muscles, he didn't necessarily control my currentgift. And while I couldn't control it that well, either, I knew that it was hungry to be shared—as ever, it wanted to devour everything in its path, even if what was in its path was me. The doctor my mother had taken me to when I was young had told me my currentgift was an expression of what I thought I deserved, and what I thought other people deserved: pain. Perhaps there was truth in that. Perhaps I was now learning that I didn't deserve it as much as I had once thought. But regardless, I did know one thing: there was no other man in the galaxy who had earned pain more than the one who stood in front of me.

I didn't send out a hesitant tendril, wondering if it would work. I threw my currentgift at Lazmet Noavek with all the force of my will, and a black cloud engulfed him like a swarm of insects. He screamed, without control, without the luxury of pride. The knife stopped moving toward my gut, but I couldn't release it, either.

Then I heard a sharp *pop* as one of the jars on the shelves that lined the walls burst, like a balloon, its contents spurting over the floor. Another one shattered right after it, and another. Soon the air was pungent with the smell of long-preserved flesh and the light was changing from greenish to white. The floor was slick, and white lumps rolled this way and that. The wriggling in my brain subsided, and hands grabbed my shoulders from behind, dragging me backward.

I screamed, "No!" I had been so close, so close to killing him—

But the hands pulled me into the hidden hallway behind me, and once I was in the dark, I knew better than to try to run back. Instead I threw myself forward, spotting the bobbing of a knot of hair that told me it was Ettrek who had grabbed me. We ran, my father's shouting chasing us into the shadows. I jumped down half a flight of stairs I knew was coming, and turned a sharp corner, only to find Yma Zetsyvis standing at the exit in the kitchen, her blue eyes wild.

"Come quickly!" she said, and together we ran to the back gate, where Teka was waiting, motioning us out.

Running through the streets around Noavek manor reminded me of the Sojourn Festival. My hand wrapped around Akos's, my face itching from blue paint. Chasing him with water cupped in my hands, though it was raining down from above. And the quiet of afterward, when I stripped my blue-stained clothes in my bathroom and realized there was something calm and still inside me that hadn't been that way since before my mother died.

Since he had kissed me in the transport vessel galley, I had thought about what the exact moment was that I fell for him. Now, dragging air into struggling lungs as I ducked around corners and under low ceilings in the tunnels of Noavek manor, I wondered whether I had fallen for him while he was lying to me, making a show of being kind so that I would reveal how to get out of the manor. And if it had been during that time, did that mean I loved someone who didn't exist? A pretend Akos, like one of the Storyteller's smoke pictures?

A group of people running would have attracted more attention than anything, so when we were a few streets away from Noavek manor, I put my hood up and slowed to a walk. Yma, too, tucked her blond hair under a black scarf, though the pale color of her gown—lavender, today—still made her wealth too obvious. We would have to address that before we reached the fringes of the city.

Teka hooked her elbow around mine, making sure my skin was covered as well as hers. But it was instinct, to draw my currentshadows away from her, focusing them on the left side of my body instead of the right. Facing down my father had reminded me what the control felt like—not like controlling the shadows themselves, more like plating my body with armor so they couldn't touch me, and letting them flow elsewhere.

"This way we're just a pair of friends walking back from the market together," she said, tipping her head toward me. "No one expects Cyra Noavek to have a friend."

Sometimes she still said things that wounded me. And not because they were lies.

We walked that way, a dozen paces behind Ettrek and Zyt, and half a dozen paces in front of Yma.

"You'd be better off walking with her," I said, tipping my head back slightly. "You two could be mother and daughter."

Teka just shrugged.

When the streets turned from stone to broken stone to dirt, we stopped to address Yma's clothing. Teka loaned her a cloak with a hood, and she tied the dark scarf around her waist to cover most of her skirt. Only a little lavender peeked out from the bottom when she was in motion. Still, we made our way quickly to the safe house, with at least one of us peering over a shoulder every few steps, as if that wasn't suspicious on its own.

When we were tucked away inside the huge space, Ettrek turned to me.

"You know, it took a lot out of me, breaking all those jars," he said. "The least you could do is not look so angry at being rescued."

Now that we were safe, I let myself break. This time, I fell apart shouting.

"I had him! I was on the verge of killing him! And you decided to *rescue me?*"

Sifa emerged from a stairwell, her hands clasped in front of her. Had she known that we would fail? I didn't even want to consider the idea.

"Killing him!" Ettrek's hair was dusted with dirt, like sugar on top of a cake. "You were about to plunge a currentblade in your own stomach!"

"These currentshadows aren't only good for making me flinch a lot, you know." I charged toward him, crushing a patch of fragile flowers under the heel of my shoe. "I had him wrapped in them. I would have killed him."

"Maybe not before he killed you," Ettrek said quietly.

"And?" I demanded. He retreated, his back colliding with Zyt's chest, and I said, "When someone asks you to trade the chance of

Lazmet Noavek's death for the life of Ryzek's Scourge . . ." and then shouted, ". . . *you do it!*"

The echo in the half-exploded space lasted a long time.

"You and the Kereseth boy both exasperate me," Yma said, undoing the clasp on the cloak she had borrowed and lowering the hood. "So eager to throw your lives away."

"It's not just his life he's willing to throw away," I snapped. "It's mine, too."

"Yes, that was quite a shock, him not saving you," Yma said. "I wasn't sure he had the fortitude. I was so concerned I thought about creating it, in him, but I was afraid of the damage I might do in the process."

"Creating it?" I said.

"Yes," she said. "The reason your family has kept me alive so long is that I twist hearts into the shapes of my choosing."

"That," I said, "explains a lot."

"Does it." Yma's tone was wry. "In any case, you are remarkably consistent, Miss Noavek. The boy has been starved, imprisoned, beaten, manipulated, threatened, and shown his friend's eyeballs in a jar at dinner, and still you think about what he allowed to happen to *you*."

"Yma," Teka said, looking sick.

"No, no. Let her get it out." I held my arms wide. "Which am I, then? Irritatingly self-sacrificial, or shockingly self-centered?"

"Do I have to choose?" She raised her eyebrows, which were so pale they almost blended into her skin. "You would die so that we all have to honor you. You are too bigheaded for the slow fade into obscurity, also known as a regular life. One thing I will say for your former paramour is that unlike you, he has no thirst for glory, at least."

I was about to respond when I noticed that Teka had covered her face. I heard a sharp sound, muffled by her palms. A sob.

"Jorek," she said.

It pulled the anger out of me, like sucking the poison from a bite. I had forgotten. Yma had forgotten, too, or she might not have chosen such specific words—*shown his friend's eyeballs in a jar.* Not only was Jorek gone, but he had suffered the same horror as Teka beforehand. It was not the way anyone should have to die.

Yma went to her in the way that only family could, wrapping her arms around her niece and clutching her close. I stood nearby, not willing to leave, but unsure how to stay. In more ways than one.

Sifa had walked over. Her hair was tucked into a bumpy braid, the same wavy-thick-smooth texture as my own.

"Did you know?" I said. I could have been asking about a dozen things, but I didn't bother to clarify.

"I suspected. I am still not sure exactly what's coming, or how to steer us. The situation has become . . . exponentially more complicated."

My chin wobbled when I spoke next: "If you don't know how to steer us . . . why did you come?"

"You won't like my answer."

As if that had ever mattered.

Sifa lifted a shoulder. "I came to be with you."

Sifa—the woman who had abandoned her husband and children to the horror of murder and kidnapping, the woman who had coaxed her son into killing Vas Kuzar and allowed Orieve Benesit to die in the name of fate—had come here, not to maneuver, but just . . . to be with me?

I wasn't sure whether to believe her or not, so I just nodded, sharply, and walked away.

The slant of light coming through the broken ceiling had taken on a burnt color, like still-cooling embers. That meant the day was done, with no plan, no path, no way back to Lazmet Noavek. Morning would come, and the time Isae Benesit had given us would run out.

CHAPTER 48 | CISI

I WAKE WITH A sour taste in my mouth. I am not sure where I am. The last time I knew anything, I was in my bathroom with blood soaking my side, and Ast had just stabbed me. I thought I would die. But wherever I am, I don't seem to be dead.

My tongue feels like it's fuzzy. I cringe a little at the feeling. Someone sticks a straw between my lips, and I drink. Water fills my mouth, and I swish it around before swallowing.

And oh—swallowing *hurts*. Not my throat, but my stomach. It's like someone tore right through my abdomen.

I open my eyes. I'm not sure why I expect to see the big crack that's above my bed at home. When I was sick as a kid I used to think about what it was shaped like. A floater? A bird? I could never decide.

There's no crack in this ceiling, though. The ceiling here is a moving image, like the ones in the walls at Assembly Headquarters. It shows a blue sky with puffy clouds drifting across it.

I lift a hand. There's a patch of tech just under my knuckles. I can feel it, stinging a little as I wiggle my fingers. It's probably monitoring my vitals, heart rate and temperature and blood sugar. There's a little exit point on top of it, attached now to a tube with clear liquid running through it. Keeping me hydrated, I assume, though it's not doing anything for the taste in my mouth.

"Miss Kereseth?"

I blink away the film covering my eyes and see a woman dressed in a crisp white uniform—shirt and pants—with a dark blue apron over the top of it. Her hair is tied back and secured with pins. She wears rubber gloves.

I feel unmoored. In my mind, I list the things I know. I am not at home. Judging by the ceiling, I am in a rich place. Assembly Headquarters? No, Othyr—Othyr is where we were last. I'm hurt. My stomach. It's like someone tore right through my abdomen. . . .

I remember his face in the mirror, right next to mine. Someone did just that.

"Ast," I croak.

"What?" The nurse frowns. "He's not here right now—he came yesterday to check on you, though."

He came to check on me? No, he came to make sure I was still unconscious, or in the hope that I was dead. A shiver runs through me. He was here while I was unconscious—what if he did something else, what if he tried to finish what he started? I imagine a pillow pressed to my mouth, a vial of poison tipped down my throat, stitches pulled from the wound in my abdomen until my guts spill out—

"No," I say, and it comes out a growl. "No—Ast did it, Ast stabbed me—"

"Miss Kereseth, I think you're confused, you've been out for a couple days—"

"I am not—"

"The security footage of your room was missing," she says softly.

Of course it was, I think, but can't say. *Ast found a way to delete the evidence—!*

"But they found the weapon, wiped of fingerprints," she continues, "in the house of a man whose currentgift allows him to put on different faces. The Othyrian police suspect he was trying to kill the chancellor and got you instead."

I squeeze my eyes shut. Of course. Ast plays at being too simple for politics, he senses currentgifts, he grew up with real-world smarts and contacts with seedy reputations, no doubt . . . of course he knew how to cover his tracks. He deleted the footage, misled the police, found a likely suspect to frame for the crime, planted the weapon. . . .

But *why*? Why would he take this risk? Just to be right? To get his way? Why did he even care so much about what happened to Thuvhe in this war?

"It was him," I say with some difficulty.

Maybe, I think as I drift off again, *it's not Thuvhe he cares about, but Shotet.*

Isae told me the story, once, of how she got the scars. I never asked her, because that wasn't the sort of thing you just *asked* about. But she told me anyway.

We had been sitting on the old, grungy sofa in my school

apartment. There were pots brewing on burners everywhere, so the corners of the room were full of vapor. We were in Shissa, so through the floor-to-ceiling windows on the far wall, all I could see were snowdrifts far below. My room was hardly even wide enough for me to stretch out my arms in both directions, but it had a good view.

She had an embroidered pillow in her lap, one I had bought from a little shop in Hessa where a friend from primary school worked. She was wearing socks I had loaned her because hers weren't warm enough. They were yellowish brown, or brownish yellow, I could never decide which, and had a lumpy heel where I'd gone wrong with mending them.

She told me that she hadn't really grown up on a pirate ship. That was just what she told people to startle them. The transporter ship she was on as a kid did some shady business every now and then, she said, but nothing to get huffy about.

And trust me, she said, *if there was something to get huffy about, my parents would be huffy.*

They had landed on Essander to dump the goods from their most recent job, and it just happened to be the planet where the Shotet were doing their seasonal scavenge. Only, scavenges weren't *supposed* to include theft and murder, according to the ethical guidelines Shotet had agreed to when the Assembly was formed.

The Shotet boarded the transporter ship, much like pirates would have done. And they blew through the vessel room by room, rifling through everything to find valuables, and killing whoever they wanted. One of the scavengers threatened Isae's mother, and when her father defended her, they both wound up dead. So Isae went at the man with a meat mallet.

A . . . meat mallet? I asked her, so shocked I couldn't help but smile. It was all right. She smiled, too.

She cracked one of them hard in the head, she said, but meat mallets are worthless against a Shotet soldier. Actually, pretty much anything was, according to her. They were lethal. And the leader of the group, a woman, must have admired Isae's gumption, because instead of killing her, she pinned Isae down and carved into her face, saying, *"Remember me."*

She hadn't mentioned Ast at the time, except to say that some of her friends were hurt or killed, too. Now, though, I knew that he had been there, and that a Shotet soldier had killed his father, and half of his friends.

Yeah, there were plenty of reasons for Ast to care what happened to Shotet in this war.

"Cee?"

Isae's voice sounds strained. She looks worn, her hair lank around her face. She grabs my hand and squeezes it. I guess Ast must not have told her I tried to send a message to the Shotet exiles, then, or she would have me arrested instead of sitting at my bedside.

"Did you . . ." My voice sounds creaky as an old door. "Did you make the alliance with Othyr?"

"You don't need to worry about that right now," she says. "Just focus on healing, okay? We almost lost you. *I* almost lost you."

"I'm fine," I say. I tap the button to raise the top half of the bed. When I'm partially upright, pain burns all the way through to my back, but I don't want to lie down again. "Tell me."

"Yes, I made the alliance," she says. "Before you say anything—we needed that weapon, Cee. The pressure to retaliate is intense."

"Pressure from where?" I say. "Ast?"

She frowns at me.

"Everywhere," she says. "From my own head, for one. From Shissa, Osoc, Hessa. From the Assembly Leader. Everywhere. They killed innocent people. What am I supposed to do?"

"Show mercy," I say, and it's enough to set her off.

"Mercy?" she demands. "*Mercy?* Where was Shotet mercy when they destroyed a hospital? Where was it when that woman held me down and sliced into my face? Where was it for my mother, my father—for *Ori?*"

"I—"

"Othyr gave us an anticurrent blast, and I'm going to use it as soon as I can," she says. "At which point I hope you'll tell me your brain was addled by painkillers, because there's no way a right-minded person would call for mercy right now."

She storms out, with a straight spine. The posture a couple seasons at the Assembly taught her, so she would fit in.

They killed innocent people, she said, almost in the same breath she talked about doing the same. And that's the problem—because to her, no Shotet is innocent. And that is the big difference between us.

I look up at the clouds projected on my ceiling. They're thicker now, closer together.

I'm stuck here, and out of options. Out of time.

I dream of the oracle Vara, showing me the sculptures in the Hall of Prophecy on Ogra. Each one is a member of my family, made of glass. Even Cyra is among them.

And I wake to Ast's face, looming over mine.

"I'm not here to hurt you," he says, when the beetle chirps—signaling to him, I'm sure, that I've moved. "Isae will be along soon. I just wanted to have a chat with you first."

He drags the stool over to my bedside, and sits, the beetle perching on his shoulder.

"You may have noticed that I didn't tell Isae that you tried to contact our enemies. That you tried to contact *Cyra Noavek*."

My face is hot. My throat burns. I want to speak. To yell. To wrap my hands around his throat.

"I didn't think it was wise to arouse her suspicions—you betray her, and in the same night, you're attacked?" he says. "But you should know that if I do decide to tell her, I'm sure she will have more sympathy for me than she will for you. Attacking the woman she loves because she turned traitor to her country . . . it's forgivable. What you did is not."

"You—" I grit my teeth. The word comes out as a growl, forced as hard as I can past the strictures of my throat and mouth.

"So don't step out of line, Cisi," he says. "What's done is done. The attack's been ordered, and I think now we can begin to get along."

I want to scream at the unfairness of it, my silence forced by the current, which supposedly gives all life. If it's such a good thing, why does it strangle me? Why does it torture Cyra? Why does it push away my brother, and empower dictators, and boggle my mother's mind?

I hear the sharp, clipped tone of Isae's voice just outside the door. I know, then, what I need to do.

If my gift can't be overcome, then maybe it needs to be put to use instead.

I push aside my anger, my grief, my worry. I push aside my pain, too, as much as I can. I remember sinking to the bottom of the pool in the temple basement when I learned to swim. The way the water burned my eyes at first. How it lifted my hair away from my head, made it feel soft. How it caressed, and pulsed with its own rhythm. How I could hear my own heartbeat.

Isae told me Ast's father went by "Wrench." He maintained their little ship. So maybe it's not comfortable things that soften Ast, but hard things: the warm metal handle of a tool his dad just put down. The vibration of the ship's engine in the wall. The prick of a grate under his bare feet.

Ast blinks, slowly.

"Hey," he says. "Stop."

"No," I say. He's comfortable enough now that I can talk, at least. "You've been chastising me for the use of my currentgift since you arrived. You watch it strangle me and you don't do anything to make sure I'm heard. Well, now I'll watch it strangle you."

"You're controlling her," Ast says. "I can't let you."

The rough sleeve of a maintenance worker's coveralls, faintly frayed. Engine oil rubbed between two fingers, smooth and faintly sticky. A screw catching in place and tightening, turn after turn.

"You try to get your way, and I try to get mine," I say, "but neither of us controls her."

"No, you're—" He leans back, and closes his eyes. "It's different."

"You're right, my methods are far more effective," I say softly.

"You think I use my gift recklessly. You have no idea how much I hold back."

I hit him with it again: the shudder of the seat beneath him as his ship passes through an atmosphere. The crinkle of the wrapper that comes around a prepackaged protein cake at a fuel station. I wrap the textures around him, metal and plastic and vapor and grease, until he may as well be living back in that ship.

He sags against the wall and just stares at me.

"You will not get in my way anymore," I say. "I will guide us away from catastrophe, and you will allow me to."

The door opens, admitting Isae, dressed in her training clothes. Her face shines with sweat. She smiles at Ast and me, likely thinking we're making peace. As if peace is what I could have with someone who attacks me, and threatens me, and takes advantage of my inability to speak.

"What's wrong?" she says, her face falling as she takes in the scene, me tense and upright, hands clenched into fists. Ast sagging, shoulders curled in, eyelids half-closed.

"Tell her," I say to him. "Tell her what you did to me."

He stares, his eyes empty.

"Tell. Her," I say slowly.

"I attacked you," he says to me. Then, to Isae, "It was me, I attacked her."

"You—what?" Isae says. "Why?"

"She was interfering," he says.

I can't sustain this level of energy for much longer. I pull back on my currentgift with a gasp. When Ast returns to himself, his face crumples into rage. Isae looks stricken.

"I'm sorry, I . . ." I pretend to choke on the words. I let myself falter, and grab my stomach with one arm, wincing. Let her see me as weak, out of control.

"I didn't mean to," I say. "But I needed—I needed you to believe me."

"She's lying to you!" Ast snaps. "Can't you see that? She's using her currentgift to manipulate you, to control you! She's been doing it this whole time!"

"Look—look at his arm," I say. "There's a bite mark, from where I fought back."

Isae's jaw tightens. She marches over to him and grabs his arm, pulling him to his feet. He goes where she directs him, maybe knowing that he can't fight a chancellor, or that I've finally beat him. She pushes up his sleeve, and there it is—a perfect impression of my teeth, an uneven half circle.

She drops his arm with a soft moan.

"I—she was trying to contact the Shotet!" he says. "She tried to send a message to—"

"Shut up," Isae says. She blinks rapidly. "I trusted you. You lied to me. You—I want you arrested. I want you *gone*."

I am slipping away. Too tired to stay. But before I go, I look at Ast, and though I know he can't see it, I smile.

CHAPTER 49 | AKOS

Akos was staring into the fire when the door opened the next morning.

He had expected, when Cyra fled without his help, to break down completely. Instead, he felt like all the excess of his life—the agonizing over blood and citizenship and family and fate—had been pared away, like meat cooked away from the bone. And now everything that had been muddled was clear.

He was not Thuvhesit or Shotet, Kereseth or Noavek, third child or second. He was a weapon against Lazmet Noavek.

The gnaw of hunger no longer bothered him, except that it left his mind and body fatigued, and less useful to him. Yma didn't come to bring him more food, so he knew she had likely helped Cyra escape, and he was grateful for that, in a distant way that applied to some other life. In this life, he wanted nothing but to accomplish his goal.

"Akos?"

The voice belonged to Vakrez. Akos rose from his place by the fire, suppressing a shiver at the cold air he found away from it.

Vakrez was frowning at him.

"Are you all right?" he said more kindly than usual.

"I'm fine," Akos said, as he stuck out his arm for Vakrez to take.

"That's not why I'm here. There wouldn't be much point, with Yma gone," Vakrez said. "Lazmet summoned me to discuss strategy, and he asked me to collect you on my way."

Akos looked for his shoes, and found them tucked under the foot of the bed. He stuffed his feet in, and raised his eyebrows at the commander when he didn't move away from the doorway.

"What?" he said.

"You seem . . ." Vakrez frowned. "Never mind."

They walked side by side to whatever room Lazmet was using for the meeting. His office, it seemed, because they climbed up a staircase with wood-paneled walls, instead of going down to the Weapons Hall. Akos had to stop at the top to catch his breath, and Vakrez waited for him without complaint.

His father greeted him with a tilted head when he walked into the office, with its soft rug and its tomes of history stacked high. The peel of the fruit that had clued Lazmet in to Cyra's infiltration of the manor sat curled on Lazmet's desk.

When Lazmet gestured for Akos to sit, he did this time, at the end of the sofa closest to the fire. He looked down at his fingers. Had his knuckles gotten thicker? Or had the rest of his hand simply begun to disappear, his body devouring the last reserves of strength and energy it had?

"Akos," Vakrez said, jostling his shoulder.

"Hmm?" Akos lifted his head.

"Pay attention," he said, eyebrows raised.

He had scolded Akos for inattention more than once. The last time, Akos remembered, had been at the soldiers' camp, after he had earned his armor, and maybe a small amount of respect from his commander. Vakrez had been lecturing about strategy. Something about how the soldier who was on his home ground always had the advantage, because he knew the terrain. Shotet soldiers therefore had to adapt quickly, as they would never be on their home ground. *Even Voa*, he said, *isn't your home. Shotet have no home.*

"Oh, don't scold him, Vakrez," Lazmet said, leaning back in his chair with a book in his lap. Akos couldn't see the spine. "He's not operating at full capacity right now."

"Why am I here?" Akos asked, blinking slowly at Lazmet.

"I was hoping you would tell me a few things about your hometown," Lazmet said. "I understand that you come from Hessa."

He was about to ask why Lazmet wanted to know about his hometown—his memories, after all, were the kind a kid would care about, like where the best sweets were, or which shop Eijeh liked to browse just so he could make eyes at the girl who worked behind the counter. But the answer, when he considered it a little bit more, was obvious.

"You're going to attack it," Akos said. The thought of Shotet swarming the steep streets of Hessa, charging into the sweet shop, maybe killing the girl who worked behind the counter, made him feel ill.

Lazmet didn't answer.

"It's not hard to figure out," Akos said. He felt far away from everything. "There are only three major cities in Thuvhe. You already hit Shissa. So it's either Osoc or Hessa next."

"You don't seem troubled," Lazmet said. "Do you expect me to believe that you feel nothing for the place where you spent the majority of your life?"

He wouldn't let himself think about the dim little spice shop that made him sneeze, or the woman who sold elaborate paper flowers in the warm months, when it didn't snow. Or the alley that was a straight shot up the hill, the best—and most dangerous—sledding path in all of Thuvhe. He wouldn't, or he would get swallowed up in it.

Lazmet wanted him to betray his home. *Shotet have no home*, Akos thought, remembering Vakrez's lecture on strategy.

But he did have a home. He had a home ground, a place no one knew as well as he did.

"It's not that I feel nothing," he said, steadying himself as much as he could. "It's that I have an offer for you."

"Oh?" Lazmet looked amused. Well, that was all right, Akos thought. Better he be amused and underestimate Akos, than be suspicious.

"You'll take me to Hessa with you, and after your attack is over, you will leave me there, at my house," Akos said. "After that, I won't come after you, and you won't come after me."

"And in return?"

"In return, I'll help you destroy the temple of Hessa."

Lazmet glanced at Vakrez. The commander looked like he was working the idea between his teeth. He sat on the other end of the sofa, somehow managing to make sinking into the cushions look graceful.

"The temple of Hessa," Lazmet said. "Why should that matter to me?"

"Judging by your Shissa attack, you want to be theatrical. Big, destructive gestures are demoralizing, as well as costing a lot of lives," Akos said. "But Hessa doesn't have grand, floating buildings you can knock out of the sky. It has the temple. It's stamped on our old currency, from before the Assembly was formed. There's nothing else to attack in Hessa *except* the temple."

The odd thing was, he knew that both men already knew this. Lazmet was old enough to remember the siege his mother had led against Hessa, the one that Hessa temple still bore the busted windows and scraped-up stones from. The one Akos's grandmother had gone into with nothing more than a meat cleaver, if the stories were true.

So Lazmet probably just wanted to see if Akos would persuade him, or bother to try. More "curiosity," more experimentation. It never stopped.

"It's a temple, not a labyrinth," Lazmet said. "I don't really need your help to attack it, now that you've told me that's what I ought to do."

Akos felt the sharp stick of panic in his chest. But he knew Hessa temple better than most Thuvhesits did, and that had to be worth something. It had to.

"By all reports, it may as well be a labyrinth for as much sense as its layout makes. You'd be hard-pressed to find a map of it, either," Akos said. "But if you and your fighting force want to run around like a bunch of idiots, giving the oblates plenty of time to summon the whole army of Hessa—the best army in all of

Thuvhe, I should add—then go right ahead."

"So the layout is nonsensical, there are no maps, and you just happen to know how to navigate it," Lazmet said with a sneer. "How convenient."

"None of this is *convenient*," Akos said, scowling. "You brought me here because you thought I had something useful to tell you about Hessa, and now I tell you I know something useful and you refuse to believe it?" Akos let out a short laugh. "I betrayed my country, I got my friend killed—I have nothing to go back to, nothing left in the world except for that house, where people will leave me alone. You made sure of that. So have your attack, have your war, have whatever you want, but *leave me alone*, and I'll give you whatever I've got."

Lazmet's eyes were fixed on his, searching, calculating. Akos imagined himself as the Armored One, tearing into his own abdomen to make a space for Lazmet to get in. He felt the wire wiggling in his head, and the involuntary twitch of his fingers that meant Lazmet was testing him. Suspicious, as always, but Akos had come to expect it.

Lazmet took in his twitching fingers. Akos felt the swoop of something like hope in his gut, and then—

"Vakrez, give me a read on him," Lazmet said.

Akos knew it would be more suspicious to object than not, so he stuck out his arm for Vakrez to take. It was getting easier and easier to imagine himself as the Armored One, the more he wanted to be away from everything and everyone. Armored Ones were solitary, separate from everything that channeled the current. Lonely, but impenetrable, just like he was. He knew most people who killed them had to find a way to stick a knife in them right under the arm or leg joint, where there was a space between the thick plates that covered its body. They had to get in far enough to make the thing bleed to death. That was how Cyra had killed it, he was sure. It was her way—find the weakness, exploit it, be done with it. It was more honorable than the way he had done it, lulling the beast to sleep, giving it relief, like he was someone to be trusted, and then poisoning it.

But that was *his* way.

Except now, there was nothing he could do except let down his currentgift shield so that Vakrez could poke his way into Akos's heart. And what he would see there was pure intention, the desire to kill Lazmet unmistakable.

Vakrez touched him, his hand cool and rough as always, and closed his eyes for a few ticks. Akos waited for the blow to fall, waited for the end of him.

"So much clearer now," Vakrez said. He opened his eyes, and looked to Lazmet. "All he wants is to escape."

Akos tried not to stare. It was a lie.

Vakrez was lying for him.

He didn't dare look at the commander. He couldn't afford to give himself away now.

"Then, my boy," Lazmet said to him, "it seems we have a deal. You take me to Hessa. And I'll let you go home."

I'll take you to my home ground, Akos thought, *and that's where you'll die.*

CHAPTER 50 | CYRA

THE NEXT MORNING, THERE was nothing left to do but leave the safe house. Leave Voa, and Lazmet, and Akos.

Give up, in other words.

We rifled through the drawers of one of the abandoned apartments to find a change of clothes for everyone, then left the safe house. We had promised Yssa, who was waiting in the ship for the signal to retrieve us, that we would meet her if we managed to escape.

I fidgeted as we walked, the rough fabric of my ill-fitting trousers rubbing at my thighs. Someone's old throw blanket had become a scarf to cover my face, and it, too, chafed. Zyt and Ettrek led the way, the knot atop Ettrek's head bobbing with each footstep, then Yma and Teka, at a respectable distance, and Sifa and me, trailing behind. As we passed beneath boarded-up windows, I listened to Yma and Teka's conversation.

"I left the house to its ruin," Yma was saying. "It's too far away for most thieves to bother breaking into it, anyway."

"Once this is over, I'll help you put it right," Teka said.

"That place is full of Uzul, anyway," Yma said, shaking her head. She had tucked her hair behind her ears, and under the collar of her jacket, so it didn't show as much, but there was no disguising that flawless white.

The sound of Uzul's name stung me, though not as much as it stung Yma, I was sure. I had not killed him, not in the way I could have, but pain had driven him to death, and I had provided that pain. Cyra Noavek, purveyor of pain, agent of agony.

We reached the building where the ship waited, tucked under its tarp on the roof with Yssa inside it. Zyt had sent her a signal the night before, just to tell her at least some of us were alive, so she had not fled the city yet. We trudged up the stairs, which still smelled of garbage, and I found myself beside Zyt again at the head of the group, my long legs giving me an advantage.

He cast a soft look at me. "I—"

"Oh, don't." I sighed. "I don't do well with sympathy."

"Can I offer you a bracing slap on the back?" Zyt said. "A gruff reassurance, maybe?"

"Do you have candy? I would take candy."

He smiled, reached into his pocket, and took out a piece of bright plastic wrap about the size of a fingertip. I squinted at it, but peeled the wrapper with my fingernail and uncovered a small piece of hard fenzu honey, recognizable due to its bright yellow color.

"Why," I said, "are you carrying candy around in your pocket?"

Zyt shrugged. He pushed the door to the rooftop open, letting Voa's hazy light into the stairwell. The sky was covered with clouds, and the city had a yellowish cast, a storm brewing. The thick fabric that covered the ship was still tied down—loosely, so Yssa could have pulled the ship free easily if she needed to. I ducked under the edge of it, and almost choked on the hard candy.

Eijeh stood on the steps that extended from the ship's hatch.

"What are you doing here?" I demanded.

"I'm not staying," he warned. He looked awkward, all his weight on one leg, one hand clasping the hem of his jacket.

"That doesn't really answer her question," Teka said from behind me.

"I'm here to warn you all," Eijeh said.

"Why? Did you inform the Shotet police on us again?" Zyt said.

"No," Eijeh said. "I—just wanted to escape. To be free of her." He nodded to me. "And then, some of my visions . . . fell together. Overlapped."

"Mine haven't," Sifa said, her brow furrowed.

"Isae Benesit imparted some of herself when she forced us— forced Ryzek, I mean—to see her memories, before he was killed," Eijeh said. "So I have a better grasp on her than you do. I know her from the inside out."

I felt Teka staring at me, quizzical, but I couldn't look away. Eijeh's pale green eyes were strange. Clearer than they had been in a long time.

"I know we're out of time," I said. "Isae Benesit promised not to pressure Ogra to deport the exiles until after my week was up."

"Deportation is not what she has in mind now," Eijeh said. "She is preparing another anticurrent blast, like the one that destroyed the sojourn ship."

Sifa lifted a hand to cover her mouth, and for the first time, I knew—not from memory, or guesswork, but *seeing*, with my own eyes—that we were the same. The same strong nose. The same fierce brow. The family Kereseth, my family.

"Anticurrent," I said, redirecting my focus. I was no little girl craving a mother. I had had one. I had killed her.

"That's what the weapon is called," Eijeh said. "The current is a creative energy, and the anticurrent is its opposite. Where the two collide, a . . . strong force results."

I snorted. *Strong force, indeed.*

Yssa stepped out of the hatch, then, edging around Sifa. She ran toward Ettrek, hugging him, then Teka, and then me— quickly, and with wincing, but still, a hug.

"You lived," she said, breathless.

"Speak for yourself," I said. "I'm just an apparition."

"If that was true, it would likely not hurt to touch you," she said, without a trace of humor. I glanced at Teka, who shrugged.

"When is this blast supposed to hit us?" Teka asked Eijeh.

I gave Eijeh a hard look. "Concrete answers only."

Eijeh sighed, and said, "This evening."

And that was when a small fleet of ships rose up from the area around Noavek manor like bubbles bobbing to the surface of a water glass. They hovered together for a moment, and if the sky had not been so empty, or if they had not borne the Noavek symbol on their wings, I might not have noticed them at all. But those were Lazmet Noavek's ships, and they were headed straight west, toward the Divide. Toward Thuvhe.

"The anticurrent blast will happen this evening," I said.

Everyone sat on the main deck of the transport vessel. Most were on the bench along one wall, where the straps for buckling ourselves in dangled from the wall, but Teka was on the steps leading up to the nav deck, and Yssa was in the captain's chair, fiddling with the ship's map. My racing currentshadows, and the pain that chased them back and forth across my body, didn't allow me such stillness. I paced.

"Yes," Eijeh said. "Visions don't come with a watch, so the timing is not exact, but based on the color of the light, it will be evening."

I squinted at him. "Is that the truth, or is that just something you're telling me to manipulate me into doing what you want?"

"Are you really going to believe my answer to that question?"

"No." I stopped for a moment, in front of him. "Why now? You've only ever cared about yourself, for your entire life. So what's gotten into you? Brain parasite?"

"Is that really constructive?" Teka said. "We should be figuring out how to save as many lives as possible. Which means activating the emergency evacuation alert again."

"Evacuation protocol is to flee toward the sojourn ship," I said. "Where would people go, if we sounded that alarm?"

"I can code the alarm with a message. That way, people with screens in their homes will at least know what's coming," Teka said. "We can tell them to just get out of the city whatever way they can."

"And the people who don't have screens in their houses?" Ettrek said. "The people who barely have lights to turn on? What about them?"

"I didn't say it was perfect." She scowled at him. "And I don't hear you suggesting anything useful."

"If we do this," Yma said to Teka, "we may not be able to flee ourselves. We may die here."

A silence fell at that. I had accepted the likelihood of death when I decided to kill my father, but now that I had my life, I wanted to keep it again. Even without Akos, even without family, even with most of Shotet hating me, what I had told Teka before was right. I had more now. I had friends. Hope for my own future, and for myself.

But I also had love for my people, broken though some of them may have been. Their stubborn will to survive. The way they looked at discarded objects, not as garbage, but as possibilities. They crash-landed through hostile atmospheres. They coasted alongside the currentstream. They were explorers, innovators, warriors, wanderers. And I belonged to them.

"Yeah," I said. "Let's do it."

"How?" Yssa asked. "Where do you activate the alarm?"

"One of two places: Noavek manor, and the amphitheater. The amphitheater is easier to access," I said. "We don't all need to go. So who goes, and who stays?"

"I'm leaving this planet," Eijeh said.

"Yeah, I got that impression based on your repeated insistence that you're not staying," I snapped.

"I will take you off-planet, Eijeh," Yssa said to him. "You are an oracle and as such, your life is valuable."

"My life's not valuable?" Ettrek said.

Yssa gave him a look.

"You two should go," I said to Zyt. "You only signed on to smuggle, not to risk your lives."

"Yeah, none of us here would ever do that," Ettrek said, rolling his eyes. "You remember most of us came here to kill Lazmet Noavek, right?"

I glanced at Teka and Sifa, in turn.

"You're an oracle, too," I said to Sifa.

"I'm not afraid," Sifa said quietly.

I was. Part of me wanted to steal a floater and flee Voa as quickly as I could, get myself out of the way of the blast. But the better part—the part that made the decisions now, it seemed—knew that I had to stay, had to fight for my people, or at least allow them a chance to fight for themselves.

And maybe Sifa was as undaunted as she appeared. Maybe knowing the future forced you to be at peace with it. But I didn't think so.

She was afraid, just as I was, just as any person would be. It was that, perhaps, that made me accept that she was here. It was the most mercy I could offer her at the moment.

"Cyra should lead the way to the amphitheater," Yma said, and I looked at her in surprise. It was rare she gave me credit for anything. Ever. She added, "I believe you're familiar with the subterranean prison."

"Not as familiar as I am with your dazzling wit," I bit back with a smile.

"You take the bait every time, don't you?" Teka said to me.

I considered that for a moment. "Yes," I said. "It's part of my charm."

Ettrek snorted. And we started to plan.

⋙⋘

Some time later, we stood on the rooftop and watched Eijeh and Yssa board a smuggler ship, courtesy of Zyt's connections to Voa's criminal underground.

Eijeh didn't bid me farewell. But he did glance back before disappearing inside the ship. His eyes met mine, and he nodded, just once.

And then my brother was gone.

CHAPTER 51 | AKOS

THE AWAKENING IN HESSA had never been Akos's favorite—he liked the quiet dark of the Deadening, with its warm ovens and bright, Bloomed hushflowers—but it had certain charms. At the very start, in the weeks before the hushflowers lost their blooms, a swarm of deadbirds flew over Hessa every morning and evening in a big cloud, whistling in unison. Their song was bright and sweet, and the undersides of their wings were pink, like Akos's blush.

They were called deadbirds because they hibernated all winter, and the first person to come across a flock during hibernation had thought they were all dead. They hardly even had heartbeats then. But when the Awakening came around, they flew all the time, dropping pink feathers everywhere. His dad collected them for his mom, and stuck them in a jar on the kitchen table for decoration.

When Lazmet Noavek's ship landed just past the feathergrass north of Hessa, it sent up a cloud of pink feathers.

At least they aren't going past the house, Akos thought. His family's home was far from where they landed, though along the same strip of feathergrass. They would approach Hessa hill from behind, where there were no houses, and steps carved from rock would lead them to the temple's back gate.

The Shotet groaned and shivered when the hatch of the ship opened. Even Lazmet seemed to brace himself. But Akos drank in the frozen air like it was the finest thing he'd ever tasted. The soldiers had laughed at him when he first came on board, stuffed into half a dozen sweaters and jackets, incapable of lowering his arms. But none of them were laughing now.

Akos pulled the strip he had torn from his blanket over his face, so only his eyes showed. He spotted the handle of a current-blade on a careless soldier's hip, and wondered if he could grab it, stab Lazmet right now before anyone attacked Hessa. But the soldier turned away, the opportunity disappearing.

Lazmet beckoned, and Akos went to the front of the pack that had come together, the soldiers drawing closer in the cold. Vakrez and Lazmet, at least, had put on more than one layer.

Akos went to the front of the group, and looked up at Hessa hill. He had told Lazmet to fly in from as far north as he could stand to go, to glide low next to the feathergrass and land, going in on foot. Sure enough, he didn't hear the sirens that would have sounded all throughout the town if somebody had seen Shotet soldiers. It was strange, how he hoped that he would succeed, and hoped that he would fail, all at once.

There were two paths to the bottom of the hill, one that went into a dip in the land and would protect them from rough wind, and another that wouldn't. Akos chose the latter. He hoped half of the soldiers froze to death on their way in, or at least got such cold fingers they couldn't handle their currentblades right.

Akos pointed his nose across the bare plains and started walking.

It wasn't a long enough walk for any of the Shotet soldiers to freeze to death, unfortunately. But by the time they got to the bottom of the hill, the people behind him had come up with their own strategies for staying warm, some better than others. They were chewing on their fingertips—not the best idea—or wrapping their hands and faces in handkerchiefs and cloths. They were huddled in groups, rotating so one person took the brunt of the wind at a time. Akos's eyelashes were frosted, and the skin around his eyes was numb, but he felt all right otherwise. The trick to walking in the cold was to just let the chill happen, trusting that your body would take care of itself. When the will to live failed, the body still fought.

The wind died down. They were shielded now by huge crags made by avalanches, and natural promontories, since this was the jagged side of Hessa hill. Still, finding the steps wasn't easy—you had to know where they were, and Akos's memory, dulled though it was by everything he'd done, held strong. He went around one of the bigger rock formations and there they were, faint indentations only as long as the ball of his foot.

"I thought you said there were steps," Vakrez said to him.

"I thought you said the Shotet were adaptable," Akos retorted, his voice muffled by fabric, and he started up the slope.

Lazmet insisted that Akos lead the way, which ruled out shoving him over the edge. Akos started the quick hop that made the steps easier to climb, only he couldn't do it. He had been deprived of food for too long to do so much as a single bounce. He slumped against the side of the hill—more of a mountain to the Shotet, he realized—to keep him balanced as he went.

"You starve him for weeks and now you want him to lead us up a mountain?" Vakrez said to Lazmet.

"Get up there and help him, then, if you're so concerned," Lazmet said.

Vakrez stepped past Lazmet and, avoiding Akos's eyes, put an arm across Akos's back. Akos was startled by how strong Vakrez was, the older man lifting him almost to his toes as they walked together on the narrow stairs. The wind wailed so loud Akos couldn't have heard him if he had whispered right in his ear, so the two men climbed in silence, Vakrez pausing every time he noticed Akos's breaths getting labored.

After a while, the steps got bigger and flatter, cutting a winding path into the mountainside. They were made for oracles, not athletes, after all.

The sun was setting, and the snow sparkled in the light, glinting as it blew across the stone. It was a simple enough sight, and one Akos had seen thousands of times, growing up. But he'd never loved it as much as he did then, at the helm of a group of invading soldiers, on the verge of murder.

It was over too soon. They made it to the top, where a few sparse trees covered their approach, bent and curled from the constant wind. Akos had to stop at the top step, and Lazmet waved the others toward the door as Vakrez held him upright.

He was just standing on his own again when Vakrez pivoted, his broad frame shielding Akos from Lazmet's view.

"Whoa," Vakrez said, "get your legs under you, boy."

And he hiked up some of Akos's layers, shoving a blade under the waistband of Akos's pants and covering the handle with a sweater.

"Just in case," Vakrez said so quietly it was almost lost to the wind.

Akos didn't intend to use a blade, but he appreciated the gesture regardless.

The smell of Hessan incense nearly made Akos fall apart. It was herbal—almost like the medicine his mom had force-fed him for his chronic cough when he was a kid, but not quite—and spicy, stinging his nose once it wasn't numb from the cold anymore. It smelled like a dozen Bloomings, and handfuls of after-school visits spent waiting for Sifa to be done meeting with someone in the Hall of Prophecy, and afternoons of snickering at the youngest oblates, who stared at Eijeh and blushed right after he grew from a child to a teenager. It smelled like home.

Akos joined the soldiers in shedding some of his outer layers, though he was careful to protect the blade Vakrez had given him every time he raised his arms. He wound up in just one sweater, dark blue and soft, and kept his multiple pairs of socks on. They were keeping his too-large boots where they were. Sweat dotted the back of his neck; he felt warm air on it when he took off his hat. His legs still felt like jelly from the climb, or maybe that was anticipation of what was next.

"You'll want to disable the power in the building before you do anything else," he said to Lazmet. "There's the main power source and a backup generator. Take the bulk of your soldiers to the main source, it's on the other side of the building and you'll run into temple guards that way. The backup generator is close, and nobody guards it."

He took out the crude map he'd drawn of the temple—just the path from the back door to the maintenance room in the basement was marked on it—and stuffed it into Lazmet's hand.

"You only labeled one of those two on here," Lazmet said, looking the map over.

"Yeah," Akos said. "I have to keep some things back, or I can't hold you to your end of the deal. I'll take you to the backup generator myself."

He wasn't surprised when Lazmet didn't get angry. That would have been a normal response—you get in a person's way at a crucial moment, and they get angry. But Lazmet wasn't normal. He wanted his world to interest him. And Akos thinking two steps ahead clearly did.

This must have been how he crafted Ryzek, Akos thought. His disapproval came in the form of horror after horror, eyeballs in jars and people lying on their own blades. But when a person did finally make him proud, even if the reason disgusted them, they wanted to do it again. And again. And again.

"Commander Noavek, you'll take the platoon to the main power source. You and you—" He pointed to two soldiers—one dark-skinned, his coarse hair pulled back, and the other slim and yellow-haired, her skin almost as pale as Akos's. "You'll come with us."

It wouldn't be easy to get this done with two soldiers with them, Akos knew, but there was nothing he could do about it, no way he could insist that Lazmet come with him alone without making the man suspicious. If he had to get them all killed, he would. He had already gone crashing through his own ethics in every possible way. What was another mark on his arm?

The cool metal of Vakrez's blade pressed to Akos's back as he walked. He led the small group down a stone hallway, past the memorial of oracles past, where a long line of names were etched into a flat slab of stone. His mother wouldn't write her own until she foresaw her own death, which was the curse all oracles had to bear.

At the end of the hallway was a lantern that glowed faint pink, the result of faded hushflower powder. He turned right there, guiding them away from the Hall of Prophecy. He thought it was safe, leading them through the dormitories of the oblates who lived at the temple, but he had miscalculated—at the end of the row of doors was a young woman with her hair piled high on her head, yawning as she tugged her sweater back over her shoulder.

Their eyes met. Akos shook his head, but he was too late— Lazmet had already seen her.

"Don't let her run," he said, sounding bored.

The yellow-haired soldier streaked past Akos with her blade outstretched, black strings of current wrapped around her clenched fist. She thrust with one arm and caught the girl with the other. A sick gurgling sound came out of her mouth, a scream aborted before it could even take shape.

Akos shuddered.

Tell me your mission, he repeated to himself as he tasted bile.

To kill Lazmet Noavek.

"Stay here," Lazmet said to the soldier in a quiet voice. "Make sure she doesn't make noise. And that no one else interferes."

Swallowing hard, Akos kept going, past the girl, wheezing now with what was left of her life, and the soldier, wiping her bloody blade on the seat of her pants.

It was a clear night, so the moon, still rising to its full height, glowed through the narrow windows they passed. There were still scars in the stone walls from the Shotet siege that happened before Akos was born. He remembered running his fingers over them when he was a kid, stretching high over his head to touch the violence he hadn't yet seen.

That violence lived in his blood, not because he was a Shotet, but because he was a Noavek. The great-grandfather who had been a mediocre blacksmith and a vicious killer. The grandmother who had murdered her own siblings. The father who put a vise around the city of Voa. The brother who twisted and warped Eijeh.

It would end here. Now.

Akos reached the door he was looking for, had been looking for since they first landed. It didn't lead to a backup generator. There was no backup generator for the temple, a fact that had caused trouble during more than one snowstorm, forcing them to host a small pack of oblates in their house until the wind died down.

No, this door led to the courtyard where the hushflowers grew. A small field of deadly poison, right there in the temple.

Akos opened it, gesturing Lazmet inside.

"After you," he said.

Akos stepped in front of the soldier before he could follow Lazmet into the courtyard, bringing the door swinging behind him. The move had surprised the man; he didn't even object as Akos slammed the door between them, and turned the bolt so he couldn't get in.

"If your intention was to trick me into poisoning myself, your timing is off," Lazmet said.

Akos turned. The hushflowers—the ones he had been counting on to make this easier, their poison blooms capable of felling Lazmet even if he, Akos, couldn't—weren't there. Their stalks were empty. The flowers had already been harvested.

The knife was still cool against Akos's back. If Vakrez hadn't given it to him, he would be as good as dead right now.

Lazmet spread his hands, gesturing to all the dying leaves that surrounded him. He stood in the middle of the narrow path of stone that ran through the courtyard, to keep the caretakers away from the death-giving blossoms. Hushflower leaves died off in the peak of the Awakening, when the weather was warmest, though the roots stayed viable for a lifetime, if cared for properly. So all the greenery around Akos's father was limp and smelled like rot and dirt, ready to lie fallow until the next Blooming. There was no poison left to kill Lazmet with.

"That's inconvenient," Akos said. "But I do have a backup plan."

He lifted his shirt, and drew Vakrez's currentblade.

"Vakrez. Now, that's a surprise. I didn't think his heart had gone that soft in my absence," Lazmet said.

His voice had lost the unctuous quality it usually had when he spoke to Akos, like he was resorting to singsong with a stubborn kid. This was not the Lazmet who found him amusing. It was the one who forced people to cut out their own eyes.

"I will have to punish him as soon as I am finished with you."

He was folding the cuffs of his sleeves over, one turn after another, so they stayed up by his elbows.

"Tell me, Akos," Lazmet said. "How do you believe this will go for you? You are starved, exhausted, and picking a fight with a man who can control every movement of your body. There is no chance you will emerge from this place alive."

"Well," Akos said, "get on with killing me, then."

He felt the squeeze around his head that meant Lazmet's currentgift was trying to worm its way in, searching out weak points. But Akos was the Armored One, and there was no getting past his currentgift.

He started toward Lazmet, crushing leaves under his boots as he went. He knew better than to delay any longer. Before the full weight of the situation could hit Lazmet, Akos swung.

His arm collided with Lazmet's armored wrist. Akos gasped from the pain of the collision, but didn't relent. He was back in the arena, only there was no jeering crowd this time, no Suzao Kuzar thirsting for his blood. Just the grit of Lazmet's teeth in the dark, and Cyra's lessons echoing in his head, telling him to think. To abandon thoughts of honor. To survive.

He felt the pressure of Lazmet's currentgift again, bearing down harder on both sides of his skull.

They broke apart. Lazmet wore armor on both wrists, chest, back. He would have to aim low, or high.

Akos bent, rushing at his father like he meant to tackle him, and stabbing low, at his legs. He felt a line of heat across the back of his neck as his own knife carved into Lazmet's thigh. Lazmet had cut him.

He ignored the blood coursing down his back, soaking his

shirt, and the pulse of pain. Lazmet was groaning, clutching his leg with one hand.

"How?" the man growled.

Akos didn't answer. He felt unsteady, the weeks of limited food catching up with him. Not everything could be buried under adrenaline. He followed, stumbling toward Lazmet again, using the unpredictability of his movement to his advantage, the way Cyra had when, suffering from severe blood loss, she had to fight Eijeh in the arena. As his world tilted, so did he, and he thrust up, at Lazmet's throat.

Lazmet grabbed his arm and yanked it hard to the side. Pain sparked in Akos's shoulder and spread through his entire body. He screamed, and the knife fell out of his hands and into the rotten leaves. He fell down, too, lying at Lazmet's feet.

Tears rolled down the sides of his face. All this planning, all this lying—the betrayal of his friends, his family, his country— Cyra—and it had come to this.

"You aren't the first son to try to kill me, you know," Lazmet said. He lifted his foot, and pressed it to the joint of Akos's injured shoulder. Even just the touch of the man's boot made Akos scream again, but he stepped down, harder, slowly putting all his weight into it. Akos's vision went black, and he fought to stay present, to stay conscious, to *think*.

He wished he had thought to ask Cyra how she did it, kept thinking in the midst of pain, because to him it felt impossible— all that was left of him were the white-hot sparks of agony.

Lazmet leaned closer, not moving his foot.

"Ryzek surprised me, too, while we sojourned together. Our holiest of rites, the scavenge, and he *dared* to attack me, imprison me—" Lazmet paused, his jaw working. "But I didn't die then— Ryzek was too weak!—and I'm not going to die now, am I?"

He twisted his toe like he was squashing a particularly stubborn bug. Akos screamed again, tears running into his hair, wrapping around his ears. He heard a distant wail, the Hessa siren going off, summoning the army to arms. It was too late, too late for him, too late for the oblate in the hallway and the temple of Hessa.

This moment had all the heft of fate in it, the weight of inevitability, set in motion from the moment Vara the oracle told him his kyerta, his life-altering truth. The revelation of his parentage hadn't released him from the future, it had *guided* him to it, pulling him to his father's side like a fish hooked through the lip. *Suffer the fate*, his mother's voice said to him, *for all else is delusion*.

He understood, now, how Cyra had felt when she demanded that he choose her, even though he hadn't known, at the time, that he really could. *I don't want to be something you "suffer,"* she had told him. There was something powerful in that quality of hers, her refusal to accept what she didn't choose, the force of her *want*.

I don't want, she had said, and he felt it now.

He didn't want this to be the end, the fate he suffered.

And in the muddle of all that pain, Akos *thought*.

He pulled his knee high, up against his chest, and kicked hard at the wound in Lazmet's leg. Lazmet grunted, taken by surprise, and let up just a little on Akos's shoulder. With a yell, Akos pushed against the ground with his free leg so his back scraped against the ground, half on the leaves and half on the stone path, and he stretched his uninjured arm up, his hand searching through the stems for Vakrez's knife.

Lazmet had stepped back, grabbing his leg with one hand. Akos felt the metal of the knife handle, and grabbed. He felt his pulse in his throat, his head, his shoulder. And, trembling and throbbing and sagging under his own weight, he pushed himself to his feet.

It wasn't fate that had brought him here. He had chosen this. He had *wanted* it.

And now he wanted Lazmet dead.

The Hessa siren wailed. He and Lazmet collided, armor against flesh. They went down, falling with a thump to the frozen ground and the waxy leaves. Akos felt another burst of pain in his shoulder, and dry heaved, his stomach too empty to throw anything up. Their arms were crossed between them, both of Lazmet's hands around his wrist, trying to push the knife away.

Honor, Akos thought, *has no place in survival.*

He bent his head and bit Lazmet's arm. He clenched his teeth as hard as he could, tasting blood, tearing flesh. Lazmet screamed, low. Akos pushed the knife against the pressure that held him away, and jerked his head, ripping skin and muscle from Lazmet's arm.

The knife went right into Lazmet's neck.

Everything stopped.

Aoseh Kereseth had broken things with his currentgift. Floater seats. Couch cushions. Tables. Mugs. Plates. One time he broke one of Akos's toys by mistake, and sat his smallest child in his lap to show him how he could fix it, like magic, with the same gift that had broken it. The toy had never looked right again, but Aoseh had done his best.

He had chased their mother around the kitchen with flour-dusted hands to put fingerprints on her clothes. He was the only one who could make Sifa laugh, a full belly laugh. The one who had kept her present, and grounded—at least, as much as that was possible, for an oracle.

Aoseh Kereseth had been loud, and messy, and affectionate. He had been Akos's father.

And this man—this armored, cold, cruel man lying an arm's length away—wasn't.

Akos lay beside Lazmet as he died, holding the arm his father had wounded to his chest, and finally wanting again.

It was a small thing—just a slight craving for survival—but it was better than nothing.

CHAPTER 52 | CYRA

I RAN MY FINGERS over the silverskin on my head. It had begun to generate electrical impulses similar to those of real nerves, so I could feel a light tapping where my touch was. It was soothing, like standing under the warm rain of Pitha.

"Quit it, Plate Head," Teka said. "You're drawing attention."

We stood in the square just outside the amphitheater. Under the reign of my brother, this place would have been packed with vendors, some from other planets—forbidden from instructing us in the use of their languages, of course—and some Shotet. The air would smell like smoke and charred meat and the burnt herbs from the tents of Essander, where everyone seemed particularly attuned to scents. I would tuck my hands into my sleeves to keep from touching anyone, fearing the crush of the crowd. My brother had been a tyrant as much as Lazmet was, but part of him had craved adoration, and it had inspired him to make concessions, on occasion. Lazmet had no such craving.

In light of that, the square was not packed with people shouting numbers at each other. Soldiers didn't stroll between the stalls, hoping to catch someone speaking a word of another language so they could extort money or threaten punishment. There were a few tables set up with goods—food, mostly, marked up to high prices—and all of them were Shotet. I doubted many outsiders wanted to be in a country involved in war, profitable though it might have been.

"It's less of a plate and more of a bowl," I said to Teka, holding my hands in a curved shape, like that of my skull.

"What?"

"The silverskin," I said, showing her my hands again. "If it's any kind of serveware, it's a bowl, not a plate."

"I didn't mean 'plate' as in 'dinner plate,'" Teka said, scowling. "I meant it as in a metal plate, like on the side of a ship—you know what? This is ridiculous. You're ridiculous."

I grinned.

I thought we would suffer for the lack of a crowd to disguise us, but there were few soldiers that I could see. Guards by the usual entrances and exits, but they were easily dealt with. And not in my typical fashion, though that had been my initial suggestion.

Sifa had proposed a more peaceful path into the amphitheater. She and Yma would approach the guards at the entrance head-on, and convince them to let her tour the arena. Yma had worn the lavender dress for the occasion, so she would look wealthy, important, worth making allowances for. This would draw the guards' attention away from us, while also giving Yma and Sifa a chance to get in themselves.

Zyt and Ettrek had pledged to create some kind of large distraction near the side door, to draw away the guards there. Teka and I had to enter through that door while the guards dealt with whatever Ettrek and Zyt did. We were too easily recognized.

"There she goes," I said to Teka, nodding to the entrance with its grand archway. Yma's lavender skirt fluttered in the wind. She drew her shawl tighter around her shoulders, and began walking through the square.

I had passed through the amphitheater's arch on my way to challenge my brother. It had been simpler, then. A single enemy, a single path forward. Now, there were tyrants and chancellors and exiles and countless factions among the people who served each of them.

And there was Akos.

Whatever that meant.

"Sifa said he's not here," Teka said to me. Like a mind reader. "Lazmet took him wherever they went. I know that's not all that reassuring, but . . . better for him not to be hit by the blast, right?"

It was. It meant that I could think clearly. But I didn't want to admit to that. I shrugged.

"I asked her for you," Teka said. "I knew you'd be too proud to do it yourself."

"Time to go," I said, ignoring her.

We started through the square, keeping pace with Sifa, who was doing her part to look casual and familiar. She paused at one of the tables to look over a platter of pan-fried feathergrass; Teka and I kept to the next row, watching her through the haze of smoke rising up from the smithy advertising free currentblade repairs with purchase.

I watched Sifa and Yma approach the entrance guard from a distance. I was sure Yma's tongue could be just as quick and persuasive as she needed to get into that amphitheater. She had spent her life lying, after all.

When the guards were both engaged enough to turn away, I led the way to the side door at a brisk walk. It was set into the wall at an angle, creating a space for a guard to stand without being visible from the street. I drew my currentblade.

The soldier was young, and tall, so for a moment I saw Akos in his stead, putting on his Shotet armor for the first time and appearing, to me, as the exact image of what I might have wanted, if I had been allowed to want normal things. But in the next moment, the soldier was shorter, thinner, and lighter-haired—not Akos.

Just before I could lash out at him, I heard screaming behind me. At the edge of the square, a cloud of smoke had risen up from one of the stalls. No—not a cloud of smoke, but one of *insects*, all taking flight at once. The screams came from the vendor, losing all of his product at once. He lunged at Zyt, who was laughing, and punched him hard in the jaw.

I sheathed my currentblade, and said, "Guard!"

The sandy-haired guard stepped out of his alcove to look at me.

"There's a fight," I said, jabbing my thumb over my shoulder.

"Not again." He groaned, and took off running.

Teka slipped in without ceremony, drawing the small screwdriver from its place in her pocket and addressing the lock on the door. I peered out at the square to make sure no one was watching us. There were only slumped vendors and furtive-looking Shotet making their purchases, and the growing brawl Zyt and Ettrek had fostered.

"Hello, darling," Teka said softly in the voice she used to speak to wires. "Would you open up for me? No, not your job? Ah."

I heard a click. The door opened, and Teka and I passed through the doorway. It locked automatically behind us, and some instinct in me told me that wasn't good for quick escapes, but there was nothing to be done about it now. We jogged down the dark hallway with its arched stone ceiling, toward the light at the end that would admit us to the bottom level of seats.

Sifa was already walking the arena floor, cooing like a bird at how large the place was, and how it never seemed as big when she was sitting in the audience, and whatever else she could think of to say. Her voice, with its slight rough character, echoed a dozen times over even before we made it to the end of the hallway. Yma was beside her, making little hums of assent.

Teka immediately started up the steps toward the control room, which was behind the second-level seats, but I stayed at the low wall that separated the first row from the arena floor, and closed my eyes. I could hear the chanting that had accompanied the edge of Ryzek's knife as it dug into me, the shouts of "Traitor!" that had met me when I challenged him again.

"Cyra?" Teka's voice pulled me free from the twists and turns of my memory.

I opened my eyes as the sky darkened.

It could have been something as ordinary as a cloud passing over the sun, but it had already been cloudy when I closed my eyes, an even pale gray in every direction. Instead, when I lifted my head, I saw a vast ship, far larger than any transport vessel or floater or military craft that Shotet possessed. It was as large as the sojourn ship, but perfectly round, more like the Thuvhesit passenger floater that Sifa had guided into the renegade safe house.

The underside of the ship was smooth and polished, like it had never been flown before, never been battered by space debris and asteroids and rough atmospheres. Dotting its belly were little white lights. They marked doors and hatches, important attachment points and docking stations, and the ship's massive outline. It was an Othyrian craft. I was sure of it. No one else would have the will and the vanity to make something so functional so beautiful.

"Cyra." Teka's voice again, fearful this time.

I locked eyes with Sifa, standing in the center of the arena. Eijeh had decided the time of his vision based on the color of the light, he said. Well, with this ship shielding Voa from the sun, it looked very much like dusk.

The attack was happening now.

"I wouldn't bother with the control room," I said, surprised by how remote my own voice sounded to me.

The soldiers who had shown Sifa into the arena fled, as if they could outrun a ship that large before the anticurrent blast hit. And perhaps there was no shame in that, in dying with hope.

I hoisted myself over the barrier that separated me from the arena, and dropped neatly to the packed earth below. I didn't know why, except that I didn't want to be standing above the arena when the anticurrent blast hit. I wanted to be where I belonged: here, with grit in the soles of my boots, where people who loved to fight stood.

And I loved to fight.

But I also loved to live.

I wouldn't say I had never thought of dying as some kind of relief, when the pain was at its worst, when I lost my true mother to the darkness I didn't yet understand. And I wouldn't say that living was always, or even often, a pleasant experience for me. But the discovery and rediscovery of other worlds, the burn and ache of muscles building strength, the feeling of Akos's warm, strong body against mine, the glint of my mother's decorative armor at night in the sojourn ship—I loved them all.

I stopped in the middle of the arena, within grasp of Sifa and Yma, but not touching them. I heard Teka's light footfalls behind me.

"Well," Teka said. "I suppose it could be worse."

I would have laughed, if it had been any further from the truth. But for Teka and Yma and me, who had come so close to other, far more horrible ways of dying, I supposed dissolving into an anticurrent blast was not so bad.

"Anticurrent," I murmured, because the word seemed so strange to me.

I looked at Sifa—at my mother, in whatever way she still was that—and for the first time, she looked genuinely surprised.

"I don't understand. Anticurrent blasts are *light*," I said. "The sojourn ship . . . it was so bright when it was destroyed. How can anticurrent be bright?"

"The current is both visible and invisible," Sifa said. "It doesn't always appear to us in a way that we understand."

I frowned down at my spread palms, where the currentshadows had collected, winding again and again around my fingers like stacks of rings.

The doctor I had seen as a child had suggested that my currentgift came about because I thought I deserved pain, and that everyone else deserved it, too. My mother, Ylira Noavek, had chafed at the mere suggestion. *This is not her fault*, she had said, before dragging me out of the office.

And Akos—when he had seen the way I kept track of what I had done on my arm, now covered, as always, by armor, he had simply asked me, *How old were you?*

He had not thought this gift was what I deserved, and neither had my mother. And maybe they were both right—maybe the doctor was the one who had been wrong, the man whose words had been echoing in my mind all my life. Maybe pain was not my currentgift, not at all. Maybe pain was just a by-product of something else.

If the anticurrent was light—

And I was plagued by dark—

Maybe *current* was my gift.

She is herself a small Ogra, the Ogran dancers had said to me, when they saw my currentgift displayed.

"Does anyone know what the word 'Ogra' actually means, in Ogran?" I said.

"It means 'the living dark,'" Sifa replied.

I laughed, a little, and as a narrow hatch opened on the underside of the ship above us, I raised my shadow-stained hands to the sky.

I pushed my currentshadows up, up, up.

Over the sizzle of the amphitheater's force field, which Akos had disabled at a touch as he lifted us to safety. His arm had been strong across my back, tightly coiled as a rope.

Over the center of Voa, where I had lived all my life, contained in spotless wood paneling and the glow of fenzu. I felt Ryzek's hands, a little sweaty as they pressed over my ears, to shield me from the screams of whoever my father was tormenting.

And higher over Voa, over even the fringes of the city where the Storyteller and his sweet purple tea lived, where the renegades had cobbled together a dinner table made of half a dozen other dinner tables.

I didn't suffer from a lack of fuel. The currentshadows had been so strong all my life, strong enough to render me incapable of attending a simple dinner party, strong enough to bow my back and force tears from my eyes, strong enough to keep me awake and pacing all through the night. Strong enough to kill, but now I understood why they killed. It wasn't because they drained the life from a person, but because they *overwhelmed* it. It was like gravity—we needed it to stay grounded, alive, but if it was too strong, it formed a black hole, from which even light could not escape.

Yes, the force of the current was too fierce for one body to contain—

Unless that body was mine.

My body, battered again and again by soldiers and brothers and enemies, but still working its way upright—

My body, a channel for the pure force of current, the hum-buzz of life that brought others to their knees—

Life is full of pain, I had told Akos, trying to draw him back from depression. *Your capacity for bearing it is greater than you believe.* And I had been right.

I had had every reason to become closed off, wrapped up tight, pushing everything that resembled life and growth and power as far away from myself as possible. It would have been easier that way, to refuse to let anything in. But I had let Akos in, trusting him when I had forgotten how to trust, and I had let Teka in, too, and maybe one day, Sifa—

I would let anyone in who dared draw near. I was like the planet Ogra, which welcomed anyone and anything that could survive life close to it.

Not because I deserved pain, and not because I was too strong to feel it, but because I was resilient enough to accept it as an inevitability.

My currentshadows shot up, up, up.

They spread, building from the tendrils around my fingers to a column in the sky that wrapped my entire body in shadow-dark. I couldn't see Teka or Sifa or Yma now, but I saw the great pillar of current that passed over and through me, toward that hatch that had opened in the Othyrian ship above.

I didn't see the anticurrent weapon, whatever its container looked like, but I did see the blast. The light spreading out from one fixed point, just as the shadow stretched upward from me.

And where they collided: agony.

I screamed, helplessly, as I had not screamed since I was too young to remember. The pain was so intense it shattered my pride, my reason, my sense of self. I heard the screaming and felt the scraping feeling of my own voice in my throat and the inferno inside me and around me, and saw the shadow and the light and the space where they met with a sharp *clap*.

My knees buckled, and arms wrapped around my waist, thin, bony ones. A head pressed between my shoulder blades, and I heard Teka's voice saying, "Hold on, hold on, hold on . . ."

I had killed her uncle, her cousin, and in some ways, her

mother, and still she stood behind me, keeping me upright.

Hands wrapped around my arms, warm and soft, and the smell of sendes leaf floated over to me, the scent of Sifa's shampoo.

The dark eyes of the one who had abandoned me, and now returned for me—

And last, the strict, pale fingers of Yma Zetsyvis on my wrist.

The current moved through all of us at once, my friend, my enemy, my mother, and me, all wrapped together in the darkness that was life itself.

5

Arzodae. Verb. In Zoldan: "To mar, as with a knife"

CHAPTER 53 | CISI

BREAKING NEWS, THE SCREEN says. *Lazmet Noavek confirmed dead in Shotet assault on Hessa, major city of Thuvhe.*

I look the nurse steadily in the eye. I want to tell her that I don't care if my intestines are spilling out on the floor, she *will* get me a wheelchair, and she *will* clear me to fly with Isae Benesit to Thuvhe. But of course I can't say that. Other people's currentgifts falter when their bodies weaken, but not mine, apparently.

Instead, I search for what might persuade her. The usual Othyrian things—fine fabrics—don't seem like the right choice. She's too hard-nosed for that. She's not someone who has let herself long for things. She would take comfort in something she can access—like a hot bath, or a comfortable chair. Water is easy for me, so I send it toward her, not the rolling waves that would work on Isae, but the still warmth of someone soaking. Buoyant and motionless.

I don't bother with subtlety. I fill the room with it. My cheeks heat and my stomach aches from the stitches that still hold my guts in.

"I'm from Hessa," I say, and it feels muffled, even though I can hear myself clearly. One of the oddities of my gift. "I need to go. Clear me."

She's nodding, blinking dully at me.

I haven't spoken to Isae since Ast's arrest. She came to assure me that it was done, that he was gone. Since he wasn't a citizen of the Assembly, he was shipped off to his home moon to await trial, and they would deal with him in whatever manner they chose. But he wouldn't be allowed to set foot on an Assembly planet again.

One day, that might mean fewer planets. There are rumors of secession over Othyr's proposed oracle oversight law. It is too soon to know about the other nation-planets, but Thuvhe has thrown itself in with Othyr, so our path through that issue, at least, is clear.

We aren't sure what happened in Shotet yet. News is slow to come out of there. What we do know is the anticurrent weapon didn't work. Something ink-dark met it in the air, right in the middle of Voa, protecting the city from its blast. No one can explain it, but I'm taking it as a sign of better things to come.

The nurse wheels me to the hospital landing pad in a small, portable bed that can be secured to the wall of an Othyrian ship. Every jostle of the bed makes shooting pains go through my abdomen, but I am just happy to be going home, so I try not to let the pain show. *The first child of the family Noavek will succumb to the blade.* Well, maybe I had succumbed, but I hadn't died. That was something.

As the nurse activates the wall magnet that will hold my bed steady during takeoff, Isae steps down from the nav deck, where she was speaking with the captain. She's dressed in comfortable clothes: a sweater with sleeves long enough to cover her hands, tight black pants, and her old boots with their red laces. She looks uncharacteristically nervous.

She offers me a handheld screen with a keyboard. "Just in case you want to say something you can't say aloud," she says.

I hold it in my lap. I'm angry with her—for not listening to me instead of Ast, for not believing me—but this reminds me why I care about her. She thinks about what I need. She wants me to be able to speak my mind.

"I'm surprised you didn't object to me coming," I say to her as unkindly as my currentgift will allow.

"I'm trying to trust your judgment from now on," she says, looking down at her fingers, twisted together. "You want to go to Hessa, so you'll go to Hessa. You wanted me to show mercy, so I'll try to do that, too, from now on."

I nod.

"I'm sorry, Cee," she almost whispers.

I feel a pang of guilt. I didn't tell her that I tried to reach out to Shotet when she decided to unleash the anticurrent weapon on the Shotet. And I haven't told her how I've been using my currentgift to soften her and persuade her since all this started. And I don't plan to confess. I would lose everything I've gained, that way. But I don't feel good about the deception.

The least I can do now is forgive her. I turn over one hand, and hold it out to her, inviting her closer. She rests her palm on mine.

"I love you," she says.

"I love you, too," I say, and it's one of the easiest things I've ever said. Sometimes I might lie to her, but this, at least, is true.

She bends to kiss me, and I touch her cheek, holding her in place for a few long moments before she pulls away. She smells like sendes leaf and soap. Like home.

I will never be heralded as the one who made Chancellor Benesit turn away from further aggressive action and invite the Shotet to peace talks in the wake of the attempted attack on Voa. It might have been one of the more destructive wars in Assembly history, if I hadn't been there. No one will call me skilled in diplomacy, or poised, or a remarkable adviser.

But that's as it should be. When all goes according to plan, I fade into the background. But I will be there, standing behind a chancellor as she maneuvers through this uneasy peace. I will be the one she looks to for guidance, for comfort when her grief and anger surge within her again and again. I will be the arm that guides the hand. No one will know.

Except me. I'll know.

CHAPTER 54 | CYRA

I WOKE TO BUZZING. A fenzu glowing blue, turning lazy circles above my head. Its iridescent wings made me think, suddenly, of Uzul Zetsyvis, who had thought so fondly of them, his cash crop and his passion.

Around me was white—white floors, white sheets, white walls, white curtains. I was not in a hospital, but a quiet house. Growing from a pot in the corner was a black flower with layer after layer of plush petals, unfolding from a dark yellow center.

I recognized the place. It was the Zetsyvis home, standing on a cliff overlooking Voa.

Something felt wrong. Off, somehow. I lifted an arm and found it to be heavy, my muscles shaking with the slight effort. I let the limb drop to the mattress, and contented myself by watching the fenzu fly, tracing paths of light in the air.

I knew what was off: I wasn't in pain. And from what I could see of my own bare arms, the currentshadows were gone.

Fear and relief intermingled within me. No pain. No currentshadows. Was it permanent? Had I expended so much energy in the anticurrent blast that my currentgift had left me forever? I closed my eyes. I couldn't allow myself to imagine that, a life without pain. I couldn't let myself hope for it.

A while later—I had no sense of how long—I heard a knock at the door. Sifa carried a mug of tea toward me.

"I suspected you might be awake," she said.

"Tell me about Voa," I said. I planted my hands, trying to push myself up. My arms felt like jelly. Sifa moved to help me, and I stopped her with a glare, struggling on my own instead.

Instead, she sat in a chair near my bed, her hands folded in her lap.

"Your currentshadows countered the anticurrent blast. The Shotet exiles arrived within days to seize control of Voa, in the power vacuum that resulted from Lazmet's death," she said. "But what you did seems to have depleted you. No, I'm not sure if the disappearance of your currentshadows is permanent," she added, answering the question I hadn't yet asked. "But you saved a lot of people, Cyra."

She sounded . . . proud. As a mother would have been.

"Don't," I said. "I'm not yours."

"I know." She sighed. "But I was hoping we might work our way toward something other than outright hostility."

I considered that.

"Maybe," I said.

She smirked a little.

"Well, in that spirit . . . look at this."

She rose to draw the curtain back from the window beside my bed. I was in the part of the house positioned on the edge of the cliff, overlooking the city of Voa. At first, all I saw was the sparkle of distant lights, the buildings of Voa. But then:

"It's noon," Sifa said.

Voa was covered—shielded by what looked like dark clouds. They were only a shade or two lighter than the Ogran sky. My currentshadows had found a home over Voa, sending it into endless night.

I felt better—physically—in the next few days than I had since I was a child. Izit by izit, my strength returned, as I ate food prepared by Sifa, Yma, and Teka in the Zetsyvis kitchen. Yma burned the bottom of almost everything she made, and presented it without apology. Sifa cooked odd-tasting Thuvhesit dishes that were packed with too many spices. Teka made uncommonly good breakfasts. I helped where I could, sitting at the counter with a knife to chop things until my arm got too tired. The weakness was infuriating to me, but the lack of pain more than made up for it.

I would have traded a dozen currentgifts for no more pain.

Sifa had assured me that Akos was alive, but in what condition, I didn't know. I searched the news out of Thuvhe for any signs of him, and found nothing. Reports of my father's death didn't mention him. It was Cisi who finally sent us news, directly from Hessa: She had found Akos at the hospital there, recovering from hypothermia. She was taking him home.

The clouds showed no sign of clearing over Voa. It was likely the entire city would be dark forever. Up here on the cliff, if you looked toward Voa, it appeared to be night. But if you turned away, toward the Divide that separated us from Thuvhe, the sun shone again. It was odd, to be living on the edge of such a thing. And to know that you yourself had created it.

And then, in the middle of the night, almost a week after the attack on Voa, I woke to pain.

At first I didn't know why I was awake. I checked the clock to be sure it wasn't time to get up and start on breakfast, since I was finally well enough to take my own turn in the kitchen. Then I felt the dull pounding in my head, with a spark of alarm.

Maybe it's just a headache, I told myself. *No need to panic, no need to—*

My fingers stung, like they had fallen asleep and blood was now returning to them. I scrambled to turn on the lamp next to my bed, and I saw it: a line of shadow traveling from wrist to fingertip.

Shaking, I threw the blankets back and looked at my bare legs. Faint shadows wrapped around my ankles, like shackles. My head and heart pounded in the same rhythm. I didn't realize I was making a noise—a horrible, heaving noise, like a dying animal—until Teka opened the door, her bright hair piled on top of her head.

She spotted the currentshadows immediately, and came to my bedside, pulling the sleeves of her sleep clothes over her hands. She sat on the bed and pulled me against her, pressing my face to her bony shoulder.

I sobbed into her shirt, and she held me in place, in silence.

"I didn't—I didn't want them back," I choked out.

"I know."

"I don't *care* if they're powerful, I don't—"

"I know that, too."

She rocked us back and forth, slowly, for a long time.

"People call them a gift," she said after a while. "What bullshit."

A few days later, I stood listening to the patter of rain on the guest-room windows, a bag on the bed in front of me. I had stuffed most of my possessions inside it, and now struggled to think past the pain in my back and legs. My currentgift's return had not been easy to adjust to.

"Aza asked me to speak with you about her request," Yma said to me. She was leaning against the doorframe, dressed all in white. "For you to accept a position of power in the new Shotet government."

"Why would she ask you? You know as well as I do that what's best for our people is no Noaveks in power, ever again."

"I know no such thing," Yma said, pinching the hem of her blouse between her trimmed, clean fingernails. "There are quite a few Noavek loyalists still among us. They might actually cooperate with us if we establish the Noavek bloodline in a high position. And unity is what we need right now."

"One problem, though," I said. "I'm not actually part of the Noavek bloodline."

Yma flapped her hand at me. "No one needs to know that."

The system of governance Aza had proposed was a blend of elected officials and monarchy, with the monarch—me, if she got her way—appointing a representative who would hold all the actual power, supported by a council. It wouldn't require me to be a ruler in the sense that my father and Ryzek had been, but I was still wary of it. Bad things happened when my family was in power.

"What about Vakrez?" I said. "He's a Noavek. A real one, in fact. And he's an adult."

"Are you going to make me say it?" Yma said, sighing.

"Say what?"

Yma rolled her eyes. "That I think you are a better option than Vakrez. He allowed himself to be controlled by both Lazmet and Ryzek. He lacks the . . . fortitude."

I raised both eyebrows.

"Did you just compliment me?" I said.

"Don't take it too much to heart," Yma replied.

I smiled a little.

"Okay," I said. "I'll do it."

"What? Just because I complimented you?"

"No." I looked out the window, at the water-streaked glass, at the dark currentshadow cloud that covered Voa. "Because I trust your judgment."

She looked, for a moment, taken aback.

Then she nodded, turned, and left without a word.

She still didn't like me, but it was possible she didn't hate me, either. I would take what I could get, for now.

CHAPTER 55 | AKOS

AKOS WALKED THE RAISED path that kept the farmers clear of the hushflowers. Half the hushflower crop from that season had been burned by Shotet invaders, but the farmers were still out there, tending what was left with their thick gloves on. It was lucky, they said, that the Shotet had come after the blooms were harvested, since they only needed the roots to survive anyway. Hessa's crops would bounce back just fine.

The temple, on the other hand . . .

Akos still couldn't bear to look up at it. Where the red glass dome had once glinted in the moonlight was now a big empty space. The Shotet had smashed it to bits. They had killed most of the oblates in the temple. They had swarmed the streets and filled the alleys. Two weeks later and Hessans were still dealing with the bodies. The dead were mostly soldiers, thanks to a brave oblate who had sounded the alarm, but some civilians, too.

He didn't dare go into town. They might recognize him, or his sleeve might pull back and show his marks. They might attack him, if they knew what he was. Kill him, even. He wouldn't blame them. He had let the Shotet in.

Mostly, though, he just couldn't stand to look at any of it. What flashes he saw on the news were plenty.

So when he walked, it was through the iceflower fields, wrapped up in his warmest clothes, even though it was Thuvhe's warmest time. The fields were a safe place. White purity blossoms were still popping off their stems and floating through the air, even now. Yellow jealousy dust was thick on the ground. It was desolate, everything gone until the Deadening time came again, but that suited him fine.

He hopped down from the raised path, onto the road. This time of year, when some of the snow went soft, it froze at night, so there was ice everywhere, and he had to be careful. The hooks on the bottom of his boots didn't always catch, and he was still off balance with his arm in the sling. His careful steps took him as far west as the feathergrass, where his family's house was nestled, safe and lonely.

Cisi's floater wasn't parked on the front lawn. When she came to visit, she parked in town and walked to the house, so nobody would know she was there. Nobody knew he was there, either, or he was sure he would be arrested by now. He may have killed Lazmet Noavek, but he'd let Shotet soldiers into Hessa temple. His arm was marked. There was armor in his bedroom. He spoke the revelatory tongue. He was too Shotet for Thuvhesits, now.

Light glowed from under the kitchen door when he walked in, so he knew Cisi was there. His mother had tried to visit him in the hospital. She had made it into the room, and he had lost himself in shouting at her, getting so wound up the doctors told Sifa to leave. Cisi had promised not to let her into the house until he was ready. Which, Akos privately thought, would be never. He was done with her. With what she had done to Cyra. With how she had stood apart from his suffering. With how she had maneuvered him into killing Vas. With all of it.

He stomped to get the ice off his boots, then loosened them and toed them off by the door. His hands were already undoing the straps and buttons that kept his kutyah coat fastened tight, and stripping the hat and goggles from his face. He had forgotten how much time it took to get dressed and undressed here. He'd gotten used to the temperate climate in Voa.

Voa was now dark. Ogra-dark, the sky stained black in the center and fading to gray out by the old soldiers' camp. The news didn't have an explanation, and neither did Akos. No one knew much about what had happened there.

What was happening now, though, was covered on a constant loop. How the Shotet exiles were now recognized as Shotet's official government, under a temporary council of advisers while they set up for elections. How Shotet had negotiated for its nationhood. How they had traded legitimacy for their land, and were now evacuating Voa. The Ograns had given them a piece of land, bigger than Voa, and far more hazardous, and were negotiating the terms of Ogran-Shotet coexistence.

And there were other things brewing in the Assembly, too. Talk of a schism. The fate-faithful planets separating from the secular ones, the oracles fleeing the latter for the former. Half a galaxy living without knowing the future, and half listening to whatever wisdom the oracles might offer. That schism existed in

Akos himself, and the idea that the galaxy might divide distressed him, because it meant that he, too, would have to choose a side, and he didn't want to.

But that was the way of things—sometimes, wounds were too deep to heal. Sometimes, people didn't want to reconcile. Sometimes, even though a solution might create worse problems than there were to begin with, people chose it anyway.

"Cee?" he called out, once he was finished hanging up all his winter clothes. He walked the dark, narrow hallway to the kitchen, peering out into the courtyard to see if the burnstones were still lit.

"Hello there." A voice spoke from his living room.

Yma Zetsyvis sat by the fireplace. She was an arm's length away from the place where his father had died. Her white hair was loose around her face, and she was elegant as ever, even dressed in armor. It was the color of sand.

He startled, more at the sight of her than the sound, cringing into the wall. And then, embarrassed by his reaction, he pushed himself away from the wall and forced himself to face her. It had been like this since Lazmet's death.

"I apologize. I couldn't think of a better way to warn you," Yma said.

"What—" He drank in a few shallow breaths. "What are you doing here?"

She smiled a little. "What, no 'Oh, you're alive, how nice'?"

"I—"

"Shh. I don't actually care." She stood. "You look better. You've been eating?"

"I—yes."

Every time he faced a meal these days, he thought of what he had done to Jorek, and it was hard to take even a single bite, hungry as he was. He made himself do it, because he didn't like to feel tired, and weak, and fragile. But it was difficult each time.

"I came to get you out of here," she said.

"It's my house," he replied.

"No, it's your parents' house," she said. "It's the place where your father died, in the shadow of a town you can't even go into anymore, thanks to certain facets of your identity being public knowledge. This isn't a good place for you to be."

Akos crossed his arms over his stomach, holding on tight. She had put into words what he already knew, what he had known since Cisi brought him here, after the attack. The bed that had belonged to him was right next to Eijeh's, and Eijeh was gone, disappeared into the streets of Voa and never spotted again. The living room still reminded him of his father's blood. And the destroyed temple—

Well.

"Where am I supposed to go?" he said in more of a whisper than anything.

Yma came to her feet and approached him, slowly, as if approaching an animal.

"You," she said, "are a Shotet. It's not the only thing you are, to be sure. You are still a Thuvhesit, and an oracle's son, and a Kereseth, and all those things. But you can't deny that a Shotet is part of what you are." She set a hand on his shoulder, gently. "And we are the ones who want you with us."

"We?" Akos snorted, ignoring the heat that had sparked behind his eyes. "What about Ara, and Cyra? They don't want me
with them."

"I can't believe I'm about to say this," Yma said. "But I don't
think you are giving your girl enough credit. Or Ara, given time."

"I don't—"

"For heaven's sake, boy, just go in the kitchen," Yma snapped.

Sitting at his kitchen table—the kitchen table where he had
spread his homework as a kid to work before dinner, where he had
climbed up to dust the burnstones with red hushflower powder,
where he had learned to chop and slice and crush ingredients for
the painkiller—was Cyra.

Her thick, wavy hair piled on one side of her head, the other
glinting silver.

Her arm wrapped in armor.

Her eyes dark as space.

"Hello," she said to him in Thuvhesit.

"Hello," he replied in Shotet.

"Cisi smuggled us into Thuvhe," Cyra said. "Border control is
very tight right now."

"Oh," he said. "Right."

"Yma and I are flying to Ogra tonight, now that I'm well
enough to travel."

"You—" Akos swallowed hard. "What happened?"

"The dark over Voa? That was me. My currentshadows." She
smiled, a bit sheepishly. It wasn't the easy smile she might have
given him a few months ago, but it was more than he expected.
She held up a hand, showing him the black shadows that still

floated over her skin, dense and dark. "It took so much out of me, the currentshadows were gone for a week. I thought they might have disappeared forever. Was devastated when they came back, actually. But I'm—dealing with it. As always."

Akos nodded.

"You're thin," she said. "Yma told me about—how it was. With Lazmet. With you."

"Cyra," he said.

"I know what he's like, you know. I saw, I heard things." She closed her eyes, shook her head. "I know."

"Cyra," he said again. "I'm so—there aren't words—"

"There are a great number of words, actually." She rose from her seat at the table, trailing her fingers along the wood as she walked around it. "In Shotet, the word just means 'regret,' but in Zoldan, there are three words. One for slights, one for regular apology, and one that means something along the lines of 'What I did cut out a piece of me.'"

Akos nodded, unable to speak.

"I thought I couldn't forgive you, that I lacked the capacity," she said. "After all, I was about to die, and you were just sitting there."

Akos winced.

"I couldn't move," he said. "I was—frozen. Numb."

"I know," she said, coming to stand in front of him, her brow furrowed. "Don't you remember, Akos, what I hide beneath this armor?" She clasped the forearm guard in front of her body. "When I showed you these marks, did you think, even for a moment, that I had done something that couldn't be forgiven?"

Akos's heart was pounding, as hard as it did when he

panicked, and he didn't know why.

"No, you didn't," she said. "You showed me mercy. Teka showed me mercy. Even Yma, in her way." She reached for him, for his cheek. He cringed away.

It was so much harder—so much harder to accept her forgiveness than her condemnation, because it meant that he had to change.

"This time, let *me* be the one to say to you—you were young, and hungry, and exhausted. In pain, and confused, and alone," she said. "And if you think that I—Cyra Noavek, Ryzek's Scourge, killer of my own mother—can't understand what happened to you, then you don't really understand who I was, and what I did."

Akos watched her carefully as she spoke, as she pulled him closer and touched her forehead to his, so they could still look at each other, breathing the same air.

"What I did," he said, "cut out a piece of me."

"It's all right," she said. "I'm all hacked up and stitched back together, too."

She pulled away.

"For now," she said, "just be my friend again, okay? And we can talk about the whole 'I'm still in love with you, what the hell do we do about it' question later."

Akos smiled.

"Show me your house," she said. "Are there embarrassing pictures of you? On the journey, your sister told me you were very particular about your socks."

And so Akos took her upstairs, his fingers laced with hers, and opened all his drawers, letting himself be thoroughly mocked.

≫≪

Dear Cisi,

I'm sorry I didn't wait for you. I wasn't sure when you'd be back, and my ride was leaving.

I hope you understand why I can't stay. There's no place for me here anymore. But let's make a deal. If you try to ease off your current-gift when you're advising Isae, I'll try to stop beating myself up about Eijeh. And Jorek. And Hessa.

Personally, I think your end is much easier, so you better take me up on it.

But I'm serious—you're not a puppet master, Cee, even though I know sometimes you want to be. Maybe power suits you, but it's got to be handled carefully, you know?

I'll be farther away from you now, on Ogra, than I ever was in Shotet, but this time will be different. This time, I can come visit. This time, I can be what I want to be, go where I want to go.

I'll miss you. Stay safe.

—Akos

P.S. Don't worry, I'll talk to Mom eventually.

CHAPTER 56 | CYRA

One Season Later

I WOKE TO A low hum, and the *tap tap tap* of a knife on a cutting board. He was facing away from me, his shoulders hunched over the narrow counter. The pile of ingredients next to him was unfamiliar—something Ogran that he had learned to use in half a dozen ways since he'd been studying under Zenka.

I stretched, my knees cracking as I straightened them. I had fallen asleep to the sound of this new concoction bubbling on the stove, but he had been sitting on the end of the bed then, reading a Shotet book with the translator close at hand in case he needed it. He had made rapid progress with Shotet characters, but there were quite a few of them to learn, and it would take seasons to master them.

"I heard that creaky knee, your sovereignty," he said.

"Good," I said through a yawn. "Then you're not as unguarded as you look."

I got up and padded over to him. There was a bandage on his arm—the tentacle of some kind of venemous Ogran plant had wrapped around him while he harvested it, and ate away at his skin like acid. The scar would stretch right across his Shotet marks, passing through them, though not entirely erasing them.

"That looks disgusting," I said, pointing to the substance he was chopping. It was grainy and black, like it was coated in engine oil. It had stained his fingertips a grayish color.

"It tastes disgusting, too," he said. "But if it does what I think it will, you'll have a painkiller that won't make you sleepy during the day."

"You don't need to dedicate so much time to painkillers," I said. "I'm managing just fine with the ones I have."

"I enjoy making them," he said. "It's not all about you, you know."

"I love it when you talk sweet to me." I wrapped my arms around his waist, breathing in the smell of fresh things that lingered on all his clothes in the afternoons, after he went to the ship's little greenhouse.

The Ograns had loaned us two ships for our sojourn this season. They were a lot smaller than the sojourn ship had been, so not all eligible Shotet could go, and those who did had been selected by lottery. But the sojourn would happen, and that was what mattered to most of us—especially the exiles, who hadn't been able to sojourn for many seasons.

The planet we would scavenge this season was Tepes. The decision was politically motivated, rather than guided by the current, as it should have been. Tepes, Ogra, and Shotet were on one

side of an ongoing debate with Othyr, Thuvhe, and Pitha about
the oracles. And the word *debate* was somewhat ill-chosen, since
the environment was, as Teka had put it, "a bit tense." Bad, in
other words.

That the galaxy would divide over this issue was no longer a
question of "if," but one of "when." The problem was that the rest
of the Assembly planets wanted to keep their oracles but impose
stringent guidelines on how they would practice, which was, for
the oracles, untenable. I wasn't sure what to think, after my deal-
ings with Sifa. But thankfully, it was not up to me.

Aza was the prime minister, responsible for most of the decision making. I consulted, when I needed to, and tried to manage
the diplomatic end of things, though I wasn't much good at it. I did
know the other planets, though. I'd spent all my life fascinated by
them. And my talent for languages was useful, since people liked
to hear foreigners make an effort.

Akos stopped chopping and turned in my arms, so I had him
pinned up against the counter. He wore one of his father's old
shirts, which was worn and patched at the elbows, and the dark
crimson color that belonged to Thuvhe.

His gray eyes—still wary, always wary—looked a little sad,
and had since the day before. Ara Kuzar was on our ship, thanks
to chance, or fate, or whatever I believed in these days. She still
wouldn't look at him, and I knew having her here was difficult for
him, though whenever I brought it up he just said, "Not as difficult
as it is for her," which was inarguable.

I tipped my chin up and kissed him, gently. He responded by
wrapping an arm across my back and lifting me into him, strong
and warm and certain.

It took a while for us to break apart.

"We pass through the currentstream today," I said. "Will you come with me?"

"In case you hadn't noticed," he said, "I'll pretty much go with you anywhere."

He tapped my nose with a gray-stained finger, leaving a mark that even I could see out of the corner of my eye.

"Did you just stain my nose right before I have to go out in public?"

He grinned, and nodded.

"I hate you," I said.

"And I love you," he replied.

"What's that on your nose?" Teka asked me.

We were on the observation deck of the ship, which was right above the nav center, where our pilots and flight techs were rushing around, preparing to pass through the currentstream. We walked to the barrier, which was waist-high and separated us from the giant window that would show us the currentstream.

The interior of the Ogran ship was dark—unsurprisingly—and uneven in places. The floor, no matter where you were, was all narrow pathways made of grate material, elevated over shallow pools of water that glowed with bioluminescent bacteria. It was beautiful, and eerie, but more than one person had fallen in and had to go to sick bay. Something new to adapt to.

Akos was already standing there. He had saved us places, as the path became more crowded, though really, people would have moved out of my way if I came near anyway. I tried not to care about that. I stood between him and Teka, and listened for the captain's shout to brace ourselves.

Akos reached for my hand as the ship drew nearer to the blue light, deep and rich in color. He would let go when we entered the currentstream, to allow me to feel its effects, agonizing though they were, but it felt good to have him there as we approached. My heart was pounding. I loved this part.

The real surprise, though, was Teka's hand seizing mine from the other side. There was a giddy smile on her face.

"I am a Shotet," she said, more to herself than to me. "I am sharp as a blade, and just as strong. . . ."

It was a variation on the other poem I had seen scrawled on a wall in Voa, the one penned as a criticism of the Noavek government:

I am a Shotet.

I am sharp as broken glass, and just as fragile.

I see all of the galaxy and never catch a glimpse of it.

I liked the other one better, because it was a reminder of my own fragility, my own tendency to see what I wanted to see. But this version was good, too.

I was surprised when Akos joined her in reciting the last lines:

"I see all of the galaxy," he said, "and it is all mine."

"Prepare yourselves!" came the shout from below.

Both Teka and Akos released my hands, almost in the same moment. And the ship was consumed by blue light.

EPILOGUE | EIJEH

W<small>E RETURN TO</small> H<small>ESSA</small> in disguise.

For a time, it seemed like too much of a risk, to us. But it was also unavoidable. So we waited until the Shotet sojourned again, and we reserved a seat on the flight under a false name, the one we bought from a criminal on P1104 after we fled from Voa.

We rent a coat from the shabby tourist shop in the main square, because we don't intend to stay long. We make the climb to the top of Hessa hill on foot, as it has always been. The Hall of Prophecy is closed for repairs, but we know all the ways in, the ones others don't know. We remember that, at least.

There is a gaping hole in the domed roof of the Hall of Prophecy, with jagged edges of red glass. We don't know what the Shotet used to break the dome, and their weapons of choice, whatever they were, have long since been cleaned up. We stand in the center of the floor, where one of our mothers once stood, barefoot, to receive the future.

We see—

A galaxy riven in two, oracles fleeing to Ogra and Tepes and Zold.

Assembly ships pursuing, pursuing, overtaking.

Small blasts of anticurrent.

Possibilities disappearing as lives find their endings.

We see—

Shotet descending on Tepes, dressed in special suits that protect against the heat.

Plugging their noses against the smell of white-hot garbage.

A man brushing sand from an intact compressor.

A woman holding a rounded piece of glass up to the sun.

We see—

Isae Benesit, wearing a gown in Thuvhesit red.

She stands behind a sheet of ice where there are hushflowers on the verge of blooming.

Behind her, in the same red, half-hidden by shadow, is Cisi Kereseth, wearing an enigmatic smile. Her head is adorned with a slim band of silver, the adornment of a chancellor's spouse.

The flowers crack open, and unfurl.

We see—

Our hands seizing the straps that cover our chest as our ship falls, falls, falls through dense atmosphere.

The lines of light that mark Ogra's surface like veins, appearing beneath us.

We are Shotet. We are not Shotet. But either way, we are an

oracle, and that cannot change, so we are returning to the temple of Ogra, to learn.

To see what we might become next.

We see—

Them.

Older. The silverskin shining on one side of her head. His gray eyes crinkled at the corners as he looks at her.

They stand in a crowd beneath a mammoth ship. It towers, in patchwork metals, over the other ships on the loading bay. A new sojourn ship.

He takes her hand. They walk toward the ship together.

ACKNOWLEDGMENTS

Thank you—

Nelson, my partner in all things, for mourning with me when I mourn, and rejoicing with me when I rejoice.

Katherine Tegen, for always being supportive, honest, and exactly what I need in an editor. ♥

Joanna Volpe, for her humor, guidance, and brainstorming superpowers.

Devin Ross, for enduring my email issues with good humor. Hilary Pecheone, for teaching me a whole lot of social media wisdom. Pouya Shahbazian, for having good instincts and patience. And Chris McEwen, for his savvy and for refereeing phone tag. Kathleen Ortiz, Maira Roman, and Veronica Grijalva, for navigating the entire world to find places for my books. Everyone at New Leaf Literary, for their general wonderfulness. Steve Younger, for keeping everything on the straight and narrow . . . but in a fun way.

Tori Hill, for her friendship and for remembering all the things!

Rosanne Romanello, for her excellent strategic mind and infectious laugh. Bess Braswell, for her good ideas and her warm heart. Cindy Hamilton, Nellie Kurtzman, Audrey Diestelkamp, and Sabrina Abballe in publicity and marketing, for all the planning and brainstorming and championing I could hope for. Mabel Hsu, for her patience with me, and her hard work. Andrea Pappenheimer, Kathy Faber, Kerry Moynagh, Kirstin Bowers, Heather Doss, Susan Yaeger, Jessica Abel, Fran Olson, Jessica Malone, Jennifer Wygand, Deborah Murphy, Jenny Sheridan, and Rick Starke in sales, for their enthusiasm and support. Brenna Franzitta, for keeping her eyes on my words and my worlds since *Divergent*; Alexandra Rakaczki, Valerie Shea, Josh Weiss, and Gwen Morton in managing editorial, for keeping every little thing on track. Amy Ryan, Joel Tippie, Erin Fitzsimmons, and Barb Fitzsimmons for taking critique and turning it into design ideas, like magic. Jean McGinley, for tirelessly working with our friends across the pond and the globe. Nicole Moulaison, Kristen Eckhardt, and Vanessa Nuttry in production, for putting this whole package together so well. And last but not least, Brian Murray, Kate Jackson, and Suzanne Murphy, for being our fearless leaders through it all.

Courtney Summers, Maurene Goo, and Somaiya Daud, for their early (and quick!) reads, thoughtful notes, and encouragement. Sarah Enni, for so. Many. Great. Chats. And for being there for me on tour . . . and everywhere else. Margie Stohl, for always looking out for my brain. Alexis Bass, Amy Lukavics, Debra Driza, Kaitlin Ward, Kara Thomas, Kate Hart, Kody Keplinger, Kristin Halbrook, Laurie Devore, Leila Austin, Lindsey Culli, Michelle Krys, Phoebe North, Samantha Mabry, Stephanie Sinkhorn,

Stephanie Kuehn, and Kirsten Hubbard, for helping me weather the hard times and emoji-celebrating the not-so-hard times. (You all give me so much more than I can say.) All the YALLpeople, for the good work we do together . . . even when I'm late with the panels, which is always. A few writerly types—they know who they are—for reaching out with kindness and wisdom at just the right moments.

My family—the one I was born into, the one I acquired later, and the one I got as a bonus when I got married—for giving me places all over the world to feel safe and loved. My friends, for helping me out of hermit mode when I need it.

My readers, for following me to new worlds.

All the women in my life, for awing me with their resilience.

GLOSSARY

altetahak – A style of Shotet combat best suited for students who are strong in build, translates to "school of the arm."

altos arva – A fruit from Trella known for its intense sweetness.

arzodae – A Zoldan word meaning literally "to mar, as with a knife," though it is actually used as a very strong apology, ie, "what I did cut a piece out of me."

Benesit – One of three fated families on the nation-planet of Thuvhe. One of the current generation is destined to be Thuvhe's chancellor.

current – Both natural phenomena and, in some cases, religious symbol, the current is an invisible power that gives people abilities and can be channeled into ships, machines, weapons, etc.

currentgift – Thought to be a result of the current flowing through a person, currentgifts are abilities, unique to each person, that develop during puberty. They are not always benevolent.

currentstream – A visual representation of the current in the sky, the brightly colored currentstream flows between and around each planet in the solar system.

elmetahak – A style of Shotet combat that has fallen out of favor, emphasizing strategic thinking. Translates to "school of the mind."

Essander – A moderately wealthy planet with a strong religious population. Its people are particularly attuned to scents.

feathergrass – A powerful plant that originated on Ogra. Causes hallucinations, particularly when ingested.

Galo – A city in Ogra that is now occupied primarily by Shotet exiles.

Hessa – One of three major cities in the nation-planet of Thuvhe, has a reputation for being rougher and poorer than the other two.

hushflower – The most significant iceflower to the Thuvhesit, the bright red hushflower can be poisonous when not diluted. Diluted, it is used both as an analgesic and for recreational purposes.

iceflower – Thuvhe's only crops, iceflowers are hardy, thick-stemmed plants with different-colored blooms, each one uniquely useful in medicines and other substances throughout the solar system.

izit – A unit of measurement, about the width of the average person's pinkie.

Kereseth – One of three fated families on the nation-planet of Thuvhe, residing in Hessa.

kutya – A massive, furry creature resembling a canine, native to Thuvhe. Thuvhesits use kutyah fur to stay warm.

kyerta – A life-altering truth. In Ogran, it literally means "that which has been crushed into a new shape."

Noavek – The only fated family of Shotet, known for their instability and brutality.

Ogra – Nicknamed "the shadow planet," Ogra is a mysterious world at the far reaches of the solar system whose atmosphere can't be penetrated by surveillance systems.

oruzo – Literally "a mirror image" in Shotet, this word means "successor" or that one person has become another.

Osoc – The coldest of the three major cities of Thuvhe, and the farthest north.

Othyr – A planet near the center of the solar system, known for its wealth and its contribution to technology, particularly in the realm of medicine.

Pitha – Also known as "the water planet," a nation-planet of highly practical people who are prized for their engineering of synthetic materials.

Pokgo – The capital city of Ogra.

season – A unit of time that has its origins in Pitha, where one revolution around the sun is jokingly referred to as "the rainy season" (since it rains constantly there).

sema – The word for a person who identifies as neither male nor female.

Shissa – The wealthiest of the three cities of Thuvhe. The buildings in Shissa hang high above the ground "like suspended raindrops."

sojourn – A seasonal journey undertaken by the Shotet people in a massive spaceship, involving one revolution around the solar system, and the scavenging of a "current favored" planet's valuable materials.

soju – A metal from Essander that blocks the flow of the current.

Tepes – Known also as "the desert planet," it is the closest nation-planet to the sun, known for being highly religious.

Thuvhe – The Assembly-recognized name for both the nation and the planet itself, also known as the "ice planet." It contains both the Thuvhesit and Shotet people.

tick – A slang term for a small unit of time, similar to a second.

Trella – A small planet of moderate means and little reverence for the oracles, Trella is mountainous and produces much of the galaxy's fruit.

Urek – The Shotet name for the planet of Thuvhe (though they refer to the nation of Thuvhe by its proper name), meaning "empty."

Voa – The capital city of Shotet, where most of the population is located.

zivatahak – A style of Shotet combat best suited for students who are quick in mind and body. Translates to "school of the heart."

Zold – A small, poor planet in the middle of the solar system known for its ascetic practices and strong national identity.

Turn the page for a sneak peek at
Veronica Roth's "The Spinners,"
an excerpt from her
masterful collection of futuristic short stories,

THE END
AND
OTHER
BEGINNINGS

THE SPINNERS

"I DIDN'T COME HERE to skewer you," she said, low and throaty. "Unless you give me a reason."

She uncurled her fingers so the weapon would retract. It made a *click click click* as all the gears shifted, but she still heard its low hum as she brought her hands up by her ears to show she meant no harm.

She was in a bar. A dirty, hot one that smelled like smoke and sweat. The floor was covered in a layer of stale peanut shells, and every surface she laid a hand on was sticky. She had busted her way in the locked door a minute or two earlier, since it was much too early for the place to be open to customers, just shy of 10:00 a.m.

The only person inside it wasn't human—which wasn't a big deal, unless they were trying to pretend to be one. Right now they were standing behind the bar with a rag in hand, as if it stood a chance against the grime.

"Not afraid of getting skewered by some kid," they said. If she hadn't been who she was, she would have called them an average man, even a boring one. Their face was rough with a salt-and-pepper beard, and there was grease under their—very human-looking—fingernails. But they had all the telltale signs of digital skin: flickering when their eyes moved, a still chest, and a shifty quality, like they didn't belong in their body.

"That's too bad," she said. "I find a healthy amount of fear improves somebody's likelihood of survival."

Flickering, flickering, as their eyes moved.

"What can we do to improve yours, then?" they said.

She smiled, all teeth. "Why don't you take off your little costume so I can get a good look at you?"

The ET shrugged. Twice. The first time was a human shrug, a *Whatever, if you insist*. The second time was a bigger one, to shuffle off its digital skin.

For a time, as a kid, she'd thought the skin was just a projection, like a hologram. But Mom had explained that wouldn't work—if it was a bigger creature, it would get itself into trouble that way—knock glasses off countertops, hit its head on doorframes, jab people with a spiked tail, whatever. The digital skin was more like . . . stuffing some of its matter into an alternate dimension. The skin was real, but it also wasn't. The ET was here, but it was also someplace else.

She didn't have to understand the science of it, anyhow. She just had to know what to look for.

The ET burst out of its skin like stuffing coming out of a busted couch cushion. Matter bubbled up from the split, gelatinous and glowing purple-blue. For a second it just looked like a heap of purple crap, but then it started to take shape, a massive torso that oozed into squat legs, a bulging head without a neck to hold it up. And stuck on the front of that head like sequins from a Bedazzler, a dozen shiny black eyes.

The smell hit her next, like a cross between stinkbug and sulfur. It was lucky Atleigh had come across a few purpuramorphs last year, because she knew to keep her face passive. They were harmless unless you commented on or otherwise reacted to their stench. Then things could get ugly.

Well. *Uglier.*

"Thanks for obliging," Atleigh said. "You know, most ETs don't bother to wear a digital skin unless they've got something to hide."

She lowered her weapon, slow, and slid it back into the holster on her belt.

"What is it that you want, kid?" the purpuramorph asked her, in a low rumble, almost subvocal. Purpuramorphs were one of the few offplanet races that didn't need some kind of tech to speak like a human. Their vocal cords—buried somewhere in that purple mush—were actually similar to her own, somehow.

Atleigh took her phone out of her pocket and lit it up. On the screen was a picture of a woman with long hair—the same auburn color as Atleigh's own. She had deep lines in her forehead, and a glint in her murky green eyes, like she was telling you to get to the goddamn point.

"You seen her? She was in here last week sometime."

A dozen glittering eyes swiveled toward the phone, and Atleigh schooled her features into neutrality as a wave of odor washed over her, so pungent it almost made her eyes water.

"And if I have?"

"I just need to know if you spotted her talking to anybody," Atleigh said.

"My customers are guaranteed a certain level of *discretion*," the purpuramorph said. "I can't go violating that just because some little girl asks me to."

Atleigh's smile turned into more of a gritted-teeth situation.

"First of all, I'm a little girl who can make your insides come out of you before you even notice it's happening," she said. "And second, that woman is my mom, and she's dead now, so if you don't tell me who she was talking to, I might do something out of grief that we'll *both* later regret, get me?"

She rested the heel of her hand on the holster at her side.

"So what's it gonna be?" she said. "Carrot, or stick? Because I gotta tell you . . ." She drew the modified gun, hooked her middle

3

finger in the metal loop just under the barrel, and tugged on it so the mechanism extended the needle again. *Click click click.* "I'm pretty fond of the stick, myself."

A couple of minutes later, Atleigh slid into the driver's side of an old green Volvo, patted the urn buckled into the seat next to her, and started the engine. She knew exactly where she was headed next.

Atleigh Kent was a bounty hunter, and her bounty was exclusively leeches.

Not all extraterrestrials were leeches—in fact, 99.9 percent of them weren't. Most of the ETs who settled on Earth were decent enough, and made things more interesting. When Atleigh saw pictures of the way her planet had been when there were only humans on it, she was always struck by how boring it was, all the same texture, like a bowl of plain oatmeal. It was better now, with beings of all shapes and sizes and colors, hearing half a dozen languages burbling or beeping or buzzing when you walked down the street.

She mostly dealt in the ones who had something to hide. Digital skin was illegal for a reason—mostly people wore it when they were on the run from something. But leeches . . .

Well. Leeches were a different story. They were a predatory race. They attached their silvery, centipede-like bodies to a person's spinal cord and took control of their body and brain. As long as they kept the back of their neck covered, they could pass for human perfectly, absorbing the host body's knowledge and experiences and integrating it into their new, joint self.

Meanwhile, the host suffered in silence, suppressed by the alien until they apparently fizzled out of existence. If the alien was attached too long, and then detached, the person was just a

4

vegetable. Their bodies could go on living, if cared for, but their minds were gone.

All the alien races were vulnerable to leeches, but none more than human beings, their ideal prey. The easiest hosts to suppress, for whatever reason.

It had happened to Atleigh's father. He—well, it hadn't really been him, but they hadn't known that at the time—had lived among them for weeks, dodging their mother and pretending at fatherhood. Then their mom had discovered the thing on their dad's neck, and tried to stab it with a kitchen knife, and he had bailed.

They had gone on the hunt, as a family, the two little girls too young to remember much before the endless road trip their childhood turned into. Their mom had learned everything she could about the thing that had taken her husband. It had taken her years to find him, in a lonely gas station in Iowa. Then she had ripped the thing off his spinal cord and gutted it. But their dad never came back to himself.

Atleigh had helped dig his grave, right there on the side of the road, by the mile marker, so they would always know where to find him. And since that day, she had been determined to save the human race, one leech at a time.

Lacey Kent's hand went to her throat, to the buttons that fastened her collar closed. Just checking on them, as she had done a dozen times in the past ten minutes as she waited for the shuttle to reach the station.

There weren't many students on the shuttle from the American Selenic Military Academy, and none that Lacey knew personally. A few teachers—including the famously volatile arachnoid, Mr. Zag—a few parents visiting ailing or troublesome children, a couple of fulguvore emissaries from their home planet, and of course, Lacey herself. She was in her sixth year, a secondary school transfer, so she didn't quite have the posture that the lifers had—she could stand up straight, sure, but when no one was looking, she sagged like an old tree.

"Headed home, Ms. Kent?" Mr. Zag's metallic voice asked. Arachnoids spoke through a complex system of pincer-clicking that no human had yet been able to decipher, so Zag had a voice box hanging from his pedicle. Even though the voice was computer-generated, Lacey thought she could hear some judgment in it. After all, she was going home in the middle of a semester.

"Yes, sir," Lacey said. "My mother just died."

"My condolences." Zag's pincers were clicking. Lacey had never gotten used to the sound. She hadn't been in Zag's class since her first year at the academy, but she still shivered when he spoke to her, the response Pavlovian. "Though perhaps it is some relief that you will not have to tell her—"

"I appreciate the sentiment," Lacey said, cutting him off. She didn't want to hear about all the things she wouldn't have to tell her mother now, because it just reminded her of what she wouldn't *get* to tell her.

Zag's multiple eyes blinked at her, but he seemed to get the hint, and fell silent.

Finally the chime went off for docking, and Lacey went to the window to look down at Peoria, Illinois, one of the shuttle's few stops. Peoria had once been home to a major machinery manufacturer that had later moved to the Chicago area. The population of the city had dwindled almost dangerously until the local government made a bid for one of the space academies. Now, by all accounts, Peoria was booming.

Lacey didn't care much about the city either way. She wasn't

6

from there—wasn't from anywhere, really, unless you counted the back of her mom's old Jeep. Her official place of birth was a town in Minnesota, and even that was just a word she wrote on official papers, not a place she felt much tied to.

She spotted the wide stretch of the Illinois River, the bridge that spanned across it, and a cluster of low buildings before the shuttle docked at the station. Then she was heaving her bag—packed carefully so nothing would wrinkle—over one shoulder, and walking through the doors to search out her sister.

Atleigh wasn't hard to find. Most families of human military students were downright proper, moneyed, all pressed collar shirts and shoes that made snapping sounds on tile. Atleigh was wearing dusty black boots—one with the laces fraying so the top of the boot was flappy around her calf—blue jeans, and a red plaid shirt over a gray T-shirt with a few holes in it. She had chopped off all her hair, so it was like a boy's, with a wave in the front where it was a little longer. She was pretty without meaning to be, freckled by the sun, and taking too big a bite out of a Snickers bar, so it bulged in her cheek.

Nearby, a pair of uptight-looking primusars draped in diamond necklaces were giving her sideways glances—not subtle when you had stalk eyes that swiveled.

When she spotted Lacey, Atleigh grinned, and pulled herself off the pillar she had been leaning against. The two girls collided somewhere in the space between them, Atleigh's hug "so tight the bears were jealous," as their mom said.

Well, she wouldn't be saying it anymore.

The sudden awareness of what she had lost—what they had both lost—kept hitting Lacey out of nowhere. She'd go along feeling all right, and then open a medicine cabinet and *wham*, her mom's name was on the bottle of painkillers Lacey took for bad

7

cramps sometimes. Or *wham*, she pulled on the black running shoes Mom had bought her for school.

The color of Atleigh's hair, and the creases at the corners of her eyes.

"Wow," Lacey said. And then, to cover it up: "Your hair's gone."

"Yup," Atleigh said. She had swallowed the giant bite of Snickers, somehow. "Supposed to be a hot summer, so I thought I'd get ahead of it."

Knowing Atleigh, that had nothing to do with the decision, but Lacey wasn't going to pry.

"I'd offer to take your bag, but I don't want to let those military school muscles go to waste." Atleigh grinned. "C'mon, let's get going."

"How's the car holding up?"

"Had to sell it."

"What about the Jeep?"

Atleigh snorted. "Not gonna drive that gas guzzler on a perpetual cross-country road trip. It's parked someplace outside Lansing. You can have it when you graduate, if you want it."

Lacey followed Atleigh to a green Volvo with a rusty bumper. She opened the back door to throw her bag inside, and saw the urn buckled into one of the seats.

Wham.

"Time for one last road trip, I guess," Atleigh remarked as she started the engine. And that was all either of them said about the catastrophic emptiness between them.

"We are not having this conversation," Atleigh had said to her mother, a few weeks before her passing.

"Yes, we are," Chloe Kent said with a grave nod. "It doesn't have to be so hard. I want my ashes to be scattered at sea. There!

8

That's basically the whole conversation."

"No," Atleigh said, pointing a finger at her. "Because you're not gonna die. You'll get old, and there'll be some kind of life-prolonging technology that will keep you going until the two of us are both ready to go. That's how it's gonna work. Hear me?"

Chloe grabbed Atleigh's finger in her fist, and smiled.

They were in an Applebee's, one of the oldest surviving chain restaurants on Earth. A plate of lukewarm mozzarella sticks was between them. The chipper waitress had just come by to make sure they were all right, to which they had both responded, wasp-ishly, at the same moment: "Fine, thanks."

"I don't want tech like that," Chloe said. She wore her hair in a braid that hung over one shoulder. She was old enough to go gray, but she hadn't yet, and maybe she never would—Atleigh was hoping, anyway, because what happened to Chloe always ended up happening to her, in time. "When it's my time to go, I want to go. And I want my girls to learn how to deal with it better than I dealt with losing your dad."

Chloe sucked down the last of her iced tea. Unsweetened, with half a dozen sugar packets mixed in until they dissolved through the force of Chloe's will alone.

"All right," Atleigh said, a little unsteadily. Her finger was still caught in her mother's hand. "At sea, then."

"And then I want you girls to take a little vacation. At least a couple days. Go sailing."

"Sailing?" Atleigh groaned. "What next, you want us to dress up in preppy polo shirts with the collars popped and scarves in our hair?"

"Absolutely." Chloe wore her most gleeful smile. "My girls, dressed like proper southern ladies. I'll laugh at you from the beyond."

"My hairpin will secretly be a blade," Atleigh said. "And the popped collar will be hiding an absurdly large throat tattoo."

"You don't have a throat tattoo."

"I'm going to get one when you die, obviously," Atleigh said. "Absurdly large. A heart with an arrow through it. Maybe some angel wings."

"Don't you dare. No daughter of mine would ever get such a cliché tattoo."

Atleigh smirked.

"Honestly," Chloe said, turning serious again. "I don't care what you wear, but go sailing, scatter my ashes, and remember what life is. Two days. Okay? That's all."

"Okay," Atleigh agreed. "But, you know. Try not to die."

"Deal." Chloe let go of Atleigh's finger.

"First stop?" Lacey asked her. She was poking the keychain charm that hung from the rearview mirror. It was cheap metal, that yellow-gold color that shows up exclusively at gas stations and airport kiosks, and depicted the three fates. "Spinners," Mom had called them, because they were passing thread to each other, one with the spindle, one measuring out the length, and the third cutting it. Birth, life, and death.

It had hung in Mom's car so long Lacey had stopped noticing it. It looked out of place in Atleigh's.

"Gotta go through Nashville. I have some things to do there while we're in the area," Atleigh said.

Lacey narrowed her eyes.

"Nashville is not 'in the area,'" she said. "It's hours out of our way."

"We're gonna have to stay overnight someplace anyway, so does it matter whether it takes us twelve hours or seventeen?"

Atleigh said, scowling a little.

"What do you have to do in Nashville that can't wait until after?"

"I don't stop needing cash just because somebody dies, okay?" Atleigh snapped. "I got a job down there. The usual thing. But I can't lose any momentum—not without Mom's help getting work."

"You have to be kidding me," Lacey said. "This isn't just *somebody dying*. This is *Mom*."

"Aw, gee, I sure am glad you reminded me, because otherwise I woulda forgot." Atleigh was leaning hard into the mild accent they had both picked up in childhood. They had spent a lot of time in the rural parts of the Midwest then, and there was a distinct twang there that had proved unshakeable. Atleigh only twanged when she was getting really angry. "I told you, I have to do this. Okay? And since I'm the one driving—"

"It's not like I don't know *how* to drive—"

"And since *this is my car*, which I paid for with my own god-damned money while you were off with a bunch of fancy astronauts at your ritzy space academy—"

"Oh, here we go." Lacey rolled her eyes. "It always comes back to me going to school. What did you want me to do, stay with you forever, hunting down aliens for cash?"

Atleigh shook her head, and went quiet.

And it was somehow worse, because it meant that she *had* wanted Lacey to stay with her forever, but she just couldn't admit it.

They made it to Nashville that night around eight o'clock, and Atleigh went that whole way without talking to Lacey once. She only broke the silence to ask Lacey if she was hungry, and pulled into a McDonald's. That in itself was a peace offering— McDonald's was Lacey's fast food of choice. Atleigh's was Wendy's.

11

They sat on the hood of the car to eat, the same way they always did, even in the winter. Atleigh hated the way the tables inside fast food places felt—tacky, like they were never really clean. One time they had wolfed down chicken sandwiches in the middle of an Indiana snowstorm.

"So how many are you up to this year?" Lacey asked. She figured it was a safe question. Atleigh was always ready to talk about leeches.

"Ten," Atleigh said. She stuffed a few fries in her mouth at once.

"Solo?"

"Yeah."

"Damn. You're a machine."

Atleigh grunted a little, and chewed. Under normal circumstances Lacey would already have been teasing her for rooting around in the fry container like a pig hunting for truffles, but she felt weird doing that now. And not even because of their argument, but because she had left. She had chosen something other than leeches. Other than Atleigh, and Mom, and even Dad. And it just wasn't the same anymore.

"Want me to look up a place for us to stay?"

Atleigh shook her head. "I got us an Airbnb."

"You . . . what?"

"You may not have realized this, Lace," Atleigh said, stuffing her burger wrapper and empty fry container in the McDonald's bag. "But motels . . . are gross."

"Yeah, I know! That's why I always sleep on top of one of my old shirts when we stay in them," Lacey said, hopping down from the hood. "I just didn't think you would plan ahead."

"The name of the place is 'Cozy Country Cottage,' so don't get too excited about it," Atleigh said. She balled up the McDonald's bag and tossed it in a nearby garbage can. "No place with alliteration in the title can possibly be any good."

It *wasn't* a great spot, as it turned out, but Atleigh had stayed in worse. She had slept in the back of the Volvo once when she found a peephole in a motel wall. She had gotten flea bites from unwashed bedsheets, and uncovered bloodstains under motel sofas. So the smaller-and-dingier-than-advertised Cozy Country Cottage wasn't so bad by comparison.

Atleigh told Lacey she was going to a meeting about a bounty, and left her at the cottage to settle in on her own. Then she drove out to the ET hideout that Gelatinous Gary (her nickname for the purpuramorph she had threatened just outside Peoria) had told her about. It was even more innocuous than their usual haunts: an old house-turned-coffee-shop with creaky floors and frilly curtains on the windows.

The young woman who smiled at her from behind the counter was flickering like a candle in the wind. Definitely digital skin, no question. She must have been newly settled, because most of them didn't give it away so easy.

"What can I get for you?" she said.

"I'm looking for a leech who was in here a couple weeks ago," Atleigh said. The young woman looked alarmed.

"Leech?" she said. "What—"

"Listen, *Riley*," Atleigh said, eyeing the woman's name tag. "I'm really tired, and I'm not in the mood for the whole rigamarole. I'm not here to get anyone in trouble, I just want to know about a guy."

Riley looked at her for a few seconds, then the friendly expression she had worn when Atleigh walked in fell away, and she crossed her arms.

"The way Violet talked about you, I thought you'd be bigger," Riley said.

Atleigh registered a moment of shock that Gelatinous Gary was actually named Violet—such a lovely name for such an unlovely thing.

"It's the shoes," Atleigh said dryly. Hidden under the flannel shirt she wore, pressed up against her spine, was the needleknife she would need if things went sour. And, judging by the hard look on Riley's face, that was a distinct possibility. Whatever Riley was under that digital skin, Atleigh was pretty sure it wasn't a purpuramorph.

"What is it you want to know?" Riley said. One of her hands was hidden under the counter. Not a good sign. Atleigh started moving her hand back, casual-like, toward her weapon.

"The leech was attached to the body of a middle-aged gentleman," Atleigh said. "A scout. He goes looking for solid hosts, get it? And the others suck down on who he tells them."

"If I had known someone like that was in here, I would have been legally obligated to report it," Riley said coolly. "So are you accusing me of breaking the law?"

"Sure, but not in a mean way." Atleigh's voice softened. "Because you gotta get by, right? So you'll do what you have to do, even if you don't like it. I understand. I've done a lot of things I don't like, Riley."

"Somehow I doubt that," Riley said, matching Atleigh's soft tone with one of her own. "From the look of you, girl, you've enjoyed every second of what you've done to my kind."

She shrugged off her skin, and what was under it was the exact same—except for the glint of silver at the back of Riley's neck.

Leech.